THE DUKE AND I

By Julia Quinn

THE BRIDGERTON PREQUELS

Because of Miss Bridgerton
The Girl with the Make-Believe Husband
The Other Miss Bridgerton
First Comes Scandal

THE BRIDGERTON SERIES

The Duke and I
The Viscount Who Loved Me
An Offer from a Gentleman
Romancing Mister Bridgerton
To Sir Phillip, With Love
When He Was Wicked
It's in His Kiss
On the Way to the Wedding
The Bridgertons: Happily Ever After

ANTHOLOGIES

The Further Observations of Lady Whistledown
Lady Whistledown Strikes Back

THE SMYTHE-SMITH QUARTET

Just Like Heaven
A Night Like This
The Sum of All Kisses
The Secrets of Sir Richard Kenworthy

The Bevelstoke Series

The Secret Diaries of Miss Miranda Cheever
What Happens in London
Ten Things I Love About You

The Two Dukes of Wyndham

The Lost Duke of Wyndham
Mr. Cavendish, I Presume

Agents of the Crown

To Catch an Heiress
How to Marry a Marquis

The Lyndon Sisters

Everything and the Moon
Brighter Than the Sun

The Splendid Trilogy

Splendid
Dancing at Midnight
Minx

Queen Charlotte (with Shonda Rhimes)

JULIA QUINN

BRIDGERTON

THE DUKE AND I

AVON

An Imprint of HarperCollins*Publishers*

"The Duke and I: The 2nd Epilogue" was originally published in *The Bridgertons: Happily Ever After* in April 2013.

HarperCollins books may be purchased for educational, business, or sales promotional use. For information, please email the Special Markets Department at SPsales@harpercollins.com.

FIRST AVON BOOKS DELUXE COLLECTOR'S EDITION PUBLISHED SEPTEMBER 2025.

Bridgerton Family Tree designed by Emily Cotler, Waxcreative Design

Library of Congress Cataloging-in-Publication Data has been applied for.

ISBN 978-0-06-344503-1

25 26 27 28 29 RTLO 10 9 8 7 6 5 4 3 2 1

For Danelle Harmon and Sabrina Jeffries,
without whom I never would have
turned this book in on time.

And for Martha
of The Romance Journal *electronic bulletin board,*
for suggesting I call it Daphne's Bad Heir Day.

And also for Paul,
even though his idea of dancing
is standing still while
he holds my hand and watches me twirl.

Bridgerton FAMILY TREE

Violet Ledger *m.* EDMUND
1766- 1764-1803

ANTHONY
1784-
The Viscount Who Loved Me
BOOK 2
featuring
Kate Sheffield
1793-

BENEDICT
1786-
An Offer From a Gentleman
BOOK 3
featuring
Sophie Beckett
1794-

COLIN
1791-
Romancing Mister Bridgerton
BOOK 4
featuring
Penelope Featherington
1796-

DAPHNE
1792-
The Duke and I
BOOK 1
featuring
Simon Basset
Duke of Hastings
1784-

ELOISE
1796-
To Sir Phillip, With Love
BOOK 5
featuring
Sir Phillip Crane
1794-

FRANCESCA
1797-
When He Was Wicked
BOOK 6
featuring
Michael Stirling
9th Earl of Kilmartin
1791-

GREGORY
1801-
On the Way to the Wedding
BOOK 8
featuring
Lucy Abernathy
1807-

HYACINTH
1803-
It's in His Kiss
BOOK 7
featuring
Gareth St. Clair
1797-

FOR MORE INFORMATION
PLEASE VISIT JULIAQUINN.COM

THE DUKE AND I

Prologue

The birth of Simon Arthur Henry Fitzranulph Basset, Earl Clyvedon, was met with great celebration. Church bells rang for hours, champagne flowed freely through the gargantuan castle that the newborn would call home, and the entire village of Clyvedon quit work to partake of the feast and holiday ordered by the young earl's father.

"This," the baker said to the blacksmith, "is no ordinary baby."

For Simon Arthur Henry Fitzranulph Basset would not spend his life as Earl Clyvedon. That was a mere courtesy title. Simon Arthur Henry Fitzranulph Basset—the baby who possessed more names than any baby could possibly need—was the heir to one of England's oldest and richest dukedoms. And his father, the ninth Duke of Hastings, had waited years for this moment.

As he stood in the hall outside his wife's confinement room, cradling the squalling infant, the duke's heart near burst with pride. Already several years past forty, he had watched his cronies—dukes and earls, all—beget heir after heir. Some had had to suffer through a few daughters before siring a precious son, but in the end, they'd all been assured that their lines would continue, that their blood would pass forward into the next generation of England's elite.

But not the Duke of Hastings. Though his wife had managed to conceive five times in the fifteen years of their marriage, only twice had she carried to full term, and both of those infants had been stillborn. After the fifth pregnancy, which had ended with a bloody miscarriage in the fifth month, surgeons and physicians alike had warned their graces that they absolutely must not make another attempt to have a child. The duchess's very life was in danger. She was too frail, too weak, and perhaps, they said gently, too old. The duke was simply going to have to reconcile himself to the fact that the dukedom would pass out of the Basset family.

But the duchess, God bless her, knew her role in life, and after a six-month recuperative period, she opened the connecting door between their bedrooms, and the duke once again commenced his quest for a son.

Five months later, the duchess informed the duke that she had conceived. The duke's immediate elation was tempered by his grim determination that nothing—absolutely nothing—would cause this pregnancy to go awry. The duchess was confined to her bed the minute it was realized that she'd missed her monthly courses. A physician was brought in to visit her every day, and halfway through the pregnancy, the duke located the most respected doctor in London and paid him a king's ransom to abandon his practice and take up residence at Clyvedon Castle temporarily.

The duke was taking no chances this time. He *would* have a son, and the dukedom *would* remain in Basset hands.

The duchess experienced pains a month early, and pillows were tucked under her hips. Gravity might keep the babe inside, Dr. Stubbs explained. The duke thought that a sound argument, and, once the doctor had retired for the evening, placed yet another pillow under his wife, raising her to a twenty-degree angle. She remained that way for a month.

And then finally, the moment of truth arrived. The household prayed for the duke, who so wanted an heir, and a few remembered to pray for the duchess, who had grown thin and frail even as her belly had grown round and wide. They tried not to be too hopeful—after all, the duchess had already delivered and buried two babes. And even if she did manage to safely deliver a child, it could be, well, a girl.

As the duchess's screams grew louder and more frequent, the duke shoved his way into her chamber, ignoring the protests of the doctor, the midwife, and her grace's maid. It was a bloody mess, but the duke was determined to be present when the babe's sex was revealed.

The head appeared, then the shoulders. All leaned forward to watch as the duchess strained and pushed, and then . . .

And then the duke knew that there was a God, and He still smiled on the Bassets. He allowed the midwife one minute to clean the babe, then took the little boy into his arms and marched into the great hall to show him off.

"I have a son!" he boomed. "A perfect little son!"

And while the servants cheered and wept with relief, the duke looked down upon the tiny little earl, and said, "You are perfect. You are a Basset. You are mine."

The duke wanted to take the boy outside to prove to everyone that he had finally sired a healthy male child, but there was a slight chill in the early April air, so he allowed the midwife to take the babe back to his mother. The duke mounted one of his prized geldings and rode off to celebrate, shouting his good fortune to all who would listen.

Meanwhile, the duchess, who had been bleeding steadily since the birth, slipped into unconsciousness, and then finally just slipped away.

The duke mourned his wife. He truly did. He hadn't loved her, of course, and she hadn't loved him, but they'd been friends in an oddly distant sort of way. The duke hadn't expected anything more from marriage than a son and an heir, and in that regard, his wife had proven herself an exemplary spouse. He arranged for fresh flowers to be laid at the base of her funereal monument every week, no matter the season, and her portrait was moved from the sitting room to the hall, in a position of great honor over the staircase.

And then the duke got on with the business of raising his son.

There wasn't much he could do in the first year, of course. The babe was too young for lectures on land management and responsibility, so the duke left Simon in the care of his nurse and went to London, where his life continued much as it had before he'd been blessed by parenthood, except that he forced everyone—even the king—to gaze upon the miniature he'd had painted of his son shortly after his birth.

The duke visited Clyvedon from time to time, then returned for good on Simon's second birthday, ready to take the young lad's education in hand. A pony had been purchased, a small gun had been selected for future use at the fox hunt, and tutors were engaged in every subject known to man.

"He's too young for all that!" Nurse Hopkins exclaimed.

"Nonsense," Hastings replied condescendingly. "Clearly, I don't expect him to master any of this anytime soon, but it is never too early to begin a duke's education."

"He's not a duke," Nurse muttered.

"He will be." Hastings turned his back on her and crouched beside his son, who was building an asymmetrical castle with a set of blocks on the floor. The duke hadn't been down to Clyvedon in several months, and was pleased with Simon's growth. He was a sturdy, healthy young boy, with glossy brown hair and clear blue eyes.

"What are you building there, son?"

Simon smiled and pointed.

Hastings looked up at Nurse Hopkins. "Doesn't he speak?"

She shook her head. "Not yet, your grace."

The duke frowned. "He's two. Shouldn't he be speaking?"

"Some children take longer than others, your grace. He's clearly a bright young boy."

"Of course he's bright. He's a Basset."

Nurse nodded. She always nodded when the duke talked about the superiority of the Basset blood. "Maybe," she suggested, "he just doesn't have anything he wants to say."

The duke didn't look convinced, but he handed Simon a toy soldier, patted him on the head, and left the house to go exercise the new mare he'd purchased from Lord Worth.

Two years later, however, he wasn't so sanguine.

"*Why isn't he talking?*" he boomed.

"I don't know," Nurse answered, wringing her hands.

"What have you done to him?"

"I haven't done anything!"

"If you'd been doing your job correctly, *he*"—the duke jabbed an angry finger in Simon's direction—"would be speaking."

Simon, who was practicing his letters at his miniature desk, watched the exchange with interest.

"He's four years old, God damn it," the duke roared. "He should be able to speak."

"He can write," Nurse said quickly. "Five children I've raised, and not a one of them took to letters the way Master Simon has."

"A fat lot of good writing is going to do him if he can't talk." Hastings turned to Simon, rage burning in his eyes. "Talk to me, damn you!"

Simon shrank back, his lower lip quivering.

"Your grace!" Nurse exclaimed. "You're scaring the child."

Hastings whipped around to face her. "Maybe he needs scaring. Maybe what he needs is a good dose of discipline. A good paddling might help him find his voice."

The duke grabbed the silver-backed brush Nurse used on Simon's hair and advanced on his son. "I'll make you talk, you stupid little—"

"*No!*"

Nurse gasped. The duke dropped the brush. It was the first time they'd ever heard Simon's voice.

"What did you say?" the duke whispered, tears forming in his eyes.

Simon's fists balled at his sides, and his little chin jutted out as he said, "Don't you h-h-h-h-h-h-h—"

The duke's face turned deathly pale. "What is he saying?"

Simon attempted the sentence again. "D-d-d-d-d-d-d—"

"My God," the duke breathed, horrified. "He's a moron."

"He's not a moron!" Nurse cried out, throwing her arms around the boy.

"D-d-d-d-d-d-d-don't you h-h-h-h-h-h-hit"—Simon took a deep breath—"*me.*"

Hastings sank onto the window seat, his head dropping into his hands. "What have I done to deserve this? What could I have possibly done . . ."

"You should be giving the boy praise!" Nurse Hopkins admonished. "Four years you've been waiting for him to speak, and—"

"And he's an idiot!" Hastings roared. "A goddamned, bloody little idiot!"

Simon began to cry.

"Hastings is going to go to a half-wit," the duke moaned. "All those years of praying for an heir, and now it's all for ruin. I should have let the title go to my cousin." He turned back to his son, who was sniffling and wiping his eyes, trying to appear strong for his father. "I can't even look at him," he gasped. "I can't even bear to look at him."

And with that, the duke stalked out of the room.

Nurse Hopkins hugged the boy close. "You're not an idiot," she whispered fiercely. "You're the smartest little boy I know. And if anyone can learn to talk properly, I know it's you."

Simon turned into her warm embrace and sobbed.

"We'll show him," Nurse vowed. "He'll eat his words if it's the last thing I do."

Nurse Hopkins proved true to her word. While the Duke of Hastings removed himself to London and tried to pretend he had no son, she spent every waking minute with Simon, sounding out words and syllables, praising him lavishly when he got something right, and giving him encouraging words when he didn't.

The progress was slow, but Simon's speech did improve. By the time he was six, "d-d-d-d-d-d-don't" had turned into "d-d-don't," and by the time he was eight, he was managing entire sentences without faltering. He still ran into trouble when he was upset, and Nurse had to remind him often that he needed to remain calm and collected if he wanted to get the words out in one piece.

But Simon was determined, and Simon was smart, and perhaps most importantly, he was damned stubborn. He learned to take breaths before each sentence, and to think about his words before he attempted to say them. He studied the feel of his mouth when he spoke correctly, and tried to analyze what went wrong when he didn't.

And finally, at the age of eleven, he turned to Nurse Hopkins, paused to collect his thoughts, and said, "I think it is time we went to see my father."

Nurse looked up sharply. The duke had not laid eyes on the boy in seven years. And he had not answered a single one of the letters Simon had sent him.

Simon had sent nearly a hundred.

"Are you certain?" she asked.

Simon nodded.

"Very well, then. I'll order the carriage. We'll leave for London on the morrow."

The trip took a day and a half, and it was late afternoon by the time their carriage rolled up to Basset House. Simon gazed at the busy London streetscape with wonder as Nurse Hopkins led him up the steps. Neither had ever visited Basset House before, and so Nurse didn't know what to do when she reached the front door other than knock.

The door swung open within seconds, and they found themselves being looked down upon by a rather imposing butler.

"Deliveries," he intoned, reaching to close the door, "are made in the rear."

"Hold there!" Nurse said quickly, jamming her foot in the door. "We are not servants."

The butler looked disdainfully at her garments.

"Well, I am, but he's not." She grabbed Simon's arm and yanked him forward. "This is Earl Clyvedon, and you'd do well to treat him with respect."

The butler's mouth actually dropped open, and he blinked several times before saying, "It is my understanding that Earl Clyvedon is dead."

"What?" Nurse screeched.

"I most certainly am not!" Simon exclaimed, with all the righteous indignation of an eleven-year-old.

The butler examined Simon, recognized immediately that he had the look of the Bassets, and ushered them in.

"Why did you think I was d-dead?" Simon asked, cursing himself for misspeaking, but not surprised. He was always most likely to stutter when he was angry.

"It is not for me to say," the butler replied.

"It most certainly is," Nurse shot back. "You can't say something like that to a boy of his years and not explain it."

The butler was silent for a moment, then finally said, "His grace has not mentioned you in years. The last I heard, he said he had no son. He looked quite pained as he said it, so no one pursued the conversation. We—the servants, that is—assumed you'd passed on."

Simon felt his jaw clench, felt his throat working wildly.

"Wouldn't he have gone into mourning?" Nurse demanded. "Did you think about that? How could you have assumed the boy was dead if his father was not in mourning?"

The butler shrugged. "His grace frequently wears black. Mourning wouldn't have altered his costume."

"This is an outrage," Nurse Hopkins said. "I demand you summon his grace at once."

Simon said nothing. He was trying too hard to get his emotions under control. He had to. There was no way he'd be able to talk with his father while his blood was racing so.

The butler nodded. "He is upstairs. I'll alert him immediately to your arrival."

Nurse started pacing wildly, muttering under her breath and referring to his grace with every vile word in her surprisingly extensive vocabulary. Simon remained in the center of the room, his arms angry sticks at his sides as he took deep breaths.

You can do this, he shouted in his mind. *You can do this.*

Nurse turned to him, saw him trying to control his temper, and immediately gasped. "Yes, that's it," she said quickly, dropping to her knees and taking his hands in hers. She knew better than anyone what would happen if Simon tried to face his father before he calmed down. "Take deep breaths. And make sure to think about your words before you speak. If you can control—"

"I see you're still mollycoddling the boy," came an imperious voice from the doorway.

Nurse Hopkins straightened and turned slowly around. She tried to think of something respectful to say. She tried to think of anything that would smooth over this awful situation. But when she looked at the duke, she saw Simon in him, and her rage began anew. The duke might look just like his son, but he was certainly no father to him.

"You, sir," she spat out, "are despicable."

"And you, madam, are fired."

Nurse lurched back.

"No one speaks to the Duke of Hastings that way," he roared. "No one!"

"Not even the king?" Simon taunted.

Hastings whirled around, not even noticing that his son had spoken clearly. "You," he said in a low voice.

Simon nodded curtly. He'd managed one sentence properly, but it had been a short one, and he didn't want to push his luck. Not when he was this upset. Normally, he could go days without a stutter, but now . . .

The way his father stared at him made him feel like an infant. An idiot infant.

And his tongue suddenly felt awkward and thick.

The duke smiled cruelly. "What do you have to say for yourself, boy? Eh? What do you have to *say*?"

"It's all right, Simon," Nurse Hopkins whispered, throwing a furious glance at the duke. "Don't let him upset you. You can do it, sweetling."

And somehow her encouraging tone made it all the worse. Simon had come here to prove himself to his father, and now his nurse was treating him like a baby.

"What's the matter?" the duke taunted. "Cat got your tongue?"

Simon's muscles clenched so hard he started to shake.

Father and son stared at each other for what felt like an eternity, until finally the duke swore and stalked toward the door. "You are my worst failure," he hissed at his son. "I don't know what I did to deserve you, but God help me if I ever lay eyes on you again."

"Your grace!" Nurse Hopkins said indignantly. This was no way to speak to a child.

"Get him out of my sight," he spat at her. "You can keep your job just so long as you keep him away from me."

"Wait!"

The duke turned slowly around at the sound of Simon's voice. "Did you say something?" he drawled.

Simon took three long breaths in through his nose, his mouth still clamped together in anger. He forced his jaw to relax and rubbed his tongue against the roof of his mouth, trying to remind himself of how it felt to speak properly. Finally, just as the duke was about to dismiss him again, he opened his mouth and said, "I am your son."

Simon heard Nurse Hopkins breathe a sigh of relief, and something he'd never seen before blossomed in his father's eyes. Pride. Not much of it, but there was something there, lurking in the depths; something that gave Simon a whisper of hope.

"I am your son," he said again, this time a little louder, "and I am not d—"

Suddenly his throat closed up. And Simon panicked.

You can do this. You can do this.

But his throat felt tight, and his tongue felt thick, and his father's eyes started to narrow . . .

"I am not d-d-d—"

"Go home," the duke said in a low voice. "There is no place for you here."

Simon felt the duke's rejection in his very bones, felt a peculiar kind of pain enter his body and creep around his heart. And, as hatred flooded his body and poured from his eyes, he made a solemn vow.

If he couldn't be the son his father wanted, then by God, he'd be the *exact opposite* . . .

Chapter 1

The Bridgertons are by far the most prolific family in the upper echelons of society. Such industriousness on the part of the viscountess and the late viscount is commendable, although one can find only banality in their choice of names for their children. Anthony, Benedict, Colin, Daphne, Eloise, Francesca, Gregory, and Hyacinth—orderliness is, of course, beneficial in all things, but one would think that intelligent parents would be able to keep their children straight without needing to alphabetize their names.

Furthermore, the sight of the viscountess and all eight of her children in one room is enough to make one fear one is seeing double—or triple—or worse. Never has This Author seen a collection of siblings so ludicrously alike in their physical regard. Although This Author has never taken the time to record eye color, all eight possess similar bone structure and the same thick, chestnut hair. One must pity the viscountess as she seeks advantageous marriages for her brood that she did not produce a single child of more fashionable coloring. Still, there are advantages to a family of such consistent looks—there can be no doubt that all eight are of legitimate parentage.

Ah, Gentle Reader, your devoted Author wishes that that were the case amid all large families . . .

LADY WHISTLEDOWN'S SOCIETY PAPERS,
26 APRIL 1813

"Ooooooooooohhhhhhhhhh!" Violet Bridgerton crumpled the single-page newspaper into a ball and hurled it across the elegant drawing room.

Her daughter Daphne wisely made no comment and pretended to be engrossed in her embroidery.

"Did you read what she said?" Violet demanded. "Did you?"

Daphne eyed the ball of paper, which now rested under a mahogany end table. "I didn't have the opportunity before you, er, finished with it."

"Read it, then," Violet wailed, her arm slicing dramatically through the air. "Read how *that woman* has maligned us."

Daphne calmly set down her embroidery and reached under the end table. She smoothed the sheet of paper out on her lap and read the paragraph about her family. Blinking, she looked up. "This isn't so bad, Mother. In fact, it's a veritable benediction compared to what she wrote about the Featheringtons last week."

"How am I supposed to find you a husband while *that woman* is slandering your name?"

Daphne forced herself to exhale. After nearly two seasons in London, the mere mention of the word *husband* was enough to set her temples pounding. She wanted to marry, truly she did, and she wasn't even holding out for a true love match. But was it really too much to hope for a husband for whom one had at least some affection?

Thus far, four men had asked for her hand, but when Daphne had thought about living the rest of her days in the company of any of them, she just couldn't do it. There were a number of men she thought might make reasonably good husbands, but the problem was—none of them was interested. Oh, they all *liked* her. Everyone liked her. Everyone thought she was funny and kind and a quick wit, and no one thought her the least bit unattractive, but at the same time, no one was dazzled by her beauty, stunned into speechlessness by her presence, or moved to write poetry in her honor.

Men, she thought with disgust, were interested only in those women who terrified them. No one seemed inclined to court someone like her. They all adored her, or so they said, because she was so easy to talk to, and she always seemed to understand how a man felt. As one of the men Daphne had thought might make a reasonably good husband had said, "Deuce take it, Daff, you're just not like regular females. You're positively normal."

Which she might have managed to consider a compliment if he hadn't proceeded to wander off in search of the latest blond beauty.

Daphne looked down and noticed that her hand was clenched into a fist. Then she looked up and realized her mother was staring at her, clearly waiting for her to say something. Since she had already exhaled, Daphne cleared her throat, and said, "I'm sure Lady Whistledown's little column is not going to hurt my chances for a husband."

"Daphne, it's been two years!"

"And Lady Whistledown has only been publishing for three months, so I hardly see how we can lay the blame at her door."

"I'll lay the blame wherever I choose," Violet muttered.

Daphne's fingernails bit her palms as she willed herself not to make a retort. She knew her mother had only her best interests at heart, she knew her mother loved her. And she loved her mother, too. In fact, until Daphne had reached marriageable age, Violet had been positively the best of mothers. She still was, when she wasn't despairing over the fact that after Daphne she had three more daughters to marry off.

Violet pressed a delicate hand to her chest. "She cast aspersions on your parentage."

"No," Daphne said slowly. It was always wise to proceed with caution when contradicting her mother. "Actually, what she said was that there could be no doubt that we are all legitimate. Which is more than one can say for most large families of the *ton*."

"She shouldn't have even brought it up," Violet sniffed.

"Mother, she's the author of a scandal sheet. It's her job to bring such things up."

"She isn't even a real person," Violet added angrily. She planted her hands on her slim hips, then changed her mind and shook her finger in the air. "Whistledown, ha! I've never heard of any Whistledowns. Whoever this depraved woman is, I doubt she's one of *us*. As if anyone of breeding would write such wicked lies."

"Of course she's one of us," Daphne said, her brown eyes filling with amusement. "If she weren't a member of the *ton*, there is no way she'd be privy to the sort of news she reports. Did you think she was some sort of impostor, peeking in windows and listening at doors?"

"I don't like your tone, Daphne Bridgerton," Violet said, her eyes narrowing.

Daphne bit back another smile. "I don't like your tone" was Violet's standard answer when one of her children was winning an argument.

But it was too much fun to tease her mother. "I wouldn't be surprised," she said, cocking her head to the side, "if Lady Whistledown was one of your friends."

"Bite your tongue, Daphne. No friend of mine would ever stoop so low."

"Very well," Daphne allowed, "it's probably not one of your friends. But I'm certain it's someone we know. No interloper could ever obtain the information she reports."

Violet crossed her arms. "I should like to put her out of business once and for all."

"If you wish to put her out of business," Daphne could not resist pointing out, "you shouldn't support her by buying her newspaper."

"And what good would that do?" Violet demanded. "Everyone else is reading it. My puny little embargo would do nothing except make me look ignorant when everyone else is chuckling over her latest gossip."

That much was true, Daphne silently agreed. Fashionable London was positively addicted to *Lady Whistledown's Society Papers*. The mysterious newspaper had arrived on the doorstep of every member of the *ton* three months earlier. For two weeks it was delivered unbidden every Monday, Wednesday, and Friday. And then, on the third Monday, butlers across London waited in vain for the pack of paperboys who normally delivered *Whistledown*, only to discover that instead of free delivery, they were selling the gossip sheet for the outrageous price of five pennies a paper.

Daphne had to admire the fictitious Lady Whistledown's savvy. By the time she started forcing people to pay for their gossip, all the *ton* was addicted. Everyone forked over their pennies, and somewhere some meddlesome woman was getting very rich.

While Violet paced the room and huffed about this "hideous slight" against her family, Daphne looked up to make certain her mother wasn't paying her any attention, then let her eyes drop to peruse the rest of the scandal sheet. *Whistledown*—as it was now called—was a curious mix of commentary, social news, scathing insult, and the occasional compliment. What set it apart from any previous society news sheets was that the author actually listed her subjects' names in full. There was no hiding behind abbreviations such as Lord S—— and Lady G——. If Lady Whistledown wanted to write about someone, she used his full name. The *ton* declared themselves scandalized, but they were secretly fascinated.

This most recent edition was typical *Whistledown.* Aside from the short piece on the Bridgertons—which was really no more than a description of the family—Lady Whistledown had recounted the events at the previous night's ball. Daphne hadn't attended, as it had been her younger sister's birthday, and the Bridgertons always made a big fuss about birthdays. And with eight children, there were a lot of birthdays to celebrate.

"You're reading that rubbish," Violet accused.

Daphne looked up, refusing to feel the least bit guilty. "It's a rather good column today. Apparently Cecil Tumbley knocked over an entire tower of champagne glasses last night."

"Really?" Violet asked, trying not to look interested.

"Mmm-hmm," Daphne replied. "She gives quite a good account of the Middlethorpe ball. Mentions who was talking to whom, what everyone was wearing—"

"And I suppose she felt the need to offer her opinions on that point," Violet cut in.

Daphne smiled wickedly. "Oh, come now, Mother. You know that Mrs. Featherington has always looked dreadful in purple."

Violet tried not to smile. Daphne could see the corners of her mouth twitching as she tried to maintain the composure she deemed appropriate for a viscountess and mother. But within two seconds, she was grinning and sitting next to her daughter on the sofa. "Let me see that," she said, snatching up the paper. "What else happened? Did we miss anything important?"

Daphne said, "Really, Mother, with Lady Whistledown as a reporter, one needn't actually *attend* any events." She waved toward the paper. "This is almost as good as actually being there. Better, probably. I'm certain we had better food last night than they did at the ball. And give that back." She yanked the paper back, leaving a torn corner in Violet's hands.

"Daphne!"

Daphne affected mock righteousness. "I was reading it."

"Well!"

"Listen to this."

Violet leaned in.

Daphne read: " 'The rake formerly known as Earl Clyvedon has finally seen fit to grace London with his presence. Although he has not yet deigned to make an appearance at a respectable evening function, the new Duke of Hastings has been spotted several times at White's and once at Tattersall's.' " She paused to take a breath. " 'His grace has resided abroad for six years. Can it be any coincidence that he has returned only now that the old duke is dead?' "

Daphne looked up. "My goodness, she *is* blunt, isn't she? Isn't Clyvedon one of Anthony's friends?"

"He's Hastings now," Violet said automatically, "and yes, I do believe he and Anthony were friendly at Oxford. And Eton as well, I think." Her brow scrunched and her blue eyes narrowed with thought. "He was something of a hellion, if my memory serves. Always at odds with his father. But reputed to be quite brilliant. I'm fairly sure that Anthony said he took a first in mathematics. Which," she added with a maternal roll of her eyes, "is more than I can say for any of *my* children."

"Now, now, Mother," Daphne teased. "I'm sure I would take a first if Oxford would only see fit to admit women."

Violet snorted. "I corrected your arithmetic papers when your governess was ill, Daphne."

"Well, maybe in history, then," Daphne said with a grin. She looked back down at the paper in her hands, her eyes straying to the new duke's name. "He sounds quite interesting," she murmured.

Violet looked at her sharply. "He's quite unsuitable for a young lady of your years is what he is."

"Funny how my 'years,' as you put it, volley back and forth between being so young that I cannot even meet Anthony's friends and being so old that you despair of my ever contracting a good marriage."

"Daphne Bridgerton, I don't—"

"—like my tone, I know." Daphne grinned. "But you love me."

Violet smiled warmly and wrapped an arm around Daphne's shoulder. "Heaven help me, I do."

Daphne gave her mother a quick peck on the cheek. "It's the curse of motherhood. You're required to love us even when we vex you."

Violet just sighed. "I hope that someday you have children—"

"—just like me, I know." Daphne smiled nostalgically and rested her head on her mother's shoulder. Her mother could be overly inquisitive, and her father had been more interested in hounds and hunting than he'd been in society affairs, but theirs had been a warm marriage, filled with love, laughter, and children. "I could do a great deal worse than follow your example, Mother," she murmured.

"Why, Daphne," Violet said, her eyes growing watery, "what a lovely thing to say."

Daphne twirled a lock of her chestnut hair around her finger, and grinned, letting the sentimental moment melt into a more teasing one. "I'm happy to follow in your footsteps when it comes to marriage and children, Mother, just so long as I don't have to have *eight*."

At that exact moment, Simon Basset, the new Duke of Hastings and the erstwhile topic of the Bridgerton ladies' conversation, was sitting at White's. His companion was none other than Anthony Bridgerton, Daphne's eldest brother. The two cut a striking pair, both tall and athletic, with thick dark hair. But where Anthony's eyes were the same deep chocolate brown as his sister's, Simon's were icy blue, with an oddly penetrating gaze.

It was those eyes as much as anything that had earned him his reputation as a man to be reckoned with. When he stared at a person, clear and unwavering, men grew uncomfortable. Women positively shivered.

But not Anthony. The two men had known each other for years, and Anthony just laughed when Simon raised a brow and turned his icy gaze upon him. "You forget, I've seen you with your head being lowered into a chamber pot," Anthony had once told him. "It's been difficult to take you seriously ever since."

To which Simon had replied, "Yes, but if I recall, you were the one holding me over that fragrant receptacle."

"One of my proudest moments, to be sure. But you had your revenge the next night in the form of a dozen eels in my bed."

Simon allowed himself a smile as he remembered both the incident and their subsequent conversation about it. Anthony was a good friend, just the sort a man would want by his side in a pinch. He'd been the first person Simon had looked up upon returning to England.

"It's damned fine to have you back, Clyvedon," Anthony said, once they'd settled in at their table at White's. "Oh, but I suppose you'll insist I call you Hastings now."

"No," Simon said rather emphatically. "Hastings will always be my father. He never answered to anything else." He paused. "I'll assume his title if I must, but I won't be called by his name."

"If you must?" Anthony's eyes widened slightly. "Most men would not sound quite so resigned about the prospect of a dukedom."

Simon raked a hand through his dark hair. He knew he was supposed to cherish his birthright and display unwavering pride in the Basset family's illustrious history, but the truth was it all made him sick inside. He'd spent his entire life not living up to his father's expectations; it seemed ridiculous now to try to live up to his name. "It's a damned burden is what it is," he finally grumbled.

"You'd best get used to it," Anthony said pragmatically, "because that's what everyone will call you."

Simon knew it was true, but he doubted if the title would ever sit well upon his shoulders.

"Well, whatever the case," Anthony added, respecting his friend's privacy by not delving further into what was obviously an uncomfortable topic, "I'm glad to have you back. I might finally get some peace next time I escort my sister to a ball."

Simon leaned back, crossing his long, muscular legs at the ankles. "An intriguing remark."

Anthony raised a brow. "One that you're certain I'll explain?"

"But of course."

"I ought to let you learn for yourself, but then, I've never been a cruel man."

Simon chuckled. "This coming from the man who dunked my head in a chamber pot?"

Anthony waved his hand dismissively. "I was young."

"And now you're a model of mature decorum and respectability?"

Anthony grinned. "Absolutely."

"So tell me," Simon drawled, "how, exactly, am I meant to make your existence that much more peaceful?"

"I assume you plan to take your place in society?"

"You assume incorrectly."

"But you *are* planning to attend Lady Danbury's ball this week," Anthony said.

"Only because I am inexplicably fond of the old woman. She says what she means, and—" Simon's eyes grew somewhat shuttered.

"And?" Anthony prompted.

Simon gave his head a little shake. "It's nothing. Just that she was rather kind to me as a child. I spent a few school holidays at her house with Riverdale. Her nephew, you know."

Anthony nodded once. "I see. So you have no intention of entering society. I'm impressed by your resolve. But allow me to warn you—even if you do not choose to attend the *ton*'s events, *they* will find you."

Simon, who had chosen that moment to take a sip of his brandy, choked on the spirit at the look on Anthony's face when he said, "they." After a few moments of coughing and sputtering, he finally managed to say, "Who, pray tell, are 'they'?"

Anthony shuddered. "Mothers."

"Not having had one myself, I can't say I grasp your point."

"Society mothers, you dolt. Those fire-breathing dragons with daughters of—God help us—marriageable age. You can run, but you'll never manage to hide from them. And I should warn you, my own is the worst of the lot."

"Good God. And here I thought Africa was dangerous."

Anthony shot his friend a faintly pitying look. "They will hunt you down. And when they find you, you will find yourself trapped in conversation with a pale young lady all dressed in white who cannot converse on topics other than the weather, who received vouchers to Almack's, and hair ribbons."

A look of amusement crossed Simon's features. "I take it, then, that during my time abroad you have become something of an eligible gentleman?"

"Not out of any aspirations to the role on my part, I assure you. If it were up to me, I'd avoid society functions like the plague. But my sister made her bow last year, and I'm forced to escort her from time to time."

"Daphne, you mean?"

Anthony looked up in surprise. "Did the two of you ever meet?"

"No," Simon admitted, "but I remember her letters to you at school, and I recalled that she was fourth in the family, so she had to start with D, and—"

"Ah, yes," Anthony said with a slight roll of his eyes, "the Bridgerton method of naming children. Guaranteed to make certain no one forgets who you are."

Simon laughed. "It worked, didn't it?"

"Say, Simon," Anthony suddenly said, leaning forward, "I've promised my mother I'll have dinner at Bridgerton House later this week with the family. Why don't you join me?"

Simon raised a dark brow. "Didn't you just warn me about society mothers and debutante daughters?"

Anthony laughed. "I'll put my mother on her best behavior, and don't worry about Daff. She's the exception that proves the rule. You'll like her immensely."

Simon narrowed his eyes. Was Anthony playing matchmaker? He couldn't tell.

As if Anthony were reading his thoughts, he laughed. "Good God, you don't think I'm trying to pair you off with Daphne, do you?"

Simon said nothing.

"You would never suit. You're a bit too brooding for her tastes."

Simon thought that an odd comment, but instead chose to ask, "Has she had any offers, then?"

"A few." Anthony kicked back the rest of his brandy, then let out a satisfied exhale. "I've allowed her to refuse them all."

"That's rather indulgent of you."

Anthony shrugged. "Love is probably too much to hope for in a marriage these days, but I don't see why she shouldn't be happy with her husband. We've had offers from one man old enough to be her father, another old enough to be her father's younger brother, one who was rather too high in the instep for our often boisterous clan, and then this week, dear God, that was the worst!"

"What happened?" Simon asked curiously.

Anthony gave his temples a weary rub. "This last one was perfectly amiable, but a rather bit dim in the head. You'd think, after our rakish days, I'd be completely without feelings—"

"Really?" Simon asked with a devilish grin. "You'd think that?"

Anthony scowled at him. "I didn't particularly enjoy breaking this poor fool's heart."

"Er, wasn't Daphne the one to do that?"

"Yes, but I had to *tell* him."

"Not many brothers would allow their sister such latitude with their marriage proposals," Simon said quietly.

Anthony just shrugged again, as if he couldn't imagine treating his sister in any other way. "She's been a good sister to me. It's the least I can do."

"Even if it means escorting her to Almack's?" Simon said wickedly.

Anthony groaned. "Even then."

"I'd console you by pointing out that this will all be over soon, but you've what, three other sisters waiting in the wings?"

Anthony positively slumped in his seat. "Eloise is due out in two years, and Francesca the year after that, but then I've a bit of a reprieve before Hyacinth comes of age."

Simon chuckled. "I don't envy you your responsibilities in that quarter." But even as he said the words, he felt a strange longing, and he wondered what it would be like to be not quite so alone in this world. He had no plans to start a family of his own, but maybe if he'd had one to begin with, his life would have turned out a bit differently.

"So you'll come for supper, then?" Anthony stood. "Informal, of course. We never take meals formally when it's just family."

Simon had a dozen things to do in the next few days, but before he could remind himself that he needed to get his affairs in order, he heard himself saying, "I'd be delighted."

"Excellent. And I'll see you at the Danbury bash first?"

Simon shuddered. "Not if I can help it. My aim is to be in and out in under thirty minutes."

"You really think," Anthony said, raising a doubtful brow, "that you're going to be able to go to the party, pay your respects to Lady Danbury, and leave?"

Simon's nod was forceful and direct.

But Anthony's snort of laughter was not terribly reassuring.

Chapter 2

The new Duke of Hastings is a most interesting character. While it is common knowledge that he was not on favorable terms with his father, even This Author is unable to learn the reason for the estrangement.

LADY WHISTLEDOWN'S SOCIETY PAPERS,
26 APRIL 1813

Later that week, Daphne found herself standing on the fringes of Lady Danbury's ballroom, far away from the fashionable crowd. She was quite content with her position.

Normally she would have enjoyed the festivities; she liked a good party as well as the next young lady, but earlier that evening, Anthony had informed her that Nigel Berbrooke had sought him out two days earlier and asked for her hand. Again. Anthony had, of course, refused (again!), but Daphne had the sinking feeling that Nigel was going to prove uncomfortably persistent. After all, two marriage proposals in two weeks did not paint a picture of a man who accepted defeat easily.

Across the ballroom she could see him looking this way and that, and she shrank further into the shadows.

She had no idea how to deal with the poor man. He wasn't very bright, but he also wasn't unkind, and though she knew she had to somehow put an end to his infatuation, she was finding it far easier to take the coward's way out and simply avoid him.

She was considering slinking into the ladies' retiring room when a familiar voice stopped her in her tracks.

"I say, Daphne, what are you doing all the way over here?"

Daphne looked up to see her eldest brother making his way toward her. "Anthony," she said, trying to decide if she was pleased to see him or annoyed that he might be coming over to meddle in her affairs. "I hadn't realized you would be in attendance."

"Mother," he said grimly. No other words were necessary.

"Ah," Daphne said with a sympathetic nod. "Say no more. I understand completely."

"She made a list of potential brides." He shot his sister a beleaguered look. "We do love her, don't we?"

Daphne choked on a laugh. "Yes, Anthony, we do."

"It's temporary insanity," he grumbled. "It has to be. There is no other explanation. She was a perfectly reasonable mother until you reached marriageable age."

"Me?" Daphne squeaked. "Then this is all my fault? You're a full eight years older than I am!"

"Yes, but she wasn't gripped by this matrimonial fervor until you came along."

Daphne snorted. "Forgive me if I lack sympathy. I received a list last year."

"Did you?"

"Of course. And lately she's been threatening to deliver them to me on a weekly basis. She badgers me on the issue of marriage far more than you could ever imagine. After all, bachelors are a challenge. Spinsters are merely pathetic. And in case you hadn't noticed, I'm female."

Anthony let out a low chuckle. "I'm your brother. I don't notice those things." He gave her a sly, sideways look. "Did you bring it?"

"My list? Heavens, no. What can you be thinking?"

His smile widened. "I brought mine."

Daphne gasped. "You didn't!"

"I did. Just to torture Mother. I'm going to peruse it right in front of her, pull out my quizzing glass—"

"You don't have a quizzing glass."

He grinned—the slow, devastatingly wicked smile that all Bridgerton males seemed to possess. "I bought one just for this occasion."

"Anthony, you absolutely cannot. She will *kill* you. And then, somehow, she'll find a way to blame *me*."

"I'm counting on it."

Daphne swatted him in the shoulder, eliciting a loud enough grunt to cause a half dozen partygoers to send curious looks in their direction.

"A solid punch," Anthony said, rubbing his arm.

"A girl can't live long with four brothers without learning how to throw one." She crossed her arms. "Let me see your list."

"After you just assaulted me?"

Daphne rolled her brown eyes and cocked her head in a decidedly impatient gesture.

"Oh, very well." He reached into his waistcoat, pulled out a folded slip of paper, and handed it to her. "Tell me what you think. I'm sure you'll have no end of cutting remarks."

Daphne unfolded the paper and stared down at her mother's neat, elegant handwriting. The Viscountess Bridgerton had listed the names of eight women. Eight very eligible, very wealthy young women.

"Precisely what I expected," Daphne murmured.

"Is it as dreadful as I think?"

"Worse. Philipa Featherington is as dumb as a post."

"And the rest of them?"

Daphne looked up at him under raised brows. "You didn't really want to get married this year, anyway, did you?"

Anthony winced. "And how was your list?"

"Blessedly out-of-date, now. Three of the five married last season. Mother is still berating me for letting them slip through my fingers."

The two Bridgertons let out identical sighs as they slumped against the wall. Violet Bridgerton was undeterred in her mission to marry off her children. Anthony, her eldest son, and Daphne, her eldest daughter, had borne the brunt of the pressure, although Daphne suspected that the viscountess might have cheerfully married off ten-year-old Hyacinth if she'd received a suitable offer.

"Good God, you look a pair of sad sorts. What are you doing so far off in the corner?"

Another instantly recognizable voice. "Benedict," Daphne said, glancing sideways at him without moving her head. "Don't tell me Mother managed to get you to attend tonight's festivities."

He nodded grimly. "She has completely bypassed cajoling and moved on to guilt. Three times this week she has reminded me I may have to provide the next viscount, if Anthony here doesn't get busy."

Anthony groaned.

"I assume that explains your flight as well to the darkest corners of the ballroom?" Benedict continued. "Avoiding Mother?"

"Actually," Anthony replied, "I saw Daff skulking in the corner and—"

"Skulking?" Benedict said with mock horror.

She shot them both an irritated scowl. "I came over to hide from Nigel Berbrooke," she explained. "I left Mother in the company of Lady Jersey, so she's not likely to pester me anytime soon, but Nigel—"

"Is more monkey than man," Benedict quipped.

"Well, I wouldn't have put it *that* way precisely," Daphne said, trying to be kind, "but he isn't terribly bright, and it's so much easier to stay out of his way than to hurt his feelings. Of course now that you lot have found me, I shan't be able to avoid him for long."

Anthony voiced a simple, "Oh?"

Daphne looked at her two older brothers, both an inch above six feet with broad shoulders and melting brown eyes. They each sported thick chestnut hair—much the same color as her own—and more to the point, they could not go anywhere in polite society without a small gaggle of twittering young ladies following them about.

And where a gaggle of twittering young ladies went, Nigel Berbrooke was sure to follow.

Already Daphne could see heads turning in their direction. Ambitious mamas were nudging their daughters and pointing to the two Bridgerton brothers, off by themselves with no company save for their sister.

"I knew I should have made for the retiring room," Daphne muttered.

"I say, what's that piece of paper in your hand, Daff?" Benedict inquired.

Somewhat absentmindedly, she handed him the list of Anthony's supposed brides.

At Benedict's loud chortle, Anthony crossed his arms, and said, "Try not to have too much fun at my expense. I predict you'll be receiving a similar list next week."

"No doubt," Benedict agreed. "It's a wonder Colin—" His eyes snapped up. "Colin!"

Yet another Bridgerton brother joined the crowd.

"Oh, Colin!" Daphne exclaimed, throwing her arms around him. "It's so *good* to see you."

"Note that we didn't receive similarly enthusiastic greetings," Anthony said to Benedict.

"You I see all the time," Daphne retorted. "Colin's been away a full year." After giving him one last squeeze, she stepped back, and scolded, "We didn't expect you until next week."

Colin's one-shoulder shrug matched his lopsided smile to perfection. "Amsterdam grew dull."

"Ah," Daphne said with a shrewd look in her eye. "Then you ran out of money."

Colin laughed and held up his hands in surrender. "Guilty as charged."

Anthony hugged his brother, and said gruffly, "It's damned fine to have you home, brother. Although the funds I sent you should have lasted you at least until—"

"Stop," Colin said helplessly, laughter still tinging his voice. "I promise you may scold me all you want tomorrow. Tonight I merely wish to enjoy the company of my beloved family."

Benedict let out a snort. "You must be completely broke if you're calling us 'beloved.' " But he leaned forward to give his brother a hearty hug all the same. "Welcome home."

Colin, always the most devil-may-care of the family, grinned, his green eyes twinkling. "Good to be back. Although I must say the weather is not nearly so fine as on the Continent, and as for the women, well, England would be hard-pressed to compete with the signorina I—"

Daphne punched him in the arm. "Kindly recall that there is a lady present, churl." But there was little ire in her voice. Of all her siblings, Colin was the closest to her in age—only eighteen months her elder. As children, they had been inseparable—and always in trouble. Colin was a natural prankster, and Daphne had never needed much convincing to go along with his schemes. "Does Mother know you're home?" she asked.

Colin shook his head. "I arrived to an empty house, and—"

"Yes, Mother put the younger ones to bed early tonight," Daphne interrupted.

"I didn't want to wait about and twiddle my thumbs, so Humboldt gave me your direction and I came here."

Daphne beamed, her wide smile lending warmth to her dark eyes. "I'm glad you did."

"Where *is* Mother?" Colin asked, craning his neck to peer over the crowd. Like all Bridgerton males, he was tall, so he didn't have to stretch very far.

"Over in the corner with Lady Jersey," Daphne replied.

Colin shuddered. "I'll wait until she's extricated herself. I have no wish to be flayed alive by that dragon."

"Speaking of dragons," Benedict said pointedly. His head didn't move, but his eyes flicked off to the left.

Daphne followed his line of vision to see Lady Danbury marching slowly toward them. She carried a cane, but Daphne swallowed nervously and steeled her shoulders. Lady Danbury's often cutting wit was legendary among the *ton*. Daphne had always suspected that a sentimental heart beat under her acerbic exterior, but still, it was always terrifying when Lady Danbury pressed one into conversation.

"No escape," Daphne heard one of her brothers groan.

Daphne shushed him and offered the old lady a hesitant smile.

Lady Danbury's brows rose, and when she was but four feet away from the group of Bridgertons, she stopped, and barked, "Don't pretend you don't see me!"

This was followed by a thump of the cane so loud that Daphne jumped back just enough to trample Benedict's toe.

"Euf," said Benedict.

Since her brothers appeared to have gone temporarily mute (except for Benedict, of course, but Daphne didn't think that grunts of pain counted as intelligible speech) Daphne swallowed, and said, "I hope I did not give that impression, Lady Danbury, for—"

"Not you," Lady Danbury said imperiously. She jabbed her cane into the air, making a perfectly horizontal line that ended perilously close to Colin's stomach. "Them."

A chorus of mumbled greetings emerged as a response.

Lady Danbury flicked the men the briefest of glances before turning back to Daphne, and saying, "Mr. Berbrooke was asking after you."

Daphne actually felt her skin turn green. "He was?"

Lady Danbury gave her a curt nod. "I'd nip that one in the bud, were I you, Miss Bridgerton."

"Did you tell him where I was?"

Lady Danbury's mouth slid into a sly, conspiratorial smile. "I always knew I liked you. And no, I did not tell him where you were."

"Thank you," Daphne said gratefully.

"It'd be a waste of a good mind if you were shackled to that nitwit," Lady Danbury said, "and the good Lord knows that the *ton* can't afford to waste the few good minds we've got."

"Er, thank you," Daphne said.

"As for you lot"—Lady Danbury waved her cane at Daphne's

brothers—"I still reserve judgment. You"—she pointed the cane at Anthony—"I'm inclined to be favorable toward, since you refused Berbrooke's suit on your sister's behalf, but the rest of you . . . Hmmph."

And with that she walked away.

" 'Hmmph?' " Benedict echoed. " 'Hmmph?' She purports to quantify my intelligence and all she comes up with is 'Hmmph?' "

Daphne smirked. "She *likes* me."

"You're welcome to her," Benedict grumbled.

"Rather sporting of her to warn you about Berbrooke," Anthony admitted.

Daphne nodded. "I believe that was my cue to take my leave." She turned to Anthony with a beseeching look. "If he comes looking for me—"

"I'll take care of it," he said gently. "Don't worry."

"Thank you." And then, with a smile to her brothers, she slipped out of the ballroom.

As Simon walked quietly through the halls of Lady Danbury's London home, it occurred to him that he was in a singularly good mood. This, he thought with a chuckle, was truly remarkable, considering the fact that he was about to attend a society ball and thus subject himself to all the horrors Anthony Bridgerton had laid out before him earlier that afternoon.

But he could console himself with the knowledge that after today, he needn't bother with such functions again; as he had told Anthony earlier that afternoon, he was only attending this particular ball out of loyalty to Lady Danbury, who, despite her curmudgeonly ways, had always been quite nice to him as a child.

His good mood, he was coming to realize, derived from the simple fact that he was pleased to be back in England.

Not that he hadn't enjoyed his journeys across the globe. He'd traveled the length and breadth of Europe, sailed the exquisitely blue seas of the Mediterranean, and delved into the mysteries of North Africa. From there he'd gone on to the Holy Land, and then, when inquiries revealed that it was not yet time to return home, he crossed the Atlantic and explored the West Indies. At that point he considered moving on to the United States of America, but the new nation had seen fit to enter into conflict with Britain, so Simon had stayed away.

Besides, that was when he'd learned that his father, ill for several years, had finally died.

It was ironic, really. Simon wouldn't have traded his years of exploration for anything. Six years gave a man a lot of time to think, a lot of time to learn what it meant to be a man. And yet the only reason the then-twenty-two-year-old Simon had left England was because his father had suddenly decided that he was finally willing to accept his son.

Simon hadn't been willing to accept his father, though, and so he'd simply packed his bags and left the country, preferring exile to the old duke's hypocritical overtures of affection.

It had all started when Simon had finished at Oxford. The duke hadn't originally wanted to pay for his son's schooling; Simon had once seen a letter written to a tutor stating that he refused to let his idiot son make a fool of the family at Eton. But Simon had had a hungry mind as well as a stubborn heart, and so he'd ordered a carriage to take him to Eton, knocked on the headmaster's door, and announced his presence.

It had been the most terrifying thing he'd ever done, but he'd somehow managed to convince the headmaster that the mix-up was the school's fault, that somehow Eton must have lost his enrollment papers and fees. He'd copied all of his father's mannerisms, raising an arrogant brow, lifting his chin, and looking down his nose, and generally appearing as if he thought he owned the world.

And the entire time, he'd been quaking in his shoes, terrified that at any moment his words would grow garbled and land on top of each other, that "I am Earl Clyvedon, and I am here to begin classes," would instead come out as, "I am Earl Clyvedon, and I am h-h-h-h-h-h—"

But it hadn't, and the headmaster, who'd spent enough years educating England's elite to immediately recognize Simon as a member of the Basset family, had enrolled him posthaste and without question. It had taken several months for the duke (who was always quite busy with his own pursuits) to learn of his son's new status and change in residence. By that point, Simon was well ensconced at Eton, and it would have looked very bad if the duke had pulled the boy out of school for no reason.

And the duke didn't like to look bad.

Simon had often wondered why his father hadn't chosen to make an overture at that time. Clearly Simon wasn't tripping over his every word at Eton; the duke would have heard from the headmaster if his son weren't able to keep up with his studies. Simon's speech still occasionally slipped, but by then he'd grown remarkably proficient in covering up his mistakes with a cough or, if he was lucky enough to be taking a meal at the time, a well-timed sip of tea or milk.

But the duke never even wrote him a letter. Simon supposed his father had grown so used to ignoring his son that it didn't even matter that he wasn't proving to be an embarrassment to the Basset name.

After Eton, Simon followed the natural progression to Oxford, where he earned the reputations of both scholar and rake. Truth be told, he hadn't deserved the label of rake any more than most of the young bucks at university, but Simon's somewhat aloof demeanor somehow fed the persona.

Simon wasn't exactly certain how it had happened, but gradually he became aware that his peers craved his approval. He was intelligent and athletic, but it seemed his elevated status had more to do with his manner than anything else. Because Simon didn't speak when words were not necessary, people judged him to be arrogant, just as a future duke should be. Because he preferred to surround himself with only those friends with whom he truly felt comfortable, people decided he was exceptionally discriminating in his choice of companions, just as a future duke should be.

He wasn't very talkative, but when he did say something, he had a quick and often ironic wit—just the sort of humor that guaranteed that people would hang on his every word. And again, because he didn't constantly run off at the mouth, as did so many of the *ton*, people were even *more* obsessed with what he had to say.

He was called "supremely confident," "heartstoppingly handsome," and "the perfect specimen of English manhood." Men wanted his opinion on any number of topics.

The women swooned at his feet.

Simon never could quite believe it all, but he enjoyed his status nonetheless, taking what was offered him, running wild with his friends, and enjoying the company of all the young widows and opera singers who sought his attention—and every escapade was all the more delicious for knowing that his father must disapprove.

But, as it turned out, his father didn't *entirely* disapprove. Unbeknownst to Simon, the Duke of Hastings had already begun to grow interested in the progress of his only son. He requested academic reports from the university and hired a Bow Street Runner to keep him apprised of Simon's extracurricular activities. And eventually, the duke stopped expecting every missive to contain tales of his son's idiocy.

It would have been impossible to pinpoint exactly when his change of heart occurred, but one day the duke realized that his son had turned out rather nicely, after all.

The duke puffed out with pride. As always, good breeding had proven true in the end. He should have known that Basset blood could not produce an imbecile.

Upon finishing Oxford with a first in mathematics, Simon came to London with his friends. He had, of course, taken bachelor's lodgings, having no wish to reside with his father. And as Simon went out in society, more and more people misinterpreted his pregnant pauses for arrogance and his small circle of friends for exclusivity.

His reputation was sealed when Beau Brummel—the then recognized leader of society—had asked a rather involved question about some trivial new fashion. Brummel's tone had been condescending and he had clearly hoped to embarrass the young lord. As all London knew, Brummel loved nothing better than to reduce England's elite into blithering idiots. And so he had pretended to care about Simon's opinion, ending his question with a drawled, "Don't you think?"

As an audience of gossips watched with baited breath, Simon, who couldn't have cared less about the specific arrangement of the Prince's cravat, simply turned his icy blue eyes on Brummel, and answered, "No."

No explanation, no elaboration, just, "No."

And then he walked away.

By the next afternoon, Simon might as well have been the king of society. The irony was unnerving. Simon didn't care for Brummel or his tone, and he would probably have delivered a more loquacious set-down if he'd been sure he could do so without stumbling over his words. And yet in this particular instance, less had most definitely proven to be more, and Simon's terse sentence had turned out to be far more deadly than any long-winded speech he might have uttered.

Word of the brilliant and devastatingly handsome Hastings heir naturally reached the duke's ears. And although he did not immediately seek Simon out, Simon began to hear bits and pieces of gossip that warned him that his relationship with his father might soon see a change. The duke had laughed when he'd heard of the Brummel incident, and said, "Naturally. He's a Basset." An acquaintance mentioned that the duke had been heard crowing about Simon's first at Oxford.

And then the two came face-to-face at a London ball.

The duke would not allow Simon to give him the cut direct.

Simon tried. Oh, how he tried. But no one had the ability to crush his confidence like his father, and as he stared at the duke, who might as well have been a mirror image, albeit slightly older version, of himself, he couldn't move, couldn't even try to speak.

His tongue felt thick, his mouth felt odd, and it almost seemed as if his stutters had spread from his mouth to his body, for he suddenly didn't even feel right in his own skin.

The duke had taken advantage of Simon's momentary lapse of reason by embracing him with a heartfelt, "Son."

Simon had left the country the very next day.

He'd known that it would be impossible to avoid his father completely if he remained in England. And he refused to act the part of his son after having been denied a father for so many years.

Besides, lately he'd been growing bored of London's wild life. Rake's reputation aside, Simon didn't really have the temperament of a true debauché. He had enjoyed his nights on the town as much as any of his dissolute cronies, but after three years in Oxford and one in London, the endless round of parties and prostitutes was growing, well, old.

And so he left.

Now, however, he was glad to be back. There was something soothing about being home, something peaceful and serene about an English springtime. And after six years of solitary travel, it was damned good to find his friends again.

He moved silently through the halls, making his way to the ballroom. He hadn't wanted to be announced; the last thing he desired was a declaration of his presence. The afternoon's conversation with Anthony Bridgerton had reaffirmed his decision not to take an active role in London society.

He had no plans to marry. Ever. And there wasn't much point in attending *ton* parties if one wasn't looking for a wife.

Still, he felt he owed some loyalty to Lady Danbury after her many kindnesses during his childhood, and truth be told, he held a great deal of affection for the forthright old lady. It would have been the height of rudeness to spurn her invitation, especially since it had come accompanied by a personal note welcoming him back to the country.

Since Simon knew his way around this house, he'd entered through a side door. If all went well, he could slip unobtrusively into the ballroom, give his regards to Lady Danbury, and leave.

But as he turned a corner, he heard voices, and he froze.

Simon suppressed a groan. He'd interrupted a lovers' tryst. Bloody hell. How to extricate himself without notice? If his presence was discovered, the ensuing scene was sure to be replete with histrionics, embarrassment, and no end of tedious emotion. Better just to melt into the shadows and let the lovers go on their merry way.

But as Simon started backing quietly up, he heard something that caught his attention.

"No."

No? Had some young lady been forced into the deserted hallway against her will? Simon had no great desire to be anyone's hero, but even he could not let such an insult pass. He craned his neck slightly, pressing his ear forward so that he might hear better. After all, he might have heard incorrectly. If no one needed saving, he certainly wasn't going to charge forward like some bullish fool.

"Nigel," the girl was saying, "you really shouldn't have followed me out here."

"But I love you!" the young man cried out in a passionate voice. "All I want is to make you my wife."

Simon nearly groaned. Poor besotted fool. It was painful to listen to.

"Nigel," she said again, her voice surprisingly kind and patient, "my brother has already told you that I cannot marry you. I hope that we may continue on as friends."

"But your brother doesn't understand!"

"Yes," she said firmly, "he does."

"Dash it all! If you don't marry me, who will?"

Simon blinked in surprise. As proposals went, this one was decidedly *un*romantic.

The girl apparently thought so, too. "Well," she said, sounding a bit disgruntled, "it's not as if there aren't dozens of other young ladies in Lady Danbury's ballroom right now. I'm sure one of them would be thrilled to marry you."

Simon leaned forward slightly so that he could get a glimpse of the scene. The girl was in shadows, but he could see the man quite clearly. His face held a hangdog expression, and his shoulders were slumped forward in defeat. Slowly, he shook his head. "No," he said forlornly, "they don't. Don't you see? They . . . they . . ."

Simon winced as the man fought for words. He didn't appear to be stuttering so much as emotionally overcome, but it was never pleasant when one couldn't get a sentence out.

"No one's as nice as you," the man finally said. "You're the only one who ever smiles at me."

"Oh, Nigel," the girl said, sighing deeply. "I'm sure that's not true."

But Simon could tell she was just trying to be kind. And as she sighed again, it became apparent to him that she would not need any rescuing. She seemed to have the situation well in hand, and while Simon felt vague pangs of sympathy for the hapless Nigel, there wasn't anything he could do to help.

Besides, he was beginning to feel like the worst sort of voyeur.

He started inching backward, keeping his eye focused on a door that he knew led to the library. There was another door on the other side of that room, one that led to the conservatory. From there he could enter the main hall and make his way to the ballroom. It wouldn't be as discreet as cutting through the back corridors, but at least poor Nigel wouldn't know that his humiliation had had a witness.

But then, just a footstep away from a clean getaway, he heard the girl squeal.

"You have to marry me!" Nigel cried out. "You have to! I'll never find anyone else—"

"Nigel, stop!"

Simon turned around, groaning. It looked like he was going to have to rescue the chit, after all. He strode back into the hall, putting his sternest, most dukish expression on his face. The words, "I believe the lady asked you to stop," rested on the tip of his tongue, but it seemed that he wasn't fated to play the hero tonight, after all, because before he could make a sound, the young lady pulled back her right arm and landed a surprisingly effective punch squarely on Nigel's jaw.

Nigel went down, his arms comically flailing in the air as his legs slid out from under him. Simon just stood there, watching in disbelief as the girl dropped to her knees.

"Oh dear," she said, her voice squeaking slightly. "Nigel, are you all right? I didn't mean to hit you so hard."

Simon laughed. He couldn't help it.

The girl looked up, startled.

Simon caught his breath. She had been in shadows until now, and all he'd been able to discern of her appearance was a wealth of thick, dark hair. But now, as she lifted her head to face him, he saw that she had large, equally dark eyes, and the widest, lushest mouth he'd ever seen. Her heart-shaped face wasn't beautiful by society standards, but something about her quite simply sucked the breath from his body.

Her brows, thick but delicately winged, drew together. "Who," she asked, not sounding at all pleased to see him, "are you?"

Chapter 3

It has been whispered to This Author that Nigel Berbrooke was seen at Moreton's Jewelry Shop purchasing a diamond solitaire ring. Can a new Mrs. Berbrooke be very far behind?

LADY WHISTLEDOWN'S SOCIETY PAPERS,
28 April 1813

The night, Daphne decided, couldn't possibly get much worse. First she'd been forced to spend the evening in the darkest corner of the ballroom (which wasn't such an easy task, since Lady Danbury clearly appreciated both the aesthetic and illuminating qualities of candles), then she'd managed to trip over Philipa Featherington's foot as she tried to make her escape, which had led Philipa, never the quietest girl in the room, to squeal, "Daphne Bridgerton! Are you hurt?" Which must have captured Nigel's attention, for his head had snapped up like a startled bird, and he'd immediately started hurrying across the ballroom. Daphne had hoped, no *prayed* that she could outrun him and make it to the ladies' retiring room before he caught up with her, but no, Nigel had cornered her in the hall and started wailing out his love for her.

It was all embarrassing enough, but now it appeared this man—this shockingly handsome and almost disturbingly poised stranger—had witnessed the entire thing. And worse, he was laughing!

Daphne glared at him as he chuckled at her expense. She'd never seen him before, so he had to be new to London. Her mother had made certain that Daphne had been introduced to, or at least been made aware of, all eligible gentlemen. Of course, this man could be married and therefore not on Violet's list of potential victims, but Daphne instinctively knew that he could not have been long in London without all the world whispering about it.

His face was quite simply perfection. It took only a moment to realize that he put all of Michelangelo's statues to shame. His eyes were oddly intense—so blue they practically glowed. His hair was thick and dark, and he was tall—as tall as her brothers, which was a rare thing.

This was a man, Daphne thought wryly, who could quite possibly steal the gaggle of twittering young ladies away from the Bridgerton men for good.

Why that annoyed her so much, she didn't know. Maybe it was because she knew a man like him would never be interested in a woman like her. Maybe it was because she felt like the veriest frump sitting there on the floor in his splendid presence. Maybe it was simply because he was standing there laughing as if she were some sort of circus amusement.

But whatever the case, an uncharacteristic peevishness rose within her, and her brows drew together as she asked, "Who are you?"

Simon didn't know why he didn't answer her question in a straightforward manner, but some devil within caused him to reply, "My intention had been to be your rescuer, but you clearly had no need of my services."

"Oh," the girl said, sounding slightly mollified. She clamped her lips together, twisting them slightly as she considered his words. "Well, thank you, then, I suppose. Pity you didn't reveal yourself ten seconds earlier. I'd rather not have had to hit him."

Simon looked down at the man on the ground. A bruise was already darkening on his chin, and he was moaning, "Laffy, oh Laffy. I love you, Laffy."

"You're Laffy, I presume?" Simon murmured, sliding his gaze up to her face. Really, she was quite an attractive little thing, and from this angle the bodice of her gown seemed almost decadently low.

She scowled at him, clearly not appreciating his attempt at subtle humor—and also clearly not realizing that his heavy-lidded gaze had rested on portions of her anatomy that were not her face. "What are we to do with him?" she asked.

" 'We?' " Simon echoed.

Her scowl deepened. "You did say you aspired to be my rescuer, didn't you?"

"So I did." Simon planted his hands on his hips and assessed the situation. "Shall I drag him out into the street?"

"Of course not!" she exclaimed. "For goodness' sake, isn't it still raining outside?"

"My dear Miss Laffy," Simon said, not particularly concerned about the condescending tone of his voice, "don't you think your concern is slightly misplaced? This man tried to attack you."

"He didn't try to attack me," she replied. "He just . . . He just . . . Oh, very well, he tried to attack me. But he would never have done me any real harm."

Simon raised a brow. Truly, women were the most contrary creatures. "And you can be sure of that?"

He watched as she carefully chose her words. "Nigel isn't capable of malice," she said slowly. "All he is guilty of is misjudgment."

"You're a more generous soul than I, then," Simon said quietly.

The girl let out another sigh, a soft, breathy sound that Simon somehow felt across his entire body. "Nigel's not a bad person," she said with quiet dignity. "It's just that he isn't always terribly bright, and perhaps he mistook kindness on my part for something more."

Simon felt a strange sort of admiration for this girl. Most women of his acquaintance would have been in hysterics at this point, but she—whoever she was—had taken the situation firmly in hand, and was now displaying a generosity of spirit that was astounding. That she could even think to defend this Nigel person was quite beyond him.

She rose to her feet, dusting her hands off on the sage green silk of her skirts. Her hair had been styled so that one thick lock fell over her shoulder, curling seductively at the top of her breast. Simon knew he should be listening to her—she was prattling on about something, as women were wont to do—but he couldn't seem to take his eyes off that single dark lock of hair. It fell like a silky ribbon across her swanlike neck, and Simon had the most appalling urge to close the distance between them and trace the line of her hair with his lips.

He'd never dallied with an innocent before, but all the world had already painted him a rake. What could be the harm? It wasn't as if he were going to ravish her. Just a kiss. Just one little kiss.

It was tempting, so deliciously, maddeningly tempting.

"Sir! Sir!"

With great reluctance, he dragged his eyes up to her face. Which was, of course, delightful in and of itself, but it was difficult to picture her seduction when she was scowling at him.

"Were you listening to me?"

"Of course," he lied.

"You weren't."

"No," he admitted.

A sound came from the back of her throat that sounded suspiciously like a growl. "Then why," she ground out, "did you say you were?"

He shrugged. "I thought it was what you wanted to hear."

Simon watched with fascinated interest as she took a deep breath and muttered something to herself. He couldn't hear her words, but he doubted any of them could be construed as complimentary. Finally, her voice almost comically even, she said, "If you don't wish to aid me, I'd prefer it if you would just leave."

Simon decided it was time to stop acting like such a boor, so he said, "My apologies. Of course I'll help you."

She exhaled, and then looked back to Nigel, who was still lying on the floor, moaning incoherently. Simon looked down, too, and for several seconds they just stood there, staring at the unconscious man, until the girl said, "I really didn't hit him very hard."

"Maybe he's drunk."

She looked dubious. "Do you think? I smelled spirits on his breath, but I've never seen him drunk before."

Simon had nothing to add to that line of thought, so he just asked, "Well, what do you want to do?"

"I suppose we could just leave him here," she said, the expression in her dark eyes hesitant.

Simon thought that was an excellent idea, but it was obvious she wanted the idiot cared for in a more tender manner. And heaven help him, but he felt the strangest compulsion to make her happy. "Here is what we're going to do," he said crisply, glad that his tone belied any of the odd tenderness he was feeling. "I am going to summon my carriage—"

"Oh, good," she interrupted. "I really didn't want to leave him here. It seemed rather cruel."

Simon thought it seemed rather generous considering the big oaf had nearly attacked her, but he kept that opinion to himself and instead continued on with his plan. "You will wait in the library while I'm gone."

"In the library? But—"

"In the library," he repeated firmly. "With the door shut. Do you really want to be discovered with Nigel's body should anyone happen to wander down this hallway?"

"His body? Good gracious, sir, you needn't make it sound as if he were dead."

"As I was saying," he continued, ignoring her comment completely, "you will remain in the library. When I return, we will relocate Nigel here to my carriage."

"And how will we do that?"

He gave her a disarmingly lopsided grin. "I haven't the faintest idea."

For a moment Daphne forgot to breathe. Just when she'd decided that her would-be rescuer was irredeemingly arrogant, he had to go and smile at her like that. It was one of those boyish grins, the kind that melted female hearts within a ten-mile radius.

And, much to Daphne's dismay, it was awfully hard to remain thoroughly irritated with a man under the influence of such a smile. After growing up with four brothers, all of whom had seemed to know how to charm ladies from birth, Daphne had thought she was immune.

But apparently not. Her chest was tingling, her stomach was turning cartwheels, and her knees felt like melted butter.

"Nigel," she muttered, desperately trying to force her attention away from the nameless man standing across from her, "I must see to Nigel." She crouched down and shook him none too gently by the shoulder. "Nigel? Nigel? You have to wake up now, Nigel."

"Daphne," Nigel moaned. "Oh, Daphne."

The dark-haired stranger's head snapped around. "Daphne? Did he say Daphne?"

She drew back, unnerved by his direct question and the rather intense look in his eyes. "Yes."

"Your name is Daphne?"

Now she was beginning to wonder if he was an idiot. "Yes."

He groaned. "Not Daphne Bridgerton."

Her face slid into a puzzled frown. "The very one."

Simon staggered back a step. He suddenly felt physically ill, as his brain finally processed the fact that she had thick, chestnut hair. The famous Bridgerton hair. Not to mention the Bridgerton nose, and cheekbones, and—Bugger it all, this was Anthony's *sister*!

Bloody hell.

There were rules among friends, commandments, really, and the most important one was Thou Shalt Not Lust After Thy Friend's Sister.

While he stood there, probably staring at her like a complete idiot, she planted her hands on her hips, and demanded, "And who are *you*?"

"Simon Basset," he muttered.

"The duke?" she squeaked.

He nodded grimly.

"Oh, dear."

Simon watched with growing horror as the blood drained from her face. "Good God, woman, you're not going to swoon, are you?" He couldn't imagine why she would, but Anthony—her brother, he reminded himself—had spent half the afternoon warning him about the effects of a young, unmarried duke on the young, unmarried female population. Anthony had specifically singled out Daphne as the exception to the rule, but still, she looked deucedly pale. "Are you?" he demanded, when she said nothing. "Going to swoon?"

She looked offended that he'd even considered the notion. "Of course not!"

"Good."

"It's just that—"

"What?" Simon asked suspiciously.

"Well," she said with a rather dainty shrug of her shoulders, "I've been warned about you."

This was really too much. "By whom?" he demanded.

She stared at him as if he were an imbecile. "By everyone."

"That, my d—" He felt something suspiciously like a stammer coming on, and so he took a deep breath to steady his tongue. He'd become a master at this kind of control. All she would see was a man who looked as if he were trying to keep his temper in check. And considering the direction of their conversation, that image could not seem terribly far-fetched.

"My dear Miss Bridgerton," Simon said, starting anew in a more even and controlled tone, "I find that difficult to believe."

She shrugged again, and he had the most irritating sensation that she was enjoying his distress. "Believe what you will," she said blithely, "but it was in the paper today."

"*What?*"

"In *Whistledown*," she replied, as if that explained anything.

"Whistle-which?"

Daphne stared at him blankly for a moment until she remembered that he was newly returned to London. "Oh, you must not know about it," she said softly, a wicked little smile crossing her lips. "Fancy that."

The duke took a step forward, his stance positively menacing.

"Miss Bridgerton, I feel I should warn you that I am within an inch of strangling the information out of you."

"It's a gossip sheet," she said, hastily backing up a step. "That's all. It's rather silly, actually, but everyone reads it."

He said nothing, just arched one arrogant brow.

Daphne quickly added, "There was a report of your return in Monday's edition."

"And what"—his eyes narrowed dangerously—"precisely"—now they turned to ice—"did it say?"

"Not very much, ah, precisely," Daphne hedged. She tried to back up a step, but her heels were already pressing against the wall. Any further and she'd be up on her tiptoes. The duke looked beyond furious, and she was beginning to think that she should try for a quick escape and just leave him here with Nigel. The two were perfect for each other—madmen, the both of them!

"Miss Bridgerton." There was a wealth of warning in his voice.

Daphne decided to take pity on him since, after all, he was new to town and hadn't had time to adjust to the new world according to *Whistledown*. She supposed she couldn't really blame him for being so upset that he'd been written about in the paper. It had been rather startling for Daphne the first time as well, and she'd at least had the warning of a month's previous *Whistledown* columns. By the time Lady Whistledown got around to writing about Daphne, it had been almost anticlimactic.

"You needn't upset yourself over it," Daphne said, attempting to lend a little compassion to her voice but probably not succeeding. "She merely wrote that you were a terrible rake, a fact which I'm sure you won't deny, since I have long since learned that men positively *yearn* to be considered rakes."

She paused and gave him the opportunity to prove her wrong and deny it. He didn't.

She continued, "And then my mother, whose acquaintance I gather you must have made at some point or another before you left to travel the world, confirmed it all."

"Did she?"

Daphne nodded. "She then forbade me ever to be seen in your company."

"Really?" he drawled.

Something about the tone of his voice—and the way his eyes seemed to have grown almost smoky as they focused on her face—made her extremely uneasy, and it was all she could do not to shut her eyes.

She refused—absolutely refused—to let him see how he'd affected her.

His lips curved into a slow smile. "Let me make certain I have this correctly. Your mother told you I am a very bad man and that you are under no circumstances to be seen with me."

Confused, she nodded.

"Then what," he asked, pausing for dramatic effect, "do you think your mother would say about *this* little scenario?"

She blinked. "I beg your pardon?"

"Well, unless you count Nigel here"—he waved his hand toward the unconscious man on the floor—"no one has actually *seen* you in my presence. And yet . . ." He let his words trail off, having far too much fun watching the play of emotions on her face to do anything but drag this moment out to its lengthiest extreme.

Of course most of the emotions on her face were varying shades of irritation and dismay, but that made the moment all the sweeter.

"And yet?" she ground out.

He leaned forward, narrowing the distance between them to only a few inches. "And yet," he said softly, knowing that she'd feel his breath on her face, "here we are, completely alone."

"Except for Nigel," she retorted.

Simon spared the man on the floor the briefest of glances before returning his wolfish gaze to Miss Bridgerton. "I'm not terribly concerned about Nigel," he murmured. "Are you?"

Simon watched as she looked down at Nigel in dismay. It had to be clear to her that her spurned suitor wasn't going to save her should Simon decide to make an amorous advance. Not that he would, of course. After all, this was Anthony's younger sister. He might have to remind himself of this at frequent intervals, but it wasn't a fact that was likely to slip his mind on a permanent basis.

Simon knew that it was past time to end this little game. Not that he thought she would report the interlude to Anthony; somehow he knew that she would prefer to keep this to herself, stewing over it in privately righteous fury, and, dare he hope it—just a touch of excitement?

But even as he knew it was time to stop this flirtation and get back to the business of hauling Daphne's idiotic suitor out of the building, he couldn't resist one last comment. Maybe it was the way her lips pursed when she was annoyed. Or maybe it was the way they parted when she was shocked. All he knew was that he was helpless against his own devilish nature when it came to this girl.

And so he leaned forward, his eyes heavy-lidded and seductive as he said, "I think I know what your mother would say."

She looked a little befuddled by his onslaught, but still she managed a rather defiant, "Oh?"

Simon nodded slowly, and he touched one finger to her chin. "She'd tell you to be very, very afraid."

There was a moment of utter silence, and then Daphne's eyes grew very wide. Her lips tightened, as if she were keeping something inside, and then her shoulders rose slightly, and then . . .

And then she laughed. Right in his face.

"Oh, my goodness," she gasped. "Oh, that was funny."

Simon was not amused.

"I'm sorry." This was said between laughs. "Oh, I'm sorry, but really, you shouldn't be so melodramatic. It doesn't suit you."

Simon paused, rather irritated that this slip of a girl had shown such disrespect for his authority. There were advantages to being considered a dangerous man, and being able to cow young maidens was supposed to be one of them.

"Well, actually, it does suit you, I ought to admit," she added, still grinning at his expense. "You looked quite dangerous. And very handsome, of course." When he made no comment, her face took on a bemused expression, and she asked, "That was your intention, was it not?"

He still said nothing, so she said, "Of course it was. And I would be remiss if I did not tell you that you would have been successful with any other woman besides me."

A comment he couldn't resist. "And why is that?"

"Four brothers." She shrugged as if that should explain everything. "I'm quite immune to your games."

"Oh?"

She gave his arm a reassuring pat. "But yours was a most admirable attempt. And truly, I'm quite flattered you thought me worthy of such a magnificent display of dukish rakishness." She grinned, her smile wide and unfeigned. "Or do you prefer rakish dukishness?"

Simon stroked his jaw thoughtfully, trying to regain his mood of menacing predator. "You're a most annoying little chit, did you know that, Miss Bridgerton?"

She gave him her sickliest of smiles. "Most people find me the soul of kindness and amiability."

"Most people," Simon said bluntly, "are fools."

Daphne cocked her head to the side, obviously pondering his words. Then she looked over at Nigel and sighed. "I'm afraid I have to agree with you, much as it pains me."

Simon bit back a smile. "It pains you to agree with me, or that most people are fools?"

"Both." She grinned again a wide, enchanting smile that did odd things to his brain. "But mostly the former."

Simon let out a loud laugh, then was startled to realize how foreign the sound was to his ears. He was a man who frequently smiled; occasionally chuckled, but it had been a very long time since he'd felt such a spontaneous burst of joy. "My dear Miss Bridgerton," he said, wiping his eyes, "if you are the soul of kindness and amiability, then the world must be a very dangerous place."

"Oh, for certain," she replied. "At least to hear my mother tell it."

"I can't imagine why I do not recall your mother," Simon murmured, "because she certainly sounds a memorable character."

Daphne raised a brow. "You don't remember her?"

He shook his head.

"Then you don't know her."

"Does she look like you?"

"That's an odd question."

"Not so very odd," Simon replied, thinking that Daphne was exactly right. It *was* an odd question, and he had no idea why he'd voiced it. But since he had, and since she had questioned it, he added, "After all, I'm told that all of you Bridgertons look alike."

A tiny, and to Simon mysterious, frown touched her face. "We do. Look alike, that is. Except for my mother. She's rather fair, actually, with blue eyes. We all get our dark hair from our father. I'm told I have her smile, though."

An awkward pause fell across the conversation. Daphne was shifting from foot to foot, not at all certain what to say to the duke, when Nigel exhibited stellar timing for the first time in his life, and sat up. "Daphne?" he said, blinking as if he couldn't see straight. "Daphne, is that you?"

"Good God, Miss Bridgerton," the duke swore, "how hard did you hit him?"

"Hard enough to knock him down, but no worse than that, I swear!" Her brow furrowed. "Maybe he *is* drunk."

"Oh, Daphne," Nigel moaned.

The duke crouched next to him, then reeled back, coughing.

"Is he drunk?" Daphne asked.

The duke staggered back. "He must have drunk an entire bottle of whiskey just to get up the nerve to propose."

"Who would have thought I could be so terrifying?" Daphne murmured, thinking of all the men who thought of her as a jolly good friend and nothing more. "How wonderful."

Simon stared at her as if she were insane, then muttered, "I'm not even going to question that statement."

Daphne ignored his comment. "Should we set our plan into action?"

Simon planted his hands on his hips and reassessed the scene. Nigel was trying to rise to his feet, but it didn't appear, to Simon's eye at least, that he was going to find success anytime in the near future. Still, he was probably lucid enough to make trouble, and certainly lucid enough to make noise, which he was doing. Quite well, actually.

"Oh, Daphne. I luff you so much, Daffery." Nigel managed to raise himself to his knees, weaving around as he shuffled toward Daphne, looking rather like a sotted churchgoer attempting to pray. "Please marry me, Duffne. You have to."

"Buck up, man," Simon grunted, grabbing him by the collar. "This is getting embarrassing." He turned to Daphne. "I'm going to have to take him outside now. We can't leave him here in the hall. He's liable to start moaning like a sickened cow—"

"I rather thought he'd already started," Daphne said.

Simon felt one corner of his mouth twist up in a reluctant smile. Daphne Bridgerton might be a marriageable female and thus a disaster waiting to happen for any man in his position, but she was certainly a good sport.

She was, it occurred to him in a rather bizarre moment of clarity, the sort of person he'd probably call friend if she were a man.

But since it was abundantly obvious—to both his eyes and his body—that she wasn't a man, Simon decided it was in both of their best interests to wrap up this "situation" as soon as possible. Aside from the fact that Daphne's reputation would suffer a deadly blow if they were discovered, Simon wasn't positive that he could trust himself to keep his hands off of her for very much longer.

It was an unsettling feeling, that. Especially for a man who so valued his self-control. Control was everything. Without it he'd never have stood up to his father or taken a first at university. Without it, he'd—

Without it, he thought grimly, he'd still be speaking like an idiot.

"I'll haul him out of here," he said suddenly. "You go back to the ballroom."

Daphne frowned, glancing over her shoulder to the hall that led back to the party. "Are you certain? I thought you wanted me to go to the library."

"That was when we were going to leave him here while I summoned the carriage. But we can't do that if he's awake."

She nodded her agreement, and asked, "Are you sure you can do it? Nigel's a rather large man."

"I'm larger."

She cocked her head. The duke, although lean, was powerfully built, with broad shoulders and firmly muscled thighs. (Daphne knew she wasn't supposed to notice such things, but, really, was it *her* fault that current fashions dictated such snug breeches?) More to the point, he had a certain air about him, something almost predatory, something that hinted of tightly controlled strength and power.

Daphne decided she had no doubt that he'd be able to move Nigel.

"Very well," she said, giving him a nod. "And thank you. It's very kind of you to help me in this way."

"I'm rarely kind," he muttered.

"Really?" she murmured, allowing herself a tiny smile. "How odd. I couldn't possibly think of anything else to call it. But then again, I've learned that men—"

"You do seem to be the expert on men," he said, somewhat acerbically, then grunted as he hauled Nigel to his feet.

Nigel promptly reached for Daphne, practically sobbing her name. Simon had to brace his legs to keep him from lunging at her.

Daphne darted back a step. "Yes, well, I do have four brothers. A better education I cannot imagine."

There was no way of knowing if the duke had intended to answer her, because Nigel chose that moment to regain his energy (although clearly not his equilibrium) and yanked himself free of Simon's grip. He threw himself onto Daphne, making incoherent, drunken noises all the way.

If Daphne hadn't had her back to the wall, she would have been knocked to the ground. As it was, she hit the wall with a bone-jarring thud, knocking all the breath from her body.

"Oh, for the love of Christ," the duke swore, sounding supremely disgusted. He hauled Nigel off Daphne, then turned to her, and asked, "Can I hit him?"

"Oh, please do go ahead," she replied, still gasping for breath. She'd tried to be kind and generous toward her erstwhile suitor, but really, enough was enough.

The duke muttered something that sounded like "good" and landed a stunningly powerful blow on Nigel's chin.

Nigel went down like a stone.

Daphne regarded the man on the floor with equanimity. "I don't think he's going to wake up this time."

Simon shook out his fist. "No."

Daphne blinked and looked back up. "Thank you."

"It was my pleasure," he said, scowling at Nigel.

"What shall we do now?" Her gaze joined his on the man on the floor—now well and truly unconscious.

"Back to the original plan," he said crisply. "We leave him here while you wait in the library. I'd rather not have to drag him out until I've a carriage waiting."

Daphne gave him a sensible nod. "Do you need help righting him, or should I proceed directly to the library?"

The duke was silent for a moment. His head tilted this way and that as he analyzed Nigel's position on the floor. "Actually, a bit of help would be greatly appreciated."

"Really?" Daphne asked, surprised. "I was sure you'd say no."

That earned her a faintly amused and superior look from the duke. "And is that why you asked?"

"No, of course not," Daphne replied, slightly offended. "I'm not so stupid as to offer help if I have no intention of giving it. I was merely going to point out that men, in my experience—"

"You have too much experience," the duke muttered under his breath.

"What?!"

"I beg your pardon," he amended. "You *think* you have too much experience."

Daphne glared at him, her dark eyes smoldering nearly to black. "That is not true, and who are you to say, anyway?"

"No, that's not quite right, either," the duke mused, completely ignoring her furious question. "I think it's more that *I* think you think you have too much experience."

"Why you—You—" As retorts went, it wasn't especially effective, but it was all Daphne could manage to get out. Her powers of speech tended to fail her when she was angry.

And she was really angry.

Simon shrugged, apparently unmoved by her furious visage. "My dear Miss Bridgerton—"

"If you call me that one more time, I swear I shall scream."

"No, you won't," he said with a rakish smile. "That would draw a crowd, and if you recall, you don't want to be seen with me."

"I am considering risking it," Daphne said, each word squeezed out between her teeth.

Simon crossed his arms and leaned lazily against the wall. "Really?" he drawled. "This I should like to see."

Daphne nearly threw up her arms in frustration. "Forget it. Forget me. Forget this entire evening. I'm leaving."

She turned around, but before she could even take a step, her movement was arrested by the sound of the duke's voice.

"I thought you were going to help me."

Drat. He had her there. She turned slowly around. "Why, yes," she said, her voice patently false, "I'd be delighted."

"You know," he said innocently, "if you didn't want to help you shouldn't have—"

"I said I'd help," she snapped.

Simon smiled to himself. She was such an easy mark. "Here is what we are going to do," he said. "I'm going to haul him to his feet and drape his right arm over my shoulders. You will go around to the other side and shore him up."

Daphne did as she was bid, grumbling to herself about his autocratic attitude. But she didn't voice a single complaint. After all, for all his annoying ways, the Duke of Hastings was helping her out of a possibly embarrassing scandal.

Of course if anyone found her in this position, she'd find herself in even worse straits.

"I have a better idea," she said suddenly. "Let's just leave him here."

The duke's head swung around to face her, and he looked as if he'd dearly like to toss her through a window—preferably one that was still closed. "I thought," he said, clearly working hard to keep his voice even, "that you didn't want to leave him on the floor."

"That was before he knocked me into the wall."

"Could you possibly have notified me of your change of heart before I expended my energy to lift him?"

Daphne blushed. She hated that men thought that women were fickle, changeable creatures, and she hated even more that she was living up to that image right then.

"Very well," he said simply, and dropped Nigel.

The sudden weight of him nearly took Daphne down to the floor as well. She let out a surprised squeal as she ducked out of the way.

"Now may we leave?" the duke asked, sounding insufferably patient.

She nodded hesitantly, glancing down at Nigel. "He looks rather uncomfortable, don't you think?"

Simon stared at her. Just stared at her. "You're concerned for his comfort?" he finally asked.

She gave her head a nervous shake, then a nod, then went back to the shake. "Maybe I should—That is to say—Here, just wait a moment." She crouched and untwisted Nigel's legs so he lay flat on his back. "I didn't think he deserved a trip home in your carriage," she explained as she rearranged his coat, "but it seemed rather cruel to leave him here in this position. There, now I'm done." She stood and looked up.

And just managed to catch sight of the duke as he walked away, muttering something about Daphne and something about women in general and something else entirely that Daphne didn't quite catch.

But maybe that was for the best. She rather doubted it had been a compliment.

Chapter 4

London is awash these days with Ambitious Mamas. At Lady Worth's ball last week This Author saw no fewer than eleven Determined Bachelors, cowering in corners and eventually fleeing the premises with those Ambitious Mamas hot on their heels.

It is difficult to determine who, precisely, is the worst of the lot, although This Author suspects the contest may come down to a near draw between Lady Bridgerton and Mrs. Featherington, with Mrs. F edging Lady B out by a nose. There are three Featherington misses on the market right now, after all, whereas Lady Bridgerton need only worry about one.

It is recommended, however, that all safety-minded people stay far, far away from the latest crop of unmarried men when Bridgerton daughters E, F, and H come of age. Lady B is not likely to look both ways when she barrels across a ballroom with three daughters in tow, and the Lord help us all should she decide to don metal-toed boots.

Lady Whistledown's Society Papers,
28 April 1813

The night, Simon decided, couldn't possibly get much worse. He wouldn't have believed it at the time, but his bizarre encounter with Daphne Bridgerton was definitely turning out to be the evening's high point. Yes, he'd been horrified to discover that he'd been lusting—even briefly—after his best friend's younger sister. Yes, Nigel Berbrooke's oafish attempts at seduction had offended every one of his rakish sensibilities. And yes, Daphne had finally exasperated him beyond endurance with her indecision over whether to treat Nigel like a criminal or care for him as she would her dearest friend.

But none of that—not one bit—compared to the torture that he'd been about to endure.

His oh-so-clever plan of slipping into the ballroom, giving his regards to Lady Danbury, and leaving unnoticed had fallen into instant ruin. He'd taken no more than two steps into the ballroom when he'd been recognized by an old friend from Oxford, who, much to Simon's dismay, had recently married. The wife was a perfectly charming young woman, but unfortunately one with rather high social aspirations, and she had quickly determined that her road to happiness lay in her position as the one to introduce the new duke to society. And Simon, even though he fancied himself a world-weary, cynical sort, discovered that he wasn't quite rude enough to directly insult the wife of his old university friend.

And so, two hours later, he'd been introduced to every unmarried lady at the ball, every *mother* of every unmarried lady at the ball, and, of course, every older married sister of every unmarried lady at the ball. Simon couldn't decide which set of women was the worst. The unmarried ladies were decidedly boring, the mothers were annoyingly ambitious, and the *sisters*—well, the sisters were so forward Simon began to wonder if he'd stumbled into a brothel. Six of them had made extremely suggestive remarks, two had slipped him notes inviting him to their boudoirs, and one had actually run her hand down his thigh.

In retrospect, Daphne Bridgerton was starting to look very good, indeed.

And speaking of Daphne, where the hell was she? He'd thought he'd caught a glimpse of her about an hour earlier, surrounded by her rather large and forbidding brothers. (Not that Simon found them individually forbidding, but he'd quickly decided that any man would have to be an imbecile to provoke them as a group.)

But since then she seemed to have disappeared. Indeed, he thought she might have been the only unmarried female at the party to whom he *hadn't* been introduced.

Simon wasn't particularly worried about her being bothered by Berbrooke after he'd left them in the hall. He'd delivered a solid punch to the man's jaw and had no doubt that he'd be out for several minutes. Probably longer, considering the vast quantities of alcohol Berbrooke had consumed earlier in the evening. And even if Daphne had been foolishly tenderhearted when it came to her clumsy suitor, she wasn't stupid enough to remain in the hallway with him until he woke up.

Simon glanced back over to the corner where the Bridgerton brothers were gathered, looking as if they were having a grand old time. They had been accosted by almost as many young women and old mothers as Simon, but at least there seemed to be some safety in numbers. Simon noticed that the young debutantes didn't seem to spend half as much time in the Bridgertons' company as they did in his.

Simon sent an irritated scowl in their direction.

Anthony, who was leaning lazily against a wall, caught the expression and smirked, raising a glass of red wine in his direction. Then he cocked his head slightly, motioning to Simon's left. Simon turned, just in time to be detained by yet another mother, this one with a trio of daughters, all of whom were dressed in monstrously fussy frocks, replete with tucks and flounces, and of course, heaps and heaps of lace.

He thought of Daphne, with her simple sage green gown. Daphne, with her direct brown eyes and wide smile . . .

"Your grace!" the mother shrilled. "Your grace!"

Simon blinked to clear his vision. The lace-covered family had managed to surround him with such efficiency that he wasn't even able to shoot a glare in Anthony's direction.

"Your grace," the mother repeated, "it is such an honor to make your acquaintance."

Simon managed a frosty nod. Words were quite beyond him. The family of females had pressed in so close he feared he might suffocate.

"Georgiana Huxley sent us over," the woman persisted. "She said I simply must introduce my daughters to you."

Simon didn't remember who Georgiana Huxley was, but he thought he might like to strangle her.

"Normally I should not be so bold," the woman went on, "but your dear, dear papa was such a friend of mine."

Simon stiffened.

"He was truly a marvelous man," she continued, her voice like nails to Simon's skull, "so conscious of his duties to the title. He must have been a marvelous father."

"I wouldn't know," Simon bit off.

"Oh!" The woman had to clear her throat several times before managing to say, "I see. Well. My goodness."

Simon said nothing, hoping an aloof demeanor would prompt her to take her leave. Damn it, where was Anthony? It was bad enough having these women acting as if he were some prize horse to be bred, but to have to stand here and listen to this woman tell him what a *good* father the old duke had been . . .

Simon couldn't possibly bear it.

"Your grace! Your grace!"

Simon forced his icy eyes back to the lady in front of him and told himself to be more patient with her. After all, she was probably only complimenting his father because she thought it was what he wanted to hear.

"I merely wanted to remind you," she said, "that we were introduced several years ago, back when you were still Clyvedon."

"Yes," Simon murmured, looking for any break in the barricade of ladies through which he might make his escape.

"These are my daughters," the woman said, motioning to the three young ladies. Two were pleasant-looking, but the third was still cloaked in baby fat and an orangey gown which did nothing for her complexion. She didn't appear to be enjoying the evening.

"Aren't they lovely?" the lady continued. "My pride and joy. And so even-tempered."

Simon had the queasy feeling that he'd heard the same words once when shopping for a dog.

"Your grace, may I present Prudence, Philipa, and Penelope."

The girls made their curtsies, not a one of them daring to meet his eye.

"I have another daughter at home," the lady continued. "Felicity. But she's a mere ten years of age, so I do not bring her to such events."

Simon could not imagine why she felt the need to share this information with him, but he just kept his tone carefully bored (this, he'd long since learned, was the best way not to show anger) and prompted, "And you are . . . ? "

"Oh, beg pardon! I am Mrs. Featherington, of course. My husband passed on three years ago, but he was your papa's, er, dearest friend." Her voice trailed off at the end of her sentence, as she remembered Simon's last reaction to mention of his father.

Simon nodded curtly.

"Prudence is quite accomplished on the pianoforte," Mrs. Featherington said, with forced brightness.

Simon noted the oldest girl's pained expression and quickly decided never to attend a musicale chez Featherington.

"And my darling Philipa is an expert watercolorist."

Philipa beamed.

"And Penelope?" some devil inside Simon forced him to ask.

Mrs. Featherington shot a panicked look at her youngest daughter, who looked quite miserable. Penelope was not terribly attractive, and her somewhat pudgy figure was not improved by her mother's choice of attire for her. But she seemed to have kind eyes.

"Penelope?" Mrs. Featherington echoed, her voice a touch shrill. "Penelope is . . . ah . . . well, she's Penelope!" Her mouth wobbled into a patently false grin.

Penelope looked as if she wanted to dive under a rug. Simon decided that if he was forced to dance, he'd ask Penelope.

"Mrs. Featherington," came a sharp and imperious voice that could only belong to Lady Danbury, "are you pestering the duke?"

Simon wanted to answer in the affirmative, but the memory of Penelope Featherington's mortified face led him to murmur, "Of course not."

Lady Danbury raised a brow as she moved her head slowly toward him. "Liar."

She turned back to Mrs. Featherington, who had gone quite green. Mrs. Featherington said nothing. Lady Danbury said nothing. Mrs. Featherington finally mumbled something about seeing her cousin, grabbed her three daughters, and scurried off.

Simon crossed his arms, but he wasn't able to keep his face completely free of amusement. "That wasn't very well done of you," he said.

"Bah. She's feathers for brains, and so do her girls, except maybe that unattractive young one." Lady Danbury shook her head. "If they'd only put her in a different color . . ."

Simon fought a chuckle and lost. "You never did learn to mind your own business, did you?"

"Never. And what fun would that be?" She smiled. Simon could tell she didn't want to, but she smiled. "And as for you," she continued. "You are a monstrous guest. One would have thought you'd possess the manners to greet your hostess by now."

"You were always too well surrounded by your admirers for me to dare even approach."

"So glib," she commented.

Simon said nothing, not entirely certain how to interpret her words. He'd always had the suspicion that she knew his secret, but he'd never been quite sure.

"Your friend Bridgerton approaches," she said.

Simon's eyes followed the direction of her nod. Anthony ambled over, and was only half a second in their presence before Lady Danbury called him a coward.

Anthony blinked. "I beg your pardon?"

"You could have come over and saved your friend from the Featherington quartet ages ago."

"But I was so enjoying his distress."

"Hmmph." And without another word (or another grunt) she walked away.

"Strangest old woman," Anthony said. "I wouldn't be surprised if she's that cursed Whistledown woman."

"You mean the gossip columnist?"

Anthony nodded as he led Simon around a potted plant to the corner where his brothers were waiting. As they walked, Anthony grinned, and said, "I noticed you speaking with a number of very proper young ladies."

Simon muttered something rather obscene and unflattering under his breath.

But Anthony only laughed. "You can't say I didn't warn you, can you?"

"It is galling to admit that you might be right about anything, so please do not ask me to do so."

Anthony laughed some more. "For that comment I shall start introducing you to the debutantes myself."

"If you do," Simon warned, "you shall soon find yourself dying a very slow and painful death."

Anthony grinned. "Swords or pistols?"

"Oh, poison. Very definitely poison."

"Ouch." Anthony stopped his stroll across the ballroom in front of two other Bridgerton men, both clearly marked by their chestnut hair, tall height, and excellent bone structure. Simon noted that one had green eyes and the other brown like Anthony, but other than that, the dim evening light made the three men practically interchangeable.

"You do remember my brothers?" Anthony queried politely. "Benedict and Colin. Benedict I'm sure you recall from Eton. He was the one who dogged our footsteps for three months when he first arrived."

"Not true!" Benedict said with a laugh.

"I don't know if you've met Colin, actually," Anthony continued. "He was probably too young to have crossed your path."

"Pleased to meet you," Colin said jovially.

Simon noted the rascally glint in the young man's green eyes and couldn't help but smile in return.

"Anthony here has said such insulting things about you," Colin continued, his grin growing quite wicked, "that I know we're sure to be great friends."

Anthony rolled his eyes. "I'm certain you can understand why my mother is convinced that Colin will be the first of her children to drive her to insanity."

Colin said, "I pride myself on it, actually."

"Mother, thankfully, has had a brief respite from Colin's tender charms," Anthony continued. "He is actually just returned from a grand tour of the Continent."

"Just this evening," Colin said with a boyish grin. He had a devil-may-care youthful look about him. Simon decided he couldn't be much older than Daphne.

"I have just returned from travels as well," Simon said.

"Yes, except yours spanned the globe, I hear," Colin said. "I should love to hear about them someday."

Simon nodded politely. "Certainly."

"Have you met Daphne?" Benedict inquired. "She's the only Bridgerton in attendance who's unaccounted for."

Simon was pondering how best to answer that question when Colin let out a snort, and said, "Oh, Daphne's accounted for. Miserable, but accounted for."

Simon followed his gaze across the ballroom, where Daphne was standing next to what had to be her mother, looking, just as Colin had promised, as miserable as could be.

And then it occurred to him—Daphne was one of those dreaded unmarried young ladies being paraded about by her mother. She'd seemed far too sensible and forthright to be such a creature, and yet of course that was what she had to be. She couldn't have been more than twenty, and as her name was still Bridgerton she was clearly a maiden. And since she had a mother—well, of course she'd be trapped into an endless round of introductions.

She looked every bit as pained by the experience as Simon had been. Somehow that made him feel a good deal better.

"One of us should save her," Benedict mused.

"Nah," Colin said, grinning. "Mother's only had her over there with Macclesfield for ten minutes."

"Macclesfield?" Simon asked.

"The earl," Benedict replied. "Castleford's son."

"Ten minutes?" Anthony asked. "Poor Macclesfield."

Simon shot him a curious look.

"Not that Daphne is such a chore," Anthony quickly added, "but when Mother gets it in her head to, ah . . ."

"Pursue," Benedict filled in helpfully.

"—a gentleman," Anthony continued with a nod of thanks toward his brother, "she can be, ah . . ."

"Relentless," Colin said.

Anthony smiled weakly. "Yes. Exactly."

Simon looked back over toward the trio in question. Sure enough, Daphne looked miserable, Macclesfield was scanning the room, presumably looking for the nearest exit, and Lady Bridgerton's eyes held a gleam so ambitious that Simon cringed in sympathy for the young earl.

"We should save Daphne," Anthony said.

"We really should," Benedict added.

"And Macclesfield," Anthony said.

"Oh, certainly," Benedict added.

But Simon noticed that no one was leaping into action.

"All talk, aren't you?" Colin chortled.

"I don't see *you* marching over there to save her," Anthony shot back.

"Hell no. But I never said we should. *You*, on the other hand . . ."

"What the devil is going on?" Simon finally asked.

The three Bridgerton brothers looked at him with identical guilty expressions.

"We *should* save Daff," Benedict said.

"We really should," Anthony added.

"What my brothers are too lily-livered to tell you," Colin said derisively, "is that they are terrified of my mother."

"It's true," Anthony said with a helpless shrug.

Benedict nodded. "I freely admit it."

Simon thought he'd never seen a more ludicrous sight. These were the Bridgerton brothers, after all. Tall, handsome, athletic, with every miss in the nation setting her cap after them, and here they were, completely cowed by a mere slip of a woman.

Of course, it *was* their mother. Simon supposed one had to make allowances for that.

"If I save Daff," Anthony explained, "Mother might get me into her clutches, and then I'm done for."

Simon choked on laughter as his mind filled with a vision of Anthony being led around by his mother, moving from unmarried lady to unmarried lady.

"Now you see why I avoid these functions like the plague," Anthony said grimly. "I'm attacked from both directions. If the debutantes and their mothers don't find me, *my* mother makes certain I find *them*."

"Say!" Benedict exclaimed. "Why don't *you* save her, Hastings?"

Simon took one look at Lady Bridgerton (who at that point had her hand firmly wrapped around Macclesfield's forearm) and decided he'd rather be branded an eternal coward. "Since we haven't been introduced, I'm sure it would be most improper," he improvised.

"I'm sure it wouldn't," Anthony returned. "You're a duke."

"So?"

"So?" Anthony echoed. "Mother would forgive any impropriety if it meant gaining an audience for Daphne with a duke."

"Now look here," Simon said hotly, "I'm not some sacrificial lamb to be slaughtered on the altar of your mother."

"You *have* spent a lot of time in Africa, haven't you?" Colin quipped.

Simon ignored him. "Besides, your sister said—"

All three Bridgerton heads swung around in his direction. Simon immediately realized he'd blundered. Badly.

"You've met Daphne?" Anthony queried, his voice just a touch too polite for Simon's comfort.

Before Simon could even reply, Benedict leaned in ever-so-slightly closer, and asked, "Why didn't you mention this?"

"Yes," Colin said, his mouth utterly serious for the first time that evening. "Why?"

Simon glanced from brother to brother and it became perfectly clear why Daphne must still be unmarried. This belligerent trio would scare off all but the most determined—or stupid—of suitors.

Which would probably explain Nigel Berbrooke.

"Actually," Simon said, "I bumped into her in the hall as I was making my way into the ballroom. It was"—he glanced rather pointedly at the Bridgertons—"rather obvious that she was a member of your family, so I introduced myself."

Anthony turned to Benedict. "Must have been when she was fleeing Berbrooke."

Benedict turned to Colin. "What did happen to Berbrooke? Do you know?"

Colin shrugged. "Haven't the faintest. Probably left to nurse his broken heart."

Or broken head, Simon thought acerbically.

"Well, that explains everything, I'm sure," Anthony said, losing his overbearing big-brother expression and looking once again like a fellow rake and best friend.

"Except," Benedict said suspiciously, "why he didn't mention it."

"Because I didn't have the chance," Simon bit off, about ready to throw his arms up in exasperation. "In case you hadn't noticed, Anthony, you have a ridiculous number of siblings, and it takes a ridiculous amount of time to be introduced to all of them."

"There are only two of us present," Colin pointed out.

"I'm going home," Simon announced. "The three of you are mad."

Benedict, who had seemed to be the most protective of the brothers, suddenly grinned. "You don't have a sister, do you?"

"No, thank God."

"If you ever have a daughter, you'll understand."

Simon was rather certain he would never have a daughter, but he kept his mouth shut.

"It can be a trial," Anthony said.

"Although Daff is better than most," Benedict put in. "She doesn't have that many suitors, actually."

Simon couldn't imagine why not.

"I'm not really sure why," Anthony mused. "I think she's a perfectly nice girl."

Simon decided this wasn't the time to mention that he'd been one inch away from easing her up against the wall, pressing his hips against hers, and kissing her senseless. If he hadn't discovered that she was a Bridgerton, frankly, he might have done exactly that.

"Daff's the best," Benedict agreed.

Colin nodded. "Capital girl. Really good sport."

There was an awkward pause, and then Simon said, "Well, good sport or not, I'm not going over there to save her, because she told me quite specifically that your mother forbade her ever to be seen in my presence."

"Mother said *that*?" Colin asked. "You must really have a black reputation."

"A good portion of it undeserved," Simon muttered, not entirely certain why he was defending himself.

"That's too bad," Colin murmured. "I'd thought to ask you to take me 'round."

Simon foresaw a long and terrifyingly roguish future for the boy.

Anthony's fist found its way to the small of Simon's back, and he started to propel him forward. "I'm sure Mother will change her mind given the proper encouragement. Let's go."

Simon had no choice but to walk toward Daphne. The alternative required making a really big scene, and Simon had long since learned that he didn't do well with scenes. Besides, if he'd been in Anthony's position, he probably would have done the exact same thing.

And after an evening with the Featherington sisters and the like, Daphne didn't sound half-bad.

"Mother!" Anthony called out in a jovial voice as they approached the viscountess. "I haven't seen you all evening."

Simon noticed that Lady Bridgerton's blue eyes lit up when she saw her son approaching. Ambitious Mama or not, Lady Bridgerton clearly loved her children.

"Anthony!" she said in return. "How nice to see you. Daphne and I were just chatting with Lord Macclesfield."

Anthony sent Lord Macclesfield a commiserating look. "Yes, I see."

Simon caught Daphne's eye for a moment and gave his head the tiniest shake. She responded with an even tinier nod, sensible girl that she was.

"And who is this?" Lady Bridgerton inquired, her eyes lighting upon Simon's face.

"The new Duke of Hastings," Anthony replied. "Surely you remember him from my days at Eton and Oxford."

"Of course," Lady Bridgerton said politely.

Macclesfield, who had been keeping scrupulously quiet, quickly located the first lull in the conversation, and burst in with, "I think I see my father."

Anthony shot the young earl an amused and knowing glance. "Then by all means, go to him."

The young earl did, with alacrity.

"I thought he detested his father," Lady Bridgerton said with a confused expression.

"He does," Daphne said baldly.

Simon choked down a laugh. Daphne raised her brows, silently daring him to comment.

"Well, he had a terrible reputation, anyway," Lady Bridgerton said.

"There seems to be quite a bit of that in the air these days," Simon murmured.

Daphne's eyes widened, and this time Simon got to raise *his* brows, silently daring *her* to comment.

She didn't, of course, but her mother gave him a sharp look, and Simon had the distinct impression that she was trying to decide whether his newly acquired dukedom made up for his bad reputation.

"I don't believe I had the chance to make your acquaintance before I left the country, Lady Bridgerton," Simon said smoothly, "but I am very pleased to do so now."

"As am I." She motioned to Daphne. "My daughter Daphne."

Simon took Daphne's gloved hand and laid a scrupulously polite kiss on her knuckles. "I am honored to officially make your acquaintance, Miss Bridgerton."

"Officially?" Lady Bridgerton queried.

Daphne opened her mouth, but Simon cut in before she could say anything. "I already told your brother about our *brief* meeting earlier this evening."

Lady Bridgerton's head turned rather sharply in Daphne's direction. "You were introduced to the duke earlier this evening? Why did you not say anything?"

Daphne smiled tightly. "We were rather occupied with the earl. And before that, with Lord Westborough. And before that, with—"

"I see your point, Daphne," Lady Bridgerton ground out.

Simon wondered how unforgivably rude it would be if he laughed.

Then Lady Bridgerton turned the full force of her smile on him—and Simon quickly learned where Daphne got that wide, wide smile from—and Simon realized that Lady Bridgerton had decided that his bad reputation could be overlooked.

A strange light appeared in her eye, and her head bobbed back and forth between Daphne and Simon.

Then she smiled again.

Simon fought the urge to flee.

Anthony leaned over slightly, and whispered in his ear, "I am *so* sorry."

Simon said between clenched teeth, "I may have to kill you."

Daphne's icicle glare said that she'd heard both of them and was not amused.

But Lady Bridgerton was blissfully oblivious, her head presumably already filling with images of a grand wedding.

Then her eyes narrowed as she focused on something behind the men. She looked so overwhelmingly annoyed that Simon, Anthony, and Daphne all twisted their necks to see what was afoot.

Mrs. Featherington was marching purposefully in their direction, Prudence and Philipa right behind. Simon noticed that Penelope was nowhere to be seen.

Desperate times, Simon quickly realized, called for desperate measures. "Miss Bridgerton," he said, whipping his head around to face Daphne, "would you care to dance?"

Chapter 5

Were you at Lady Danbury's ball last night? If not, shame on you. You missed witnessing quite the most remarkable coup of the season. It was clear to all partygoers, and especially to This Author, that Miss Daphne Bridgerton has captured the interest of the newly returned to England Duke of Hastings.

One can only imagine the relief of Lady Bridgerton. How mortifying it will be if Daphne remains on the shelf for yet another season! And Lady B—with three more daughters to marry off. Oh, the horror.

Lady Whistledown's Society Papers,
30 April 1813

There was no way Daphne could refuse. First of all, her mother was impaling her with her deadly I-Am-Your-Mother-Don't-You-Dare-Defy-Me gaze.

Secondly, the duke had clearly not given Anthony the entire story of their meeting in the dimly lit hallway; to make a show of refusing to dance with him would certainly raise undue speculation.

Not to mention that Daphne really didn't particularly relish getting drawn into a conversation with the Featheringtons, which was sure to happen if she didn't make immediate haste for the dance floor.

And finally, she kind of sort of just a little teeny bit actually *wanted* to dance with the duke.

Of course the arrogant boor didn't even give her the chance to accept. Before Daphne could manage an "I'd be delighted," or even a mere, "Yes," he had her halfway across the room.

The orchestra was still producing those awful noises it makes while the musicians were getting ready to begin, so they were forced to wait a moment before they actually danced.

"Thank God you didn't refuse," the duke said with great feeling.

"When would I have had the opportunity?"

He grinned at her.

Daphne answered that with a scowl. "I wasn't given the opportunity to accept, either, if you recall."

He raised a brow. "Does that mean I must ask you again?"

"No, of course not," Daphne replied, rolling her eyes. "That would be rather childish of me, don't you think? And besides, it would cause a terrible scene, which I don't think either of us desires."

He cocked his head and gave her a rather assessing glance, as if he had analyzed her personality in an instant and decided she might just be acceptable. Daphne found the experience somewhat unnerving.

Just then the orchestra ceased its discordant warm-up and struck the first notes of a waltz.

Simon groaned. "Do young ladies still need permission to waltz?"

Daphne found herself smiling at his discomfort. "How long have you been away?"

"Five years. Do they?"

"Yes."

"Do you have it?" He looked almost pained at the prospect of his escape plan falling apart.

"Of course."

He swept her into his arms and whirled her into the throng of elegantly clad couples. "Good."

They had made a full circle of the ballroom before Daphne asked, "How much of our meeting did you reveal to my brothers? I saw you with them, you know."

Simon only smiled.

"What are you grinning about?" she asked suspiciously.

"I was merely marveling at your restraint."

"I beg your pardon?"

He shrugged slightly, his shoulders rising as his head tilted to the right. "I hadn't thought you the most patient of ladies," he said, "and here it took you a full three and a half minutes before asking me about my conversation with your brothers."

Daphne fought a blush. The truth was, the duke was a most accomplished dancer, and she'd been enjoying the waltz too much even to think of conversation.

"But since you asked," he said, mercifully sparing her from having to make a comment, "all I told them was that I ran into you in the hall and that, given your coloring, I instantly recognized you as a Bridgerton and introduced myself."

"Do you think they believed you?"

"Yes," he said softly, "I rather think they did."

"Not that we have anything to hide," she added quickly.

"Of course not."

"If there is any villain in this piece it is most certainly Nigel."

"Of course."

She chewed on her lower lip. "Do you think he's still out in the hall?"

"I certainly have no intention of finding out."

There was an awkward moment of silence, and then Daphne said, "It has been some time since you have attended a London ball, has it not? Nigel and I must have been quite a welcome."

"You were a welcome sight. He was not."

She smiled slightly at the compliment. "Aside from our little escapade, have you been enjoying your evening?"

Simon's answer was so unequivocally in the negative that he actually snorted a laugh before saying it.

"Really?" Daphne replied, her brows arching with curiosity. "Now *that* is interesting."

"You find my agony interesting? Remind me never to turn to you should I ever fall ill."

"Oh, please," she scoffed. "It can't have been that bad."

"Oh, it can."

"Certainly not as bad as *my* evening."

"You did look rather miserable with your mother and Macclesfield," he allowed.

"How kind of you to point it out," she muttered.

"But I still think my evening was worse."

Daphne laughed, a light musical sound that warmed Simon's bones. "What a sad pair we are," she said. "Surely we can manage a conversation on a topic other than our respective terrible evenings."

Simon said nothing.

Daphne said nothing.

"Well, I can't think of anything," he said.

Daphne laughed again, this time with more gaiety, and Simon once again found himself mesmerized by her smile.

"I give in," she gasped. "What has turned your evening into such a dreadful affair?"

"What or *whom*?"

" 'Whom'?" she echoed, tilting her head as she looked at him. "This grows even more interesting."

"I can think of any number of adjectives to describe all of the 'whoms' I have had the pleasure of meeting this evening, but 'interesting' is not one of them."

"Now, now," she chided, "don't be rude. I did see you chatting with my brothers, after all."

He nodded gallantly, tightening his hand slightly at her waist as they swung around in a graceful arc. "My apologies. The Bridgertons are, of course, excluded from my insults."

"We are all relieved, I'm sure."

Simon cracked a smile at her deadpan wit. "I live to make Bridgertons happy."

"Now *that* is a statement that may come back to haunt you," she chided. "But in all seriousness, what has you in such a dither? If your evening has gone that far downhill since our interlude with Nigel, you're in sad straits, indeed."

"How shall I put this," he mused, "so that I do not completely offend you?"

"Oh, go right ahead," she said blithely. "I promise not to be offended."

Simon grinned wickedly. "A statement that may come back to haunt *you*."

She blushed slightly. The color was barely noticeable in the shadowy candlelight, but Simon had been watching her closely. She didn't say anything, however, so he added, "Very well, if you must know, I have been introduced to every single unmarried lady in the ballroom."

A strange snorting sound came from the vicinity of her mouth. Simon had the sneaking suspicion that she was laughing at him.

"I have also," he continued, "been introduced to all of their mothers."

She gurgled. She actually gurgled.

"Bad show," he scolded. "Laughing at your dance partner."

"I'm sorry," she said, her lips tight from trying not to smile.

"No, you're not."

"All right," she admitted, "I'm not. But only because I have had to suffer the same torture for two years. It's difficult to summon too much pity for a mere evening's worth."

"Why don't you just find someone to marry and put yourself out of your misery?"

She shot him a sharp look. "Are you asking?"

Simon felt the blood leave his face.

"I thought not." She took one look at him and let out an impatient exhale. "Oh, for goodness' sake. You can start breathing now, your grace. I was only teasing."

Simon wanted to make some sort of dry, cutting, and utterly ironic comment, but the truth was, she had so startled him that he couldn't utter a word.

"To answer your question," she continued, her voice a touch more brittle than he was accustomed to hearing from her, "a lady must consider her options. There is Nigel, of course, but I think we must agree he is not a suitable candidate."

Simon shook his head.

"Earlier this year there was Lord Chalmers."

"Chalmers?" He frowned. "Isn't he—"

"On the darker side of sixty? Yes. And since I would someday like to have children, it seemed—"

"Some men that age can still sire brats," Simon pointed out.

"It wasn't a risk I was prepared to take," she returned. "Besides—" She shuddered slightly, a look of revulsion passing over her features. "I didn't particularly care to have children with *him*."

Much to his annoyance, Simon found himself picturing Daphne in bed with the elderly Chalmers. It was a disgusting image, and it left him feeling faintly furious. At whom, he didn't know; maybe at himself for even bothering to imagine the damned thing, but—

"Before Lord Chalmers," Daphne continued, thankfully interrupting his rather unpleasant thought process, "there were two others, both just as repulsive."

Simon looked at her thoughtfully. "Do you want to marry?"

"Well, of course." Her face registered her surprise. "Doesn't everyone?"

"I don't."

She smiled condescendingly. "You think you don't. All men think they don't. But you will."

"No," he said emphatically. "I will never marry."

She gaped at him. Something in the duke's tone of voice told her that he truly meant what he said. "What about your title?"

Simon shrugged. "What about it?"

"If you don't marry and sire an heir, it will expire. Or go to some beastly cousin."

That caused him to raise an amused brow. "And how do you know that my cousins are beastly?"

"All cousins who are next in line for a title are beastly." She cocked her head in a mischievous manner. "Or at least they are according to the men who actually *possess* the title."

"And this is information you've gleaned from your extensive knowledge of men?" he teased.

She shot him a devastatingly superior grin. "Of course."

Simon was silent for a moment, and then he asked, "Is it worth it?"

She looked bemused by his sudden change of subject. "Is what worth it?"

He let go of her hand just long enough to wave at the crowd. "This. This endless parade of parties. Your mother nipping at your heels."

Daphne let out a surprised chuckle. "I doubt she'd appreciate the metaphor." She fell silent for a moment, her eyes taking on a faraway look as she said, "But yes, I suppose it is worth it. It has to be worth it."

She snapped back to attention and looked back to his face, her dark eyes meltingly honest. "I want a husband. I want a family. It's not so silly when you think about it. I'm fourth of eight children. All I know are large families. I shouldn't know how to exist outside of one."

Simon caught her gaze, his eyes burning hot and intense into hers. A warning bell sounded in his mind. He wanted her. He wanted her so desperately he was straining against his clothing, but he could never, ever so much as touch her. Because to do so would be to shatter every last one of her dreams, and rake or not, Simon wasn't certain he could live with himself if he did that.

He would never marry, never sire a child, and that was all she wanted out of life.

He might enjoy her company; he wasn't certain he could deny himself that. But he had to leave her untouched for another man.

"Your grace?" she asked quietly. When he blinked, she smiled and said, "You were woolgathering."

He inclined his head graciously. "Merely pondering your words."

"And did they meet with your approval?"

"Actually, I can't remember the last time I conversed with someone with such obvious good sense." He added in a slow voice, "It's good to know what you want out of life."

"Do you know what you want?"

Ah, how to answer that. There were some things he knew he could not say. But it was so easy to talk to this girl. Something about her put his mind at ease, even as his body tingled with desire. By all rights they should not have been having such a frank conversation so soon into an acquaintance, but somehow it just felt natural.

Finally, he just said, "I made some decisions when I was younger. I try to live my life according to those vows."

She looked ravenously curious, but good manners prevented her from questioning him further. "My goodness," she said with a slightly forced smile, "we've grown serious. And here I thought all we meant to debate was whose evening was less pleasant."

They were both trapped, Simon realized. Trapped by their society's conventions and expectations.

And that's when an idea popped into his mind. A strange, wild, and appallingly wonderful idea. It was probably also a dangerous idea, since it would put him in her company for long periods of time, which would certainly leave him in a perpetual state of unfulfilled desire, but Simon valued his self-control above all else, and he was certain he could control his baser urges.

"Wouldn't you like a respite?" he asked suddenly.

"A respite?" she echoed bemusedly. Even as they twirled across the floor, she looked from side to side. "From this?"

"Not precisely. This, you'd still have to endure. What I envision is more of a respite from your mother."

Daphne choked on her surprise. "You're going to remove my mother from the social whirl? Doesn't that seem a touch extreme?"

"I'm not talking about removing your mother. Rather, I want to remove you."

Daphne tripped over her feet, and then, just as soon as she'd regained her balance, she tripped over his. "I beg your pardon?"

"I had hoped to ignore London society altogether," he explained, "but I'm finding that may prove to be impossible."

"Because you've suddenly developed a taste for ratafia and weak lemonade?" she quipped.

"No," he said, ignoring her sarcasm, "because I've discovered that half of my university friends married in my absence, and their wives seem to be obsessed with throwing the perfect party—"

"And you've been invited?"

He nodded grimly.

Daphne leaned in close, as if she were about to tell him a grave secret. "You're a duke," she whispered. "You can say no."

She watched with fascination as his jaw tightened. "These men," he said, "their husbands—they are my friends."

Daphne felt her lips moving into an unbidden grin. "And you don't want to hurt their wives' feelings."

Simon scowled, clearly uncomfortable with the compliment.

"Well, I'll be," she said mischievously. "You might just be a nice person after all."

"I'm hardly nice," he scoffed.

"Perhaps, but you're hardly cruel, either."

The music drew to a close, and Simon took her arm and guided her to the perimeter of the ballroom. Their dance had deposited them on the opposite side of the room from Daphne's family, so they had time to continue their conversation as they walked slowly back to the Bridgertons.

"What I was trying to say," he said, "before you so skillfully diverted me, was that it appears I must attend a certain number of London events."

"Hardly a fate worse than death."

He ignored her editorial. "You, I gather, must attend them as well."

She gave him a single regal nod.

"Perhaps there is a way that I might be spared the attentions of the Featheringtons and the like, and at the same time, you might be spared the matchmaking efforts of your mother."

She looked at him intently. "Go on."

"We"—he leaned forward, his eyes mesmerizing hers—"will form an attachment."

Daphne said nothing. Absolutely nothing. She just stared at him as if she were trying to decide if he were the rudest man on the face of the earth or simply mad in the head.

"Not a true attachment," Simon said impatiently. "Good God, what sort of man do you think I am?"

"Well, I *was* warned about your reputation," she pointed out. "And you yourself tried to terrify me with your rakish ways earlier this evening."

"I did no such thing."

"Of course you did." She patted his arm. "But I forgive you. I'm sure you couldn't help it."

Simon gave her a startled look. "I don't believe I have ever been condescended to by a woman before."

She shrugged. "It was probably past time."

"Do you know, I'd thought that you were unmarried because your brothers had scared off all your suitors, but now I wonder if you did it all on your own."

Much to his surprise, she just laughed. "No," she said, "I'm unmarried because everyone sees me as a friend. No one ever has any romantic interest in me." She grimaced. "Except Nigel."

Simon pondered her words for a few moments, then realized that his plan could work to her benefit even more than he'd originally imagined. "Listen," he said, "and listen quickly because we're almost back to your family, and Anthony looks as if he's about to bolt in our direction any minute now."

They both glanced quickly to the right. Anthony was still trapped in conversation with the Featheringtons. He did not look happy.

"Here is my plan," Simon continued, his voice low and intense. "We shall pretend to have developed a tendre for each other. I won't have quite so many debutantes thrown in my direction because it will be perceived that I am no longer available."

"No it won't," Daphne replied. "They won't believe you're unavailable until you're standing up before the bishop, taking your vows."

The very thought made his stomach churn. "Nonsense," he said. "It may take a bit of time, but I'm sure I will eventually be able to convince society that I am not anyone's candidate for marriage."

"Except mine," Daphne pointed out.

"Except yours," he agreed, "but we will know that isn't true."

"Of course," she murmured. "Frankly, I do not believe that this will work, but if you're convinced . . ."

"I am."

"Well, then, what do I gain?"

"For one thing, your mother will stop dragging you from man to man if she thinks you have secured my interest."

"Rather conceited of you," Daphne mused, "but true."

Simon ignored her gibe. "Secondly," he continued, "men are always more interested in a woman if they think other men are interested."

"Meaning?"

"Meaning, quite simply, and pardon my *conceit*"—he shot her a sardonic look to show that he hadn't missed her earlier sarcasm—

"but if all the world thinks I intend to make you my duchess, all of those men who see you as nothing more than an affable friend will begin to view you in a new light."

Her lips pursed. "Meaning that once you throw me over, I shall have hordes of suitors at my beck and call?"

"Oh, I shall allow you to be the one to cry off," he said gallantly.

He noticed she didn't bother to thank him.

"I still think I'm gaining much more from this arrangement than you," she said.

He squeezed her arm slightly. "Then you'll do it?"

Daphne looked at Mrs. Featherington, who looked like a bird of prey, and then at her brother, who looked as if he had swallowed a chicken bone. She'd seen those expressions dozens of times before—except on the faces of her own mother and some hapless potential suitor.

"Yes," she said, her voice firm. "Yes, I'll do it."

"What do you suppose is taking them so long?"

Violet Bridgerton tugged on her eldest son's sleeve, unable to take her eyes off of her daughter—who appeared to have thoroughly captured the attention of the Duke of Hastings—only one week in London and already the catch of the season.

"I don't know," Anthony replied, looking gratefully at the backs of the Featheringtons as they moved on to their next victim, "but it feels as if it's been hours."

"Do you think he likes her?" Violet asked excitedly. "Do you think our Daphne truly has a chance to be a duchess?"

Anthony's eyes filled with a mixture of impatience and disbelief. "Mother, you told Daphne she wasn't even to be *seen* with him, and now you're thinking of marriage?"

"I spoke prematurely," Violet said with a blithe wave of her hand. "Clearly he is a man of great refinement and taste. And how, may I ask, do you know what I said to Daphne?"

"Daff told me, of course," Anthony lied.

"Hmmph. Well, I am certain that Portia Featherington won't be forgetting this evening anytime soon."

Anthony's eyes widened. "Are you trying to marry Daphne off so that she might be happy as a wife and a mother, or are you just trying to beat Mrs. Featherington to the altar?"

"The former, of course," Violet replied in a huff, "and I am offended you would even imply otherwise." Her eyes strayed off of Daphne and the duke for just long enough to locate Portia Featherington and her daughters. "But I certainly shan't mind seeing the look on her face when she realizes that *Daphne* will make the season's greatest match."

"Mother, you are hopeless."

"Certainly not. Shameless, perhaps, but never hopeless."

Anthony just shook his head and muttered something under his breath.

"It's impolite to mumble," Violet said, mostly just to annoy him. Then she spotted Daphne and the duke. "Ah, here they come. Anthony, behave yourself. Daphne! Your grace!" She paused as the couple made their way to her side. "I trust you enjoyed your dance."

"Very much," Simon murmured. "Your daughter is as graceful as she is lovely."

Anthony let out a snort.

Simon ignored him. "I hope we may have the pleasure of dancing together again very soon."

Violet positively glowed. "Oh, I'm *sure* Daphne would *adore* that." When Daphne didn't answer with all possible haste, she added, quite pointedly, "Wouldn't you, Daphne?"

"Of course," Daphne said demurely.

"I'm certain your mother would never be so lax as to allow me a second waltz," Simon said, looking every inch the debonair duke, "but I do hope she will permit us to take a stroll around the ballroom."

"You just took a stroll around the ballroom," Anthony pointed out.

Simon ignored him again. He said to Violet, "We shall, of course, remain in your sight at all times."

The lavender silk fan in Violet's hand began to flutter rapidly. "I should be delighted. I mean, Daphne should be delighted. Shouldn't you, Daphne?"

Daphne was all innocence. "Oh, I should."

"And I," Anthony snapped, "should take a dose of laudanum, for clearly I am fevered. What the devil is going on?"

"Anthony!" Violet exclaimed. She turned hastily to Simon. "Don't mind him."

"Oh, I never do," Simon said affably.

"Daphne," Anthony said pointedly, "I should be delighted to act as your chaperon."

"Really, Anthony," Violet cut in, "they hardly need one if they are to remain here in the ballroom."

"Oh, I *insist*."

"You two run along," Violet said to Daphne and Simon, waving her hand at them. "Anthony will be with you in just a moment."

Anthony tried to follow immediately, but Violet grabbed onto his wrist. Hard. "What the devil do you think you're doing?" she hissed.

"Protecting my sister!"

"From the duke? He can't be that wicked. Actually, he reminds me of you."

Anthony groaned. "Then she definitely needs my protection."

Violet patted him on the arm. "Don't be so overprotective. If he attempts to spirit her out onto the balcony, I promise you may dash out to rescue her. But until that unlikely event occurs, please allow your sister her moment of glory."

Anthony glared at Simon's back. "Tomorrow I will kill him."

"Dear me," Violet said, shaking her head, "I had no idea you could be so high-strung. One would think, as your mother, I would know these things, especially since you are my firstborn, and thus I have known you for the longest of any of my children, but—"

"Is that Colin?" Anthony interrupted, his voice strangled.

Violet blinked, then squinted her eyes. "Why, yes, it is. Isn't it lovely that he returned early? I could hardly believe my eyes when I saw him an hour ago. In fact, I—"

"I'd better go to him," Anthony said quickly. "He looks lonely. Good-bye, Mother."

Violet watched as Anthony ran off, presumably to escape her chattering lecture. "Silly boy," she murmured to herself. None of her children seemed to be on to any of her tricks. Just blather on about nothing in particular, and she could be rid of any of them in a trice.

She let out a satisfied sigh and resumed her watch of her daughter, now on the other side of the ballroom, her hand nestled comfortably in the crook of the duke's elbow. They made a most handsome couple.

Yes, Violet thought, her eyes growing misty, her daughter would make an excellent duchess.

Then she let her gaze wander briefly over to Anthony, who was now right where she wanted him—out of her hair. She allowed herself a secret smile. Children were so easy to manage.

Then her smile turned to a frown as she noticed Daphne walking back toward her—on the arm of another man. Violet's eyes immediately scanned the ballroom until she found the duke.

Dash it all, what the devil was he doing dancing with Penelope Featherington?

Chapter 6

It has been reported to This Author that the Duke of Hastings mentioned no fewer than six times yestereve that he has no plans to marry. If his intention was to discourage the Ambitious Mamas, he made a grave error in judgment. They will simply view his remarks as the greatest of challenges.

And in an interesting side note, his half dozen anti-matrimony remarks were all uttered before he made the acquaintance of the lovely and sensible Miss (Daphne) Bridgerton.

Lady Whistledown's Society Papers,
30 April 1813

The following afternoon found Simon standing on the front steps of Daphne's home, one hand rapping the brass knocker on the door, the other wrapped around a large bouquet of fiendishly expensive tulips. It hadn't occurred to him that his little charade might require his attention during the daylight hours, but during their stroll about the ballroom the previous night, Daphne had sagely pointed out that if he did not call upon her the next day, no one—least of all her mother—would truly believe he was interested.

Simon accepted her words as truth, allowing that Daphne almost certainly had more knowledge in this area of etiquette than he did. He'd dutifully found some flowers and trudged across Grosvenor Square to Bridgerton House. He'd never courted a respectable woman before, so the ritual was foreign to him.

The door was opened almost immediately by the Bridgertons' butler. Simon gave him his card. The butler, a tall thin man with a hawkish nose, looked at it for barely a quarter second before nodding, and murmuring, "Right this way, your grace."

Clearly, Simon thought wryly, he had been expected.

What was unexpected, however, was the sight that awaited him when he was shown into the Bridgertons' drawing room.

Daphne, a vision in ice-blue silk, perched on the edge of Lady Bridgerton's green damask sofa, her face decorated with another one of those wide wide smiles.

It would have been a lovely sight, had she not been surrounded by at least a half dozen men, one of whom had actually descended to one knee, gales of poetry spewing from his mouth.

Judging from the florid nature of the prose, Simon fully expected a rosebush to sprout from the nitwit's mouth at any moment.

The entire scene, Simon decided, was most disagreeable.

He fixed his gaze on Daphne, who was directing her magnificent smile at the buffoon reciting poetry, and waited for her to acknowledge him.

She didn't.

Simon looked down at his free hand and noticed that it was curled into a tight fist. He scanned the room slowly, trying to decide on which man's face to use it.

Daphne smiled again, and again not at him.

The idiot poet. Definitely the idiot poet. Simon tilted his head slightly to the side as he analyzed the young swain's face. Would his fist fit best in the right eye socket or the left? Or maybe that was too violent. Maybe a light clip to the chin would be more appropriate. At the very least, it might actually shut the man up.

"This one," the poet announced grandly, "I wrote in your honor last night."

Simon groaned. The last poem he had recognized as a rather grandiose rendition of a Shakespearean sonnet, but an original work was more than he could bear.

"Your grace!"

Simon looked up to realize that Daphne had finally noticed that he had entered the room.

He nodded regally, his cool look very much at odds with the puppy-dog faces of her other suitors. "Miss Bridgerton."

"How lovely to see you," she said, a delighted smile crossing her face.

Ah, that was more like it. Simon straightened the flowers and started to walk toward her, only to realize that there were three young suitors in his path, and none appeared inclined to move. Simon pierced the first one with his haughtiest stare, which caused the boy—really, he looked all of twenty, hardly old enough to be called a *man*—to cough in a most unattractive manner and scurry off to an unoccupied window seat.

Simon moved forward, ready to repeat the procedure with the next annoying young man, when the viscountess suddenly stepped into his path, wearing a dark blue frock and a smile that might possibly rival Daphne's in its brightness.

"Your grace!" she said excitedly. "What a pleasure to see you. You honor us with your presence."

"I could hardly imagine myself anywhere else," Simon murmured as he took her gloved hand and kissed it. "Your daughter is an exceptional young lady."

The viscountess sighed contentedly. "And such lovely, lovely flowers," she said, once she was finished with her little revel of maternal pride. "Are they from Holland? They must have been terribly dear."

"Mother!" Daphne said sharply. She extricated her hand from the grasp of a particularly energetic suitor and made her way over. "What can the duke possibly say to that?"

"I could tell her how much I paid for them," he said with a devilish half-smile.

"You wouldn't."

He leaned forward, lowering his voice so that only Daphne could hear. "Didn't you remind me last night that I'm a duke?" he murmured. "I thought you told me I could do anything I wanted."

"Yes, but not that," Daphne said with a dismissive wave of her hand. "You would never be so crass."

"Of course the duke would not be crass!" her mother exclaimed, clearly horrified that Daphne would even mention the word in his presence. "What are you talking about? Why would he be crass?"

"The flowers," Simon said. "The cost. Daphne thinks I shouldn't tell you."

"Tell me later," the viscountess whispered out of the side of her mouth, "when she's not listening." Then she moved back over to the green damask sofa where Daphne had been sitting with her suitors and cleared it out in under three seconds. Simon had to admire the military precision with which she managed the maneuver.

"There now," the viscountess said. "Isn't that convenient? Daphne, why don't you and the duke sit right there?"

"You mean where Lord Railmont and Mr. Crane were sitting just moments ago?" Daphne asked innocently.

"Precisely," her mother replied, with what Simon considered to be an admirable lack of obvious sarcasm. "Besides, Mr. Crane said that he has to meet his mother at Gunter's at three."

Daphne glanced at the clock. "It's only two, Mother."

"The traffic," Violet said with a sniff, "is nothing short of dreadful these days. Far too many horses on the road."

"It ill becomes a man," Simon said, getting into the spirit of the conversation, "to keep his mother waiting."

"Well said, your grace." Violet beamed. "You can be sure that I have expressed that very same sentiment to my own children."

"And in case you're not sure," Daphne said with a smile, "I'd be happy to vouch for her."

Violet merely smiled. "If anyone should know, it would be you, Daphne. Now, if you will excuse me, I have business to attend to. Oh, Mr. Crane! Mr. Crane! Your mother would never forgive me if I did not shoo you out in time." She bustled off, taking the hapless Mr. Crane by the arm and leading him toward the door, barely giving him time to say farewell.

Daphne turned to Simon with an amused expression. "I can't quite decide if she is being terribly polite or exquisitely rude."

"Exquisitely polite, perhaps?" Simon asked mildly.

She shook her head. "Oh, definitely not that."

"The alternative, of course, is—"

"Terribly rude?" Daphne grinned and watched as her mother looped her arm through Lord Railmont's, pointed him toward Daphne so that he could nod his good-bye, and led him from the room. And then, as if by magic, the remaining beaux murmured their hasty farewells and followed suit.

"Remarkably efficient, isn't she?" Daphne murmured.

"Your mother? She's a marvel."

"She'll be back, of course."

"Pity. And here I thought I had you well and truly in my clutches."

Daphne laughed. "I don't know how anyone considered you a rake. Your sense of humor is far too superb."

"And here we rakes thought we were so wickedly droll."

"A rake's humor," Daphne stated, "is essentially cruel."

Her comment surprised him. He stared at her intently, searching her brown eyes, and yet not really knowing what it was he was looking for. There was a narrow ring of green just outside her pupils, the color as deep and rich as moss. He'd never seen her in the daylight before, he realized.

"Your grace?" Daphne's quiet voice snapped him out of his daze.

Simon blinked. "I beg your pardon."

"You looked a thousand miles away," she said, her brow wrinkling.

"I've been a thousand miles away." He fought the urge to return his gaze to her eyes. "This is entirely different."

Daphne let out a little laugh, the sound positively musical. "You have, haven't you? And here I've never even been past Lancashire. What a provincial I must seem."

He brushed aside her remark. "You must forgive my woolgathering. We were discussing my lack of humor, I believe?"

"We were not, and you well know it." Her hands found their way to her hips. "I specifically told you that you were in possession of a sense of humor far superior to that of the average rake."

One of his brows lifted in a rather superior manner. "And you wouldn't classify your brothers as rakes?"

"They only *think* they are rakes," she corrected. "There is a considerable difference."

Simon snorted. "If Anthony isn't a rake, I pity the woman who meets the man who is."

"There is more to being a rake than seducing legions of women," Daphne said blithely. "If a man can't do more than poke his tongue into a woman's mouth and kiss—"

Simon felt his throat close up, but somehow he managed to sputter, "You should not be speaking of such things."

She shrugged.

"You shouldn't even *know* about them," he grunted.

"Four brothers," she said by way of an explanation. "Well, three, I suppose. Gregory is too young to count."

"Someone ought to tell them to hold their tongues around you."

She shrugged again, this time with only one shoulder. "Half the time they don't even notice I'm there."

Simon couldn't imagine *that*.

"But we seem to have veered away from the original subject," she said. "All I meant to say is that a rake's humor has its basis in cruelty. He needs a victim, for he cannot imagine ever laughing at himself. You, your grace, are rather clever with the self deprecating remark."

"I just don't know whether to thank you or throttle you."

"Throttle me? Good heavens, why?" She laughed again, a rich, throaty sound that Simon felt deep in his gut.

He exhaled slowly, the long whoosh of air just barely steadying his pulse. If she continued laughing, he wasn't going to be able to answer to the consequences.

But she just kept looking at him, her wide mouth curved into one of those smiles that looked as if it were perpetually on the verge of laughter.

"I am going to throttle you," he growled, "on general principle."

"And what principle is that?"

"The general principle of *man*," he blustered.

Her brows lifted dubiously. "As opposed to the general principle of woman?"

Simon looked around. "Where is your brother? You're far too cheeky. Surely someone needs to take you in hand."

"Oh, I'm sure you'll be seeing more of Anthony. In fact I'm rather surprised he hasn't made an appearance yet. He was quite irate last night. I was forced to listen to a full hour's lecture on your many faults and sins."

"The sins are almost certainly exaggerated."

"And the faults?"

"Probably true," Simon admitted sheepishly.

That remark earned him another smile from Daphne. "Well, true or not," she said, "he thinks you're up to something."

"I *am* up to something."

Her head tilted sarcastically as her eyes rolled upward. "He thinks you're up to something nefarious."

"I'd like to be up to something nefarious," he muttered.

"What was that?"

"Nothing."

She frowned. "I think we should tell Anthony about our plan."

"And what could possibly be the benefit to that?"

Daphne remembered the full-hour grilling she'd endured the previous night, and just said, "Oh, I think I'll let you figure that out for yourself."

Simon merely raised his brows. "My dear Daphne . . ."

Her lips parted slightly in surprise.

"Surely you're not going to force me to call you Miss Bridgerton." He sighed dramatically. "After all that we've been through."

"We've been through nothing, you ridiculous man, but I suppose you may call me Daphne nonetheless."

"Excellent." He nodded in a condescending manner. "You may call me 'your grace.' "

She swatted him.

"Very well," he replied, his lips twitching at the corners. "Simon, if you must."

"Oh I must," Daphne said, rolling her eyes, "clearly, I must."

He leaned toward her, something odd and slightly hot sparking in the depths of his pale eyes. "Must you?" he murmured. "I should be very excited to hear it."

Daphne had the sudden sense that he was talking about something far more intimate than the mere mention of his given name. A strange, tingling sort of heat shot down her arms, and without thinking, she jumped back a step. "Those flowers are quite lovely," she blurted out.

He regarded them lazily, rotating the bouquet with his wrist. "Yes, they are, aren't they?"

"I adore them."

"They're not for you."

Daphne choked on air.

Simon grinned. "They're for your mother."

Her mouth slowly opened in surprise, a short little gasp of air passing through her lips before she said, "Oh, you clever clever man. She will positively melt at your feet. But this will come back to haunt you, you know."

He gave her an arch look. "Oh really?"

"Really. She will be more determined than ever to drag you to the altar. You shall be just as beleaguered at parties as if we hadn't concocted this scheme."

"Nonsense," he scoffed. "Before I would have had to endure the attentions of dozens of Ambitious Mamas. Now I must deal with only one."

"Her tenacity might surprise you," Daphne muttered. Then she twisted her head to look out the partially open door. "She must truly like you," she added. "She's left us alone far longer than is proper."

Simon pondered that and leaned forward to whisper, "Could she be listening at the door?"

Daphne shook her head. "No, we would have heard her shoes clicking down the hall."

Something about that statement made him smile, and Daphne found herself smiling right along with him. "I really should thank you, though," she said, "before she returns."

"Oh? Why is that?"

"Your plan is a brilliant success. At least for me. Did you notice how many suitors came to call this morning?"

He crossed his arms, the tulips dangling upside down. "I noticed."

"It's brilliant, really. I've never had so many callers in a single afternoon before. Mother was beside herself with pride. Even Humboldt—he's our butler—was beaming, and I've never seen him so much as smile before. Ooops! Look, you're dripping." She leaned down and righted the flowers, her forearm grazing the front of his coat. She immediately jumped back, startled by both the heat and power of him.

Good God, if she could sense all that through his shirt and coat, what must he be like—

Daphne colored red. Deep, dark red.

"I should give my entire fortune for those thoughts," Simon said, his brows rising in question.

Thankfully, Violet chose that moment to sail into the room. "I'm terribly sorry for abandoning you for so long," she said, "but Mr. Crane's horse threw a shoe, so naturally I had to accompany him to the stables and find a groom to repair the damage."

In all their years together—which, Daphne thought acerbically, naturally constituted her entire life—Daphne had never known her mother to step foot in the stables.

"You are truly an exceptional hostess," Simon said, holding out the flowers. "Here, these are for you."

"For me?" Violet's mouth fell open in surprise, and a strange little breathy sound escaped her lips. "Are you certain? Because I—" She looked over at Daphne, and then at Simon, and then finally back at her daughter. "Are you certain?"

"Absolutely."

Violet blinked rapidly, and Daphne noticed that there were actually tears in her mother's eyes. No one ever gave her flowers, she realized. At least not since her father had died ten years earlier. Violet was such a mother—Daphne had forgotten that she was a woman as well.

"I don't know what to say," Violet sniffled.

"Try 'thank you,' " Daphne whispered in her ear, her grin lending warmth to her voice.

"Oh, Daff, you are the *worst.*" Violet swatted her in the arm, looking more like a young woman than Daphne had ever seen her. "But thank you, your grace. These are beautiful blooms, but more importantly, it was a most thoughtful gesture. I shall treasure this moment always."

Simon looked as if he were about to say something, but in the end he just smiled and inclined his head.

Daphne looked at her mother, saw the unmistakable joy in her cornflower blue eyes, and realized with a touch of shame that none of her own children had ever acted in such a thoughtful manner as this man standing beside her.

The Duke of Hastings. Daphne decided then and there that she'd be a fool if she didn't fall in love with him.

Of course it would be nice if he returned the sentiment.

"Mother," Daphne said, "would you like me to fetch you a vase?"

"What?" Violet was still too busy sniffing blissfully at her flowers to pay attention to her daughter's words. "Oh. Yes, of course. Ask Humboldt for the cut crystal from my grandmother."

Daphne flashed a grateful smile at Simon and headed for the door, but before she could take more than two steps, the large and forbidding form of her eldest brother materialized in the doorway.

"Daphne," Anthony growled. "Just the person I needed to see."

Daphne decided the best strategy was simply to ignore his churlish mood. "In just a moment, Anthony," she said sweetly. "Mother has asked me to fetch a vase. Hastings has brought her flowers."

"Hastings is here?" Anthony looked past her to the duo further in the room. "What are you doing here, Hastings?"

"Calling on your sister."

Anthony pushed past Daphne and strode into the room, looking rather like a thundercloud on legs. "I did not give you leave to court my sister," he bellowed.

"I did," Violet said. She shoved the flowers in Anthony's face, wiggling them so as to deposit the greatest amount of pollen on his nose. "Aren't these lovely?"

Anthony sneezed and pushed them aside. "Mother, I am trying to have a conversation with the duke."

Violet looked at Simon. "Do you want to have this conversation with my son?"

"Not particularly."

"Fine, then. Anthony, be quiet."

Daphne clapped her hand over her mouth, but a snuffly-giggly sound escaped nonetheless.

"You!" Anthony jabbed a finger in her direction. "Be quiet."

"Perhaps I should fetch that vase," Daphne mused.

"And leave me to the tender mercies of your brother?" Simon said in a mild voice. "I think not."

Daphne raised a brow. "Do you imply that you are not man enough to deal with him?"

"Nothing of the sort. Merely that he ought to be your problem, not mine, and—"

"What the *hell* is going on here?" Anthony roared.

"Anthony!" Violet exclaimed. "I will not tolerate such unbecoming language in my drawing room."

Daphne smirked.

Simon did nothing more than cock his head, regarding Anthony with a curious stare.

Anthony threw a dark scowl at both of them before turning his attention to his mother. "He is not to be trusted. Do you have any idea what is happening here?" he demanded.

"Of course I do," Violet replied. "The duke is paying a call upon your sister."

"And I brought flowers for your mother," Simon said helpfully.

Anthony gazed longingly at Simon's nose. Simon had the distinct impression that Anthony was imagining smashing it in.

Anthony whipped his head around to face his mother. "Do you understand the extent of his reputation?"

"Reformed rakes make the best husbands," Violet said.

"Rubbish and you know it."

"He's not a true rake, anyway," Daphne added.

The look Anthony shot at his sister was so comically malevolent Simon nearly laughed. He managed to restrain himself, but mostly just because he was fairly certain that any show of humor would cause Anthony's fist to lose its battle with his brain, with Simon's face emerging as the conflict's primary casualty.

"You don't know," Anthony said, his voice low and nearly shaking with rage. "You don't know what he has done."

"No more than what you have done, I'm sure," Violet said slyly.

"Precisely!" Anthony roared. "Good God, I know *exactly* what is going on in his brain right now, and it has nothing to do with poetry and roses."

Simon pictured laying Daphne down on a bed of rose petals. "Well, maybe roses," he murmured.

"I'm going to kill him," Anthony announced.

"These are tulips, anyway," Violet said primly, "from Holland. And Anthony, you really must summon control of your emotions. This is most unseemly."

"He is not fit to lick Daphne's boots."

Simon's head filled with more erotic images, this time of himself licking her toes. He decided not to comment.

Besides, he had already decided that he wasn't going to allow his thoughts to wander in such directions. Daphne was Anthony's sister, for God's sake. He couldn't seduce her.

"I refuse to listen to another disparaging word about his grace," Violet stated emphatically, "and that is the end of the subject."

"But—"

"I don't like your tone, Anthony Bridgerton!"

Simon thought he heard Daphne choke on a chuckle, and he wondered what that was all about.

"If it would please Your Motherhood," Anthony said in excruciatingly even tones, "I would like a private word with his grace."

"This time I'm really going to get that vase," Daphne announced, and dashed from the room.

Violet crossed her arms, and said to Anthony, "I will not have you mistreat a guest in my home."

"I shan't lay so much as a hand on him," Anthony replied. "I give you my word."

Having never had a mother, Simon was finding this exchange fascinating. Bridgerton House was, after all, technically Anthony's house, not his mother's, and Simon was impressed that Anthony had refrained from pointing this out. "It's quite all right, Lady Bridgerton," he interjected. "I'm sure Anthony and I have much to discuss."

Anthony's eyes narrowed. "Much."

"Very well," Violet said. "You're going to do what you want no matter what I say, anyway. But I'm not leaving." She plopped down onto the sofa. "This is my drawing room, and I'm comfortable here. If the two of you want to engage in that asinine interchange that passes for conversation among the males of our species, you may do so elsewhere."

Simon blinked in surprise. Clearly there was more to Daphne's mother than met the eye.

Anthony jerked his head toward the door, and Simon followed him into the hall.

"My study is this way," Anthony said.

"You have a study here?"

"I *am* the head of the family."

"Of course," Simon allowed, "but you do reside elsewhere."

Anthony paused and turned an assessing stare on Simon. "It cannot have escaped your notice that my position as head of the Bridgerton family carries with it serious responsibilities."

Simon looked him evenly in the eye. "Meaning Daphne?"

"Precisely."

"If I recall," Simon said, "earlier this week you told me you wanted to introduce us."

"That was before I thought you'd be interested in her!"

Simon held his tongue as he preceded Anthony into his study, remaining silent until Anthony shut the door. "Why," he asked softly, "would you assume I would not be interested in your sister?"

"Besides the fact that you have sworn to me that you will never marry?" Anthony drawled.

He had a good point. Simon hated that he had such a good point. "Besides that," he snapped.

Anthony blinked a couple of times, then said, "No one is interested in Daphne. At least no one we'd have her marry."

Simon crossed his arms and leaned back against the wall. "You don't hold her in terribly high regard, do y—?"

Before he could even finish the query, Anthony had him by the throat. "Don't you dare insult my sister."

But Simon had learned quite a bit about self-defense on his travels, and it took him only two seconds to reverse their positions. "I wasn't insulting your sister," he said in a malevolent voice. "I was insulting you."

Strange gurgling sounds were coming from Anthony's throat, so Simon let him go. "As it happens," he said, brushing his hands against each other, "Daphne explained to me why she has not attracted any suitable suitors."

"Oh?" Anthony asked derisively.

"Personally, I think it has everything to do with your and your brothers' apelike ways, but she tells me it is because all London views her as a friend, and none sees her as a romantic heroine."

Anthony was silent for a long moment before saying, "I see." Then, after another pause, he added thoughtfully, "She's probably right."

Simon said nothing, just watched his friend as he sorted all of this out. Finally, Anthony said, "I still don't like your sniffing about her."

"Good God, you make me sound positively canine."

Anthony crossed his arms. "Don't forget, we ran in the same pack after we left Oxford. I know exactly what you've done."

"Oh, for the love of Christ, Bridgerton, we were twenty! All men are idiots at that age. Besides, you know damn well that h—h—"

Simon felt his tongue grow awkward, and faked a coughing fit to cover his stammer. Damn. This happened so infrequently these days, but when it did, it was always when he was upset or angry. If he lost control over his emotions, he lost control over his speech. It was as simple as that.

And unfortunately, episodes such as this only served to make him upset and angry with himself, which in turn exacerbated the stammer. It was the worst sort of vicious circle.

Anthony looked at him quizzically. "Are you all right?"

Simon nodded. "Just a bit of dust in my throat," he lied.

"Shall I ring for tea?"

Simon nodded again. He didn't particularly want tea, but it seemed the sort of thing one would ask for if one truly did have dust in one's throat.

Anthony tugged at the bellpull, then turned back to Simon and asked, "You were saying?"

Simon swallowed, hoping the gesture would help him to regain control over his ire. "I merely meant to point out that you know better than anyone that at least half of my reputation is undeserved."

"Yes, but I was there for the half that *was* deserved, and while I don't mind your occasionally socializing with Daphne, I don't want you courting her."

Simon stared at his friend—or at least the man he thought was his friend—in disbelief. "Do you really think I'd seduce your sister?"

"I don't know what to think. I know you plan never to marry. I know that Daphne *does*." Anthony shrugged. "Frankly, that's enough for me to keep you two on opposite sides of the dance floor."

Simon let out a long breath. While Anthony's attitude was irritating as hell, he supposed it was understandable, and in fact even laudable. After all, the man was only acting in the best interests of his sister. Simon had difficulty imagining being responsible for anyone save himself, but he supposed that if he had a sister, he'd be damned picky about who courted her as well.

Just then, a knock sounded at the door.

"Enter!" Anthony called out.

Instead of the maid with tea, Daphne slipped into the room. "Mother told me that the two of you are in beastly moods, and I should leave you alone, but I thought I ought to make certain neither of you had killed the other."

"No," Anthony said with a grim smile, "just a light strangle."

To Daphne's credit, she didn't bat an eyelash. "Who strangled whom?"

"I strangled him," her brother replied, "then he returned the favor."

"I see," she said slowly. "I'm sorry to have missed the entertainment."

Simon couldn't suppress a smile at her remark. "Daff," he began.

Anthony whirled around. "You call her Daff?" His head snapped back to Daphne. "Did you give him permission to use your given name?"

"Of course."

"But—"

"I think," Simon interrupted, "that we are going to have to come clean."

Daphne nodded somberly. “I think you’re right. If you recall, I told you so.”

“How genteel of you to mention it,” Simon murmured.

She smiled gamely. “I could not resist. With four brothers, after all, one must always seize the moment when one may say, ‘I told you so.’ ”

Simon looked from sibling to sibling. “I don’t know which one of you I pity more.”

“What the devil is going on?” Anthony demanded, and then added as an aside, “And as for your remark, pity me. I am a far more amiable brother than she is a sister.”

“Not true!”

Simon ignored the squabble and focused his attention on Anthony. “You want to know what the devil is going on? It’s like this . . .”

Chapter 7

Men are sheep. Where one goes, the rest will soon follow.
LADY WHISTLEDOWN'S SOCIETY PAPERS,
30 April 1813

All in all, Daphne thought, Anthony was taking this rather well. By the time Simon had finished explaining their little plan (with, she had to admit, frequent interruptions on her part), Anthony had raised his voice only seven times.

That was about seven fewer than Daphne would have predicted.

Finally, after Daphne begged him to hold his tongue until she and Simon were done with their story, Anthony gave a curt nod, crossed his arms, and clamped his mouth shut for the duration of the explanation. His frown was enough to shake the plaster off the walls, but true to his word, he remained utterly silent.

Until Simon finished with, "And that's that."

There was silence. Dead silence. For a full ten seconds, nothing but silence, although Daphne would have sworn she could hear her eyes moving in their sockets as they darted back from Anthony to Simon.

And then finally, from Anthony: "Are you *mad*?"

"I thought this might be his reaction," Daphne murmured.

"Are you both completely, irrevocably, abominably *insane*?" Anthony's voice rose to a roar. "I don't know which of you is more clearly the idiot."

"Will you hush!" Daphne hissed. "Mother will hear you."

"*Mother* would perish of heart failure if she knew what you were about," Anthony retorted, but he did use a softer tone.

"But *Mother* is not going to hear of it, is she?" Daphne shot back.

"No, she's not," Anthony replied, his chin jutting forward, "because your little scheme is finished as of this very moment."

Daphne crossed her arms. "You can't do anything to stop me."

Anthony jerked his head toward Simon. "I can kill *him*."

"Don't be ridiculous."

"Duels have been fought for less."

"By idiots!"

"I'm not disputing the title as regards to *him*."

"If I might interrupt," Simon said quietly.

"He's your best friend!" Daphne protested.

"Not," Anthony said, the single syllable brimming with barely contained violence, "anymore."

Daphne turned to Simon with a huff. "Aren't you going to *say* anything?"

His lips quirked into an amused half-smile. "And when would I have had the chance?"

Anthony turned to Simon. "I want you out of this house."

"Before I may defend myself?"

"It's my house, too," Daphne said hotly, "and I want him to stay."

Anthony glared at his sister, exasperation evident in every inch of his posture. "Very well," he said, "I'll give you two minutes to state your case. No more."

Daphne glanced hesitantly at Simon, wondering if he'd want to use the two minutes himself. But all he did was shrug, and say, "Go right ahead. He's *your* brother."

She took a fortifying breath, planted her hands on her hips without even realizing it, and said, "First of all, I must point out that I have far more to gain from this alliance than his grace. He says he wishes to use me to keep the other women—"

"And their mothers," Simon interrupted.

"—and their mothers at bay. But frankly"—Daphne glanced at Simon as she said this—"I think he's wrong. The women aren't going to stop pursuing him just because they think he might have formed an attachment with another young lady—especially when that young lady is *me*."

"And what is wrong with you?" Anthony demanded.

Daphne started to explain, but then she caught a strange glance pass between the two men. "What was that all about?"

"Nothing," Anthony muttered, looking a trifle sheepish.

"I explained to your brother your theory on why you have not had more suitors," Simon said gently.

"I see." Daphne pursed her lips as she tried to decide whether that was something she ought to be irritated about. "Hmmph. Well, he should have figured that out on his own."

Simon made an odd snorting sound that might have been a laugh.

Daphne leveled a sharp look at both men. "I do hope my two minutes do not include all of these interruptions."

Simon shrugged. "He's the timekeeper."

Anthony clutched at the edge of the desk, probably, Daphne thought, to keep himself from going for Simon's throat. "And *he*," he said menacingly, "is going to find himself headfirst through the goddamned window if he doesn't shut up."

"Did you know I have always suspected that men were idiots," Daphne ground out, "but I was never positive until today."

Simon grinned.

"Allowing for interruptions," Anthony bit off, shooting yet another deadly glare in Simon's direction even as he spoke to Daphne, "you have a minute and a half left."

"Fine," she snapped. "Then I'll reduce this conversation to one single fact. Today I had six callers. Six! Can you recall the last time I had six callers?"

Anthony just stared at her blankly.

"I can't," Daphne continued, in fine form now. "Because it *has never happened.* Six men marched up our steps, knocked on our door, and gave Humboldt their cards. Six men brought me flowers, engaged me in conversation, and one even recited poetry."

Simon winced.

"And do you know *why*?" she demanded, her voice rising dangerously. "Do you?"

Anthony, in his somewhat belatedly arrived wisdom, held his tongue.

"It is all because *he*"—she jabbed her forefinger toward Simon—"was kind enough to feign interest in me last night at Lady Danbury's ball."

Simon, who had been leaning casually against the edge of the desk, suddenly straightened. "Well, now," he said quickly, "I wouldn't quite put it that way."

She turned to him, her eyes remarkably steady. "And how would you put it?"

He didn't get much past, "I—" before she added, "Because I can assure you those men have never seen fit to call on me before."

"If they are so myopic," Simon said quietly, "why do you care for their regard?"

She fell silent, drawing back slightly. Simon had the sinking suspicion that he might have said something very, very wrong, but he wasn't positive until he saw her blinking rapidly.

Oh, damn.

Then she wiped one of her eyes. She coughed as she did it, trying to hide the maneuver by pretending to cover her mouth, but Simon still felt like the worst sort of heel.

"Now look what you've done," Anthony snapped. He placed a comforting hand on his sister's arm, all the while glaring at Simon. "Pay him no mind, Daphne. He's an ass."

"Maybe," she sniffled. "But he's an intelligent ass."

Anthony's mouth fell open.

She shot him a testy look. "Well, if you didn't want me to repeat it, you shouldn't have said it."

Anthony let out a weary sigh. "Were there really six men here this afternoon?"

She nodded. "Seven including Hastings."

"And," he asked carefully, "were any of them men you might be interested in marrying?"

Simon realized that his fingers were gouging small holes in his thigh and forced himself to move his hand to the desk.

Daphne nodded again. "They are all men with whom I have enjoyed a previous friendship. It is only that they never viewed me as a candidate for romance before Hastings led the way. I might, if given the opportunity, develop an attachment for one of them."

"But—" Simon quickly shut his mouth.

"But what?" Daphne asked, turning to him with curious eyes.

It occurred to him that what he wanted to say was that if those men had only noticed Daphne's charms because a duke had shown interest in her, then they were idiots, and thus she shouldn't even contemplate marrying them. But considering that *he* had been the one to originally point out that his interest would gain her more suitors—well, frankly, it seemed a bit self-defeating to mention it.

"Nothing," he finally said, raising a hand in a don't-mind-me motion. "It doesn't signify."

Daphne looked at him for a few moments, as if waiting for him to change his mind, and then turned back to her brother. "Do you admit the wisdom of our plan, then?"

" 'Wisdom' might be a bit of a stretch, but"—Anthony looked pained to say it—"I can see where you might think it might benefit you."

"Anthony, I have to find a husband. Besides the fact that Mother is pestering me to death, I *want* a husband. I want to marry and have a family of my own. I want it more than you could ever know. And thus far, no one acceptable has asked."

Simon had no idea how Anthony could possibly hold out against the warm pleading in her dark eyes. And sure enough, Anthony sagged against the desk and let out a weary groan. "Very well," he said, closing his eyes as if he couldn't believe what he was saying, "I shall agree to this if I must."

Daphne jumped up and threw her arms around him. "Oh, Anthony, I knew you were the very best of brothers." She gave him a kiss on the cheek. "You're just occasionally misguided."

Anthony's eyes floated heavenward before focusing on Simon. "Do you see what I have to put up with?" he asked with a shake of his head. His tone was that particular timbre used only from one beleaguered male to another.

Simon chuckled to himself as he wondered when he'd turned from evil seducer back into good friend.

"But," Anthony said loudly, causing Daphne to back up, "I am placing some conditions on this."

Daphne didn't say anything, just blinked as she waited for her brother to continue.

"First of all, this goes no further than this room."

"Agreed," she said quickly.

Anthony looked pointedly at Simon.

"Of course," he replied.

"Mother would be devastated if she learned the truth."

"Actually," Simon murmured, "I rather think your mother would applaud our ingenuity, but since you have quite obviously known her longer, I bow to your discretion."

Anthony shot him a frosty look. "Second, under no circumstances are the two of you to be alone together. Ever."

"Well, that should be easy," Daphne said, "as we wouldn't be allowed to be alone if we were courting in truth, anyway."

Simon recalled their brief interlude in the hall at Lady Danbury's house, and found it a pity that he wasn't to be allowed any more private time with Daphne, but he recognized a brick wall when he saw one, especially when said wall happened to be named Anthony Bridgerton. So he just nodded and murmured his assent.

"Third—"

"There is a *third*?" Daphne asked.

"There would be thirty if I could think of them," Anthony growled.

"Very well," she acceded, looking most aggrieved. "If you must."

For a split second Simon thought Anthony might strangle her.

"What are you laughing about?" Anthony demanded.

It was only then that Simon realized that he had snorted a laugh. "Nothing," he said quickly.

"Good," Anthony grunted, "because the third condition is this: If I ever, even once, catch you in any behavior that compromises her . . . If I ever even catch you kissing her bloody hand without a chaperon, I shall tear your head off."

Daphne blinked. "Don't you think that's a bit excessive?"

Anthony leveled a hard stare in her direction. "No."

"Oh."

"Hastings?"

Simon had no choice but to nod.

"Good," Anthony replied gruffly. "And now that we're done with that, you"—he cocked his head rather abruptly toward Simon—"can leave."

"Anthony!" Daphne exclaimed.

"I assume this means I am disinvited for supper this evening?" Simon asked.

"Yes."

"No!" Daphne jabbed her brother in the arm. "Is Hastings invited for supper? Why did you not say something?"

"It was days ago," Anthony grumbled. "Years."

"It was Monday," Simon said.

"Well, then you must join us," Daphne said firmly. "Mother will be so delighted. And you"—she poked her brother in the arm—"stop thinking about how you may poison him."

Before Anthony could reply, Simon waved off her words with a chuckle. "Do not worry on my behalf, Daphne. You forget that I attended school with him for nearly a decade. He never did understand the principles of chemistry."

"I shall kill him," Anthony said to himself. "Before the week is out, I shall kill him."

"No you won't," Daphne said blithely. "By tomorrow you will have forgotten all of this and will be smoking cheroots at White's."

"I don't think so," Anthony said ominously.

"Of course you will. Don't you agree, Simon?"

Simon studied his best friend's face and realized he was seeing something new. Something in his eyes. Something serious.

Six years ago, when Simon had left England, he and Anthony had been boys. Oh, they'd thought they were men. They'd gambled and whored and strutted about society, consumed with their own importance, but now they were different.

Now they were men in truth.

Simon had felt the change within himself during his travels. It had been a slow transformation, wrought over time as he faced new challenges. But now he realized that he'd returned to England still picturing Anthony as that twenty-two-year-old boy he'd left behind.

He'd done his friend a great disservice, he'd realized, in failing to realize that he, too, had grown up. Anthony had responsibilities Simon had never even dreamed of. He had brothers to guide, sisters to protect. Simon had a dukedom, but Anthony had a *family*.

There was a grave difference, and Simon found that he couldn't fault his friend for his overprotective and indeed somewhat mulish behavior.

"I think," Simon said slowly, finally answering Daphne's question, "that your brother and I are both different people than we were when we ran wild six years ago. And I think that might not be such a bad thing."

Several hours later, the Bridgerton household was in chaos.

Daphne had changed into an evening dress of dark green velvet that someone had once said almost made her eyes look not quite brown, and was presently idling about in the great hall, trying to find a way to calm her mother's racing nerves.

"I cannot *believe*," Violet said, one hand fluttering on her chest, "that Anthony forgot to tell me he invited the duke to dinner. I had no time to prepare. None at all."

Daphne eyed the menu in her hand, which began with turtle soup and marched through three more courses before finishing with lamb à la bechamel (followed, of course, by a choice of four desserts). She tried to keep her voice free of sarcasm as she said, "I do not think the duke will have cause to complain."

"I pray that he won't," Violet replied. "But if I had known he was coming, I would have made sure we had a beef dish as well. One cannot entertain without a beef dish."

"He knows this is an informal meal."

Violet shot her an acerbic look. "No meal is informal when a duke is calling."

Daphne regarded her mother thoughtfully. Violet was wringing her hands and gnashing her teeth. "Mother," Daphne said, "I don't think the duke is the sort to expect us to dramatically alter our family supper plans on his behalf."

"He might not expect it," Violet said, "but I do. Daphne, there are certain rules in society. Expectations. And frankly, I do not understand how you can be quite so calm and disinterested."

"I'm not disinterested!"

"You certainly don't look nervous." Violet eyed her suspiciously. "How can you not be nervous? For goodness' sake, Daphne, this man is thinking of marrying you."

Daphne caught herself just before she groaned. "He has never said as much, Mother."

"He didn't have to. Why else would he have danced with you last night? The only other lady he so honored was Penelope Featherington, and we both know that that had to be out of pity."

"I *like* Penelope," Daphne said.

"I like Penelope, too," Violet returned, "and I long for the day her mother realizes that a girl of her complexion cannot be dressed in tangerine satin, but that is beside the point."

"What *is* the point?"

"I don't know!" Violet very nearly wailed.

Daphne shook her head. "I'm going to find Eloise."

"Yes, do that," Violet said distractedly, "and make sure Gregory is clean. He never washes behind his ears. And Hyacinth—Good God, what are we to do about Hyacinth? Hastings will not expect a ten-year-old at the table."

"Yes, he will," Daphne replied patiently. "Anthony told him we were dining as a family."

"Most families do not allow their younger children to dine with them," Violet pointed out.

"Then that is their problem." Daphne finally gave in to her exasperation and let out a loud sigh. "Mother, I spoke to the duke. He understands that this is not a formal meal. And he specifically told me that he was looking forward to a change of pace. He has no family himself, so he has never experienced anything like a Bridgerton family dinner."

"God help us." Violet's face went utterly pale.

"Now, Mother," Daphne said quickly, "I know what you're thinking, and I assure you that you don't have to worry about Gregory putting creamed potatoes on Francesca's chair again. I'm certain he has outgrown such childish behavior."

"He did it last week!"

"Well, then," Daphne said briskly, not missing a beat, "then I'm sure he's learned his lesson."

The look Violet gave her daughter was dubious in the extreme.

"Very well, then," Daphne said, her tone considerably less businesslike, "then I will simply threaten him with death if he does anything to upset you."

"Death won't scare him," Violet mused, "but perhaps I can threaten to sell his horse."

"He'll never believe you."

"No, you're right. I'm far too softhearted." Violet frowned. "But he might believe me if I told him he would be forbidden to go on his daily ride."

"That might work," Daphne agreed.

"Good. I shall go off and scare some sense into him." Violet took two steps then turned around. "Having children is such a challenge."

Daphne just smiled. She knew it was a challenge her mother adored.

Violet cleared her throat softly, signaling a more serious turn of conversation. "I do hope this supper goes well, Daphne. I think Hastings might be an excellent match for you."

" 'Might'?" Daphne teased. "I thought dukes were good matches even if they had two heads and spit while they talked." She laughed. "Out of both mouths!"

Violet smiled benignly. "You might find this difficult to believe, Daphne, but I don't want to see you married off to just anyone. I may introduce you to no end of eligible men, but that is only because I would like you to have as many suitors as possible from which to choose a husband." Violet smiled wistfully. "It is my fondest dream to see you as happy as I was with your father."

And then, before Daphne could reply, Violet disappeared down the hall.

Leaving Daphne with second thoughts.

Maybe this plan with Hastings wasn't such a good idea, after all. Violet was going to be crushed when they broke off their faux alliance. Simon had said that Daphne might be the one to do the jilting, but she was beginning to wonder if perhaps it wouldn't be better the other way around. It would be mortifying for Daphne to be thrown over by Simon, but at least that way she wouldn't have to endure Violet's bewildered chorus of "Why?"

Violet was going to think she was insane for letting him get away.

And Daphne would be left wondering if maybe her mother was right.

Simon had not been prepared for supper with the Bridgertons. It was a loud, raucous affair, with plenty of laughter and thankfully, only one incident involving a flying pea.

(It had looked as if the pea in question had originated at Hyacinth's end of the table, but the littlest Bridgerton had looked so innocent and angelic that Simon had difficulty believing she had actually aimed the legume at her brother.)

Thankfully, Violet had not noticed the flying pea, even though it sailed right over her head in a perfect arc.

But Daphne, who was sitting directly across from him, most certainly had, because her napkin flew up to cover her mouth with remarkable alacrity. Judging from the way her eyes were crinkling at the corners, she was definitely laughing under the square of linen.

Simon spoke little throughout the meal. Truth be told, it was far easier to listen to the Bridgertons than actually try to converse with them, especially considering the number of malevolent stares he was receiving from Anthony and Benedict.

But Simon had been seated clear at the opposite end of the table from the two eldest Bridgertons (no accident on Violet's part, he was sure) so it was relatively simple to ignore them and instead enjoy Daphne's interactions with the rest of her family. Every now and then one of them would ask him a direct question, and he would answer, and then he would return to his demeanor of quiet observation.

Finally, Hyacinth, who was seated to Daphne's right, looked him straight in the eye, and said, "You don't talk much, do you?"

Violet choked on her wine.

"The duke," Daphne said to Hyacinth, "is being far more polite than we are, constantly jumping into the conversation and interrupting one another as if we're afraid we might not be heard."

"I'm not afraid I might not be heard," Gregory said.

"I'm not afraid of that, either," Violet commented dryly. "Gregory, eat your peas."

"But Hyacinth—"

"Lady Bridgerton," Simon said loudly, "may I trouble you for another helping of those delicious peas?"

"Why certainly." Violet shot an arch look at Gregory. "Notice how the duke is eating his peas."

Gregory ate his peas.

Simon smiled to himself as he spooned another portion of peas onto his plate, thankful that Lady Bridgerton had not decided to serve dinner *à la russe*. It would have been difficult to stave off Gregory's certain accusation of Hyacinth as a pea-tosser if he'd had to summon a footman to serve him.

Simon busied himself with his peas, since he really had no choice but to finish off every last one. He stole a glance at Daphne, however, who was wearing a secret little smile. Her eyes were brimming with infectious good humor, and Simon soon felt the corners of his mouth turning up as well.

"Anthony, why are you scowling?" asked one of the other Bridgerton girls—Simon thought it might be Francesca, but it was hard to say. The two middle ones looked amazingly alike, right down to their light eyes, so like their mother's.

"I'm not scowling," Anthony snapped, but Simon, having been on the receiving end of those scowls for the better part of an hour, rather thought he was lying.

"You are, too," either Francesca or Eloise said.

Anthony's tone of reply was condescending in the extreme. "If you think I am going to say, 'Am not,' you are sadly mistaken."

Daphne laughed into her napkin again.

Simon decided life was more amusing than it had been in ages.

"Do you know," Violet suddenly announced, "that I think this might be one of the most pleasant evenings of the year. Even"—she sent a knowing glance down the table at Hyacinth—"if my youngest is tossing peas down the table."

Simon looked up just as Hyacinth cried out, "How did you know?"

Violet shook her head as she rolled her eyes. "My dear children," she said, "when will you learn that I know everything?"

Simon decided he had a great deal of respect for Violet Bridgerton.

But even still, she managed to completely confuse him with a question and a smile. "Tell me, your grace," she said, "are you busy tomorrow?"

Despite her blond and blue-eyed coloring, she looked so like Daphne as she asked him this question that he was momentarily befuddled. Which had to be the only reason he didn't bother to think before he stammered, "N-no. Not that I recall."

"Excellent!" Violet exclaimed, beaming. "Then you must join us on our outing to Greenwich."

"Greenwich?" Simon echoed.

"Yes, we've been planning a family outing for several weeks now. We thought we'd take a boat, then perhaps have a picnic on the shores of the Thames." Violet smiled at him confidently. "You'll come, won't you?"

"Mother," Daphne interjected, "I'm certain the duke has any number of commitments."

Violet gave Daphne a look so frigid Simon was surprised that neither one of them turned to ice. "Nonsense," Violet replied. "He just said himself that he wasn't busy." She turned back to Simon. "And we shall be visiting the Royal Observatory as well, so you needn't worry that this will be a mindless jaunt. It's not open to the public, of course, but my late husband was a great patron, so we are assured entry."

Simon looked at Daphne. She just shrugged and apologized with her eyes.

He turned back to Violet. "I'd be delighted."

Violet beamed and patted him on the arm.

And Simon had the sinking sensation that his fate had just been sealed.

Chapter 8

It has reached This Author's ears that the entire Bridgerton family (plus one duke!) embarked upon a journey to Greenwich on Saturday.

It has also reached This Author's ears that the aforementioned duke, along with a certain member of the Bridgerton family, returned to London very wet indeed.

LADY WHISTLEDOWN'S SOCIETY PAPERS, 3 May 1813

"If you apologize to me one more time," Simon said, leaning his head back against his hands, "I may have to kill you."

Daphne shot him an irritated look from her position in her deck chair on the small yacht her mother had commissioned to take the entire family—and the duke, of course—to Greenwich. "Pardon me," she said, "if I am polite enough to apologize for my mother's quite obvious manipulations. I thought that the purpose of our little charade was to shield you from the tender mercies of matchmaking mothers."

Simon waved off her comment, as he settled deeper into his own chair. "It would only be a problem if I were not enjoying myself."

Daphne's chin lurched backward slightly in surprise. "Oh," she said (stupidly, in her opinion). "That's nice."

He laughed. "I am inordinately fond of boat travel, even if it is just down to Greenwich, and besides, after spending so much time at sea, I rather fancy a visit to the Royal Observatory to see the Greenwich Meridian." He cocked his head in her direction. "Do you know much about navigation and longitude?"

She shook her head. "Very little, I'm afraid. I must confess I'm not even certain what this meridian here at Greenwich *is*."

"It's the point from which all longitude is measured. It used to be that sailors and navigators measured longitudinal distance from their point of departure, but in the last century, the astronomer royal decided to make Greenwich the starting point."

Daphne raised her brows. "That seems rather self-important of us, don't you think, positioning ourselves at the center of the world?"

"Actually, it's quite convenient to have a universal reference point when one is attempting to navigate the high seas."

She still looked doubtful. "So everyone simply agreed on Greenwich? I find it difficult to believe that the French wouldn't have insisted upon Paris, and the Pope, I'm sure, would have preferred Rome . . ."

"Well, it wasn't an agreement, precisely," he allowed with a laugh. "There was no official treaty, if that is what you mean. But the Royal Observatory publishes an excellent set of charts and tables each year—it's called the *Nautical Almanac*. And a sailor would have to be insane to attempt to navigate the ocean without one on board. And since the *Nautical Almanac* measures longitude with Greenwich as zero . . . well, everyone else has adopted it as well."

"You seem to know quite a bit about this."

He shrugged. "If you spend enough time on a ship, you learn."

"Well, I'm afraid it wasn't the sort of thing one learned in the Bridgerton nursery." She cocked her head to the side in a somewhat self-deprecating manner. "Most of my learning was restricted to what my governess knew."

"Pity," he murmured. Then he asked, "Only most?"

"If there was something that interested me, I could usually find several books to read on the topic in our library."

"I would wager then, that your interests did not lie in abstract mathematics."

Daphne laughed. "Like you, you mean? Hardly, I'm afraid. My mother always said that it was a wonder I could add high enough to put shoes on my feet."

Simon winced.

"I know, I know," she said, still smiling. "You sorts who excel at arithmetic simply don't understand how we lesser mortals can look at a page of numbers and not know the answer—or at least how to *get* to the answer—instantly. Colin is the same way."

He smiled, because she was exactly right. "What, then, were your favorite subjects?"

"Hmm? Oh, history and literature. Which was fortunate, since we had no end of books on those topics."

He took another sip of his lemonade. "I've never had any great passion for history."

"Really? Why not, do you think?"

Simon pondered that for a moment, wondering if perhaps his lack of enthusiasm for history was due to his distaste for his dukedom and all the tradition that wrapped around it. His father had been so passionate about the title . . .

But of course all he said was, "Don't know, really. Just didn't like it, I suppose."

They fell into a few moments of companionable silence, the

gentle river wind ruffling their hair. Then Daphne smiled, and said, "Well, I won't apologize again, since I'm too fond of my life to sacrifice it needlessly at your hands, but I am glad that you're not miserable after my mother browbeat you into accompanying us."

The look he gave her was vaguely sardonic. "If I hadn't wanted to join you, there is nothing your mother could have said that would have secured my presence."

She snorted. "And this from a man who is feigning a courtship to *me*, of all people, all because he's too polite to refuse invitations from his friends' new wives."

A rather irritable scowl immediately darkened his features. "What do you mean, *you* of all people?"

"Well, I . . ." She blinked in surprise. She had no idea *what* she meant. "I don't know," she finally said.

"Well, stop saying it," he grumbled, then settled back into his chair.

Daphne's eyes inexplicably focused on a wet spot on the railing as she fought to keep an absurd smile off her face. Simon was so sweet when he was grumpy.

"What are you looking at?" he asked.

Her lips twitched. "Nothing."

"Then what are you smiling about?"

That she most certainly was not going to reveal. "I'm not smiling."

"If you're not smiling," he muttered, "then you're either about to suffer a seizure or sneeze."

"Neither," she said in a breezy voice. "Just enjoying the excellent weather."

Simon was leaning his head against the back of the chair, so he just rolled it to the side so he could look at her. "And the company's not that bad," he teased.

Daphne shot a pointed look at Anthony, who was leaning against the rail on the opposite side of the deck, glowering at them both. "*All* of the company?" she asked.

"If you mean your belligerent brother," Simon replied, "I'm actually finding his distress most amusing."

Daphne fought a smile and didn't win. "That's not very kind-hearted of you."

"I never said I was kind. And look—" Simon tipped his head ever so slightly in Anthony's direction. Anthony's scowl had, unbelievably, turned even blacker. "He knows we're talking about him. It's killing him."

"I thought you were friends."

"We *are* friends. This is what friends do to one another."

"Men are mad."

"Generally speaking," he agreed.

She rolled her eyes. "I thought the primary rule of friendship was that one was not supposed to dally with one's friend's sister."

"Ah, but I'm not dallying. I'm merely *pretending* to dally."

Daphne nodded thoughtfully and glanced at Anthony. "And it's still killing him—even though he knows the truth of the matter."

"I know." Simon grinned. "Isn't it brilliant?"

Just then Violet came sailing across the deck. "Children!" she called out. "Children! Oh, pardon me, your grace," she added when she spied him. "It's certainly not fair for me to lump you with my children."

Simon just smiled and waved off her apology.

"The captain tells me we're nearly there," Violet explained. "We should gather up our things."

Simon rose to his feet and extended a helpful hand to Daphne, who took it gratefully, wobbling as she stood.

"I haven't my sea legs yet," she laughed, clutching his arm to steady herself.

"And here we're merely on the river," he murmured.

"Beast. You're not supposed to point out my lack of grace and balance."

As she spoke, she turned her face toward his, and in that instant, with the wind catching her hair and painting her cheeks pink, she looked so enchantingly lovely that Simon nearly forgot to breathe.

Her lush mouth was caught somewhere between a laugh and a smile, and the sun glinted almost red on her hair. Here on the water, away from stuffy ballrooms, with the fresh air swirling about them, she looked natural and beautiful and just being in her presence made Simon want to grin like an idiot.

If they hadn't been about to pull into dock, with her entire family running around them, he would have kissed her. He knew he couldn't dally with her, and he knew he would never marry her, and still he found himself leaning toward her. He didn't even realize what he was doing until he suddenly felt off-balance and lurched back upright.

Anthony, unfortunately, caught the entire episode, and he rather brusquely insinuated himself between Simon and Daphne, grasping her arm with far more strength than grace. "As your eldest brother," he growled, "I believe it is my honor to escort you ashore."

Simon just bowed and let Anthony have his way, too shaken and angered by his momentary loss of control to argue.

The boat settled next to the dock, and a gangplank was put into place. Simon watched as the entire Bridgerton family disembarked, then he brought up the rear, following them onto the grassy banks of the Thames.

At the top of the hill stood the Royal Observatory, a stately old building of rich red brick. Its towers were topped with gray domes, and Simon had the sense that he was, as Daphne had put it, at the very center of the world. Everything, he realized, was measured from this point.

After having crossed a good portion of the globe, the thought was rather humbling.

"Do we have everyone?" the viscountess called out. "Hold still, everyone, so I may be sure we are all present and accounted for." She started counting heads, finally ending on herself with a triumphant, "Ten! Good, we're all here."

"Just be glad she doesn't make us line up by age any longer."

Simon looked to the left to see Colin grinning at him.

"As a method of keeping order, age worked when it still corresponded with height. But then Benedict gained an inch on Anthony, and then Gregory outgrew Francesca—" Colin shrugged. "Mother simply gave up."

Simon scanned the crowd and lifted one shoulder in a shrug. "I'm just trying to figure out where I'd fit in."

"Somewhere near Anthony, if I had to hazard a guess," Colin replied.

"God forbid," Simon muttered.

Colin glanced at him with a mix of amusement and curiosity.

"Anthony!" Violet called out. "Where's Anthony?"

Anthony indicated his location with a rather ill-tempered grunt.

"Oh, there you are, Anthony. Come and escort me in."

Anthony reluctantly let go of Daphne's arm and walked to his mother's side.

"She's shameless, isn't she?" Colin whispered.

Simon thought it best not to comment.

"Well, don't disappoint her," Colin said. "After all her machinations, the least you can do is go and take Daphne's arm."

Simon turned to Colin with a quirked eyebrow. "You might be just as bad as your mother."

Colin just laughed. "Yes, except that at least I don't *pretend* to be subtle."

Daphne chose that moment to walk over. "I find myself without an escort," she said.

"Imagine that," Colin returned. "Now, if the two of you will excuse me, I'm off to find Hyacinth. If I'm forced to escort Eloise, I may have to swim back to London. She's been a wretch ever since she attained the age of fourteen."

Simon blinked in confusion. "Didn't you just return from the Continent last week?"

Colin nodded. "Yes, but Eloise's fourteenth birthday was a year and a half ago."

Daphne swatted him on the elbow. "If you're lucky, I won't tell her you said that."

Colin just rolled his eyes and disappeared into the small crowd, bellowing Hyacinth's name.

Daphne laid her hand in the crook of Simon's elbow as he offered her his arm, then asked, "Have we scared you off yet?"

"I beg your pardon?"

She offered him a rueful smile. "There is nothing quite as exhausting as a Bridgerton family outing."

"Oh, that." Simon stepped quickly to the right to avoid Gregory, who was racing after Hyacinth, yelling something about mud and revenge. "It's, ah, a new experience."

"Very politely put, your grace," Daphne said admiringly. "I'm impressed."

"Yes, well—" He jumped back as Hyacinth barreled by, squealing at such a pitch that Simon was certain that dogs would start howling from there to London. "I have no siblings, after all."

Daphne let out a dreamy sigh. "No siblings," she mused. "Right now it sounds like heaven." The faraway look remained in her eyes for a few more seconds, then she straightened and shook off her reverie. "Be that as it may, however—" Her hand shot out just as Gregory ran past, catching the boy firmly by the upper arm. "Gregory Bridgerton," she scolded, "you should know better than to run thus through a crowd. You're liable to knock someone over."

"How did you do that?" Simon asked.

"What, catch him?"

"Yes."

She shrugged. "I have years of practice."

"Daphne!" Gregory whined. His arm, after all, was still attached to her hand.

She let go. "Now, slow down."

He took two exaggerated steps then broke into a trot.

"No scolding for Hyacinth?" Simon asked.

Daphne motioned over her shoulder. "It appears my mother has Hyacinth in hand."

Simon saw that Violet was shaking her finger quite vehemently at Hyacinth. He turned back to Daphne. "What were you about to say before Gregory appeared on the scene?"

She blinked. "I have no idea."

"I believe you were about to go into raptures at the thought of having no siblings."

"Oh, of course." She let out a little laugh as they followed the rest of the Bridgertons up the hill toward the observatory. "Actually, believe it or not, I was going to say that while the concept of eternal solitude is, at times, tempting, I think I would be quite lonely without family."

Simon said nothing.

"I cannot imagine having only one child myself," she added.

"Sometimes," Simon said in a dry voice, "one has little choice in the matter."

Daphne's cheeks turned an immediate red. "Oh, I'm so sorry," she stammered, her feet absolutely refusing to take a step. "I'd forgotten. Your mother . . ."

Simon paused beside her. "I didn't know her," he said with a shrug. "I didn't mourn her."

But his blue eyes were strangely hollow and shuttered, and Daphne somehow knew that his words were false.

And at the same time, she knew that he believed them one hundred percent.

And she wondered—what could have happened to this man to make him lie to himself for so many years?

She studied his face, her head tilting slightly as she took in his features. The wind had brought color to his cheeks and ruffled his dark hair. He looked rather uncomfortable under her scrutiny, and finally he just grunted, and said, "We're falling behind."

Daphne looked up the hill. Her family was a good distance ahead of them. "Yes, of course," she said, straightening her shoulders. "We should get going."

But as she trudged up the hill, she wasn't thinking of her family, or of the observatory, or even of longitude. Instead, she was wondering why she had the most bizarre urge to throw her arms around the duke and never let go.

Several hours later, they were all back on the grassy banks of the Thames, enjoying the last bites of an elegant yet simple luncheon that had been prepared by the Bridgertons' cook. As he had the night before, Simon spoke little, instead observing the often boisterous interactions of Daphne's family.

But Hyacinth apparently had other ideas.

"Good day, your grace," she said, seating herself next to him on the blanket one of the footmen had laid out for their picnic. "Did you enjoy your tour of the observatory?"

Simon couldn't quite suppress a smile as he answered, "Indeed I did, Miss Hyacinth. And you?"

"Oh, very much so. I especially appreciated your lecture on longitude and latitude."

"Well, I don't know that I'd call it a *lecture*," Simon said, the word making him feel just the slightest bit old and stodgy.

Across the blanket, Daphne was grinning at his distress.

Hyacinth just smiled flirtatiously—*flirtatiously*?—and said, "Did you know that Greenwich also has a most romantic history?"

Daphne started to shake with laughter, the little traitor.

"Really?" Simon managed to get out.

"Indeed," Hyacinth replied, using such cultured tones that Simon briefly wondered if there were actually a forty-year-old matron inside her ten-year-old body. "It was here that Sir Walter Raleigh laid his cloak upon the ground so that Queen Elizabeth would not have to dirty her slippers in a puddle."

"Is that so?" Simon stood and scanned the area.

"Your grace!" Hyacinth's face reverted to ten-year-old impatience as she jumped to her feet. "What are you doing?"

"Examining the terrain," he replied. He cast a secret glance at Daphne. She was looking up at him with mirth and humor and something else that made him feel about ten feet tall.

"But what are you looking for?" Hyacinth persisted.

"Puddles."

"Puddles?" Her face slowly transformed into one of utter delight as she grasped his meaning. "Puddles?"

"Indeed. If I'm going to have to ruin a cloak to save your slippers, Miss Hyacinth, I'd like to know about it in advance."

"But you're not wearing a cloak."

"Heavens above," Simon replied, in such a voice that Daphne burst into laughter below him. "You do not mean that I will be forced to remove my *shirt*?"

"No!" Hyacinth squealed. "You don't have to remove anything! There aren't any puddles."

"Thank heavens," Simon breathed, clasping one hand to his chest for added effect. He was having far more fun with this than he would have ever dreamed possible. "You Bridgerton ladies are very demanding, did you know that?"

Hyacinth viewed him with a mixture of suspicion and glee. Suspicion finally won out. Her hands found their way to her little hips as she narrowed her eyes and asked, "Are you funning me?"

He smiled right at her. "What do you think?"

"I think you are."

"I think I'm lucky there aren't any puddles about."

Hyacinth pondered that for a moment. "If you decide to marry my sister—" she said.

Daphne choked on a biscuit.

"—then you have my approval."

Simon choked on air.

"But if you don't," Hyacinth continued, smiling shyly, "then I'd be much obliged if you'd wait for me."

Luckily for Simon, who had little experience with young girls and not a clue how to respond, Gregory came dashing by and yanked on Hyacinth's hair. She immediately took off after him, her eyes narrowed with the single-minded determination to get even.

"I never thought I'd say this," Daphne said, laughter in her voice, "but I believe you have just been saved by my younger brother."

"How old is your sister?" Simon asked.

"Ten, why?"

He shook his head in bewilderment. "Because for a moment, I could have sworn she was forty."

Daphne smiled. "Sometimes she is so like my mother it's frightening."

At that moment, the woman in question stood and began to summon her children back to the boat. "Come along!" Violet called out. "It's growing late!"

Simon looked at his pocket watch. "It's three."

Daphne shrugged as she rose to her feet. "To her that's late. According to Mother, a lady should always be home at five o'clock."

"Why?"

She reached down to pick up the blanket. "I have no idea. To get ready for the evening, I suppose. It's one of those rules I've grown up with and deemed best not to question." She straightened, holding the soft blue blanket to her chest, and smiled. "Are we ready to go?"

Simon held out his arm. "Certainly."

They took a few steps toward the boat, and then Daphne said, "You were very good with Hyacinth. You must have spent a great deal of time with children."

"None," he said tersely.

"Oh," she said, a puzzled frown decorating her face. "I knew you had no siblings, but I had assumed you must have met some children on your travels."

"No."

Daphne held silent for a moment, wondering if she should pursue the conversation. Simon's voice had grown hard and forbidding, and his face . . .

He didn't look like the same man who had teased Hyacinth mere minutes earlier.

But for some reason—maybe because it had been such a lovely afternoon, maybe it was just because the weather was fine—she faked a sunny smile and said, "Well, experience or no, you clearly have the touch. Some adults don't know how to talk to children, you know."

He said nothing.

She patted his arm. "You'll make some lucky child an excellent father someday."

His head whipped around to face her, and the look in his eyes nearly froze her heart. "I believe I told you I have no intention of marrying," he bit off. "Ever."

"But surely you—"

"Therefore it is unlikely that I shall ever have children."

"I . . . I see." Daphne swallowed and attempted a shaky smile, but she had a feeling she didn't manage anything more than a slight quivering of her lips. And even though she knew that their courtship was nothing more than a charade, she felt a vague sense of disappointment.

They reached the edge of the dock, where most of the rest of the Bridgertons were milling about. A few had already boarded, and Gregory was dancing on the gangplank.

"Gregory!" Violet called out, her voice sharp. "Stop that at once!"

He stilled, but didn't move from his position.

"Either get on the boat or come back to the dock."

Simon slipped his arm from Daphne's, muttering, "That gangplank looks wet." He started moving forward.

"You heard Mother!" Hyacinth called out.

"Oh, Hyacinth," Daphne sighed to herself. "Can't you just keep out of it?"

Gregory stuck out his tongue.

Daphne groaned, then noticed that Simon was still walking toward the gangplank. She hurried to his side, whispering, "Simon, I'm sure he'll be fine."

"Not if he slips and gets caught in the ropes." He motioned with his chin to a tangled mess of ropes that were hanging off the boat.

Simon reached the end of the gangplank, walking casually, as if he hadn't a worry in the world. "Are you going to get moving?" he called out, stepping out onto the narrow piece of wood. "So that I might cross?"

Gregory blinked. "Don't you have to escort Daphne?"

Simon groaned and moved forward, but just then, Anthony, who had already boarded the small yacht, appeared at the top of the gangplank.

"Gregory!" he called out sharply. "Get on this boat at once!"

From down on the dock, Daphne watched with horror as Gregory spun around in surprise, losing his footing on the slippery wood. Anthony leapt forward, making a frantic grab with his arms, but Gregory had already slid to his bottom, and Anthony caught only air.

Anthony fought for balance as Gregory slid down the gangplank, clipping Simon rather neatly in the shins.

"Simon!" Daphne croaked, running forward.

Simon went tumbling into the murky water of the Thames, just as Gregory wailed a heartfelt, "I'm sorry!" He scooted up the gangplank backwards on his behind—rather like a crab, actually—not at all looking where he was going.

Which probably explained why he had no idea that Anthony—who had almost managed to regain his balance—was only a few short feet behind him.

Gregory rammed into Anthony with a thud on his part and a

grunt on Anthony's, and before anyone knew it, Anthony was sputtering in the water, right next to Simon.

Daphne clapped a hand to her mouth, her eyes wide as saucers.

Violet yanked on her arm. "I highly suggest you don't laugh."

Daphne pinched her lips together in an effort to comply, but it was difficult. "*You're* laughing," she pointed out.

"I'm not," Violet lied. Her entire neck was quivering with the exertion required to keep her laughter inside. "And besides, I'm a *mother*. They wouldn't dare do anything to *me*."

Anthony and Simon came stalking out of the water, dripping and glaring at each other.

Gregory crawled the rest of the way up the gangplank and disappeared over the edge.

"Maybe you should intercede," Violet suggested.

"Me?" Daphne squeaked.

"It looks as if they might come to blows."

"But why? It was all Gregory's fault."

"Of course," Violet said impatiently, "but they're *men*, and they're both furious and embarrassed, and they can't very well take it out on a boy of twelve."

Sure enough, Anthony was muttering, "I could have taken care of him," just as Simon growled, "If you hadn't surprised him . . ."

Violet rolled her eyes, and said to Daphne, "Any man, you'll soon learn, has an insurmountable need to blame someone else when he is made to look a fool."

Daphne rushed forward, fully intending to attempt to reason with the two men, but one close look at their faces told her that nothing she could possibly say could imbue them with as much intelligence and sensibility as a woman would have in such a situation, so she simply pasted on a bright smile, grabbed Simon's arm, and said, "Escort me up?"

Simon glared at Anthony.

Anthony glared at Simon.

Daphne yanked.

"This isn't over, Hastings," Anthony hissed.

"Far from it," Simon hissed back.

Daphne realized that they were simply looking for an excuse to come to blows. She yanked harder, prepared to dislocate Simon's shoulder if need be.

After one last burning glare, he acquiesced and followed her up into the boat.

It was a very long trip home.

Later that night, as Daphne prepared for bed, she found herself oddly restless. Sleep, she could already tell, would prove impossible, so she pulled on a robe and wandered downstairs in search of warm milk and some company. With so many siblings, she thought wryly, surely *someone* had to be up and about.

On her way to the kitchen, however, she heard rustlings in Anthony's study, so she poked her head in. Her eldest brother was hunched over his desk, ink spots on his fingers from the correspondence he was answering. It was uncommon to find him here so late into the evening. He'd preferred to keep his study at Bridgerton House even after he'd moved into his bachelor's lodgings, but he usually took care of his business matters during the day.

"Don't you have a secretary to do that?" Daphne asked with a smile.

Anthony looked up. "Damned fool got married and moved to Bristol," he muttered.

"Ah." She walked into the room and perched on a chair opposite the desk. "That would explain your presence here in the wee hours of the morning."

Anthony glanced up at the clock. "Midnight is hardly wee. And besides, it took me all afternoon just to get the Thames out of my hair."

Daphne tried not to smile.

"But you're right," Anthony said with a sigh, setting down his quill. "It's late, and there's nothing here that won't keep until the morning." He leaned back and stretched out his neck. "What are you doing up and about?"

"Couldn't sleep," Daphne explained with a shrug. "I came downstairs for some hot milk and heard you cursing."

Anthony let out a grunt. "It's this bloody quill. I swear I—" He smiled sheepishly. "I suppose 'I swear' pretty much takes care of it, eh?"

Daphne smiled in return. Her brothers had never minded their language around her. "So you'll be heading home soon, then?"

He nodded. "Although that warm milk you mentioned sounds rather nice. Why don't you ring for it?"

Daphne stood. "I've a better idea. Why don't we get it ourselves? We're not complete idiots. We should be able to warm some milk. And besides, the servants are probably in bed."

Anthony followed her out the door. "Very well, but you shall have to do all the work. I haven't the faintest idea how to boil milk."

"I don't think one is supposed to let it boil," Daphne said with a frown. She rounded the last corner on the way to the kitchen and pushed open the door. The room was dark, save for moonlight glowing through the windows. "Find a lamp while I find some milk," she said to Anthony. Her face took on a slight smirk. "You *can* light a lamp, can't you?"

"Oh, I believe I can manage that," he said good-naturedly.

Daphne smiled to herself as she fumbled about in the dark, pulling a small pot from the hanging rack above her. She and Anthony usually had an easy, joking relationship, and it was nice to see him back to his normal self again. He'd been in such a beastly mood for the past week, with most of his sour temper directed squarely at her.

And Simon, of course, but Simon was rarely present to receive Anthony's scowls.

A light flickered to life behind her, and Daphne turned to see Anthony smiling triumphantly. "Have you found the milk," he asked, "or must I venture out in search of a cow?"

She laughed and held up a bottle. "Found it!" She wandered over to the enclosed range, a rather modern-looking contraption that Cook had purchased earlier in the year. "Do you know how to work this?" she asked.

"No idea. You?"

Daphne shook her head. "None." She reached forward and gingerly touched the surface of the stove top. "It's not hot."

"Not even a little bit?"

She shook her head. "It's rather cold, actually."

Brother and sister were silent for a few seconds.

"You know," Anthony finally said, "cold milk might be quite refreshing."

"I was just thinking that very thing!"

Anthony grinned and found two mugs. "Here, you pour."

Daphne did, and soon they were seated on stools, gulping down the fresh milk. Anthony drained his mug in short order, and poured another. "You need some more?" he asked, wiping off his milk mustache.

"No, I'm barely halfway to the bottom," Daphne said, taking another sip. She licked at her lips, fidgeting in her chair. Now that she was alone with Anthony, and he seemed like he was back in his usual good humor, it seemed like a good time to . . . Well, the truth was . . .

Oh, blast, she thought to herself, *just go ahead and ask him.*

"Anthony?" she said, a touch hesitantly. "Could I ask you a question?"

"Of course."

"It's about the duke."

Anthony's mug hit the table with a loud thunk. "What about the duke?"

"I know you don't like him . . ." she began, her words trailing off.

"It's not that I don't like him," Anthony said with a weary sigh. "He's one of my closest friends."

Daphne's brows rose. "One would be hard-pressed to deduce that based on your recent behavior."

"I just don't trust him around women. Around you in particular."

"Anthony, you must know that that is one of the silliest things you have ever said. The duke might have been a rake—I suppose he might still be a rake for all I know—but he would never seduce me, if only because I'm your sister."

Anthony looked unconvinced.

"Even if there weren't some male code of honor about such things," Daphne persisted, barely resisting the urge to roll her eyes, "he knows you'd kill him if he touched me. The man isn't stupid."

Anthony refrained from commenting, instead saying, "What was it you wanted to ask me?"

"Actually," Daphne said slowly, "I was wondering if you knew why the duke was so opposed to marriage."

Anthony spit his milk halfway across the table. "For Christ's sake, Daphne! I thought we agreed that this was just a charade! Why are you even thinking about marrying him?"

"I'm not!" she insisted, thinking that she might be lying but unwilling to examine her feelings closely enough to be sure. "I'm just curious," she muttered defensively.

"You had better not be thinking about trying to get him to marry you," Anthony said with a grunt, "because I'll tell you right now he'll never do it. Never. Do you understand me, Daphne? He won't marry you."

"I would have to be a half-wit not to understand you," she grumbled.

"Good. Then that's the end of it."

"No, it's not!" she returned. "You still haven't answered my question."

Anthony leveled a stony stare at her across the table.

"About why he won't get married," she prodded.

"Why are you so interested?" he asked wearily.

The truth, Daphne feared, lay a little too close to Anthony's accusations, but she just said, "I'm curious, and besides, I think I have a right to know, since, if I don't find an acceptable suitor soon, I may become a pariah after the duke drops me."

"I thought *you* were supposed to jilt *him*," Anthony said suspiciously.

Daphne snorted. "Who is going to believe *that*?"

Anthony didn't immediately jump to her defense, which Daphne found vaguely annoying. But he did say, "I don't know why Hastings refuses to marry. All I know is that he has maintained this opinion for as long as I've known him."

Daphne opened her mouth to speak, but Anthony cut her off by adding, "*And* he's stated it in such a way so that I do not believe his is the weak vow of the beleaguered bachelor."

"Meaning?"

"Meaning that unlike most men, when he says he will never marry, he means it."

"I see."

Anthony let out a long, tired breath, and Daphne noticed tiny lines of concern around his eyes that she'd never seen before. "Choose a man from your new crowd of suitors," he said, "and forget Hastings. He's a good man, but he's not for you."

Daphne latched on to the first part of his sentence. "But you think he's a good—"

"He's not for you," Anthony repeated.

But Daphne couldn't help thinking that maybe, just maybe, Anthony might be wrong.

Chapter 9

The Duke of Hastings was espied yet again with Miss Bridgerton. (That is Miss Daphne Bridgerton, for those of you who, like This Author, find it difficult to differentiate between the multitudes of Bridgerton offspring.) It has been some time since This Author has seen a couple so obviously devoted to one another.

It does seem odd, however, that, with the exception of the Bridgerton family outing to Greenwich, which was reported in this newspaper ten days earlier, they are seen together only at evening functions. This Author has it on the best authority that while the duke called upon Miss Bridgerton at her home a fortnight ago, this courtesy has not been repeated, and indeed, they have not been seen riding together in Hyde Park even once!

LADY WHISTLEDOWN'S SOCIETY PAPERS,
14 May 1813

Two weeks later, Daphne found herself in Hampstead Heath, standing on the fringes of Lady Trowbridge's ballroom, far away from the fashionable crowd. She was quite content with her position.

She didn't want to be at the center of the party. She didn't want to be found by the dozens of suitors now clamoring to claim her in a dance. In all truth, she didn't want to be in Lady Trowbridge's ballroom at all.

Because Simon was not there.

This did not mean that she was destined to spend the evening as a wallflower. All of Simon's predictions in regard to her burgeoning popularity had proven correct, and Daphne, who had always been the girl everyone liked but no one adored, was suddenly proclaimed the season's Incomparable. Everyone who cared to air an opinion on the subject (and this being the *ton*, that meant everyone) declared that they always knew that Daphne was special and were just waiting for everyone else to notice. Lady Jersey told everyone who would listen that she had been predicting Daphne's success for months, and the only mystery was why no one had listened to her sooner.

Which was, of course, hogwash. While Daphne had certainly never been the object of Lady Jersey's scorn, not one Bridgerton could recall ever hearing Lady Jersey refer to her (as she was presently doing) as "Tomorrow's Treasure."

But even though Daphne's dance card was now full within minutes of her arrival at any ball, and even though men fought for the privilege of fetching her a glass of lemonade (Daphne had almost laughed out loud the first time *that* had happened), she found that no evening was truly memorable unless Simon was at her side.

It didn't matter that he seemed to find it necessary to mention at least once every evening that he was adamantly opposed to the institution of marriage. (Although, to his credit, he usually mentioned this in conjunction with his thankfulness to Daphne for saving him from the multitudes of Ambitious Mamas.) And it didn't matter that he occasionally fell silent and was even almost rude to certain members of society.

All that seemed to matter were those moments when they were not quite alone (they were never alone), but still somehow left to their own devices. A laughing conversation in a corner, a waltz around a ballroom. Daphne could look into his pale blue eyes and almost forget that she was surrounded by five hundred onlookers, all of whom were inordinately interested in the state of her courtship.

And she could almost forget that her courtship was a complete sham.

Daphne hadn't tried to talk to Anthony about Simon again. Her brother's hostility was apparent every time the duke's name was brought up in conversation. And when he and Simon actually met—well, Anthony usually managed a certain level of cordiality, but that was all he seemed able to muster.

And yet even amidst all this anger, Daphne could see faint glimmers of the old friendship between them. She could only hope that when all this was over—and she was married off to some boring but affable earl who never quite managed to make her heart sing—that the two men would be friends again.

At Anthony's somewhat forceful request, Simon had elected not to attend every social event to which Violet and Daphne had RSVPed in the affirmative. Anthony said that the only reason he had agreed to this ridiculous scheme was so that Daphne might find a husband among all her new suitors. Unfortunately, in Anthony's opinion (and fortunately in Daphne's) none of these eager young gentlemen dared to approach her in Simon's presence.

"A fat lot of good this is doing," were Anthony's exact words.

Actually, those exact words had been appended a fair amount of cursing and invective, but Daphne had seen no reason to dwell on this. Ever since the incident at—or rather *in*—the Thames, Anthony had spent a great deal of time applying expletives to Simon's name.

But Simon had seen Anthony's point, and Simon had told Daphne that he wanted her to find a suitable husband.

And so Simon stayed away.

And Daphne was miserable.

She supposed she should have known that this was going to happen. She should have realized the dangers of being courted—even falsely—by the man society had recently dubbed The Devastating Duke.

The moniker had begun when Philipa Featherington had pronounced him "devastatingly handsome," and since Philipa didn't know the meaning of the word "whisper," all the *ton* bore witness to her statement. Within minutes some droll young buck just down from Oxford had shortened and alliterated, and The Devastating Duke was born.

Daphne found the name woefully ironic. For The Devastating Duke was devastating her heart.

Not that he meant to. Simon treated her with nothing but respect and honor and good humor. Even Anthony was forced to admit that he'd been given no cause to complain in that quarter. Simon never tried to get Daphne alone, never did anything more than kiss her gloved hand (and much to Daphne's dismay, that had only happened twice).

They had become the best of companions, their conversations ranging from comfortable silences to the wittiest of repartée. At every party, they danced together twice—the maximum permitted without scandalizing society.

And Daphne knew, without a shadow of a doubt, that she was falling in love.

The irony was exquisite. She had, of course, begun spending so much time in Simon's company specifically so that she might attract other men. For his part, Simon had begun spending time in *her* company so that he might avoid marriage.

Come to think of it, Daphne thought, sagging against the wall, the irony was exquisitely painful.

Although Simon was still quite vocal on the subject of marriage and his determination never to enter that blessed state, she did on occasion catch him looking at her in ways that made her think he might desire her. He never repeated any of the risqué comments he'd made before he'd learned she was a Bridgerton, but sometimes she caught him looking at her in the same hungry, feral way he'd done that first evening. He turned away, of course, as soon as she noticed, but it was always enough to set her skin tingling and shorten her breath with desire.

And his eyes! Everyone likened their color to ice, and when Daphne watched him converse with other members of society, she could see why. Simon wasn't as loquacious with others as he was with her. His words were more clipped, his tone more brusque, and his eyes echoed the hardness in his demeanor.

But when they were laughing together, just the two of them poking fun at some silly society rule, his eyes changed. They grew softer, gentler, more at ease. In her more fanciful moments, she almost thought they looked as if they were melting.

She sighed, leaning even more heavily against the wall. It seemed her fanciful moments were coming closer and closer together these days.

"Ho, there, Daff, why are you skulking in the corner?"

Daphne looked up to see Colin approaching, his usual cocky smile firmly in place on his handsome face. Since his return to London, he had taken the town by storm, and Daphne could easily name a dozen young ladies who were *positive* they were in love with him and *desperate* for his attention. She wasn't worried about her brother's returning any of their affections, however; Colin obviously had many more wild oats to sow before he settled down.

"I'm not skulking," she corrected. "I'm avoiding."

"Avoiding whom? Hastings?"

"No, of course not. He's not here tonight, anyway."

"Yes, he is."

Since this was Colin, whose primary purpose in life (after chasing loose women and betting on horses, of course) was to torment his sister, Daphne meant to act blasé, but still she lurched to attention as she asked, "He is?"

Colin nodded slyly and motioned with his head toward the ballroom entrance. "I saw him enter not fifteen minutes ago."

Daphne narrowed her eyes. "Are you bamming me? He told me quite specifically that he wasn't planning to attend tonight."

"And you still came?" Colin laid both his hands on his cheeks and faked surprise.

"Of course I did," she retorted. "My life does not revolve around Hastings."

"Doesn't it?"

Daphne had the sinking feeling that he was not being facetious. "No, it doesn't," she replied, lying through her teeth. Her life might not revolve around Simon, but her thoughts certainly did.

Colin's emerald eyes grew uncharacteristically serious. "You've got it bad, don't you?"

"I have no idea what you mean."

He smiled knowingly. "You will."

"Colin!"

"In the meantime"—he motioned back toward the ballroom's entrance—"why don't you go and locate him? Clearly my scintillating company pales in comparison. I can see that your feet are already inching away from me."

Horrified that her body would betray her in such a way, Daphne looked down.

"Ha! Made you look."

"Colin Bridgerton," Daphne ground out, "sometimes I swear I think you're no more than three years old."

"An interesting concept," he mused, "and one that would place you at the tender age of one and a half, little sister."

Lacking a suitably cutting retort, Daphne just fixed upon him her blackest scowl.

But Colin only laughed. "An attractive expression to be sure, sis, but one you might want to remove from your cheeks. His Devastatingness is heading this way."

Daphne refused to fall for his bait this time. He wasn't going to Make Her Look.

Colin leaned forward and whispered conspiratorially, "This time I'm not kidding, Daff."

Daphne held her scowl.

Colin chuckled.

"Daphne!" Simon's voice. Right at her ear.

She whirled around.

Colin's chuckles grew more heartfelt. "You really ought to have more faith in your favorite brother, dear sis."

"*He's* your favorite brother?" Simon asked, one dark brow raised in disbelief.

"Only because Gregory put a toad in my bed last night," Daphne bit off, "and Benedict's standing has never recovered from the time he beheaded my favorite doll."

"Makes me wonder what Anthony's done to deny him even an honorable mention," Colin murmured.

"Don't you have somewhere else to be?" Daphne asked pointedly.

Colin shrugged. "Not really."

"Didn't," she asked through clenched teeth, "you just tell me you promised a dance to Prudence Featherington?"

"Gads, no. You must have misheard."

"Perhaps Mother is looking for you, then. In fact, I'm certain I hear her calling your name."

Colin grinned at her discomfort. "You're not supposed to be so obvious," he said in a stage whisper, purposely loud enough for Simon to hear. "He'll figure out that you like him."

Simon's entire body jerked with barely contained mirth.

"It's not his company I'm trying to secure," Daphne said acidly. "It's yours I'm trying to avoid."

Colin clapped a hand over his heart. "You wound me, Daff." He turned to Simon. "Oh, how she wounds me."

"You missed your calling, Bridgerton," Simon said genially. "You should have been on the stage."

"An interesting idea," Colin replied, "but one that would surely give my mother the vapors." His eyes lit up. "Now that's an idea. And just when the party was growing tedious. Good eve to you both." He executed a smart bow and walked off.

Daphne and Simon remained silent as they watched Colin disappear into the crowd. "The next shriek you hear," Daphne said blandly, "will surely be my mother's."

"And the thud will be her body hitting the floor in a dead faint?"

Daphne nodded, a reluctant smile playing across her lips. "But of course." She waited a moment before saying, "I wasn't expecting you this evening."

He shrugged, the black cloth of his evening jacket wrinkling slightly with the movement. "I was bored."

"You were bored so you decided to come all the way out to Hampstead Heath to attend Lady Trowbridge's annual ball?" Her eyebrows arched up. Hampstead Heath was a good seven miles from Mayfair, at least an hour's drive in the best of conditions, more on nights like tonight, when all the *ton* was clogging the roads. "Forgive me if I start to question your sanity."

"I'm starting to question it myself," he muttered.

"Well, whatever the case," she said with a happy sigh, "I'm glad you're here. It's been a ghastly evening."

"Really?"

She nodded. "I have been plagued by questions about you."

"Well, now, this grows interesting."

"Think again. The first person to interrogate me was my mother. She wants to know why you never call upon me in the afternoon."

Simon frowned. "Do you think it's necessary? I rather thought my undivided attention at these evening affairs would be enough to perpetrate the ruse."

Daphne surprised herself by managing not to growl in frustration. He didn't need to make this sound like such a chore. "Your undivided attention," she said, "would have been enough to fool anyone but my mother. And she probably wouldn't have said anything except that your lack of calls was reported in *Whistledown*."

"Really?" Simon asked with great interest.

"Really. So now you'd better call tomorrow or everyone will start to wonder."

"I'd like to know who that woman's spies are," Simon murmured, "and then I'd like to hire them for myself."

"What do you need spies for?"

"Nothing. But it seems a shame to let such stellar talent go to waste."

Daphne rather doubted that the fictitious Lady Whistledown would agree that any talents were being wasted, but she didn't particularly want to get into a discussion of the merits and evils of that newspaper, so she just shrugged off his comment. "And then," she continued, "once my mother was through with me, everyone else set in, and they were even worse."

"Heaven forfend."

She turned an acerbic look on him. "All but one of the questioners were female, and although they all vehemently professed their happiness on my behalf, they were clearly trying to deduce the probability of our not becoming betrothed."

"You told them all I was desperately in love with you, I assume?"

Daphne felt something lurch in her chest. "Yes," she lied, offering him a too-sweet smile. "I have a reputation to maintain, after all."

Simon laughed. "So then, who was the lone male doing the questioning?"

Daphne pulled a face. "It was another duke, actually. A bizarre old man who claimed to have been friends with your father."

Simon's face went suddenly tight.

She just shrugged, not having seen the change in his expression. "He went on and on about what a *good duke* your father was." She let out a little laugh as she tried to imitate the old man's voice. "I had no idea you dukes had to look out for one another so much. We don't want an incompetent duke making the title look bad, after all."

Simon said nothing.

Daphne tapped her finger against her cheek in thought. "Do you know, I've never heard you mention your father, actually."

"That is because I don't choose to discuss him," Simon said curtly.

She blinked with concern. "Is something wrong?"

"Not at all," he said, his voice clipped.

"Oh." She caught herself chewing on her lower lip and forced herself to stop. "I won't mention it then."

"I said there is *nothing wrong.*"

Daphne kept her expression impassive. "Of course."

There was a long, uncomfortable silence. Daphne picked awkwardly at the fabric of her skirts before finally saying, "Lovely flowers Lady Trowbridge used for decoration, don't you think?"

Simon followed the motion of her hand toward a large arrangement of pink and white roses. "Yes."

"I wonder if she grew them."

"I haven't the faintest."

Another awkward silence.

"Roses are so difficult to grow."

This time his reply was just a grunt.

Daphne cleared her throat, and then, when he didn't even so much as look at her, asked, "Have you tried the lemonade?"

"I don't drink lemonade."

"Well, I do," she snapped, deciding she'd had enough. "And I'm thirsty. So if you will excuse me, I'm going to fetch myself a glass and leave you to your black mood. I'm certain you can find someone more entertaining than I."

She turned to leave, but before she could take a step, she felt a heavy hand on her arm. She looked down, momentarily mesmerized by the sight of his white-gloved hand resting against the peach silk of her gown. She stared at it, almost waiting for it to move, to travel down the length of her arm until it reached the bare skin of her elbow.

But of course he wouldn't do that. He only did such things in her dreams.

"Daphne, please," he said, "turn around."

His voice was low, and there was an intensity to it that made her shiver.

She turned, and as soon as her eyes met his, he said, “Please accept my apologies.”

She nodded.

But he clearly felt the need to explain further. “I did not . . .” He stopped and coughed quietly into his hand. “I was not on good terms with my father. I—I don’t like to talk about him.”

Daphne stared at him in fascination. She’d never seen him at such a loss for words.

Simon let out an irritated exhale. It was strange, Daphne thought, because it seemed as if he were irritated with himself.

“When you brought him up . . .” He shook his head, as if deciding to try a different avenue of conversation. “It grabs at my mind. I can’t stop thinking about him. It—it—it makes me extremely angry.”

“I’m sorry,” she said, knowing her confusion must show on her face. She thought she should say more, but she didn’t know what words to use.

“Not at you,” he said quickly, and as his pale blue eyes focused on hers, something seemed to clear in them. His face seemed to relax as well, especially the tight lines that had formed around his mouth. He swallowed uncomfortably. “I’m angry at myself.”

“And apparently at your father as well,” she said softly.

He said nothing. She hadn’t expected him to, she realized. His hand was still on her arm, and she covered it with her own. “Would you like to get a bit of air?” she asked gently. “You look as if you might need it.”

He nodded. “You stay. Anthony will have my head if I take you out onto the terrace.”

“Anthony can hang for all I care.” Daphne’s mouth tightened with irritation. “I’m sick of his constant hovering, anyway.”

"He is only trying to be a good brother to you."

Her lips parted in consternation. "Whose side are you on, anyway?"

Deftly ignoring her question, he said, "Very well. But just a short walk. Anthony I can take on, but if he enlists the aid of your brothers, I'm a dead man."

There was a door leading out to the terrace a few yards away. Daphne nodded toward it, and Simon's hand slid down her arm and around the crook of her elbow.

"There are probably dozens of couples out on the terrace, anyway," she said. "He'll have nothing about which to complain."

But before they could make their way outside, a loud male voice sounded from behind them. "Hastings!"

Simon halted and turned around, grimly realizing that he had grown used to the name. In no time, he'd be thinking of it as his own.

Somehow that concept made him ill.

An older man leaning on a cane hobbled his way toward them. "That's the duke I told you about," Daphne said. "Of Middlethorpe, I believe."

Simon nodded curtly, having no desire to speak.

"Hastings!" the old man said, patting him on the arm. "I have wanted to make your acquaintance for so very long. I am Middlethorpe. Your father was a good friend of mine."

Simon just nodded again, the motion almost military in its precision.

"He missed you, you know. While you were off traveling."

A rage began to build in his mouth, a rage that rendered his tongue swollen and his cheeks tight and rigid. He knew, beyond a shadow of a doubt, that if he tried to speak, he would sound just as he'd done when he was a lad of eight.

And there was no way he'd shame himself in such a way in front of Daphne.

Somehow—he'd never know how, maybe it was because he'd never had much trouble with vowels aside from "I"—he managed to say, "Oh?" He was pleased that his voice came out sharp and condescending.

But if the old man heard the rancor in his tone, he made no reaction to it. "I was with him when he died," Middlethorpe said.

Simon said nothing.

Daphne—bless her—leapt into the fray with a sympathetic, "My goodness."

"He asked me to pass along some messages to you. I have several letters in my house."

"Burn them."

Daphne gasped and grabbed Middlethorpe by the arm. "Oh, no, don't do that. He might not want to see them now, but surely he will change his mind in the future."

Simon blasted her with an icy glare before turning back to Middlethorpe. "I said burn them."

"I—ah—" Middlethorpe looked hopelessly confused. He must have been aware that the Basset father and son were not on good terms, but clearly the late duke had not revealed to him the true depth of the estrangement. He looked to Daphne, sensing a possible ally, and said to her, "In addition to the letters, there were things he asked me to tell him. I could tell them to him now."

But Simon had already dropped Daphne's arm and stalked outside.

"I'm so sorry," Daphne said to Middlethorpe, feeling the need to apologize for Simon's atrocious behavior. "I'm sure he doesn't mean to be rude."

Middlethorpe's expression told her that he *knew* Simon meant to be rude.

But Daphne still said, "He's a bit sensitive about his father."

Middlethorpe nodded. "The duke warned me he'd react this way. But he laughed as he said it, then made a joke about the Basset pride. I must confess I didn't think he was completely serious."

Daphne looked nervously through the open door to the terrace. "Apparently he was," she murmured. "I had best see to him."

Middlethorpe nodded.

"Please don't burn those letters," she said.

"I would never dream of it. But—"

Daphne had already taken a step toward the terrace door and turned around at the halting tone of the old man's voice. "What is it?" she asked.

"I'm not a well man," Middlethorpe said. "I—The doctor says it could be anytime now. May I trust the letters into your safekeeping?"

Daphne stared at the duke with a mix of shock and horror. Shock because she could not believe he would trust such personal correspondence to a young woman he'd known for barely an hour. Horror because she knew that if she accepted them, Simon might never forgive her.

"I don't know," she said in a strained voice. "I'm not sure I'm the right person."

Middlethorpe's ancient eyes crinkled with wisdom. "I think you might be exactly the right person," he said softly. "And I believe you'll know when the time is right to give him the letters. May I have them delivered to you?"

Mutely, she nodded. She didn't know what else to do.

Middlethorpe lifted his cane and pointed it out toward the terrace. "You'd best go to him."

Daphne caught his gaze, nodded, and scurried outside. The terrace was lit by only a few wall sconces, so the night air was dim, and it was only with the aid of the moon that she saw Simon off in the corner. His stance was wide and angry, and his arms were crossed across his chest. He was facing the endless lawn that stretched out past the terrace, but Daphne sincerely doubted he saw anything aside from his own raging emotions.

She moved silently toward him, the cool breeze a welcome change from the stagnant air in the overcrowded ballroom. Light murmurs of voices drifted through the night, indicating that they were not alone on the terrace, but Daphne saw no one else in the dim light. Clearly the other guests had elected to sequester themselves in dark corners. Or maybe they had descended the steps to the garden and were sitting on the benches below.

As she walked to him, she thought about saying something like, "You were very rude to the duke," or "Why are you so angry at your father?" but in the end she decided this was not the time to probe into Simon's feelings, and so when she reached his side, she just leaned against the balustrade, and said, "I wish I could see the stars."

Simon looked at her, first with surprise, then with curiosity.

"You can never see them in London," she continued, keeping her voice purposefully light. "Either the lights are too bright, or the fog has rolled in. Or sometimes the air is just too filthy to see through it." She shrugged and glanced back up at the sky, which was overcast. "I'd hoped that I'd be able to see them here in Hampstead Heath. But alas, the clouds do not cooperate."

There was a very long moment of silence. Then Simon cleared his throat, and asked, "Did you know that the stars are completely different in the southern hemisphere?"

Daphne hadn't realized how tense she was until she felt her entire body relax at his query. Clearly, he was trying to force their evening back into normal patterns, and she was happy to let him. She looked at him quizzically, and said, "You're joking."

"I'm not. Look it up in any astronomy book."

"Hmmm."

"The interesting thing," Simon continued, his voice sounding less strained as he moved further into the conversation, "is that even if you're not a scholar of astronomy—and I'm not—"

"And obviously," Daphne interrupted with a self-deprecating smile, "neither am I."

He patted her hand, and smiled, and Daphne noticed with relief that his happiness reached his eyes. Then her relief turned into something a little more precious—joy. Because she had been the one to chase the shadows from his eyes. She wanted to banish them forever, she realized.

If only he would let her . . .

"You'd notice the difference anyway," he said. "That's what's so strange. I never cared to learn the constellations and yet when I was in Africa, I looked up into the sky—and the night was so clear. You've never seen a night like that."

Daphne stared at him, fascinated.

"I looked up into the sky," he said with a bewildered shake of his head, "and it looked wrong."

"How can a sky look wrong?"

He shrugged, lifting one of his hands in an unknowing gesture. "It just did. All the stars were in the wrong place."

"I suppose I should want to see the southern sky," Daphne mused. "If I were exotic and dashing, and the sort of female men write poetry about, I suppose I should want to travel."

"You *are* the sort of female men write poetry about," Simon reminded her with a slightly sarcastic tilt to his head. "It was just bad poetry."

Daphne laughed. "Oh, don't tease. It was exciting. My first day with six callers and Neville Binsby actually wrote poetry."

"Seven callers," Simon corrected, "including me."

"Seven including you. But you don't really count."

"You wound me," he teased, doing a fair imitation of Colin. "Oh, how you wound me."

"Perhaps you should consider a career in the theater as well."

"Perhaps not," he replied.

She smiled gently. "Perhaps not. But what I was going to say is that, boring English girl that I am, I have no desire to go anywhere else. I'm happy here."

Simon shook his head, a strange, almost electric light appearing in his eyes. "You're not boring. And"—his voice dropped down to an emotional whisper—"I'm glad you're happy. I haven't known many truly happy people."

Daphne looked up at him, and it slowly dawned on her that he had moved closer. Somehow she doubted he even realized it, but his body was swaying toward hers, and she was finding it nigh near impossible to pull her eyes from his.

"Simon?" she whispered.

"There are people here," he said, his voice oddly strangled.

Daphne turned her head to the corners of the terrace. The murmuring voices she'd heard earlier were gone, but that just might mean that their erstwhile neighbors were eavesdropping.

In front of her the garden beckoned. If this were a London ball, there would have been no place to go past the terrace, but Lady Trowbridge prided herself on being different, and thus always hosted her annual ball at her second residence in Hampstead Heath. It was less than ten miles from Mayfair, but it might as well have been in another world. Elegant homes dotted wide patches of green, and in Lady Trowbridge's garden, there were trees and flowers, shrubs and hedges—dark corners where a couple could lose themselves.

Daphne felt something wild and wicked take hold. "Let's walk in the garden," she said softly.

"We can't."

"We must."

"We can't."

The desperation in Simon's voice told her everything she needed to know. He wanted her. He desired her. He was *mad* for her.

Daphne felt as if her heart was singing the aria from *The Magic Flute*, somersaulting wildly as it tripped past high C.

And she thought—what if she kissed him? What if she pulled him into the garden and tilted her head up and felt his lips touch hers? Would he realize how much she loved him? How much he could grow to love her? And maybe—just maybe he'd realize how happy she made him.

Then maybe he'd stop talking about how determined he was to avoid marriage.

"I'm going for a walk in the garden," she announced. "You may come if you wish."

As she walked away—slowly, so that he might catch up with her—she heard him mutter a heartfelt curse, then she heard his footsteps shortening the distance between them.

"Daphne, this is insanity," Simon said, but the hoarseness in his voice told her he was trying harder to convince himself of that than he was her.

She said nothing, just slipped farther into the depths of the garden.

"For the love of God, woman, will you listen to me?" His hand closed hard around her wrist, whirling her around. "I promised your brother," he said wildly. "I made a vow."

She smiled the smile of a woman who knows she is wanted. "Then leave."

"You know I can't. I can't leave you out in the garden unprotected. Someone could try to take advantage of you."

Daphne gave her shoulders a dainty little shrug and tried to wiggle her hand free of his grasp.

But his fingers only tightened.

And so, although she knew it was not his intention, she let herself be drawn to him, slowly moving closer until they were but a foot apart.

Simon's breathing grew shallow. "Don't do this, Daphne."

She tried to say something witty; she tried to say something seductive. But her bravado failed her at the last moment. She'd never been kissed before, and now that she had all but invited him to be the first, she didn't know what to do.

His fingers loosened slightly around her wrist, but then they tugged, pulling her along with him as he stepped behind a tall, elaborately carved hedge.

He whispered her name, touched her cheek.

Her eyes widened, lips parted.

And in the end, it was inevitable.

Chapter 10

Many a woman has been ruined by a single kiss.
LADY WHISTLEDOWN'S SOCIETY PAPERS,
14 May 1813

Simon wasn't sure at what moment he knew he was going to kiss her. It was probably something he never knew, just something he felt.

Up until that very last minute he'd been able to convince himself that he was only pulling her behind the hedge to scold her, upbraid her for careless behavior that would only land both of them in serious trouble.

But then something had happened—or maybe it had been happening all along, and he'd just been trying too hard not to notice it. Her eyes changed; they almost glowed. And she opened her mouth—just the tiniest bit, barely enough for a breath, but it was enough that he couldn't take his eyes off of her.

His hand snaked up her arm, over the pale satin fabric of her glove, across bare skin, and then finally past the wispy silk of her sleeve. It stole around to her back, pulling her closer, squeezing out the distance between them. He wanted her closer. He wanted her around him, atop him, beneath him. He wanted her so much it terrified him.

He molded her to him, his arms wrapping around her like a vise. He could feel the length of her now, every last inch. She was considerably shorter than he was, so her breasts flattened against the bottom of his ribs, and his thigh—

He shuddered with desire.

His thigh wedged between her legs, his firm muscles feeling the heat that was pouring from her skin.

Simon groaned, a primitive sound that mixed need with frustration. He wasn't going to be able to have her this night—he wasn't able to have her ever, and he needed to make this touch last him a lifetime.

The silk of her dress was soft and flimsy beneath his fingers, and as his hands roved along her back, he could feel every elegant line of her.

And then somehow—to his dying day he would never know how—he stepped away from her. Just an inch, but it was enough for the cool night air to slide between their bodies.

"No!" she cried out, and he wondered if she had any idea the invitation she made with that simple word.

His hands cupped her cheeks, holding her steady so that he might drink in the sight of her. It was too dark to see the exact colors that made her unforgettable face, but Simon knew that her lips were soft and pink, with just a tinge of peach at the corners. He knew that her eyes were made up of dozens of shades of brown, with that one enchanting circle of green constantly daring him to take a closer look, to see if it was really there or just a figment of his imagination.

But the rest—how she would feel, how she would taste—he could only imagine.

And Lord, how he'd been imagining it. Despite his composed demeanor, despite all of his promises to Anthony, he burned for her. When he saw her across a crowded room, his skin grew hot, and when he saw her in his dreams, he went up in flames.

Now—now that he had her in his arms, her breath fast and uneven with desire, her eyes glazed with need she couldn't possibly comprehend—now he thought he might explode.

And so kissing her became a matter of self-preservation. It was simple. If he did not kiss her now, if he did not *consume* her, he would die. It sounded melodramatic, but at the moment he would have sworn it to be true. The hand of desire twisting around his gut would burst into flame and take him along with it.

He needed her that much.

When his lips finally covered hers, he was not gentle. He was not cruel, but the pulse of his blood was too ragged, too urgent, and his kiss was that of a starving lover, not that of a gentle suitor.

He would have forced her mouth open, but she, too, was caught up in the passion of the moment, and when his tongue sought entry, he found no resistance.

"Oh, my God, Daphne," he moaned, his hands biting into the soft curve of her buttocks, pulling her closer, needing her to feel the pulse of desire that had pooled in his groin. "I never knew . . . I never dreamed . . ."

But that was a lie. He had dreamed. He'd dreamed in vivid detail. But it was nothing next to the real thing.

Every touch, every movement made him want her even more, and as each second passed, he felt his body wresting control from his mind. It no longer mattered what was right, what was proper. All that mattered was that she was here, in his arms, and he wanted her.

And, his body realized, she wanted him, too.

His hands clutched at her, his mouth devoured her. He couldn't get enough.

He felt her gloved hand slide hesitantly over his upper back, lightly resting at the nape of his neck. His skin prickled where she touched him, then burned.

And it wasn't enough. His lips left her mouth, trailing down her neck to the soft hollow above her collarbone. She moaned at each touch, the soft mewling sounds firing his passion even more.

With shaking hands, he reached for the delicately scalloped neckline of her gown. It was a gentle fit, and he knew it would take no more than the lightest push to ease the delicate silk down over the swell of her breast.

It was a sight he had no right to see, a kiss he did not deserve to make, but he couldn't help himself.

He gave her the opportunity to stop him. He moved with agonizing slowness, stopping before he bared her to give her one last chance to say no. But instead of maidenly dismay, she arched her back and let out the softest, most arousing rush of breath.

Simon was undone.

He let the fabric of her dress fall away, and in a staggering, shuddering moment of desire, just gazed at her. And then, as his mouth descended to claim her as his prize, he heard—

"You bastard!"

Daphne, recognizing the voice before he did, shrieked and jerked away. "Oh, my God," she gasped. "Anthony!"

Her brother was only ten feet away, and closing the distance fast. His brows were knit together into a mask of utter fury, and as he launched himself at Simon, he let out a primeval warrior cry unlike anything Daphne had ever heard in her life. It barely sounded human.

She just had time to cover herself before Anthony's body crashed into Simon's with such force that she, too, was knocked to the ground by someone's flailing arm.

"I'll kill you, you bloody—" The rest of Anthony's rather violent curse was lost as Simon flipped him over, knocking the breath from him.

"Anthony, no! Stop!" Daphne cried, still clutching at the bodice of her gown, even though she'd already yanked it up and it was in no danger of falling down.

But Anthony was a man possessed. He pummeled Simon, his rage showing on his face, in his fists, in the primitive grunts of fury that emanated from his mouth.

And as for Simon—he was defending himself, but he wasn't really fighting back.

Daphne, who had been standing aside, feeling like a helpless idiot, suddenly realized that she had to intervene. Otherwise, Anthony was going to kill Simon, right there in Lady Trowbridge's garden. She reached down to try to wrest her brother away from the man she loved, but at that moment they suddenly rolled over in a quick flipping motion, clipping Daphne in the knees and sending her sprawling into the hedge.

"Yaaaaaaaahhhhhhh!" she howled, pain stabbing her in more parts of her body than she would have thought possible.

Her cry must have contained a sharper note of agony than she'd thought she'd let slip, because both men immediately stilled.

"Oh, my God!" Simon, who had been at the top of the altercation when Daphne fell over, rushed to her aid. "Daphne! Are you all right?"

She just whimpered, trying not to move. The brambles were cutting into her skin, and every movement just elongated the scratches.

"I think she's hurt," Simon said to Anthony, his voice sharp with worry. "We need to lift her straight out. If we twist, she's likely to become even more entangled."

Anthony gave a curt, businesslike nod, his fury at Simon temporarily put aside. Daphne was in pain, and she had to come first.

"Just hold still, Daff," Simon crooned, his voice soft and soothing. "I'm going to put my arms around you. Then I'm going to lift you forward and pull you out. Do you understand?"

She shook her head. "You'll scratch yourself."

"I have long sleeves. Don't worry about me."

"Let me do it," Anthony said.

But Simon ignored him. While Anthony stood by helplessly, Simon reached into the tangled bramble of the hedge, and slowly pushed his gloved hands through the mess, trying to wedge his coat-covered arms between the prickly branches and Daphne's bare, tortured skin. When he reached her sleeves, however, he had to stop to disentangle the razor-sharp points from the silk of her dress. Several branches had poked straight through the fabric and were biting her skin.

"I can't get you completely loose," he said. "Your dress will tear."

She nodded, the movement jerky. "I don't care," she gasped. "It's already ruined."

"But—" Even though Simon had just been in the process of pulling that very same dress down to her waist, he still felt uncomfortable pointing out that the fabric was likely to fall right off her body once the branches were done tearing through the silk. Instead, he turned to Anthony, and said, "She'll need your coat."

Anthony was already shrugging out of it.

Simon turned back to Daphne and locked his eyes on hers. "Are you ready?" he asked softly.

She nodded, and maybe it was his imagination, but he thought she seemed a little calmer now that her eyes were focused on his face.

After making sure that no branches were still stuck to her skin, he pushed his arms farther back into the bramble, and then around her body until his hands met and locked together behind her back.

"On the count of three," he murmured.

She nodded again. "One . . . Two . . ."

He yanked her up and out, the force sending them both sprawling.

"You said three!" Daphne yelled.

"I lied. I didn't want you to tense up."

Daphne might have wanted to pursue the argument, but it was at that moment that she realized that her dress was in tatters, and she squealed as her arms flew up to cover herself.

"Take this," Anthony said, thrusting his coat at her. Daphne gratefully accepted and wrapped herself in Anthony's superfine coat. It fit him to perfection, but on her it hung so loose that she could easily wrap herself up.

"Are you all right?" he asked gruffly.

She nodded.

"Good." Anthony turned to Simon. "Thank you for pulling her out."

Simon said nothing, but his chin dipped in acknowledgment of Anthony's remark.

Anthony's eyes darted back to Daphne. "Are you certain you're all right?"

"It stings a little," she admitted, "and I'll surely need to apply a salve when I get home, but it's nothing I can't bear."

"Good," Anthony said again. Then he drew back his fist and slammed it into Simon's face, easily knocking his unsuspecting friend to the ground.

"That," Anthony spat out, "is for defiling my sister."

"Anthony!" Daphne shrieked. "Stop this nonsense right now! He didn't defile me."

Anthony swung around and glared at her, his eyes burning. "I saw your—"

Daphne's stomach churned, and for a moment she feared she'd actually cast up her accounts. Good God, Anthony had seen her breast! Her brother! It was unnatural.

"Stand up," Anthony grunted, "so I can hit you again."

"Are you mad?" Daphne cried out, jumping between him and Simon, who was still on the ground, his hand clutching his injured eye. "Anthony, I swear if you hit him again, I shall not forgive you."

Anthony pushed her aside, and not gently. "The next one," he spit, "is for betraying our friendship."

Slowly, and to Daphne's horror, Simon rose to his feet.

"No!" she yelled, jumping back between them.

"Get out of the way, Daphne," Simon ordered softly. "This is between us."

"It most certainly is not! In case no one recalls, I'm the one who—" She stopped herself in mid-sentence. There was no point in speaking. Neither man was listening to her.

"Get out of the way, Daphne," Anthony said, his voice frighteningly still. He didn't even look at her; his gaze remained focused over her head, straight into Simon's eyes.

"This is ridiculous! Can we not all discuss this like adults?" She looked from Simon to her brother, then whipped her head back to Simon. "Merciful heavens! Simon! Look at your eye!"

She hurried to him, reaching up to his eye, which was already swelling shut.

Simon remained impassive, not moving even a muscle under her concerned touch. Her fingers skimmed lightly over his swollen skin, oddly soothing. He ached for her still, although this time not with desire. She felt so good next to him, good and honorable and pure.

And he was about to do the most dishonorable thing he'd ever done in his life.

When Anthony finished with his violence, finished with his fury, and finally demanded that Simon marry his sister, Simon was going to say no.

"Move out of the way, Daphne," he said, his voice strange in his own ears.

"No, I—"

"*Move!*" he roared.

She fled, pressing her back up against the very hedge in which she'd been caught, staring in horror at the two men.

Simon nodded grimly at Anthony. "Hit me."

Anthony looked stunned by the request.

"Do it," Simon said. "Get it over with."

Anthony's fist fell slack. He didn't move his head, but his eyes flitted to Daphne. "I can't," he blurted out. "Not when he's just standing there asking for it."

Simon took a step forward, bringing his face mockingly close. "Do it now. Make me pay."

"You'll pay at the altar," Anthony replied.

Daphne gasped, the sound drawing Simon's attention. Why was she surprised? Surely she understood the consequences of, if not their actions, their stupidity in getting caught?

"I won't force him," Daphne said.

"I will," Anthony bit out.

Simon shook his head. "By tomorrow I'll be on the Continent."

"You're leaving?" Daphne asked. The stricken sound of her voice sliced a guilty knife through Simon's heart.

"If I stay, you'll forever be tainted by my presence. It's best if I'm gone."

Her lower lip was trembling. It killed him that it was trembling. A single word fell from her lips. It was his name, and it was filled with a longing that squeezed his heart in two.

It took Simon a moment to summon the words: "I can't marry you, Daff."

"Can't or won't?" Anthony demanded.

"Both."

Anthony punched him again.

Simon hit the ground, stunned by the force of the blow to his chin. But he deserved every sting, every shot of pain. He didn't want to look at Daphne, didn't want to catch even the barest of glances at her face, but she knelt beside him, her gentle hand sliding behind his shoulder to help him right himself.

"I'm sorry, Daff," he said, forcing himself to look at her. He felt odd and off-balance, and he could see out of only one eye, but she'd come to his aid, even after he'd rejected her, and he owed her that much. "I'm so sorry."

"Save your pathetic words," Anthony spat. "I'll see you at dawn."

"No!" Daphne cried out.

Simon looked up at Anthony and gave him the briefest of nods. Then he turned back to Daphne, and said, "If it c-could be anybody, Daff, it would be you. I p-promise you that."

"What are you talking about?" she asked, bewilderment turning her dark eyes to frantic orbs. "What do you mean?"

Simon just closed his eye and sighed. By this time tomorrow he'd be dead, because he sure as hell wasn't going to raise a pistol at Anthony, and he rather doubted that Anthony's temper would have cooled enough for him to shoot into the air.

And yet—in a bizarre, pathetic sort of way, he would be getting what he'd always wanted out of life. He'd have his final revenge against his father.

Strange, but even so, this wasn't how he'd thought it would end. He'd thought—Well, he didn't know what he'd thought—most men avoided trying to predict their own deaths—but it wasn't this. Not with his best friend's eyes burning with hatred. Not on a deserted field at dawn.

Not with dishonor.

Daphne's hands, which had been stroking him so gently, wrapped around his shoulders and shook. The motion jolted his watery eye open, and he saw that her face was very close to his—close and furious.

"What is the matter with you?" she demanded. Her face was like he'd never seen it before, eyes flashing with anger, and anguish, and even a little desperation. "He's going to kill you! He's going to meet you on some godforsaken field tomorrow and shoot you dead. And you're acting like you want him to."

"I d-don't w-w-want to d-die," he said, too exhausted in mind and body to even care that he'd stammered. "B-but I can't marry you."

Her hands fell off his shoulders, and she lurched away. The look of pain and rejection in her eyes was almost impossible to bear. She looked so forlorn, wrapped up in her brother's too-big coat, pieces of twigs and brambles still caught in her dark hair. When she opened her mouth to speak, it looked as if her words were ripped from her very soul. "I-I've always known that I wasn't the sort of woman men dream of, but I never thought anyone would prefer death to marriage with me."

"No!" Simon cried out, scrambling to his feet despite the dull aches and stinging pains that jolted his body. "Daphne, it's not like that."

"You've said enough," Anthony said in a curt voice, stepping between them. He placed his hands on his sister's shoulders, steering her away from the man who had broken her heart and possibly damaged her reputation for eternity.

"Just one more thing," Simon said, hating the pleading, pathetic look he knew must be in his eyes. But he had to talk to Daphne. He had to make sure she understood.

But Anthony just shook his head.

"Wait." Simon laid a hand on the sleeve of the man who had once been his closest friend. "I can't fix this. I've made—" He let out a ragged breath, trying to collect his thoughts. "I've made vows, Anthony. I can't marry her. I can't fix this. But I can tell her—"

"Tell her what?" Anthony asked with a complete lack of emotion.

Simon lifted his hand from Anthony's sleeve and raked it through his hair. He couldn't tell Daphne. She wouldn't understand. Or worse, she would, and then all he'd have was her pity. Finally, aware that Anthony was looking at him with an impatient expression, he said, "Maybe I can make it just a little bit better."

Anthony didn't move.

"Please." And Simon wondered if he'd ever put such depth of meaning behind that word before.

Anthony was still for several seconds, and then he stepped aside.

"Thank you," Simon said in a solemn voice, sparing Anthony the briefest of glances before focusing on Daphne.

He'd thought perhaps that she'd refuse to look at him, insulting him with her scorn, but instead he found her chin up, eyes defiant and daring. Never had he admired her more.

"Daff," he began, not at all sure what to say but hoping that the words somehow came out right and in one piece. "It—it isn't you. If it could be anyone it would be you. But marriage to me would destroy you. I could never give you what you want. You'd die a little every day, and it would kill me to watch."

"You could never hurt me," she whispered.

He shook his head. "You have to trust me."

Her eyes were warm and true as she said softly, "I do trust you. But I wonder if you trust me."

Her words were like a punch to the gut, and Simon felt impotent and hollow as he said, "Please know that I never meant to hurt you."

She remained motionless for so long that Simon wondered if she'd stopped breathing. But then, without even looking at her brother, she said, "I'd like to go home now."

Anthony put his arms around her and turned her away, as if he could protect her simply by shielding her from the sight of him. "We'll get you home," he said in soothing tones, "tuck you into bed, give you some brandy."

"I don't want brandy," Daphne said sharply, "I want to think."

Simon thought Anthony looked a bit bewildered by the statement, but to his credit, all he did was give her upper arm an affectionate squeeze, and say, "Very well, then."

And Simon just stood there, battered and bloodied, until they disappeared into the night.

Chapter 11

Lady Trowbridge's annual ball at Hampstead Heath on Saturday evening was, as always, a highlight of the gossip season. This Author spied Colin Bridgerton dance with all three of the Featherington sisters (not at once, of course) although it must be said that this most dashing Bridgerton did not appear to be charmed by his fate. Additionally, Nigel Berbrooke was seen courting a woman who was not Miss Daphne Bridgerton—perhaps Mr. Berbrooke has finally realized the futility of his pursuit.

And speaking of Miss Daphne Bridgerton, she made an early departure. Benedict Bridgerton informed the curious that she had the headache, but This Author spied her earlier in the evening, while she was talking to the elderly Duke of Middlethorpe, and she appeared to be in perfect health.

Lady Whistledown's Society Papers,
17 May 1813

It was, of course, impossible to sleep.

Daphne paced the length of her room, her feet wearing treads in the blue-and-white carpet that had lain in her room since childhood. Her mind was spinning in a dozen different directions, but one thing was clear.

She had to stop this duel.

She did not, however, underestimate the difficulties involved in carrying out that task. For one thing, men tended to be mulish idiots when it came to things like honor and duels, and she rather doubted that either Anthony or Simon would appreciate her interference. Secondly, she didn't even know where the duel was to take place. The men hadn't discussed that out in Lady Trowbridge's garden. Daphne assumed that Anthony would send word to Simon by a servant. Or maybe Simon got to choose the location since he was the one who'd been challenged. Daphne was certain there had to be some sort of etiquette surrounding duels, but she certainly didn't know what it was.

Daphne paused by the window and pushed the curtain aside to peer out. The night was still young by the standards of the *ton*; she and Anthony had left the party prematurely. As far as she knew, Benedict, Colin, and her mother were all still at Lady Trowbridge's house. The fact that they had not yet returned (Daphne and Anthony had been home for nearly two hours) Daphne took as a good sign. If the scene with Simon had been witnessed, surely the gossip would have raged across the ballroom in seconds, causing her mother to rush home in disgrace.

And maybe Daphne would make it through the night with only her dress in shreds—and *not* her reputation.

But concern for her good name was the least of her worries. She needed her family home for another reason. There was no way she'd be able to stop this duel on her own. Only an idiot would ride through London in the wee hours of the morning and try to reason with two belligerent men by herself. She was going to need help.

Benedict, she feared, would immediately take Anthony's side of the whole thing; in fact, she'd be surprised if Benedict didn't act as Anthony's second.

But Colin—Colin might come around to her way of thinking. Colin would grumble, and Colin would probably say that Simon deserved to be shot at dawn, but if Daphne begged, he would help her.

And the duel had to be stopped. Daphne didn't understand what was going on in Simon's head, but he was clearly anguished about something, probably something having to do with his father. It had long been obvious to her that he was tortured by some inner demon. He hid it well, of course, especially when he was with her, but too often she'd seen a desperate bleak look in his eyes. And there had to be a reason why he fell silent with such frequency. Sometimes it seemed to Daphne that she was the only person with whom he was ever truly relaxed enough to laugh and joke and make small talk.

And maybe Anthony. Well, maybe Anthony before all of *this*.

But despite it all, despite Simon's rather fatalistic attitude in Lady Trowbridge's garden, she didn't think he wanted to die.

Daphne heard the sound of wheels on cobbles and rushed back to the open window just in time to see the Bridgerton carriage rolling past the house on its way to the mews.

Wringing her hands, she hurried across the room and pressed her ear to the door. It wouldn't do for her to go downstairs; Anthony thought she was asleep, or at least tucked into her bed and contemplating her actions of the evening.

He'd said he wasn't going to say anything to their mother. Or at least he wasn't until he could determine what she knew. Violet's delayed return home led Daphne to believe that there hadn't been any huge or dreadful rumors circulating about her, but that didn't mean that she was off scot-free. There would be whispers. There were always whispers. And whispers, if left unchecked, could quickly grow into roars.

Daphne knew that she would have to face her mother eventually. Sooner or later Violet would hear something. The *ton* would make certain she heard something. Daphne just hoped that by the time Violet was assaulted by rumors—most of them regrettably true—her daughter would already be safely betrothed to a duke.

People would forgive anything if one was connected to a duke.

And that would be the crux of Daphne's strategy to save Simon's life. He wouldn't save himself, but he might save *her*.

Colin Bridgerton tiptoed down the hall, his boots moving silently over the runner carpet that stretched across the floor. His mother had gone off to bed, and Benedict was ensconced with Anthony in the latter's study. But he wasn't interested in any of them. It was Daphne he wanted to see.

He knocked softly on her door, encouraged by the pale shaft of light that glowed at the bottom. Clearly she'd left several candles burning. Since she was far too sensible ever to fall asleep without snuffing her candles, she was still awake.

And if she were still awake, then she'd have to talk to him.

He raised his hand to knock again, but the door swung open on well-oiled hinges, and Daphne silently motioned for him to enter.

"I need to talk to you," she whispered, her words coming out in a single, urgent rush of air.

"I need to talk to you, too."

Daphne ushered him in, and then, after a quick glance up and down the hall, shut the door. "I'm in big trouble," she said.

"I know."

The blood drained from her face. "You do?"

Colin nodded, his green eyes for once deadly serious. "Do you remember my friend Macclesfield?"

She nodded. Macclesfield was the young earl her mother had

insisted upon introducing her to a fortnight ago. The very night she'd met Simon.

"Well, he saw you disappear into the gardens tonight with Hastings."

Daphne's throat felt suddenly scratchy and swollen, but she managed to get out, "He did?"

Colin nodded grimly. "He won't say anything. I'm sure of it. We've been friends for nearly a decade. But if he saw you, someone else might have as well. Lady Danbury was looking at us rather queerly when he was telling me what he'd seen."

"Lady Danbury saw?" Daphne asked sharply.

"I don't know if she did or if she didn't. All I know is that"—Colin shuddered slightly—"she was looking at me as if she knew my every transgression."

Daphne gave her head a little shake. "That's just her way. And if she did see anything, she won't say a word."

"Lady Danbury?" Colin asked doubtfully.

"She's a dragon, and she can be rather cutting, but she isn't the sort to ruin someone just for the fun of it. If she saw something, she'll confront me directly."

Colin looked unconvinced.

Daphne cleared her throat several times as she tried to figure out how to phrase her next question. "What exactly did he see?"

Colin eyed her suspiciously. "What do you mean?"

"Exactly what I said," Daphne very nearly snapped, her nerves stretched taut by the long and stressful evening. "What did he see?"

Colin's back straightened and his chin jolted back in a defensive manner. "Exactly what I said," he retorted. "He saw you disappear into the gardens with Hastings."

"But that's all?"

"That's all?" he echoed. His eyes widened, then narrowed. "What the hell happened out there?"

Daphne sank onto an ottoman and buried her face in her hands. "Oh, Colin, I'm in such a tangle."

He didn't say anything, so she finally wiped her eyes, which weren't exactly crying but did feel suspiciously wet, and looked up. Her brother looked older—and harder—than she'd ever before seen him. His arms were crossed, his legs spread in a wide and implacable stance, and his eyes, normally so merry and mischievous, were as hard as emeralds. He'd clearly been waiting for her to look up before speaking.

"Now that you're done with your display of self-pity," he said sharply, "suppose you tell me what you and Hastings did tonight in Lady Trowbridge's garden."

"Don't use that tone of voice with me," Daphne snapped back, "and don't accuse me of indulging in self-pity. For the love of God, a man is going to die tomorrow. I'm entitled to be a little upset."

Colin sat down on a chair opposite her, his face immediately softening into an expression of extreme concern. "You'd better tell me everything."

Daphne nodded and proceeded to relate the events of the evening. She didn't, however, explain the precise extent of her disgrace. Colin didn't need to know exactly what Anthony had seen; the fact that she'd been caught in a compromising position ought to be enough.

She finished with, "And now there is going to be a duel, and Simon is going to die!"

"You don't know that, Daphne."

She shook her head miserably. "He won't shoot Anthony. I'd bet my life on it. And Anthony—" Her voice caught, and she had to swallow before continuing. "Anthony is so furious. I don't think he'll delope."

"What do you want to do?"

"I don't know. I don't even know where the duel is to be held. All I know is that I have to stop it!"

Colin swore under his breath, then said softly, "I don't know if you can, Daphne."

"I must!" she cried out. "Colin, I can't sit here and stare at the ceiling while Simon dies." Her voice broke, and she added, "I love him."

He blanched. "Even after he rejected you?"

She nodded dejectedly. "I don't care if that makes me a pathetic imbecile, but I can't help it. I still love him. He needs me."

Colin said quietly, "If that were true, don't you think he would have agreed to marry you when Anthony demanded it?"

Daphne shook her head. "No. There's something else I don't know about. I can't really explain it, but it was almost as if a part of him wanted to marry me." She could feel herself growing agitated, feel her breath starting to come in jerky gasps, but still she continued. "I don't know, Colin. But if you could have seen his face, you'd understand. He was trying to protect me from something. I'm sure of it."

"I don't know Hastings nearly as well as Anthony," Colin said, "or even as well as you, but I've never even heard the barest hint of a whisper about some deep, dark secret. Are you certain—" He broke off in the middle of his sentence, and let his head fall into his hands for a moment before looking back up. When he spoke again, his voice was achingly gentle. "Are you certain you might not be imagining his feelings for you?"

Daphne took no offense. She knew her story sounded a fantasy. But she knew in her heart that she was right. "I don't want him to die," she said in a low voice. "In the end, that's all that's important."

Colin nodded, but then asked one last question. "You don't want him to die, or you don't want him to die on your account?"

Daphne stood on shaky feet. "I think you'd better leave," she said, using every last bit of her energy to keep her voice steady. "I can't believe you just asked that of me."

But Colin didn't leave. He just reached over and squeezed his sister's hand. "I'll help you, Daff. You know I'd do anything for you."

And Daphne just fell into his arms and let out all the tears she'd been keeping so valiantly inside.

Thirty minutes later, her eyes were dried and her mind was clear. She'd needed to cry; she realized that. There'd been too much trapped inside her—too much feeling, too much confusion, hurt, and anger. She'd had to let it out. But now there was no more time for emotion. She needed to keep a cool head and remain focused on her goal.

Colin had gone off to question Anthony and Benedict, whom he'd said were talking in low and intense voices in Anthony's study. He'd agreed with her that Anthony had most probably asked Benedict to act as his second. It was Colin's job to get them to tell him where the duel was to take place. Daphne had no doubt that Colin would succeed. He'd always been able to get anybody to tell him anything.

Daphne had dressed in her oldest, most comfortable riding habit. She had no idea how the morning would play out, but the last thing she wanted was to be tripping over lace and petticoats.

A swift knock on her door brought her to attention, and before she could even reach for the knob, Colin entered the room. He, too, had changed out of his evening clothes.

"Did you find out everything?" Daphne asked urgently.

His nod was sharp and brief. "We don't have much time to lose. I assume you want to try to get there before anyone else arrives?"

"If Simon gets there before Anthony, maybe I can convince him to marry me before anyone even pulls out a gun."

Colin let out a tense breath. "Daff," he began, "have you considered the possibility that you might not succeed?"

She swallowed, her throat feeling like it had a cannonball lodged in it. "I'm trying not to think about that."

"But—"

Daphne cut him off. "If I think about it," she replied in a strained voice, "I might lose my focus. I might lose my nerve. And I can't do that. For Simon's sake, I can't do that."

"I hope he knows what he has in you," Colin said quietly. "Because if he doesn't, I may have to shoot him myself."

Daphne just said, "We'd better go."

Colin nodded, and they were off.

Simon guided his horse along Broad Walk, making his way to the farthest, most remote corner in the new Regent's Park. Anthony had suggested, and he had agreed, that they carry out their business far from Mayfair. It was dawn, of course, and no one was likely to be out, but there was no reason to be flaunting a duel in Hyde Park.

Not that Simon much cared that dueling was illegal. After all, he wouldn't be around to suffer the legal consequences.

It was, however, a damned distasteful way to die. But Simon didn't see any alternatives. He had disgraced a gently bred lady whom he could not marry, and now he must suffer the consequences. It was nothing Simon had not known before he'd kissed her.

As he made his way to the designated field, he saw that Anthony and Benedict had already dismounted and were waiting for him. Their chestnut hair ruffled in the breeze, and their faces looked grim.

Almost as grim as Simon's heart.

He brought his horse to a halt a few yards away from the Bridgerton brothers and dismounted.

"Where is your second?" Benedict called out.

"Didn't bother with it," Simon replied.

"But you have to have a second! A duel isn't a duel without one."

Simon just shrugged. "There didn't seem a point. You brought the guns. I trust you."

Anthony walked toward him. "I don't want to do this," he said.

"You don't have a choice."

"But you do," Anthony said urgently. "You could marry her. Maybe you don't love her, but I know you like her well enough. Why won't you marry her?"

Simon thought about telling them everything, all the reasons he'd sworn never to take a wife and perpetuate his line. But they wouldn't understand. Not the Bridgertons, who only knew that family was good and kind and true. They didn't know anything about cruel words and shattered dreams. They didn't know the impossible feeling of rejection.

Simon then thought about saying something cruel, something that would make Anthony and Benedict despise him and get this mockery of a duel over with more quickly. But that would require him to malign Daphne, and he just couldn't do that.

And so, in the end, all he did was look up into the face of Anthony Bridgerton, the man who had been his friend since his earliest days at Eton, and said, "Just know it isn't Daphne. Your sister is the finest woman I've ever had the privilege to know."

And then, with a nod to both Anthony and Benedict, he picked up one of the two pistols in the case Benedict had laid on the ground, and began his long walk to the north side of the field.

"Waaaaaaaaaaaiiiiiiittttttttt!"

Simon gasped and whirled around. Dear God, it was Daphne!

She was bent low over her mare, in full gallop as she raced across the field, and for one stunned moment Simon forgot to be absolutely furious with her for interfering with the duel and instead just marveled at how utterly magnificent she looked in the saddle.

By the time she yanked on the reins and brought the horse to a halt right in front of him, however, his rage was back in full force.

"What the *hell* do you think you're doing?" he demanded.

"Saving your miserable life!" Her eyes flashed fire at him, and he realized he'd never seen her so angry.

Almost as angry as he was. "Daphne, you little idiot. Do you realize how dangerous this little stunt was?" Without realizing what he was doing, his hands wrapped around her shoulders and started to shake. "One of us could have shot you."

"Oh, please," she scoffed. "You hadn't even reached your end of the field."

She had a point, but he was far too furious to acknowledge it. "And riding here in the dead of night by yourself," he yelled. "You should know better."

"I do know better," she shot back. "Colin escorted me."

"Colin?" Simon's head whipped back and forth as he looked for the youngest of her older brothers. "I'm going to kill him!"

"Would that be before or after Anthony shoots you through the heart?"

"Oh, definitely before," Simon growled. "Where is he? Bridgerton!" he bellowed.

Three chestnut heads swiveled in his direction.

Simon stomped across the grass, murder in his eyes. "I meant the idiot Bridgerton."

"That, I believe," Anthony said mildly, tilting his chin toward Colin, "would refer to you."

Colin turned a deadly stare in his direction. "And I was supposed to let her stay at home and cry her eyes out?"

"Yes!" This came from three different sources.

"Simon!" Daphne yelled, tripping across the grass after him. "Get back here!"

Simon turned to Benedict. "Get her out of here."

Benedict looked undecided.

"Do it," Anthony ordered.

Benedict held still, his eyes darting back and forth between his brothers, his sister, and the man who'd shamed her.

"For the love of Christ," Anthony swore.

"She deserves to have her say," Benedict said, and crossed his arms.

"What the hell is wrong with you two?" Anthony roared, glaring at his two younger brothers.

"Simon," Daphne said, gasping for breath after her race across the field, "you must listen to me."

Simon tried to ignore her tugs on his sleeve. "Daphne, leave it. There's nothing you can do."

Daphne looked pleadingly at her brothers. Colin and Benedict were obviously sympathetic, but there was little they could do to help her. Anthony still looked like an angry god.

Finally she did the only thing she could think of to delay the duel. She punched Simon.

In his good eye.

Simon howled in pain as he staggered back. "What the hell was that for?"

"Fall down, you idiot," she hissed. If he was prostrate on the ground, Anthony couldn't very well shoot him.

"I am certainly not going to fall down!" He clutched his eye as he muttered, "Good God, being felled by a woman. Intolerable."

"Men," Daphne grunted. "Idiots, all." She turned to her brothers, who were staring at her with identical expressions of open-mouthed shock. "What are you looking at?" she snapped.

Colin started to clap.

Anthony smacked him in the shoulder.

"Might I have one, single, tiny, ever-so-brief moment with his grace?" she asked, half the words mere hisses.

Colin and Benedict nodded and walked away. Anthony didn't move.

Daphne glared at him. "I'll hit you, too."

And she might have done it too, except that Benedict returned and nearly yanked Anthony's arm out of the socket as he pulled him away.

She stared at Simon, who was pressing his fingers against his eyebrow, as if that might lessen the pain in his eye.

"I can't believe you punched me," he said.

She glanced back at her brothers to make sure they'd moved out of earshot. "It seemed like a good idea at the time."

"I don't know what you hoped to accomplish here," he said.

"I should think that would be abundantly obvious."

He sighed, and in that moment he looked weary and sad and infinitely old. "I've already told you I cannot marry you."

"You have to."

Her words emerged with such urgency and force that he looked up, his eyes on sharp alert. "What do you mean?" he asked, his voice a study in control.

"I mean that we were seen."

"By whom?"

"Macclesfield."

Simon relaxed visibly. "He won't talk."

"But there were others!" Daphne bit her lip. It wasn't necessarily a lie. There might have been others. In fact, there probably *were* others.

"Whom?"

"I don't know," she admitted. "But I've heard rumblings. By tomorrow it will be all over London."

Simon swore so viciously that Daphne actually took a step back.

"If you don't marry me," she said in a low voice, "I will be ruined."

"That's not true." But his voice lacked conviction.

"It is true, and you know it." She forced her eyes to meet his. Her entire future—and his life!—was riding on this moment. She couldn't afford to falter. "No one will have me. I shall be packed away to some godforsaken corner of the country—"

"You know your mother would never send you away."

"But I will never marry. You know that." She took a step forward, forcing him to acknowledge her nearness. "I will be forever branded as used goods. I'll never have a husband, never bear children—"

"Stop!" Simon fairly yelled. "For the love of God, just stop."

Anthony, Benedict, and Colin all started at his shout, but Daphne's frantic shake of her head kept them in their places.

"Why can't you marry me?" she asked in a low voice. "I know you care for me. What is it?"

Simon wrapped his hand across his face, his thumb and forefinger pressing mercilessly into his temples. Christ, he had a headache.

And Daphne—dear God, she kept moving closer. She reached out and touched his shoulder, then his cheek. He wasn't strong enough. Dear God, he wasn't going to be strong enough.

"Simon," she pleaded, "save me."

And he was lost.

Chapter 12

A duel, a duel, a duel. Is there anything more exciting, more romantic . . . or more utterly moronic?

It has reached This Author's ears that a duel took place earlier this week in Regent's Park. Because dueling is illegal, This Author shall not reveal the names of the perpetrators, but let it be known that This Author frowns heavily upon such violence.

Of course, as this issue goes to press, it appears that the two dueling idiots (I am loath to call them gentlemen; that would imply a certain degree of intelligence, a quality which, if they ever possessed it, clearly eluded them that morning) are both unharmed.

One wonders if perhaps an angel of sensibility and rationality smiled down upon them that fateful morn.

If so, it is the belief of This Author that This Angel ought to shed her influence on a great many more men of the ton. Such an action could only make for a more peaceful and amiable environment, leading to a vast improvement of our world.

LADY WHISTLEDOWN'S SOCIETY PAPERS,
19 May 1813

Simon raised ravaged eyes to meet hers. "I'll marry you," he said in a low voice, "but you need to know—"

His sentence was rendered incomplete by her exultant shout and fierce hug. "Oh, Simon, you won't be sorry," she said, her words coming out in a relieved rush. Her eyes sparkled with unshed tears, but they glowed with joy. "I'll make you happy. I promise you. I'll make you so happy. You won't regret this."

"Stop!" Simon ground out, pushing her away. Her unfeigned joy was too much to bear. "You have to listen to me."

She stilled, and her face grew apprehensive.

"You listen to what I have to say," he said in a harsh voice, "and then decide if you want to marry me."

Her bottom lip caught between her teeth, and she gave the barest of nods.

Simon took in a shaky breath. How to tell her? *What* to tell her? He couldn't tell her the truth. Not all of it, at least. But she had to understand . . . If she married him . . .

She'd be giving up more than she'd ever dreamed.

He had to give her the opportunity to refuse him. She deserved that much. Simon swallowed, guilt sliding uncomfortably down his throat. She deserved much more than that, but that was all he could give her.

"Daphne," he said, her name as always soothing his frazzled mouth, "if you marry me . . ."

She stepped toward him and reached out her hand, only to pull it back at his burning glare of caution. "What is it?" she whispered. "Surely nothing could be so awful that—"

"I can't have children."

There. He'd done it. And it was almost the truth.

Daphne's lips parted, but other than that, there was no indication that she'd even heard him.

He knew his words would be brutal, but he saw no other way to force her understanding. "If you marry me, you will never have children. You will never hold a baby in your arms and know it is yours, that you created it in love. You will never—"

"How do you know?" she interrupted, her voice flat and unnaturally loud.

"I just do."

"But—"

"I cannot have children," he repeated cruelly. "You need to understand that."

"I see." Her mouth was quivering slightly, as if she wasn't quite sure if she had anything to say, and her eyelids seemed to be blinking a bit more than normal.

Simon searched her face, but he couldn't read her emotions the way he usually could. Normally her expressions were so open, her eyes startlingly honest—it was as if he could see to her very soul and back. But right now she looked shuttered and frozen.

She was upset—that much was clear. But he had no idea what she was going to say. No idea how she would react.

And Simon had the strangest feeling that Daphne didn't know, either.

He became aware of a presence to his right, and he turned to see Anthony, his face torn between anger and concern.

"Is there a problem?" Anthony asked softly, his eyes straying to his sister's tortured face.

Before Simon could reply, Daphne said, "No."

All eyes turned to her.

"There will be no duel," she said. "His grace and I will be getting married."

"I see." Anthony looked as if he wanted to react with considerably more relief, but his sister's solemn face forced a strange quietude on the scene. "I'll tell the others," he said, and walked off.

Simon felt a rush of something utterly foreign fill his lungs. It was air, he realized dumbly. He'd been holding his breath. He hadn't even realized he'd been holding his breath.

And something else filled him as well. Something hot and terrible, something triumphant and wonderful. It was emotion, pure and undiluted, a bizarre mix of relief and joy and desire and dread. And Simon, who'd spent most of his life avoiding such messy feelings, had no idea what to do about it.

His eyes found Daphne's. "Are you certain?" he asked, his voice whisper soft.

She nodded, her face strangely devoid of emotion. "You're worth it." Then she walked slowly back to her horse.

And Simon was left wondering if he had just been snatched up into heaven—or perhaps led to the darkest corner of hell.

Daphne spent the rest of the day surrounded by her family. Everyone was, of course, thrilled by the news of her engagement. Everyone, that was, except her older brothers, who while happy for her, were somewhat subdued. Daphne didn't blame them. She felt rather subdued herself. The events of the day had left them all exhausted.

It was decided that the wedding must take place with all possible haste. (Violet had been informed that Daphne *might* have been seen kissing Simon in Lady Trowbridge's garden, and that was enough for her to immediately send a request to the archbishop for a special license.) Violet had then immersed herself in a whirlwind of party details; just because the wedding was to be small, she'd announced, it didn't have to be shabby.

Eloise, Francesca, and Hyacinth, all vastly excited at the prospect of dressing up as bridesmaids, kept up a steady stream of questions. How had Simon proposed? Did he get down on one knee? What color would Daphne wear and when would he give her a ring?

Daphne did her best to answer their questions, but she could barely concentrate on her sisters, and by the time afternoon slipped into the eve, she was reduced to monosyllables. Finally, after Hyacinth asked her what color roses she wanted for her bouquet, and Daphne answered, "Three," her sisters gave up talking to her and left her alone.

The enormity of her actions had left Daphne nearly speechless. She had saved a man's life. She had secured a promise of marriage from the man she adored. And she had committed herself to a life without children.

All in one day.

She laughed, somewhat desperately. It made one wonder what she could do tomorrow as an encore.

She wished she knew what had gone through her head in those last moments before she'd turned to Anthony, and said, "There will be no duel," but in all truth, she wasn't sure it was anything she could possibly remember. Whatever had been racing through her mind—it hadn't been made up of words or sentences or conscious thought. It had been as if she was enveloped by color. Reds and yellows, and a swirling mishmash of orange where they met. Pure feeling and instinct. That's all there had been. No reason, no logic, nothing even remotely rational or sane.

And somehow, as all of that churned violently within her, she'd known what she had to do. She might be able to live without the children she hadn't yet borne, but she couldn't live without Simon. The children were amorphous, unknown beings she couldn't picture or touch.

But Simon—Simon was real and he was *here*. She knew how it felt to touch his cheek, to laugh in his presence. She knew the sweet taste of his kiss, and the wry quirk of his smile.

And she loved him.

And although she barely dared think it, maybe he was wrong. Maybe he *could* have children. Maybe he'd been misled by an incompetent surgeon, or maybe God was just waiting for the right time to bestow a miracle. She'd be unlikely to mother a brood the size of the Bridgertons, but if she could have even one child she knew she'd feel complete.

She wouldn't mention these thoughts to Simon, though. If he thought she was holding out even the tiniest hope for a child, he wouldn't marry her. She was sure of it. He'd gone to such lengths to be brutally honest. He wouldn't allow her to make a decision if he didn't think she had the facts absolutely straight.

"Daphne?"

Daphne, who had been sitting listlessly on the sofa in the Bridgertons' drawing room, looked up to see her mother gazing at her with an expression of deep concern.

"Are you all right?" Violet asked.

Daphne forced a weary smile. "I'm just tired," she replied. And she was. It hadn't even occurred to her until that very moment that she hadn't slept in over thirty-six hours.

Violet sat beside her. "I thought you'd be more excited. I know how much you love Simon."

Daphne turned surprised eyes to her mother's face.

"It's not hard to see," Violet said gently. She patted her on the hand. "He's a good man. You've chosen well."

Daphne felt a wobbly smile coming on. She *had* chosen well. And she would make the best of her marriage. If they weren't blessed with children—well, she reasoned, she might have turned out to be barren, anyway. She knew of several couples who had never had children, and she doubted any of them had known of their deficiencies prior to their marriage vows. And with seven brothers and sisters, she was sure to have plenty of nieces and nephews to hug and spoil.

Better to live with the man she loved than to have children with one she didn't.

"Why don't you take a nap?" Violet suggested. "You look terribly tired. I hate seeing such dark smudges below your eyes."

Daphne nodded and stumbled to her feet. Her mother knew best. Sleep was what she needed. "I'm sure I'll feel much better in an hour or two," she said, a wide yawn escaping her mouth.

Violet stood and offered her daughter her arm. "I don't think you're going to be able to make it up the stairs on your own," she said, smiling as she led Daphne out of the room and up the stairs. "And I sincerely doubt we'll see you in an hour or two. I shall give everyone explicit instructions that you are not to be disturbed until morning."

Daphne nodded sleepily. "Thaz good," she mumbled, stumbling into her room. "Morningsh good."

Violet steered Daphne to the bed and helped her into it. The shoes she pulled off, but that was all. "You might as well sleep in your clothes," she said softly, then bent to kiss her daughter on the forehead. "I can't imagine I'll be able to move you enough to get you out of them."

Daphne's only reply was a snore.

Simon, too, was exhausted. It wasn't every day that a man resigned himself to death. And then to be saved by—and betrothed to!—the woman who had occupied his every dream for the past two weeks.

If he weren't sporting two black eyes and a sizable bruise on his chin, he'd have thought he'd dreamed the whole thing.

Did Daphne realize what she'd done? What she was denying herself? She was a levelheaded girl, not given to foolish dreams and flights of fancy; he didn't think she would have agreed to marry him without sorting through all the consequences.

But then again, she'd reached her decision in under a minute. How could she have thought everything through in under a minute?

Unless she fancied herself in love with him. Would she give up her dream of a family because she loved him?

Or maybe she did it out of guilt. If he'd died in that duel, he was sure Daphne could come up with some line of reasoning that would make it seem her fault. Hell, he *liked* Daphne. She was one of the finest people he knew. He didn't think he could live with her death on his conscience. Perhaps she felt the same way about him.

But whatever her motives, the simple truth was that come this Saturday (Lady Bridgerton had already sent him a note informing him that the engagement would not be an extended one) he would be bound to Daphne for life.

And she to him.

There was no stopping it now, he realized. Daphne would never back out of the marriage at this point, and neither would he. And to his utter surprise, this almost fatalistic certainty felt . . .

Good.

Daphne would be his. She knew of his shortcomings, she knew what he could not give her, and she had still chosen him.

It warmed his heart more than he would ever have thought possible.

"Your grace?"

Simon looked up from his slouchy position in his study's leather chair. Not that he needed to; the low, even voice was obviously that of his butler. "Yes, Jeffries?"

"Lord Bridgerton is here to see you. Shall I inform him that you are not at home?"

Simon pulled himself to his feet. Damn, but he was tired. "He won't believe you."

Jeffries nodded. "Very well, sir." He took three steps, then turned around. "Are you certain you wish to receive a guest? You do seem to be a trifle, er, indisposed."

Simon let out a single humorless chuckle. "If you are referring to my eyes, Lord Bridgerton would be the one responsible for the larger of the two bruises."

Jeffries blinked like an owl. "The larger, your grace?"

Simon managed a half-smile. It wasn't easy. His entire face hurt. "I realize it's difficult to discern, but my right eye is actually a touch worse off than the left."

Jeffries swayed closer, clearly intrigued.

"Trust me."

The butler straightened. "Of course. Shall I show Lord Bridgerton to the drawing room?"

"No, bring him here." At Jeffries's nervous swallow, Simon added, "And you needn't worry for my safety. Lord Bridgerton isn't likely to add to my injuries at this juncture. Not," he added in a mutter, "that he'd find it easy to find a spot he hasn't already injured."

Jeffries's eyes widened, and he scurried out of the room.

A moment later Anthony Bridgerton strode in. He took one look at Simon, and said, "You look like hell."

Simon stood and raised a brow—not an easy feat in his current condition. "This surprises you?"

Anthony laughed. The sound was a little mirthless, a little

hollow, but Simon heard a shadow of his old friend. A shadow of their old friendship. He was surprised by how grateful he was for that.

Anthony motioned to Simon's eyes. "Which one is mine?"

"The right," Simon replied, gingerly touching his abused skin. "Daphne packs quite a punch for a girl, but she lacks your size and strength."

"Still," Anthony said, leaning forward to inspect his sister's handiwork, "she did quite a nice job."

"You should be proud of her," Simon grunted. "Hurts like the devil."

"Good."

And then they were silent, with so much to say and no idea how to say it.

"I never wanted it to be like this," Anthony finally said.

"Nor I."

Anthony leaned against the edge of Simon's desk, but he shifted uncomfortably, looking oddly ill at ease in his own body. "It wasn't easy for me to let you court her."

"You knew it wasn't real."

"You *made* it real last night."

What was he to say? That Daphne had been the seducer, not he? That she'd been the one to lead him off the terrace and dance into the darkness of the night? None of that mattered. He was far more experienced than Daphne. He should have been able to stop.

He said nothing.

"I hope we may put this behind us," Anthony said.

"I'm certain that would be Daphne's fondest wish."

Anthony's eyes narrowed. "And is it now your aim in life to grant her fondest wishes?"

All but one, Simon thought. *All but the one that really matters.* "You know that I will do everything in my capabilities to keep her happy," he said quietly.

Anthony nodded. "If you hurt her—"

"I will never hurt her," Simon vowed, his eyes blazing.

Anthony regarded him with a long and even stare. "I was prepared to kill you for dishonoring her. If you damage her soul, I guarantee you will never find peace as long as you live. Which," he added, his eyes turning slightly harder, "would not be long."

"Just long enough to put me in excruciating pain?" Simon asked mildly.

"Exactly."

Simon nodded. Even though Anthony was threatening torture and death, Simon could not help but respect him for it. Devotion to one's sister was an honorable thing.

Simon wondered if Anthony perhaps saw something in him that no one else did. They had known each other for over half of their lives. Did Anthony somehow see the darkest corners of his soul? The anguish and fury he tried so hard to keep hidden?

And if so, was that why he worried for his sister's happiness?

"I give you my word," Simon said. "I will do everything in my power to keep Daphne safe and content."

Anthony nodded curtly. "See that you do." He pushed himself away from the desk and walked to the door. "Or you'll be seeing me."

He left.

Simon groaned and sank back into the leather chair. When had his life grown so damned complicated? When had friends become enemies and flirtations grown to lust?

And what the hell was he going to do with Daphne? He didn't want to hurt her, couldn't bear to hurt her, actually, and yet he was doomed to do so simply by marrying her. He burned for her, ached for the day when he could lay her down and cover her body with his, slowly entering her until she moaned his name—

He shuddered. Such thoughts could not possibly be advantageous to his health.

"Your grace?"

Jeffries again. Simon was too tired to look up, so he just made an acknowledging motion with his hand.

"Perhaps you would like to retire for the evening, your grace."

Simon managed to look at the clock, but that was only because he didn't have to move his head to do it. It was barely seven in the evening. Hardly his usual bedtime. "It's early yet," he mumbled.

"Still," the butler said pointedly, "perhaps you'd like to retire."

Simon closed his eyes. Jeffries had a point. Maybe what he needed was a long engagement with his feather mattress and fine linen sheets. He could escape to his bedroom, where he might manage to avoid seeing a Bridgerton for an entire night.

Hell, the way he felt, he might hole up there for days.

Chapter 13

It's marriage for the Duke of Hastings and Miss Bridgerton!

This Author must take this opportunity to remind you, dear reader, that the forthcoming nuptials were predicted in this very column. It has not escaped the note of This Author that when this newspaper reports a new attachment between an eligible gentleman and an unmarried lady, the odds in the betting books at gentleman's clubs change within hours, and always in favor of marriage.

Although This Author is not allowed in White's, she has reason to believe that the official odds concerning the marriage of the duke and Miss Bridgerton were 2–1 for.

Lady Whistledown's Society Papers,
21 May 1813

The rest of the week flew by in a rush. Daphne didn't see Simon for several days. She might have thought he'd left town, except that Anthony told her he'd been over to Hastings House to settle the details of the marriage contract.

Much to Anthony's surprise, Simon had refused to accept even a penny as dowry. Finally, the two men had decided that Anthony would put the money his father had put aside for Daphne's marriage in a separate estate with himself as the trustee. It would be hers to spend or save as she liked.

"You can pass it along to your children," Anthony suggested.

Daphne only smiled. It was either that or cry.

A few days after that, Simon called upon Bridgerton House in the afternoon. It was two days before the wedding.

Daphne waited in the drawing room after Humboldt announced his arrival. She sat primly on the edge of the damask sofa, her back straight and her hands clasped together in her lap. She looked, she was sure, the very model of genteel English womanhood.

She felt a bundle of nerves.

Correction, she thought, as her stomach turned itself inside out, a bundle of nerves with frayed edges.

She looked down at her hands and realized that her fingernails were leaving red, crescent-shaped indentations on her palms.

Second correction, a bundle of nerves with frayed edges with an arrow stuck through them. Maybe a flaming arrow at that.

The urge to laugh was almost as overwhelming as it was inappropriate. She had never felt nervous at seeing Simon before. In fact, that had been possibly the most remarkable aspect of their friendship. Even when she caught him gazing at her with smoldering heat, and she was sure that her eyes reflected the same need, she had felt utterly comfortable with him. Yes, her stomach flipped and her skin tingled, but those were symptoms of desire, not of unease. First and foremost, Simon had been her friend, and Daphne knew that the easy, happy feeling she'd experienced whenever he was near was not something to be taken for granted.

She was confident that they would find their way back to that sense of comfort and companionship, but after the scene in Regent's Park, she very much feared that this would occur later rather than sooner.

"Good day, Daphne."

Simon appeared in the doorway, filling it with his marvelous presence. Well, perhaps his presence wasn't quite as marvelous as usual. His eyes still sported matching purple bruises, and the one on his chin was starting to turn an impressive shade of green.

Still, it was better than a bullet in the heart.

"Simon," Daphne replied. "How nice to see you. What brings you to Bridgerton House?"

He gave her a surprised look. "Aren't we betrothed?"

She blushed. "Yes, of course."

"It was my impression that men were supposed to visit their betrothed." He sat down across from her. "Didn't Lady Whistledown say something to that effect?"

"I don't think so," Daphne murmured, "but I'm certain my mother must have done."

They both smiled, and for a moment Daphne thought that all would be well again, but as soon as the smiles faded, an uncomfortable silence fell across the room.

"Are your eyes feeling any better?" she finally asked. "They don't look quite as swollen."

"Do you think?" Simon turned so that he was facing a large gilt mirror. "I rather think the bruises have turned a spectacular shade of blue."

"Purple."

He leaned forward, not that that brought him appreciably closer to the mirror. "Purple then, but I suppose it might be a debatable fact."

"Do they hurt?"

He smiled humorlessly. "Only when someone pokes at them."

"I shall refrain from doing so, then," she murmured, her lips quirking in a telltale twitch. "It shall be difficult, of course, but I shall persevere."

"Yes," he said, with a perfectly deadpan expression, "I've often been told I make women want to poke me in the eye."

Daphne's smile was one of relief. Surely if they could joke about such things, everything would go back to the way it was.

Simon cleared his throat. "I did have a specific reason for coming to see you."

Daphne gazed at him expectantly, waiting for him to continue.

He held out a jeweler's box. "This is for you."

Her breath caught in her throat as she reached for the small, velvet-covered box. "Are you certain?" she asked.

"I believe betrothal rings are considered quite *de rigueur*," he said quietly.

"Oh. How stupid of me. I didn't realize . . ."

"That it was a betrothal ring? What did you think it was?"

"I *wasn't* thinking," she admitted sheepishly. He'd never given her a gift before. She'd been so taken aback by the gesture she'd completely forgotten that he owed her a betrothal ring.

"Owed." She didn't like that word, didn't like that she'd even thought it. But she was fairly certain that that was what Simon must have been thinking when he'd picked out the ring.

This depressed her.

Daphne forced a smile. "Is this a family heirloom?"

"No!" he said, with enough vehemence to make her blink.

"Oh."

Yet another awkward silence.

He coughed, then said, "I thought you might like something of your own. All of the Hastings jewelry was chosen for someone else. This I chose for you."

Daphne thought it a wonder she didn't melt on the spot. "That's so sweet," she said, just barely managing to stifle a sentimental sniffle.

Simon squirmed in his seat, which didn't surprise her. Men did so hate to be called sweet.

"Aren't you going to open it?" he grunted.

"Oh, yes, of course." Daphne shook her head slightly as she snapped back to attention. "How silly of me." Her eyes had glazed over slightly as she stared at the jeweler's box. Blinking a few times to clear her vision, she carefully released the box's clasp and opened it.

And couldn't possibly say anything besides, "Oh, my goodness," and even that came out with more breath than voice.

Nestled in the box was a stunning band of white gold, adorned with a large marquis-cut emerald, flanked on either side by a single, perfect diamond. It was the most beautiful piece of jewelry Daphne had ever seen, brilliant but elegant, obviously precious but not overly showy.

"It's beautiful," she whispered. "I love it."

"Are you certain?" Simon removed his gloves, then leaned forward and took the ring out of the box. "Because it is your ring. You shall be the one to wear it, and it should reflect your tastes, not mine."

Daphne's voice shook slightly as she said, "Clearly, our tastes coincide."

Simon breathed a small sigh of relief and picked up her hand. He hadn't realized how much it meant to him that she liked the ring until that very moment. He hated that he felt so nervous around her when they'd been such easy friends for the past few weeks. He hated that there were silences in their conversations, when before she'd been the only person with whom he never felt the need to pause and take stock of his words.

Not that he was having any trouble speaking now. It was just that he didn't seem to know what to say.

"May I put it on?" he asked softly.

She nodded and started to remove her glove.

But Simon stilled her fingers with his own, then took over the task. He gave the tip of each finger a tug, then slowly slid the glove from her hand. The motion was unabashedly erotic, clearly an abbreviated version of what he wanted to do: remove every stitch from her body.

Daphne gasped as the edge of the glove trailed past the tips of her fingers. The sound of her breath rushing across her lips made him want her all the more.

With tremulous hands, he slid the ring on her finger, easing it over her knuckle until it rested in place.

"It fits perfectly," she said, moving her hand this way and that so that she could see how it reflected the light.

Simon, however, didn't let go of her hand. As she moved, her skin slid along his, creating a warmth that was oddly soothing. Then he lifted her hand to his mouth and dropped a gentle kiss on her knuckles. "I'm glad," he murmured. "It suits you."

Her lips curved—a hint of that wide smile he'd come to adore. Maybe a hint that all would be well between them.

"How did you know I like emeralds?" she asked.

"I didn't," he admitted. "They reminded me of your eyes."

"Of my—" Her head cocked slightly as her mouth twisted into what could only be described as a scolding grin. "Simon, my eyes are brown."

"They're mostly brown," he corrected.

She twisted until she was facing the gilt mirror he'd used earlier to inspect his bruises and blinked a few times. "No," she said slowly, as if she were speaking to a person of considerably small intellect, "they're brown."

He reached out and brushed one gentle finger along the bottom edge of her eye, her delicate lashes tickling his skin like a butterfly kiss. "Not around the edge."

She gave him a look that was mostly dubious, but a little bit hopeful, then let out a funny little breath and stood. "I'm going to look for myself."

Simon watched with amusement as she stood and marched over to the mirror and put her face close to the glass. She blinked several times, then held her eyes open wide, then blinked some more.

"Oh, my goodness!" she exclaimed. "I've never seen that!"

Simon stood and moved to her side, leaning with her against the mahogany table that stood in front of the mirror. "You'll soon learn that I am always right."

She shot him a sarcastic look. "But how did you notice that?"

He shrugged. "I looked very closely."

"You . . ." She seemed to decide against finishing her statement, and leaned back against the table, opening her eyes wide to inspect them again. "Fancy that," she murmured. "I have green eyes."

"Well, I wouldn't go so far as to say—"

"For today," she interrupted, "I refuse to believe they are anything but green."

Simon grinned. "As you wish."

She sighed. "I was always so jealous of Colin. Such beautiful eyes wasted on a man."

"I'm sure the young ladies who fancy themselves in love with him would disagree."

Daphne gave him a smirky glance. "Yes, but they don't signify, do they?"

Simon caught himself wanting to laugh. "Not if you say so."

"You'll soon learn," she said archly, "that I am always right."

This time he did laugh. There was no way he could have held it in. He finally stopped, realizing that Daphne was silent. She was regarding him warmly, though, her lips curved into a nostalgic smile.

"This was nice," she said, placing her hand on his. "Almost like it used to be, don't you think?"

He nodded, turning his hand palm up so that he could clasp hers.

"It will be like this again, won't it?" Her eyes showed a flicker of trepidation. "We'll go back to the way it was, won't we? Everything will be exactly the same."

"Yes," he said, even though he knew it could not be true. They might find contentment, but it would never be just as it was.

She smiled, closed her eyes, and rested her head against his shoulder. "Good."

Simon watched their reflection for several minutes. And he almost believed he would be able to make her happy.

The next evening—Daphne's last night as Miss Bridgerton—Violet knocked on her bedroom door.

Daphne was sitting on her bed, mementos of her childhood spread out before her, when she heard the rap. "Come in!" she called out.

Violet poked her head in, an awkward smile pasted on her face. "Daphne," she said, sounding queasy, "do you have a moment?"

Daphne looked at her mother with concern. "Of course." She stood as Violet edged into the room. Her mother's skin was a remarkable match with her yellow dress.

"Are you quite all right, Mother?" Daphne inquired. "You look a little green."

"I'm fine. I just—" Violet cleared her throat and steeled her shoulders. "It's time we had a talk."

"Ohhhhhh," Daphne breathed, her heart racing with anticipation. She'd been waiting for this. All her friends had told her that the night before one's wedding, one's mother delivered all the secrets of marriage. At the last possible moment, one was admitted into the company of womanhood, and told all those wicked and delicious facts that were kept so scrupulously from the ears of unmarried girls. Some of the young ladies of her set had, of course, already married, and Daphne and her friends had tried to get them to reveal what no one else would, but the young matrons had just giggled and smiled, saying, "You'll find out soon."

"Soon" had become "now," and Daphne couldn't wait.

Violet, on the other hand, looked as if she might lose the contents of her stomach at any moment.

Daphne patted a spot on her bed. "Would you like to sit here, Mother?"

Violet blinked in a rather distracted manner. "Yes, yes, that would be fine." She sat down, half-on and half-off the bed. She didn't look very comfortable.

Daphne decided to take pity on her and begin the conversation. "Is this about marriage?" she asked gently.

Violet's nod was barely perceptible.

Daphne fought to keep the fascinated glee out of her voice. "The wedding night?"

This time Violet managed to bob her chin up and down an entire inch. "I really don't know how to tell this to you. It's highly indelicate."

Daphne tried to wait patiently. Eventually her mother would get to the point.

"You see," Violet said haltingly, "there are things you need to know. Things that will occur tomorrow night. Things"—she coughed—"that involve your husband."

Daphne leaned forward, her eyes widening.

Violet scooted back, clearly uncomfortable with Daphne's obvious interest. "You see, your husband . . . that is to say, Simon, of course, since he will be your husband . . ."

Since Violet showed no sign of finishing that thought, Daphne murmured, "Yes, Simon will be my husband."

Violet groaned, her cornflower blue eyes glancing everywhere but Daphne's face. "This is very difficult for me."

"Apparently so," Daphne muttered.

Violet took a deep breath and sat up straight, her narrow shoulders thrown back as if she were steeling herself for the most unpleasant task. "On your wedding night," she began, "your husband will expect you to do your marital duty."

This was nothing Daphne didn't already know.

"Your marriage must be consummated."

"Of course," Daphne murmured.

"He will join you in your bed."

Daphne nodded. She knew this as well.

"And he will perform certain"—Violet groped for a word, her hands actually waving through the air—"*intimacies* upon your person."

Daphne's lips parted slightly, her short indrawn breath the room's only sound. This was finally getting interesting.

"I am here to tell you," Violet said, her voice turning quite brisk, "that your marital duty need not be unpleasant."

But what *was* it?

Violet's cheeks blazed. "I know that some women find the, er, act distasteful, but—"

"They do?" Daphne asked curiously. "Then why do I see so many maids sneaking off with the footmen?"

Violet instantly went into outraged employer mode. "Which maid was that?" she demanded.

"Don't try to change the subject," Daphne warned. "I've been waiting for this all week."

Some of the steam went out of her mother. "You have?"

Daphne's look was pure what-did-you-expect. "Well, of course."

Violet sighed and mumbled, "Where was I?"

"You were telling me that some women find their marital duty unpleasant."

"Right. Well. Hmmm."

Daphne looked down at her mother's hands and noticed that she'd practically shredded a handkerchief.

"All I really want you to know," Violet said, the words tumbling out as if she could not wait to be rid of them, "is that it needn't be unpleasant at all. If two people care for one another—and I believe that the duke cares for you very much—"

"And I for him," Daphne interrupted softly.

"Of course. Right. Well, you see, given that you do care for each other, it will probably be a very lovely and special moment." Violet started scooting to the foot of the bed, the pale yellow silk of her skirts spreading along the quilts as she moved. "And you shouldn't be nervous. I'm sure the duke will be very gentle."

Daphne thought of Simon's scorching kiss. "Gentle" didn't seem to apply. "But—"

Violet stood up like a shot. "Very well. Have a good night. That's what I came here to say."

"*That's all?*"

Violet dashed for the door. "Er, yes." Her eyes shifted guiltily. "Were you expecting something else?"

"Yes!" Daphne ran after her mother and threw herself against the door so she couldn't escape. "You can't leave telling me only that!"

Violet glanced longingly at the window. Daphne gave thanks that her room was on the second floor; otherwise, she wouldn't have put it past her mother to try to make a getaway that way.

"Daphne," Violet said, her voice sounding rather strangled.

"But what do I *do*?"

"Your husband will know," Violet said primly.

"I don't want to make a fool of myself, Mother."

Violet groaned. "You won't. Trust me. Men are . . ."

Daphne seized upon the half-finished thought. "Men are what? What, Mother? What were you going to say?"

By now Violet's entire face had turned bright red, and her neck and ears had progressed well into the pinks. "Men are easily pleased," she mumbled. "He won't be disappointed."

"But—"

"But enough!" Violet finally said firmly. "I have told you everything my mother told me. Don't be a nervous ninny, and do it enough so you'll have a baby."

Daphne's jaw dropped. "*What?*"

Violet chuckled nervously. "Did I forget to mention the bit about the baby?"

"Mother!"

"Very well. Your marital duty—the, er, consummation, that is—is how you have a baby."

Daphne sank against the wall. "So you did this eight times?" she whispered.

"No!"

Daphne blinked in confusion. Her mother's explanations had been impossibly vague, and she still didn't know what marital duty was, precisely, but something wasn't adding up. "But wouldn't you have had to do it eight times?"

Violet began to fan herself furiously. "Yes. No! Daphne, this is very personal."

"But how could you have had eight children if you—"

"I did it more than eight times," Violet ground out, looking as if she wanted to melt right into the walls.

Daphne stared at her mother in disbelief. "You did?"

"Sometimes," Violet said, barely even moving her lips, and certainly not moving her eyes off a single spot on the floor, "people just do it because they like to."

Daphne's eyes grew very wide. "They do?" she breathed.

"Er, yes."

"Like when men and women kiss?"

"Yes, exactly," Violet said, sighing with relief. "Very much like—" Her eyes narrowed. "Daphne," she said, her voice suddenly shrill, "have you kissed the duke?"

Daphne felt her skin turning a shade that rivaled her mother's. "I might have done," she mumbled.

Violet shook her finger at her daughter. "Daphne Bridgerton, I cannot believe you would do such a thing. You know very well I warned you about allowing men such liberties!"

"It hardly signifies now that we're to be married!"

"But still—" Violet gave a deflating sigh. "Never mind. You're right. It doesn't signify. You're to be married, and to a duke no less, and if he kissed you, well, then, that was to be expected."

Daphne just stared at her mother in disbelief. Violet's nervous, halting chatter was very much out of character.

"Now then," Violet announced, "as long as you don't have any more questions, I'll just leave you to your, er,"—she glanced distractedly at the mementos Daphne had been shuffling through—"whatever it is that you're doing."

"But I do have more questions!"

Violet, however, had already made her escape.

And Daphne, no matter how desperately she wanted to learn the secrets of the marital act, wasn't about to chase her mother down the hall—in full view of all the family and servants—to find out.

Besides, her mother's talk had raised a new set of worries. Violet had said that the marital act was a requirement for the creation of children. If Simon couldn't have children, did that mean he couldn't perform those intimacies her mother had mentioned?

And dash it all, what *were* those intimacies? Daphne suspected they had something to do with kissing, since society seemed so determined to make sure that young ladies keep their lips pure and chaste. And, she thought, a blush stealing over her cheeks as she remembered her time in the gardens with Simon, they might have something to do with a woman's breasts as well.

Daphne groaned. Her mother had practically ordered her not to be nervous, but she didn't see how she could be otherwise—not when she was expected to enter into this contract without the slightest idea of how to perform her duties.

And what of Simon? If he could not consummate the marriage, would it even *be* a marriage?

It was enough to make a new bride very apprehensive, indeed.

In the end, it was the little details of the wedding that Daphne remembered. There were tears in her mother's eyes (and then eventually on her face), and Anthony's voice had been oddly hoarse when he stepped forward to give her away. Hyacinth had strewn her rose petals too quickly, and there were none left by the time she reached the altar. Gregory sneezed three times before they even got to their vows.

And she remembered the look of concentration on Simon's face as he repeated his vows. Each syllable was uttered slowly and carefully. His eyes burned with intent, and his voice was low but true. To Daphne, it sounded as if nothing in the world could possibly be as important as the words he spoke as they stood before the archbishop.

Her heart found comfort in this; no man who spoke his vows with such intensity could possibly view marriage as a mere convenience.

Those whom God hath joined together, let no man put asunder.

A shiver raced down Daphne's spine, causing her to sway. In just a moment, she would belong to this man forever.

Simon's head turned slightly, his eyes darting to her face. *Are you all right?* his eyes asked.

She nodded, a tiny little jog of her chin that only he could see. Something blazed in his eyes—could it be relief?

I now pronounce you—

Gregory sneezed for a fourth time, then a fifth and sixth, completely obliterating the archbishop's "man and wife." Daphne felt a horrifying bubble of mirth pushing up her throat. She pressed her lips together, determined to maintain an appropriately serious facade. Marriage, after all, was a solemn institution, and not one to be treating as a joke.

She shot a glance at Simon, only to find that he was looking at her with a queer expression. His pale eyes were focused on her mouth, and the corners of his lips began to twitch.

Daphne felt that bubble of mirth rising ever higher.

You may kiss the bride.

Simon grabbed her with almost desperate arms, his mouth crashing down on hers with a force that drew a collective gasp from the small assemblage of guests.

And then both sets of lips—bride and groom—burst into laughter, even as they remained entwined.

Violet Bridgerton later said it was the oddest kiss she'd ever been privileged to view.

Gregory Bridgerton—when he finished sneezing—said it was disgusting.

The archbishop, who was getting on in years, looked perplexed.

But Hyacinth Bridgerton, who at ten should have known the least about kisses of anyone, just blinked thoughtfully, and said, "I think it's nice. If they're laughing now, they'll probably be laughing forever." She turned to her mother. "Isn't that a good thing?"

Violet took her youngest daughter's hand and squeezed it. "Laughter is always a good thing, Hyacinth. And thank you for reminding us of that."

And so it was that the rumor was started that the new Duke and Duchess of Hastings were the most blissfully happy and devoted couple to be married in decades. After all, who could remember another wedding with so much laughter?

Chapter 14

We are told that the wedding of the Duke of Hastings and the former Miss Bridgerton, while small, was most eventful. Miss Hyacinth Bridgerton (ten years of age) whispered to Miss Felicity Featherington (also aged ten) that the bride and groom actually laughed aloud during the ceremony. Miss Felicity then repeated this information to her mother, Mrs. Featherington, who then repeated it to the world.

This Author shall have to trust Miss Hyacinth's account, since This Author was not invited to view the ceremony.

LADY WHISTLEDOWN'S SOCIETY PAPERS,
24 May 1813

There was to be no wedding trip. There hadn't, after all, been any time to plan one. Instead, Simon had made arrangements for them to spend several weeks at Clyvedon Castle, the Bassets' ancestral seat. Daphne thought this a fine idea; she was eager to get away from London and the inquiring eyes and ears of the *ton.*

Besides, she was oddly eager to see the place where Simon had grown up.

She found herself imagining him as a young boy. Had he been as irrepressible as he now was with her? Or had he been a quiet child, with the reserved demeanor he showed to most of society?

The new couple left Bridgerton House amidst cheers and hugs, and Simon quickly bundled Daphne into his finest carriage. Although it was summer, there was a chill in the air, and he carefully tucked a blanket over her lap. Daphne laughed. "Isn't that a bit much?" she teased. "I'm unlikely to catch a chill on the few short blocks to your home."

He regarded her quizzically. "We travel to Clyvedon."

"Tonight?" She could not disguise her surprise. She had assumed they would embark on their journey the following day. The village of Clyvedon was located near Hastings, all the way down on England's southeastern coast. It was already late afternoon; by the time they reached the castle, it would be the middle of the night.

This was not the wedding night Daphne had envisioned.

"Wouldn't it make more sense to rest here in London for one night, and then travel on to Clyvedon?" she asked.

"The arrangements have already been made," he grunted.

"I . . . see." Daphne made a valiant attempt to hide her disappointment. She was silent for a full minute as the carriage lurched into motion, the well-sprung wheels unable to disguise the bumps from the uneven cobbles beneath them. As they swung around the corner to Park Lane, she asked, "Will we be stopping at an inn?"

"Of course," Simon replied. "We need to eat supper. It wouldn't do for me to starve you on our first day of our marriage, would it?"

"Will we be spending the night at this inn?" Daphne persisted.

"No, we—" Simon's mouth clamped shut into a firm line, then inexplicably softened. He turned to her with an expression of heart-melting tenderness. "I've been a bear, haven't I?"

She blushed. She always blushed when he looked at her like that. "No, no, it's just that I was surprised that—"

"No, you're right. We will rest the night at an inn. I know of a good one halfway down to the coast. The Hare and Hounds. The food is hot, and the beds are clean." He touched her on the chin. "I shan't abuse you by forcing you to make the entire trip to Clyvedon in one day."

"It's not that I'm not hardy enough for the trip," she said, her face coloring even further as she considered her next words. "It's just that we did get married today, and if we don't stop at an inn, we'll be here in the carriage when night falls, and—"

"Say no more," he said, placing a finger to her lips.

Daphne nodded gratefully. She didn't really wish to discuss their wedding night like this. Besides, it seemed the sort of topic that the husband ought to bring up, not the wife. After all, Simon was certainly the more knowledgeable of the two on that subject.

He couldn't possibly be any *less* knowledgeable, she thought with a disgruntled grimace. Her mother, despite all her hemming and hawing, had managed to tell her absolutely nothing. Well, except for the bit about the creation of children, not that Daphne understood any of the particulars. But on the other hand, maybe—

Daphne's breath caught in her throat. What if Simon couldn't— Or what if he didn't want to—

No, she decided firmly, he definitely wanted to. Moreover, he definitely wanted *her*. She hadn't imagined the fire in his eyes or the fierce pounding of his heart that night in the gardens.

She glanced out the window, watching as London melted into the countryside. A woman could go mad obsessing over such things. She was going to put this from her mind. She was absolutely, positively, forever going to put this from her mind.

Well, at least until that night.

Her wedding night.

The thought made her shiver.

Simon glanced over at Daphne—his wife, he reminded himself, although it was still a bit difficult to believe. He'd never planned to have a wife. In fact, he'd planned quite specifically *not* to have one. And yet here he was, with Daphne Bridgerton—no, Daphne *Basset*. Hell, she was the Duchess of Hastings, that's what she was.

That was probably the strangest of all. His dukedom hadn't had a duchess in his lifetime. The title sounded odd, rusty.

Simon let out a long, calming exhale, letting his eyes rest on Daphne's profile. Then he frowned. "Are you cold?" he asked. She'd been shivering.

Her lips were slightly parted, so he saw her tongue press up against the roof of her mouth to make an N sound, then she moved ever so slightly and said, "Yes. Yes, but just a touch. You needn't—"

Simon tucked the blanket a bit more closely around her, wondering why on earth she would lie about such an innocuous fact. "It's been a long day," he murmured, not because he felt it—although, when he did stop to think about it, it *had* been a long day—but because it seemed like the right type of soothing remark for the moment.

He'd been thinking a lot about soothing remarks and gentle consideration. He was going to try to be a good husband to her. She deserved at least that much. There were a lot of things he wasn't going to be able to give Daphne, true and complete happiness unfortunately among them, but he could do his best to keep her safe and protected and relatively content.

She had chosen him, he reminded himself. Even knowing that

she would never have children, she had chosen him. Being a good and faithful husband seemed the least he could do in return.

"I enjoyed it," Daphne said softly.

He blinked and turned to her with a blank expression. "I beg your pardon?"

A shadow of a smile touched her lips. It was a sight to behold, something warm and teasing and just a little bit mischievous. It sent jolts of desire straight to his midsection, and it was all he could do to concentrate on her words as she said, "You said it had been a long day. I said I enjoyed it."

He looked at her blankly.

Her face screwed up with such enchanting frustration that Simon felt a smile tugging at his lips. "*You* said it had been a long day," she said yet again. "*I* said I enjoyed it." When he still didn't speak, she let out a little snort and added, "Perhaps this will all seem more clear if I point out that I implied the words 'yes' and 'but' as in 'Yeeeessss, but I enjoyed it.'"

"I see," he murmured, with all the solemnity he could muster.

"I suspect you see a great deal," she muttered, "and ignore at least half of it."

He quirked a brow, which caused her to grumble to herself, which of course caused him to want to kiss her.

Everything made him want to kiss her.

It was starting to grow quite painful, that.

"We should be at the inn by nightfall," he said crisply, as if a businesslike mien would relieve his tension.

It didn't, of course. All it did was remind him that he'd put off his wedding night by a full day. A full day of wanting, needing, of his body screaming for release. But he was damned if he was going to take her in some roadside inn, no matter how clean and tidy it might be.

Daphne deserved better. This was her one and only wedding night, and he *would* make it perfect for her.

She shot him a slightly startled look at the sudden change of subject. "That will be nice."

"The roads really aren't safe these days after dark," he added, trying not to remind himself that he'd originally planned on pushing straight through to Clyvedon.

"No," she agreed.

"And we'll be hungry."

"Yes," she said, starting to look puzzled at his current obsession with their newly scheduled stop at the inn. Simon couldn't blame her, but it was either discuss the travel plans to death or grab her and take her right there in the carriage.

Which was *not* an option.

So he said, "They have good food."

She blinked, once, before pointing out, "You said that."

"So I did." He coughed. "I believe I'll take a nap."

Her dark eyes widened, and her entire face actually bobbed forward as she asked, "Right now?"

Simon gave a brisk nod. "I do seem to be repeating myself, but I did, as you so thoughtfully reminded me, say it had been a long day."

"Indeed." She watched him curiously as he shifted in his seat, looking for the most comfortable position. Finally, she asked, "Are you truly going to be able to fall asleep here in the moving carriage? Don't you find the ride a bit bumpy?"

He shrugged. "I'm quite good at falling asleep whenever I wish to. Learned how on my travels."

"It's a talent," she murmured.

"Jolly good one," he agreed. Then he closed his eyes and faked sleep for the better part of three hours.

Daphne stared at him. Hard. He was faking it. With seven siblings, she knew every trick in the book, and Simon was definitely *not* asleep.

His chest was rising and falling in an admirably even manner, and his breath contained just the right amount of whoosh and wheeze to sound like he was almost but not quite snoring.

But Daphne knew better.

Every time she moved, made a rustling sound, or breathed just a little too loudly, his chin moved. It was barely perceptible, but it was there. And when she yawned, making a low, sleepy, moaning noise, she saw his eyes move under his closed lids.

There was something to admire, however, in the fact that he'd managed to keep up the charade for over two hours.

She'd never lasted past twenty minutes herself.

If he wanted to feign sleep, she decided in a rare fit of magnanimity, she might as well let him. Far be it from her to ruin such a marvelous performance.

With one last yawn—a loud one, just to watch his eyes snap to attention under his eyelids—she turned to the carriage window, drawing the heavy velvet curtain back so she could peer outside. The sun sat orange and fat on the western horizon, about one-third of it already resting below the edge of the earth.

If Simon had been correct in his estimation of their traveling time—and she had the feeling that he was frequently correct about such things; people who liked mathematics usually were—then they should be almost at the halfway point of their journey. Almost to The Hare and Hounds.

Almost to her wedding night.

Good God, she was going to *have* to stop thinking in such melodramatic terms. This was getting ridiculous.

"Simon?"

He didn't move. This irritated her.

"Simon?" A little louder this time.

The corner of his mouth twitched slightly, pulling down into a tiny frown. Daphne was positive he was trying to decide if she'd spoken too loudly for him to continue to feign sleep.

"Simon!" She poked him. Hard, right where his arm joined with his chest. There was no way he could possibly think a person could sleep through that.

His eyelids fluttered open, and he made a funny little breathy sound—the sort people made when they woke up.

He was *good*, Daphne thought with reluctant admiration.

He yawned. "Daff?"

She didn't mince words. "Are we there yet?"

He rubbed nonexistent sleep from his eyes. "I beg your pardon?"

"Are we *there* yet?"

"Uhhh . . ." He glanced around the inside of the carriage, not that that would tell him anything. "Aren't we still moving?"

"Yes, but we could be close."

Simon let out a little sigh and peered out the window. He was facing east, so the sky looked considerably darker than it had through Daphne's window. "Oh," he said, sounding surprised. "Actually, it's just up ahead."

Daphne did her best not to smirk.

The carriage rolled to a halt, and Simon hopped down. He exchanged some words with the driver, presumably informing him that they had changed their plans and now intended to spend the night. Then he reached up for Daphne's hand and helped her down.

"Does this meet with your approval?" he asked, with a nod and a wave toward the inn.

Daphne didn't see how she could render judgment without

seeing the interior, but she said yes, anyway. Simon led her inside, then deposited her by the door when he went to deal with the innkeeper.

Daphne watched the comings and goings with great interest. Right now a young couple—they looked to be landed gentry—were being escorted into a private dining room, and a mother was ushering her brood of four up the stairs. Simon was arguing with the innkeeper, and a tall, lanky gentleman was leaning against a—

Daphne swung her head back toward her husband. Simon was arguing with the innkeeper? Why on earth would he do that? She craned her neck. The two men were speaking in low tones, but it was clear that Simon was most displeased. The innkeeper looked as if he might die of shame at his inability to please the Duke of Hastings.

Daphne frowned. This didn't look right.

Should she intervene?

She watched them argue a few moments longer. Clearly, she should intervene.

Taking steps that weren't hesitant yet could never be called determined, she made her way over to her husband's side. "Is anything amiss?" she inquired politely.

Simon spared her a brief glance. "I thought you were waiting by the door."

"I was." She smiled brightly. "I moved."

Simon scowled and turned back to the innkeeper.

Daphne let out a little cough, just to see if he would turn around. He didn't. She frowned. She didn't like being ignored. "Simon?" She poked him in the back. "Simon?"

He turned slowly around, his face pure thundercloud.

Daphne smiled again, all innocence. "What is the problem?"

The innkeeper held his hands up in supplication and spoke

before Simon could make any explanations. "I have but one room left," he said, his voice a study in abject apology. "I had no idea his grace planned to honor us with his presence this eve. Had I known, I would never have let that last room out to Mrs. Weatherby and her brood. I assure you"—the innkeeper leaned forward and gave Daphne a commiserating look "I would have sent them right on their way!"

The last sentence was accompanied by a dramatic whooshing wave of both hands that made Daphne a touch seasick. "Is Mrs. Weatherby the woman who just walked by here with four children?"

The innkeeper nodded. "If it weren't for the children, I'd—"

Daphne cut him off, not wanting to hear the remainder of a sentence that would obviously involve booting an innocent woman out into the night. "I see no reason why we cannot make do with one room. We are certainly not as high in the instep as that."

Beside her, Simon's jaw clenched until she would swear she could hear his teeth grinding.

He wanted separate rooms, did he? It was enough to make a new bride feel extremely unappreciated.

The innkeeper turned to Simon and waited for his approval. Simon gave a curt nod, and the innkeeper clapped his hands together in delight (and presumably relief; there was little worse for business than an irate duke on one's premises). He grabbed the key and scurried out from behind his desk. "If you'll follow me . . ."

Simon motioned for Daphne to go first, so she swept past him and climbed the stairs behind the innkeeper. After only a couple of twists and turns, they were deposited in a large, comfortably furnished room with a view of the village.

"Well, now," Daphne said, once the innkeeper had seen himself out, "this seems nice enough."

Simon's reply was a grunt.

"How articulate of you," she murmured, then disappeared behind the dressing screen.

Simon watched her for several seconds before it occurred to him where she'd gone. "Daphne?" he called out, his voice strangling on itself. "Are you changing your clothing?"

She poked her head out. "No. I was just looking around."

His heart continued to thud, although perhaps not at quite as rapid a pace. "Good," he grunted. "We'll be wanting to go down for supper soon."

"Of course." She smiled—a rather annoyingly winning and confident smile, in his opinion. "Are you hungry?" she asked.

"Extremely."

Her smile wobbled just a touch at his curt tone. Simon gave himself a mental scolding. Just because he was irate with himself didn't mean he had to extend the anger toward her. She'd done nothing wrong. "And you?" he asked, keeping his voice gentle.

She emerged fully from behind the screen and perched at the end of the bed. "A bit," she admitted. She swallowed nervously. "But I'm not certain I could eat anything."

"The food was excellent the last time I ate here. I assure you—"

"It's not the quality of the food that worries me," she interrupted. "It's my nerves."

He stared at her blankly.

"Simon," she said, obviously trying to hide the impatience in her voice (but not, in Simon's opinion, succeeding), "we were married this morning."

Realization finally dawned. "Daphne," he said gently, "you needn't worry."

She blinked. "I needn't?"

He drew a ragged breath. Being a gentle, caring husband was

not as easy as it sounded. "We will wait until we reach Clyvedon to consummate the marriage."

"We will?"

Simon felt his eyes widen in surprise. Surely she didn't sound disappointed? "I'm not going to take you in some roadside inn," he said. "I have more respect for you than that."

"You're not? You do?"

His breath stopped. She *did* sound disappointed.

"Uh, no."

She inched forward. "Why not?"

Simon stared at her face for several moments, just sat there on the bed and stared at her. Her dark eyes were huge as they returned his regard, filled with tenderness and curiosity and a touch of hesitation. She licked her lips—surely just another sign of nerves, but Simon's frustrated body reacted to the seductive movement with an instant quickening.

She smiled tremulously but didn't quite meet his eye. "I wouldn't mind."

Simon remained frozen, curiously rooted to the spot as his body screamed, *Tackle her! Haul her onto the bed! Do anything, just get her under you!*

And then, just when his urges began to outweigh his honor, she let out a small, tortured cry and jumped to her feet, turning her back on him as she covered her mouth with her hand.

Simon, who had just swiped one arm through the air to yank her to him, found himself off-balance and facedown on the bed. "Daphne?" he mumbled into the mattress.

"I should have known," she whimpered. "I'm so sorry."

She was sorry? Simon pushed himself back up. She was whimpering? What the hell was going on? Daphne never whimpered.

She turned back around, regarding him with stricken eyes.

Simon would have been more concerned, except that he couldn't even begin to imagine what had so suddenly upset her. And if he couldn't imagine it, he tended to believe it wasn't serious.

Arrogant of him, but there you had it.

"Daphne," he said with controlled gentleness, "what is wrong?"

She sat down opposite him and placed a hand on his cheek. "I'm so insensitive," she whispered. "I should have known. I should never have said anything."

"Should have known what?" he ground out.

Her hand fell away. "That you can't—that you couldn't—"

"Can't *what*?"

She looked down at her lap, where her hands were attempting to wring each other to shreds. "Please don't make me say it," she said.

"This," Simon muttered, "has got to be why men avoid marriage."

His words were meant more for his ears than hers, but she heard them and, unfortunately, reacted to them with another pathetic moan.

"What the hell is going on?" he finally demanded.

"You're unable to consummate the marriage," she whispered.

It was a wonder his erection didn't die off in that instant. Frankly, it was a wonder he was even able to strangle out the words: "I beg your pardon?"

She hung her head. "I'll still be a good wife to you. I'll never tell a soul, I promise."

Not since childhood, when his stuttering and stammering had attacked his every word, had Simon been so at a loss for speech.

She thought he was *impotent*?

"Why—why—why—?" A stutter? Or plain old shock? Simon thought shock. His brain didn't seem able to focus on anything other than that single word.

"I know that men are very sensitive about such things," Daphne said quietly.

"Especially when it's not true!" Simon burst out.

Her head jerked up. "It's not?"

His eyes narrowed to slits. "Did your brother tell you this?"

"No!" She slid her gaze away from his face. "My mother."

"Your mother?" Simon choked out. Surely no man had ever suffered so on his wedding night. "Your mother told you I'm *impotent*?"

"Is that the word for it?" Daphne asked curiously. And then, at his thunderous glare, she hastily added, "No, no, she didn't say it in so many words."

"What," Simon asked, his voice clipped, "did she say, exactly?"

"Well, not much," Daphne admitted. "It was rather annoying, actually, but she did explain to me that the marital act—"

"She called it an act?"

"Isn't that what everyone calls it?"

He waved off her question. "What else did she say?"

"She told me that the, ah, whatever it is *you* wish to call it—"

Simon found her sarcasm oddly admirable under the circumstances.

"—is related in some manner to the procreation of children, and—"

Simon thought he might choke on his tongue. "In some manner?"

"Well, yes." Daphne frowned. "She really didn't provide me with any specifics."

"Clearly."

"She did try her best," Daphne pointed out, thinking she ought at least to try to come to her mother's defense. "It was very embarrassing for her."

"After eight children," he muttered, "you'd think she'd be over that by now."

"I don't think so," Daphne said, shaking her head. "And then when I asked her if she'd participated in this"—she looked up at him with an exasperated expression. "I really don't know what else to call it but an act."

"Go right ahead," he said with a wave, his voice sounding awfully strained.

Daphne blinked with concern. "Are you all right?"

"Just fine," he choked.

"You don't sound fine."

He waved his hand some more, giving Daphne the odd impression that he couldn't speak.

"Well," she said slowly, going back to her earlier story, "I asked her if that meant she'd participated in this act eight times, and she became very embarrassed, and—"

"You asked her that?" Simon burst out, the words escaping his mouth like an explosion.

"Well, yes." Her eyes narrowed. "Are you laughing?"

"No," he gasped.

Her lips twisted into a small scowl. "You certainly look as if you're laughing."

Simon just shook his head in a decidedly frantic manner.

"Well," Daphne said, clearly disgruntled. "I thought my question made perfect sense, seeing as she has eight children. But then she told me that—"

He shook his head and held up a hand, and now he looked like he didn't know whether to laugh or cry. "Don't tell me. I beg of you."

"Oh." Daphne didn't know what to say to that, so she just clamped her hands together in her lap and shut her mouth.

Finally, she heard Simon take a long, ragged breath, and say, "I know I'm going to regret asking you this. In fact, I regret it already, but *why* exactly did you assume I was"—he shuddered—"unable to perform?"

"Well, you said you couldn't have children."

"Daphne, there are many, many other reasons why a couple might be unable to have children."

Daphne had to force herself to stop grinding her teeth. "I really *hate* how stupid I feel right now," she muttered.

He leaned forward and pried her hands apart. "Daphne," he said softly, massaging her fingers with his, "do you have any idea what happens between a man and a woman?"

"I haven't a clue," she said frankly. "You'd think I would, with three older brothers, and I thought I'd finally learn the truth last night when my mother "

"Don't say anything more," he said in the oddest voice. "Not another word. I couldn't bear it."

"But—"

His head fell into his hands, and for a moment Daphne thought he might be crying. But then, as she sat there castigating herself for making her husband weep on his wedding day, she realized that his shoulders were shaking with laughter.

The fiend.

"Are you laughing at me?" she growled.

He shook his head, not looking up.

"Then what are you laughing about?"

"Oh, Daphne," he gasped, "you have a lot to learn."

"Well, I never disputed *that*," she grumbled. Really, if people weren't so intent on keeping young women completely ignorant of the realities of marriage, scenes like this could be avoided.

He leaned forward, his elbows resting on his knees. His eyes grew positively electric. "I can teach you," he whispered.

Daphne's stomach did a little flip.

Never once taking his eyes off of hers, Simon took her hand and raised it to his lips. "I assure you," he murmured, flicking his tongue down the line of her middle finger, "I am perfectly able to satisfy you in bed."

Daphne suddenly found it difficult to breathe. And when had the room grown so hot? "I-I'm not sure I know what you mean."

He yanked her into his arms. "You will."

Chapter 15

London seems terribly quiet this week, now that society's favorite duke and that duke's favorite duchess have departed for the country. This Author could report that Mr. Nigel Berbrooke was seen asking Miss Penelope Featherington to dance, or that Miss Penelope, despite her mother's gleeful urging and her eventual acceptance of his offer, did not seem terribly enamored with the notion.

But really, who wants to read about Mr. Berbrooke or Miss Penelope? Let us not fool ourselves. We are all still ravenously curious about the duke and duchess.

LADY WHISTLEDOWN'S SOCIETY PAPERS,
28 May 1813

It was like being in Lady Trowbridge's garden all over again, Daphne thought wildly, except that this time there would be no interruptions—no furious older brothers, no fear of discovery, nothing but a husband, a wife, and the promise of passion.

Simon's lips found hers, gentle but demanding. With each touch, each flick of his tongue, she felt flutterings within her, tiny spasms of need that were building in pitch and frequency.

"Have I told you," he whispered, "how enamored I am of the corner of your mouth?"

"N-no," Daphne said tremulously, amazed that he'd ever even once examined it.

"I adore it," he murmured, and then went to show her how. His teeth scraped along her lower lip until his tongue darted out and traced the curve of the corner of her mouth.

It tickled, and Daphne felt her lips spreading into a wide, open-mouthed smile. "Stop," she giggled.

"Never," he vowed. He pulled back, cradling her face in his hands. "You have the most beautiful smile I've ever seen."

Daphne's initial reaction was to say, "Don't be silly," but then she thought—*Why ruin such a moment*?—and so she just said, "Really?"

"Really." He dropped a kiss on her nose. "When you smile it takes up half your face."

"Simon!" she exclaimed. "That sounds horrible."

"It's enchanting."

"Distorted."

"Desirable."

She grimaced, but somehow she laughed at the same time. "Clearly, you have no knowledge of the standards of female beauty."

He arched a brow. "As pertains to you, my standards are the only ones that count any longer."

For a moment she was speechless, then she collapsed against him, a torrent of laughter shaking both of their bodies. "Oh, Simon," she gasped, "you sounded so fierce. So wonderfully, perfectly, absurdly fierce."

"Absurd?" he echoed. "Are you calling me absurd?"

Her lips tightened to prevent another giggle, but they weren't entirely successful.

"It's almost as bad as being called impotent," he grumbled.

Daphne was instantly serious. "Oh, Simon. You know I didn't . . ."

She gave up trying to explain, and instead just said, "I'm so sorry about that."

"Don't be." He waved off her apology. "Your mother I may have to kill, but you have nothing to apologize for."

A horrified giggle escaped her lips. "Mother did try her best, and if I hadn't been confused because you said ”

"Oh, so now it's all my fault?" he said with mock outrage. But then his expression grew sly, seductive. He moved closer, angling his body so that she had to arch backwards. "I suppose I'll just have to work doubly hard to prove my capabilities."

One of his hands slid to the small of her back, supporting her as he lowered her onto the bed. Daphne felt the breath leave her body as she looked up into his intensely blue eyes. The world seemed somehow different when one was lying down. Darker, more dangerous. And all the more thrilling because Simon was looming above her, filling her vision.

And in that moment, as he slowly closed the distance between them, he became her entire world.

This time his kiss wasn't light. He didn't tickle; he devoured. He didn't tease; he possessed.

His hands slipped under her, cradling her derrière, pressing it up against his arousal. "Tonight," he whispered, his voice hoarse and hot in her ear, "I will make you mine."

Daphne's breath started coming faster and faster, each little gasp of air impossibly loud to her ears. Simon was so close, every inch of him covering her intimately. She'd imagined this night a thousand times since that moment in Regent's Park when he'd said he would marry her, but it had never occurred to her that the sheer weight of his body on hers would be so thrilling. He was large and hard and exquisitely muscled; there was no way she could escape his seductive onslaught, even if she'd wanted to.

How strange it was to feel such titillating joy at being so powerless. He could do with her whatever he desired—and she wanted to let him.

But when his body shuddered, and his lips tried to say her name but didn't get beyond "D-D-Daph—" she realized that she possessed her own kind of control. He wanted her so much he couldn't breathe, needed her so badly he couldn't speak.

And somehow, as she reveled in her newfound strength, she found that her body seemed to know what to do. Her hips arched up to meet his, and as his hands pushed her skirts up over her waist, her legs snaked around his, pulling him ever closer to the cradle of her femininity.

"My God, Daphne," Simon gasped, hauling his shaking body up on his elbows. "I want to—I can't—"

Daphne grabbed at his back, trying to pull him back down to her. The air felt cool where his body had just been.

"I can't go slow," he grunted.

"I don't care."

"I do." His eyes burned with wicked intention. "We seem to be getting ahead of ourselves."

Daphne just stared at him, trying to catch her breath. He'd sat up, and his eyes were raking across her body as one of his hands slid up the length of her leg to her knee.

"First of all," he murmured, "we need to do something about all of your clothes."

Daphne gasped with shock as he stood, pulling her to her feet along with him. Her legs were weak, her balance nonexistent, but he held her upright, his hands bunching her skirts around her waist. He whispered in her ear, "It's difficult to strip you naked when you're lying down."

One of his hands found the curve of her buttocks, and started massaging her in a circular motion. "The question," he mused, "is do I push the dress up, or pull it down?"

Daphne prayed that he wasn't expecting her to actually answer his question, because she couldn't make a sound.

"Or," he said slowly, one finger slipping under the ribboned bodice of her dress, "both?"

And then, before she had even a moment to react, he'd pushed her dress down so that the entire garment encircled her waist. Her legs were bare, and were it not for her thin silk chemise, she would have been completely naked.

"Now this is a surprise," Simon murmured, palming one of her breasts through the silk. "Not an entirely unwelcome one, of course. Silk is never as soft as skin, but it does have its advantages."

Daphne's breath fled as she watched him slide the silk slowly from side to side, the sweet friction causing her nipples to pucker and harden.

"I had no idea," Daphne whispered, her every breath sliding hot and moist across her lips.

Simon went to work on her other breast. "No idea of what?"

"That you were so wicked."

He smiled, slow and full of the devil. His lips moved to her ear, whispering, "You were my best friend's sister. Utterly forbidden. What was I to do?"

Daphne shivered with desire. His breath touched only her ear, but her skin prickled across her entire body.

"I could do nothing," he continued, edging one strap of her chemise off her shoulder, "except imagine."

"You thought about me?" Daphne whispered, her body thrilling at the notion. "You thought about this?"

His hand at her hip grew tight. "Every night. Every moment before I fell asleep, until my skin burned and my body begged for release."

Daphne felt her legs wobble, but he held her up.

"And then when I was asleep . . ." He moved to her neck, his hot breath as much of a kiss as the touch of his lips. "That's when I was truly naughty."

A moan escaped her lips, strangled and incoherent and full of desire.

The second chemise strap fell off her shoulder just as Simon's lips found the tantalizing hollow between her breasts. "But tonight—" he whispered, pushing the silk down until one breast was bared, and then the other. "Tonight all of my dreams come true."

Daphne had time only to gasp before his mouth found her breast and fastened on her hardened nipple.

"This is what I wanted to do in Lady Trowbridge's garden," he said. "Did you know that?"

She shook her head wildly, grabbing on to his shoulders for support. She was swaying from side to side, barely able to hold her head straight. Spasms of pure feeling were shooting through her body, robbing her of breath, of balance, even of thought.

"Of course you didn't," he murmured. "You're such an innocent."

With deft and knowing fingers, Simon slid the rest of her clothes from her body, until she was nude in his arms. Gently, because he knew she had to be almost as nervous as she was excited, he lowered her onto the bed.

His motions were uncontrolled and jerky as he yanked at his own clothing. His skin was on fire, his entire body burning with need. Never once, however, did he take his eyes off of her. She lay sprawled on the bed, a temptation like none he'd ever seen. Her skin glowed peachy smooth in the flickering candlelight, and her hair, long since released from its coiffure, fell around her face in wild abandon.

His fingers, which had removed her clothing with such finesse and speed, now felt awkward and clumsy as he tried to make sense of his own buttons and knots.

As his hands moved to his trousers, he saw that she was pulling the bedsheets over her. "Don't," he said, barely recognizing his own voice.

Her eyes met his, and he said, "I'll be your blanket."

He peeled the rest of his clothing off, and before she could utter a word, he moved to the bed, covering her body with his. He felt her gasp with surprise at the feel of him, and then her body stiffened slightly.

"Shhh," he crooned, nuzzling her neck while one of his hands made soothing circles on the side of her thigh. "Trust me."

"I do trust you," she said in a shaky voice. "It's just that—"

His hand moved up to her hip. "Just that what?"

He could hear the grimace in her voice as she said, "Just that I wish I weren't so utterly ignorant."

A low rumble of a laugh shook his chest.

"Stop that," she griped, swatting him on the shoulder.

"I'm not laughing at you," Simon insisted.

"You're certainly laughing," she muttered, "and don't tell me you're laughing *with* me, because that excuse *never* works."

"I was laughing," he said softly, lifting himself up on his elbows so that he could look into her face, "because I was thinking how very glad *I* am of your ignorance." He lowered his face down until his lips brushed hers in a feather-light caress. "I am honored to be the only man to touch you thus."

Her eyes shone with such purity of feeling that Simon was nearly undone. "Truly?" she whispered.

"Truly," he said, surprised by how gruff his voice sounded. "Although honor is most likely only the half of it."

She said nothing, but her eyes were enchantingly curious.

"I might have to kill the next man who so much as looks at you sideways," he grumbled.

To his great surprise, she burst out laughing. "Oh, Simon," she gasped, "it is so perfectly splendidly *wonderful* to be the object of such irrational jealousy. Thank you."

"You'll thank me later," he vowed.

"And perhaps," she murmured, her dark eyes suddenly far more seductive than they had any right to be, "you'll thank me as well."

Simon felt her thighs slide apart as he settled his body against hers, his manhood hot against her belly. "I already do," he said, his words melting into her skin as he kissed the hollow of her shoulder. "Believe me, I already do."

Never had he been so thankful for the hard-won control he had learned to exert over himself. His entire body ached to plunge into her and finally make her his in truth, but he knew that this night—their wedding night—was for Daphne, not for him.

This was her first time. He was her first lover—her *only* lover, he thought with uncharacteristic savagery—and it was his responsibility to make certain that this night brought her nothing but exquisite pleasure.

He knew she wanted him. Her breath was erratic, her eyes glazed with need. He could hardly bear to look at her face, for every time he saw her lips, half-open and panting with desire, the urge to slam into her nearly overwhelmed him.

So instead he kissed her. He kissed her everywhere, and ignored the fierce pounding of his blood every time he heard her gasp or mewl with desire. And then finally, when she was writhing and moaning beneath him, and he knew she was mad for him, he slipped his hand between her legs and touched her.

The only sound he could make was her name, and even that came out as a half-groan. She was more than ready for him, hotter and wetter than he'd ever dreamed. But still, just to be sure—or maybe it was because he couldn't resist the perverse impulse to torture himself—he slid one long finger inside her, testing her warmth, tickling her sheath.

"Simon!" she gasped, bucking beneath him. Already her muscles were tightening, and he knew that she was nearly to completion. Abruptly, he removed his hand, ignoring her whimper of protest.

He used his thighs to nudge hers further apart, and with a shuddering groan, positioned himself to enter her. "This m-may hurt a little," he whispered hoarsely, "but I p-promise you—"

"Just *do* it," she groaned, her head tossing wildly from side to side.

And so he did. With one powerful thrust, he entered her fully. He felt her maidenhead give way, but she didn't seem to flinch from pain. "Are you all right?" he groaned, his every muscle tensing just to keep himself from moving within her.

She nodded, her breath coming in shallow gasps. "It feels very odd," she admitted.

"But not bad?" he asked, almost ashamed by the desperate note in his voice.

She shook her head, a tiny, feminine smile touching her lips. "Not bad at all," she whispered. "But before . . . when you . . . with your fingers . . ."

Even in the dull candlelight he could see that her cheeks burned with embarrassment. "Is this what you want?" he whispered, pulling out until he was only halfway within her.

"No!" she cried out.

"Then perhaps *this* is what you want." He plunged back in.

She gasped. "Yes. No. Both."

He began to move within her, his rhythm deliberately slow and even. With each thrust, he pushed a gasp from her lips, each little moan the perfect pitch to drive him wild.

And then her moans grew into squeals and her gasps into pants, and he knew that she was near her peak. He moved ever faster, his teeth gritted as he fought to maintain his control as she spiralled toward completion.

She moaned his name, and then she screamed it, and then her entire body went rigid beneath him. She clutched at his shoulders, her hips rising off the bed with a strength he could barely believe. Finally, with one last, powerful shudder, she collapsed beneath him, oblivious to everything but the power of her own release.

Against his better judgment, Simon allowed himself one last thrust, burying himself to the hilt, savoring the sweet warmth of her body.

Then, taking her mouth in a searingly passionate kiss, he pulled out and spent himself on the sheets next to her.

It was to be only the first of many nights of passion. The newlyweds traveled down to Clyvedon, and then, much to Daphne's extreme embarrassment, sequestered themselves in the master suite for more than a week.

(Of course Daphne was not so embarrassed that she made anything more than a halfhearted attempt to actually *leave* the suite.)

Once they emerged from their honeymoonish seclusion, Daphne was given a tour of Clyvedon—which was much needed, since all she'd seen upon arrival was the route from the front door to the duke's bedroom. She then spent several hours introducing herself to the upper servants. She had, of course, been formally introduced to the staff upon her arrival, but Daphne thought it best to meet the more important members of the staff in a more individual manner.

Since Simon had not resided at Clyvedon for so many years, many of the newer servants did not know him, but those who had been at Clyvedon during his childhood seemed—to Daphne—to be almost ferociously devoted to her husband. She laughed about it to Simon as they privately toured the garden, and had been startled to find herself on the receiving end of a decidedly shuttered stare.

"I lived here until I went to Eton," was all he said, as if that ought to be explanation enough.

Daphne was made instantly uncomfortable by the flatness in his voice. "Did you never travel to London? When we were small, we often—"

"I lived here exclusively."

His tone signaled that he desired—no, *required*—an end to the conversation, but Daphne threw caution to the winds, and decided to pursue the topic, anyway. "You must have been a darling child," she said in a deliberately blithe voice, "or perhaps an extremely mischievous one, to have inspired such long-standing devotion."

He said nothing.

Daphne plodded on. "My brother—Colin, you know—is much the same way. He was the very devil when he was small, but so insufferably charming that all servants adored him. Why, one time—"

Her mouth froze, half-open. There didn't seem much point in continuing. Simon had turned on his heel and walked away.

He wasn't interested in roses. And he'd never pondered the existence of violets one way or another, but now Simon found himself leaning on a wooden fence, gazing out over Clyvedon's famed flower garden as if he were seriously considering a career in horticulture.

All because he couldn't face Daphne's questions about his childhood.

But the truth was, he hated the memories. He despised the reminders. Even staying here at Clyvedon was uncomfortable. The only reason he'd brought Daphne down to his childhood home was because it was the only one of his residences within a two-day drive from London that was ready for immediate occupancy.

The memories brought back the feelings. And Simon didn't want to feel like that young boy again. He didn't want to remember the number of times he'd sent letters to his father, only to wait in vain for a response. He didn't want to remember the kind smiles of the servants—kind smiles that were always accompanied by pitying eyes. They'd loved him, yes, but they'd also felt sorry for him.

And the fact that they'd hated his father on his behalf—well, somehow that had never made him feel better. He hadn't been—and, to be honest, still wasn't—so noble-minded that he didn't take a certain satisfaction in his father's lack of popularity, but that never took away the embarrassment or the discomfort.

Or the shame.

He'd wanted to be admired, not pitied. And it hadn't been until he'd struck out on his own by traveling unheralded to Eton that he'd had his first taste of success.

He'd come so far; he'd travel to hell before he went back to the way he'd been.

None of this, of course, was *Daphne's* fault. He knew she had no ulterior motives when she asked about his childhood. How could she? She knew nothing of his occasional difficulties with speech. He'd worked damned hard to hide it from her.

No, he thought with a weary sigh, he'd rarely had to work hard at all to hide it from Daphne. She'd always set him at ease, made him feel free. His stammer rarely surfaced these days, but when it did it was always during times of stress and anger.

And whatever life was about when he was with Daphne, it wasn't stress and anger.

He leaned more heavily against the fence, guilt forcing his posture into a slouch. He'd treated her abominably. It seemed he was fated to do that time and again.

"Simon?"

He'd felt her presence before she'd spoken. She'd approached from behind, her booted feet soft and silent on the grass. But he knew she was there. He could smell her gentle fragrance and hear the wind whispering through her hair.

"These are beautiful roses," she said. It was, he knew, her way of soothing his peevish mood. He knew she was dying to ask more. But she was wise beyond her years, and much as he liked to tease her about it, she did know a lot about men and their idiot tempers. She wouldn't say anything more. At least not today.

"I'm told my mother planted them," he replied. His words came out more gruffly than he would have liked, but he hoped she saw them as the olive branch he'd meant them to be. When she didn't say anything, he added by way of an explanation, "She died at my birth."

Daphne nodded. "I'd heard. I'm sorry."

Simon shrugged. "I didn't know her."

"That doesn't mean it wasn't a loss."

Simon considered his childhood. He had no way of knowing if his mother would have been more sympathetic to his difficulties than his father had been, but he figured there was no way she could have made it worse. "Yes," he murmured, "I suppose it was."

Later that day, while Simon was going over some estate accounts, Daphne decided it was as good a time as any to get to know Mrs. Colson, the housekeeper. Although she and Simon had not yet discussed where they would reside, Daphne couldn't imagine that they wouldn't spend some time there at Clyvedon, Simon's ancestral home, and if there was one thing she'd learned from her mother, it was that a lady simply *had* to have a good working relationship with her housekeeper.

Not that Daphne was terribly worried about getting along with Mrs. Colson. She had met the housekeeper briefly when Simon had introduced her to the staff, and it had been quickly apparent that she was a friendly, talkative sort.

She stopped by Mrs. Colson's office—a tiny little room just off the kitchen—a bit before teatime. The housekeeper, a handsome woman in her fifties, was bent over her small desk, working on the week's menus.

Daphne gave the open door a knock. "Mrs. Colson?"

The housekeeper looked up and immediately stood. "Your grace," she said, bobbing into a small curtsy. "You should have called for me."

Daphne smiled awkwardly, still unused to her elevation from the ranks of mere misses. "I was already up and about," she said, explaining her unorthodox appearance in the servants' domain. "But if you have a moment, Mrs. Colson, I was hoping we might get to know one another better, since you have lived here for many years, and I hope to do so for many to come."

Mrs. Colson smiled at Daphne's warm tone. "Of course, your grace. Was there anything in particular about which you cared to inquire?"

"Not at all. But I still have much to learn about Clyvedon if I am to manage it properly. Perhaps we could take tea in the yellow room? I do so enjoy the décor. It's so warm and sunny. I had been hoping to make that my personal parlor."

Mrs. Colson gave her an odd look. "The last duchess felt the same way."

"Oh," Daphne replied, not certain whether that ought to make her feel uncomfortable.

"I've given special care to that room over the years," Mrs. Colson continued. "It does get quite a bit of sun, being on the south side. I had all of the furniture reupholstered three years ago." Her chin rose in a slightly proud manner. "Went all the way to London to get the same fabric."

"I see," Daphne replied, leading the way out of the office. "The late duke must have loved his wife very much, to order such a painstaking conservation of her favorite room."

Mrs. Colson didn't quite meet her eyes. "It was my decision," she said quietly. "The duke always gave me a certain budget for the upkeep of the house. I thought it the most fitting use of the money."

Daphne waited while the housekeeper summoned a maid and gave her instructions for the tea. "It's a lovely room," she announced once they had exited the kitchen, "and although the current duke never had the opportunity to know his mother, I'm sure he'll be quite touched that you have seen fit to preserve her favorite room."

"It was the least I could do," Mrs. Colson said as they strolled across the hall. "I have not always served the Basset family, after all."

"Oh?" Daphne asked curiously. Upper servants were notoriously loyal, often serving a single family for generations.

"Yes, I was the duchess's personal maid." Mrs. Colson waited outside the doorway of the yellow room to allow Daphne to precede her. "And before that her companion. My mother was her nurse.

Her grace's family was kind enough to allow me to share her lessons."

"You must have been quite close," Daphne murmured.

Mrs. Colson nodded. "After she died I occupied a number of different positions here at Clyvedon until I finally became housekeeper."

"I see." Daphne smiled at her and then took a seat on the sofa. "Please sit," she said, motioning to the chair across from her.

Mrs. Colson seemed hesitant with such familiarity, but eventually sat. "It broke my heart when she died," she said. She gave Daphne a slightly apprehensive look. "I hope you don't mind my telling you so."

"Of course not," Daphne said quickly. She was ravenously curious about Simon's childhood. He said so little, and yet she sensed that it all meant so much. "Please, tell me more. I would love to hear about her."

Mrs. Colson's eyes grew misty. "She was the kindest, gentlest soul this earth has ever known. She and the duke—well, it wasn't a love match, but they got on well enough. They were friends in their own way." She looked up. "They were both very much aware of their duties as duke and duchess. Took their responsibilities quite seriously."

Daphne nodded understandingly.

"She was so determined to give him a son. She kept trying even after the doctors all told her she mustn't. She used to cry in my arms every month when her courses came."

Daphne nodded again, hoping the motion would hide her suddenly strained expression. It was difficult to listen to stories about not being able to have children. But she supposed she was going to have to get used to it. It was going to be even more strenuous to answer questions about it.

And there *would* be questions. Painfully tactful and hideously pitying questions.

But Mrs. Colson thankfully didn't notice Daphne's distress. She sniffled as she continued her story. "She was always saying things like how was she to be a proper duchess if she couldn't give him a son. It broke my heart. Every month it broke my heart."

Daphne wondered if her own heart would shatter every month. Probably not. She, at least, knew for a fact that she wouldn't have children. Simon's mother had her hopes crushed every four weeks.

"And of course," the housekeeper continued, "everyone talked as if it were *her* fault there was no baby. How could they know that, I ask you? It's not always the woman who is barren. Sometimes it's the man's fault, you know."

Daphne said nothing.

"I told her this time and again, but still she felt guilty. I said to her—" The housekeeper's face turned pink. "Do you mind if I speak frankly?"

"Please do."

She nodded. "Well, I said to her what my mother said to me. A womb won't quicken without strong, healthy seed."

Daphne held her face in an expressionless mask. It was all she could manage.

"But then she finally had Master Simon." Mrs. Colson let out a maternal sigh, then looked to Daphne with an apprehensive expression. "I beg your pardon," she said hastily. "I shouldn't be calling him that. He's the duke now."

"Don't stop on my account," Daphne said, happy to have something to smile about.

"It's hard to change one's ways at my age," Mrs. Colson said with a sigh. "And I'm afraid a part of me will always remember him as that poor little boy." She looked up at Daphne and shook her head. "He would have had a much easier time of it if the duchess had lived."

"An easier time of it?" Daphne murmured, hoping that would be all the encouragement Mrs. Colson would need to explain further.

"The duke just never understood that poor boy," the housekeeper said forcefully. "He stormed about and called him stupid, and—"

Daphne's head snapped up. "The duke thought Simon was stupid?" she interrupted. That was preposterous. Simon was one of the smartest people she knew. She'd once asked him a bit about his studies at Oxford and had been stunned to learn that his brand of mathematics didn't even use *numbers*.

"The duke never could see the world beyond his own nose," Mrs. Colson said with a snort. "He never gave that boy a chance."

Daphne felt her body leaning forward, her ears straining for the housekeeper's words. What had the duke done to Simon? And was this the reason he turned to ice every time his father's name was mentioned?

Mrs. Colson pulled out a handkerchief and dabbed at her eyes. "You should have seen the way that boy worked to improve himself. It broke my heart. It simply broke my heart."

Daphne's hands clawed at the sofa. Mrs. Colson was *never* going to get to the point.

"But nothing he ever did was good enough for the duke. This is just my opinion of course, but—"

Just then a maid entered with tea. Daphne nearly screamed with frustration. It took a good two minutes for the tea to be set up and poured, and all the while Mrs. Colson chitchatted about the biscuits, and did Daphne prefer them plain or with coarse sugar on top.

Daphne had to pry her hands off the sofa, lest she puncture holes in the upholstery Mrs. Colson had worked so hard to preserve. Finally, the maid left, and Mrs. Colson took a sip of her tea, and said, "Now then, where were we?"

"You were talking about the duke," Daphne said quickly. "The late duke. That nothing my husband did was ever good enough for him and in your opinion—"

"My goodness, you *were* listening." Mrs. Colson beamed. "I'm so flattered."

"But you were saying . . ." Daphne prompted.

"Oh yes, of course. I was simply going to say that I have long held the opinion that the late duke never forgave his son for not being perfect."

"But Mrs. Colson," Daphne said quietly, "none of us is perfect."

"Of course not, but—" The housekeeper's eyes floated up for a brief second in an expression of disdain toward the late duke. "If you'd known his grace, you would understand. He'd waited so long for a son. And in his mind, the Basset name was synonymous with perfection."

"And my husband wasn't the son he wanted?" Daphne asked.

"He didn't want a son. He wanted a perfect little replica of himself."

Daphne could no longer contain her curiosity. "But what did Simon do that was so repugnant to the duke?"

Mrs. Colson's eyes widened in surprise, and one of her hands floated to her chest. "Why, you don't know," she said softly. "Of course you wouldn't know."

"*What?*"

"He couldn't speak."

Daphne's lips parted in shock. "I beg your pardon?"

"He couldn't speak. Not a word until he was four, and then it was all stutters and stammers. It broke my heart every time he opened his mouth. I could see that there was a bright little boy inside. He just couldn't get the words out right."

"But he speaks so well now," Daphne said, surprised by the defensiveness in her voice. "I've never heard him stammer. Or if I have, I-I-I didn't notice it. See! Look, I just did it myself. Everyone stammers a bit when they're flustered."

"He worked very hard to improve himself. It was seven years, I recall. For seven years he did nothing but practice his speech with his nurse." Mrs. Colson's face wrinkled with thought. "Let's see, what was her name? Oh yes, Nurse Hopkins. She was a saint, she was. As devoted to that boy as if he'd been her own. I was the housekeeper's assistant at the time, but she often let me come up and help him practice his speech."

"Was it difficult for him?" Daphne whispered.

"Some days I thought he'd surely shatter from the frustration of it. But he was so stubborn. Heavens, but he was a stubborn boy. I've never seen a person so single-minded." Mrs. Colson shook her head sadly. "And his father still rejected him. It—"

"Broke your heart," Daphne finished for her. "It would have broken mine, as well."

Mrs. Colson took a sip of her tea during the long, uncomfortable silence that followed. "Thank you very much for allowing me to take tea with you, your grace," she said, misinterpreting Daphne's quietude for displeasure. "It was highly irregular of you to do so, but very . . ."

Daphne looked up as Mrs. Colson searched for the correct word.

"Kind," the housekeeper finally finished. "It was very kind of you."

"Thank you," Daphne murmured distractedly.

"Oh, but I haven't answered any of your questions about Clyvedon," Mrs. Colson said suddenly.

Daphne gave her head a little shake. "Another time, perhaps," she said softly. She had too much to think on just then.

Mrs. Colson, sensing her employer desired privacy, stood, bobbed a curtsy, and silently left the room.

Chapter 16

The stifling heat in London this week has certainly put a crimp in society functions. This Author saw Miss Prudence Featherington swoon at the Huxley ball, but it is impossible to discern whether this temporary lack of verticality was due to the heat or the presence of Mr. Colin Bridgerton, who has been cutting quite a swash through society since his return from the Continent.

The unseasonable heat has also made a casualty of Lady Danbury, who quit London several days ago, claiming that her cat (a long-haired, bushy beast) could not tolerate the weather. It is believed that she has retired to her country home in Surrey.

One would guess that the Duke and Duchess of Hastings are unaffected by these rising temperatures; they are down on the coast, where the sea wind is always a pleasure. But This Author cannot be certain of their comfort; contrary to popular belief, This Author does not have spies in all the important households, and certainly not outside of London!

Lady Whistledown's Society Papers, 2 June 1813

It was odd, Simon reflected, how they'd not been married even a fortnight and yet had already fallen into comfortable patterns and routines. Just now, he stood barefoot in the doorway of his dressing room, loosening his cravat as he watched his wife brush her hair.

And he'd done the exact same thing yesterday. There was something oddly comforting in that.

And both times, he thought with a hint of a leer, he'd been planning how to seduce her into bed. Yesterday, of course, he'd been successful.

His once expertly tied cravat lying limp and forgotten on the floor, he took a step forward.

Today he'd be successful, too.

He stopped when he reached Daphne's side, perching on the edge of her vanity table. She looked up and blinked owlishly.

He touched his hand to hers, both of their fingers wrapped around the handle of the hairbrush. "I like to watch you brush your hair," he said, "but I like to do it myself better."

She stared at him in an oddly intent fashion. Slowly, she relinquished the brush. "Did you get everything done with your accounts? You were tucked away with your estate manager for quite a long time."

"Yes, it was rather tedious but necessary, and—" His face froze. "What are you looking at?"

Her eyes slid from his face. "Nothing," she said, her voice unnaturally staccato.

He gave his head a tiny shake, the motion directed more at himself than at her, then he began to brush her hair. For a moment it had seemed as if she were staring at his mouth.

He fought the urge to shudder. All through his childhood, people had stared at his mouth. They'd gazed in horrified fascination, occasionally forcing their eyes up to his, but always returning to his mouth, as if unable to believe that such a normal-looking feature could produce such gibberish.

But he had to be imagining things. Why would Daphne be looking at his mouth?

He pulled the brush gently through her hair, allowing his fingers to trail through the silky strands as well. "Did you have a nice chat with Mrs. Colson?" he asked.

She flinched. It was a tiny movement, and she hid it quite well, but he noticed it nonetheless. "Yes," she said, "she's very knowledgeable."

"She should be. She's been here forev—*what* are you looking at?"

Daphne practically jumped in her chair. "I'm looking at the mirror," she insisted.

Which was true, but Simon was still suspicious. Her eyes had been fixed and intent, focused on a single spot.

"As I was saying," Daphne said hastily, "I'm certain Mrs. Colson will prove invaluable as I adjust to the management of Clyvedon. It's a large estate, and I have much to learn."

"Don't make too much of an effort," he said. "We won't spend much time here."

"We won't?"

"I thought we would make London our primary residence." At her look of surprise, he added, "You'll be closer to your family, even when they retire to the country. I thought you'd like that."

"Yes, of course," she said. "I do miss them. I've never been away from them for so long before. Of course I've always known that when I married I would be starting my own family, and—"

There was an awful silence.

"Well, you're my family now," she said, her voice sounding just a bit forlorn.

Simon sighed, the silver-backed hairbrush halting its path through her dark hair. "Daphne," he said, "your family will always be your family. I can never take their place."

"No," she agreed. She twisted around to face him, her eyes like warm chocolate as she whispered, "But you can be something more."

And Simon realized that all his plans to seduce his wife were moot, because clearly *she* was planning to seduce *him.*

She stood, her silk robe slipping from her shoulders. Underneath she wore a matching negligee, one that revealed almost as much as it hid.

One of Simon's large hands found its way to the side of her breast, his fingers in stark contrast with the sage green fabric of her nightgown. "You like this color, don't you?" he said in a husky voice.

She smiled, and he forgot to breathe.

"It's to match my eyes," she teased. "Remember?"

Simon managed a returning smile, although how he didn't know. He'd never before thought it possible to smile when one was about to expire from lack of oxygen. Sometimes the need to touch her was so great it hurt just to look at her.

He pulled her closer. He *had* to pull her closer. He would have gone insane if he hadn't. "Are you telling me," he murmured against her neck, "that you purchased this just for me?"

"Of course," she replied, her voice catching as his tongue traced her earlobe. "Who else is going to see me in it?"

"No one," he vowed, reaching around to the small of her back and pressing her firmly against his arousal. "No one. Not ever."

She looked slightly bemused by his sudden burst of possessiveness. "Besides," she added, "it's part of my trousseau."

Simon groaned. "I love your trousseau. I adore it. Have I told you that?"

"Not in so many words," she gasped, "but it hasn't been too difficult to figure it out."

"Mostly," he said, nudging her toward the bed as he tore off his shirt, "I like you out of your trousseau."

Whatever Daphne had meant to say—and he was certain she'd meant to say something, because her mouth opened in a most delightful manner—was lost as she toppled onto the bed.

Simon covered her in an instant. He put his hands on either side of her hips, then slid them up, pushing her arms over her head. He paused on the bare skin of her upper arms, giving them a gentle squeeze.

"You're very strong," he said. "Stronger than most women."

The look Daphne gave him was just a bit arch. "I don't want to hear about most women."

Despite himself, Simon chuckled. Then, with movements quick as lightning, his hands flew to her wrists and pinned them above her head. "But not," he drawled, "as strong as I."

She gasped with surprise, a sound he found particularly thrilling, and he quickly circled both her wrists with one of his hands, leaving the other free to roam her body.

And roam he did.

"If you aren't the perfect woman," he groaned, sliding the hem of her nightgown up over her hips, "then the world is—"

"Stop," she said shakily. "You know I'm not perfect."

"I do?" His smile was dark and wicked as he slid his hand under one of her buttocks. "You must be misinformed, because this"—he gave her a squeeze—"is perfect."

"Simon!"

"And as for these—" He reached up and covered one of her breasts with his hand, tickling the nipple through the silk. "Well, I don't need to tell you how I feel about these."

"You're mad."

"Quite possibly," he agreed, "but I have excellent taste. And you"—he leaned down quite suddenly and nipped at her mouth—"taste quite good."

Daphne giggled, quite unable to help herself.

Simon wiggled his brows. "Dare you mock me?"

"Normally I would," she replied, "but not when you've got both my arms pinned over my head."

Simon's free hand went to work on the fastenings of his trousers. "Clearly I married a woman of great sense."

Daphne gazed at him with pride and love as she watched his words trip effortlessly from his lips. To hear him speak now, one could never guess that he'd stammered as a child.

What a remarkable man she'd married. To take such a hindrance and beat it with sheer force of will—he had to be the strongest, most disciplined man she knew.

"I am so glad I married you," she said in a rush of tenderness. "So very proud you're mine."

Simon stilled, obviously surprised by her sudden gravity. His voice grew low and husky. "I'm proud you're mine as well." He yanked at his trousers. "And I'd show you how proud," he grunted, "if I could get these damned things off."

Daphne felt another bubble of laughter welling up in her throat. "Perhaps if you used two hands . . ." she suggested.

He gave her an I'm-not-as-stupid-as-*that* sort of look. "But that would require my letting you go."

She cocked her head coyly. "What if I promised not to move my arms?"

"I wouldn't even begin to believe you."

Her smile turned wickedly suggestive. "What if I promised I *would* move them?"

"Now, *that* sounds interesting." He leapt off the bed with an odd combination of grace and frantic energy and managed to get himself naked in under three seconds. Hopping back on, he stretched out on his side, all along the length of her. "Now then, where were we?"

Daphne giggled again. "Right about here, I believe."

"A-ha," he said with a comically accusing expression. "You haven't been paying attention. We were right"—he slid atop her, his weight pressing her into the mattress—"here."

Her giggles exploded into full-throated laughter.

"Didn't anyone tell you not to laugh at a man when he's trying to seduce you?"

If she'd had any chance of stopping her laughter before, it was gone now. "Oh, Simon," she gasped, "I do love you."

He went utterly still. "What?"

Daphne just smiled and touched his cheek. She understood him so much better now. After facing such rejection as a child, he probably didn't realize he was worthy of love. And he probably wasn't certain how to give it in return. But she could wait. She could wait forever for this man.

"You don't have to say anything," she whispered. "Just know that I love you."

The look in Simon's eyes was somehow both overjoyed and stricken. Daphne wondered if anyone had ever said the words "I love you" to him before. He'd grown up without a family, without the cocoon of love and warmth she'd taken for granted.

His voice, when he found it, was hoarse and nearly broken, "D-Daphne, I—"

"Shhh," she crooned, placing a finger to his lips. "Don't say anything now. Wait until it feels right."

And then she wondered if perhaps she had said the most hurtful words imaginable—for Simon, did speaking *ever* feel right?

"Just kiss me," she whispered hurriedly, eager to move past what she was afraid might be an awkward moment. "Please, kiss me."

And he did.

He kissed her with ferocious intensity, burning with all the passion and desire that flowed between them. His lips and hands left no spot untouched, kissing, squeezing, and caressing until her nightgown lay tossed on the floor and the sheets and blankets were twisted into coils at the foot of the bed.

But unlike every other night, he never did quite render her senseless. She'd been given too much to think about that day—nothing, not even the fiercest cravings of her body, could stop the frantic pace of her thoughts. She was swimming in desire, every nerve expertly brought to a fever pitch of need, and yet still her mind whirred and analyzed.

When his eyes, so blue they glowed even in the candlelight, burned into hers, she wondered if that intensity were due to emotions he didn't know how to express through words. When he gasped her name, she couldn't help but listen for another tiny stammer. And when he sank into her, his head thrown back until the cords of his neck stood out in harsh relief, she wondered why he looked like he was in so much pain.

Pain?

"Simon?" she asked tentatively, worry putting a very slight damper on her desire. "Are you all right?"

He nodded, his teeth gritted together. He fell against her, his hips still moving in their ancient rhythm, and whispered against her ear, "I'll take you there."

It wouldn't be that difficult, Daphne thought, her breath catching as he captured the tip of her breast in his mouth. It was never that difficult. He seemed to know exactly how to touch her, when to move, and when to tease by remaining tauntingly in place. His fingers slipped between their bodies, tickling her hot skin until her hips were moving and grinding with the same force as his.

She felt herself sliding toward that familiar oblivion. And it felt so good . . .

"Please," he pleaded, sliding his other hand underneath her so that he might press her even more tightly against him. "I need you to—Now, Daphne, now!"

And she did. The world exploded around her, her eyes squeezing so tightly shut that she saw spots, and stars, and brilliant streaming bursts of light. She heard music—or maybe that was just her own high-pitched moan as she reached completion, providing a melody over the powerful pounding of her heart.

Simon, with a groan that sounded as if it were ripped from his very soul, yanked himself out of her with barely a second to spare before he spilled himself—as he always did—on the sheets at the edge of the bed.

In a moment he would turn to her and pull her into his arms. It was a ritual she'd come to cherish. He would hold her tightly against him, her back to his front, and nuzzle his face in her hair. And then, after their breathing had settled down to an even sigh, they would sleep.

Except tonight was different. Tonight Daphne felt oddly restless. Her body was blissfully weary and sated, but something felt wrong. Something niggled at the back of her mind, teasing her subconscious.

Simon rolled over and scooted his body next to hers, pushing her toward the clean side of the bed. He always did that, using his body as a barrier so that she would never roll into the mess he made. It was a thoughtful gesture, actually, and—

Daphne's eyes flew open. She almost gasped.

A womb won't quicken without strong, healthy seed.

Daphne hadn't given a thought to Mrs. Colson's words when the housekeeper had uttered the saying that afternoon. She'd been too consumed with the tale of Simon's painful childhood, too concerned with how she could bring enough love into his life to banish the bad memories forever.

Daphne sat up abruptly, the blankets falling to her waist. With shaking fingers she lit the candle that sat on her bedside table.

Simon opened a sleepy eye. "What's wrong?"

She said nothing, just stared at the wet spot on the other side of the bed.

His seed.

"Daff?"

He'd told her he couldn't have children. He'd *lied* to her.

"Daphne, what's wrong?" He sat up. His face showed his concern.

Was that, too, a lie?

She pointed. "What is that?" she asked, her voice so low it was barely audible.

"What is what?" His eyes followed the line of her finger and saw only the bed. "What are you talking about?"

"Why can't you have children, Simon?"

His eyes grew shuttered. He said nothing.

"*Why*, Simon?" She practically shouted the words.

"The details aren't important, Daphne."

His tone was soft, placating, with just a hint of condescension. Daphne felt something inside of her snap.

"Get out," she ordered.

His mouth fell open. "This is my bedroom."

"Then I'll get out." She stormed out of the bed, whipping one of the bedsheets around her.

Simon was on her heels in a heartbeat. "Don't you *dare* leave this room," he hissed.

"You lied to me."

"I never—"

"You lied to me," she screamed. "You lied to me, and I will never forgive you for that!"

"Daphne—"

"You took advantage of my stupidity." She let out a disbelieving breath, the kind that came from the back of one's throat, right before it closed up in shock. "You must have been so delighted when you realized how little I knew about marital relations."

"It's called making love, Daphne," he said.

"Not between us, it's not."

Simon nearly flinched at the rancor in her voice. He stood, utterly naked, in the middle of the room, desperately trying to come up with some way to salvage the situation. He still wasn't even certain what she knew, or what she *thought* she knew. "Daphne," he said, very slowly so that he would not let his emotions trip up his words, "perhaps you should tell me exactly what this is about."

"Oh, we're going to play *that* game, are we?" She snorted derisively. "Very well, let me tell you a story. Once upon a time, there was—"

The scathing anger in her voice was like a dagger in his gut. "Daphne," he said, closing his eyes and shaking his head, "don't do it like this."

"Once upon a time," she said, louder this time, "there was a young lady. We'll call her Daphne."

Simon strode to his dressing room and yanked on a robe. There were some things a man didn't want to deal with naked.

"Daphne was very, very stupid."

"Daphne!"

"Oh, very well." She flipped her hand through the air dismissively. "Ignorant, then. She was very, very ignorant."

Simon crossed his arms.

"Daphne knew nothing about what happened between a man and a woman. She didn't know what they did, except that they did it in a bed, and that at some point, the result would be a baby."

"This is enough, Daphne."

The only sign that she heard him was the dark, flashing fury in her eyes. "But you see, she didn't really *know* how that baby was made, and so when her husband told her he couldn't have children—"

"I told you that before we married. I gave you every option to back out. Don't you forget that," he said hotly. "Don't you *dare* forget it."

"You made me feel sorry for you!"

"Oh now, *that's* what a man wants to hear," he sneered.

"For the love of God, Simon," she snapped, "you know I didn't marry you *because* I felt sorry for you."

"Then why?"

"Because I loved you," she replied, but the acid in her voice made the declaration rather brittle. "And because I didn't want to see you die, which you seemed stupidly bent upon doing."

He had no ready comment, so he just snorted and glared at her.

"But don't try to make this about *me*," she continued hotly. "I'm not the one who lied. You said you can't have children, but the truth is you just *won't* have them."

He said nothing, but he knew the answer was in his eyes.

She took a step toward him, advancing with barely controlled fury. "If you truly couldn't have children, it wouldn't matter where your seed landed, would it? You wouldn't be so frantic every night to make certain it ended up anywhere but inside me."

"You don't know anything ab-bout this, Daphne." His words were low and furious, and only slightly damaged.

She crossed her arms. "Then tell me."

"I will never have children," he hissed. "*Never.* Do you understand?"

"No."

He felt rage rising within him, roiling in his stomach, pressing against his skin until he thought he would burst. It wasn't rage against her, it wasn't even against himself. It was, as always, directed at the man whose presence—or lack thereof—had always managed to rule his life.

"My father," Simon said, desperately fighting for control, "was not a loving man."

Daphne's eyes held his. "I know about your father," she said.

That caught him by surprise. "What do you know?"

"I know that he hurt you. That he rejected you." Something flickered in her dark eyes—not quite pity, but close to it. "I know that he thought you were stupid."

Simon's heart slammed in his chest. He wasn't certain how he was able to speak—he wasn't certain how he was able to breathe—but he somehow managed to say, "Then you know about—"

"Your stammer?" she finished for him.

He thanked her silently for that. Ironically, "stutter" and "stammer" were two words he'd never been able to master.

She shrugged. "He was an idiot."

Simon gaped at her, unable to comprehend how she could dismiss decades of rage with one blithe statement. "You don't understand," he said, shaking his head. "You couldn't possibly. Not with a family like yours. The only thing that mattered to him was blood. Blood and the title. And when I didn't turn out to be perfect—Daphne, he told people I was dead!"

The blood drained from her face. "I didn't know it was like that," she whispered.

"It was worse," he bit off. "I sent him letters. Hundreds of letters, begging him to come visit me. He didn't answer one."

"Simon—"

"D-did you know I didn't speak until I was four? No? Well, I didn't. And when he visited, he shook me, and threatened to beat my voice out of me. *That* was my f-father."

Daphne tried not to notice that he was beginning to stumble over his words. She tried to ignore the sick feeling in her stomach, the anger that rose within her at the hideous way Simon had been treated. "But he's gone now," she said in a shaky voice. "He's gone, and you're here."

"He said he couldn't even b-bear to look at me. He'd spent years praying for an heir. Not a *son*," he said, his voice rising dangerously, "an heir. And f-for what? Hastings would go to a half-wit. His precious dukedom would b-be ruled by an idiot!"

"But he was wrong," Daphne whispered.

"I don't care if he was wrong!" Simon roared. "All he cared about was the title. He never gave a single thought to me, about how I must feel, trapped with a m-mouth that didn't w-work!"

Daphne stumbled back a step, unsteady in the presence of such anger. This was the fury of decades-old resentment.

Simon very suddenly stepped forward and pressed his face very close to hers. "But do you know what?" he asked in an awful voice. "I shall have the last laugh. He thought that there could be nothing worse than Hastings going to a half-wit—"

"Simon, you're not—"

"Are you even listening to me?" he thundered.

Daphne, frightened now, scurried back, her hand reaching for the doorknob in case she needed to escape.

"Of course I know I'm not an idiot," he spat out, "and in the end,

I think h-he knew it, too. And I'm sure that brought him g-great comfort. Hastings was safe. N-never mind that I was not suffering as I once had. Hastings—*that's* what mattered."

Daphne felt sick. She knew what was coming next.

Simon suddenly smiled. It was a cruel, hard expression, one she'd never seen on his face before. "But Hastings dies with me," he said. "All those cousins he was so worried about inheriting . . ." He shrugged and let out a brittle laugh. "They all had girls. Isn't that something?"

Simon shrugged. "Maybe that was why my f-father suddenly decided I wasn't such an idiot. He knew I was his only hope."

"He knew he'd been wrong," Daphne said with quiet determination. She suddenly remembered the letters she'd been given by the Duke of Middlethorpe. The ones written to him by his father. She'd left them at Bridgerton House, in London. Which was just as well, since that meant she didn't have to decide what to do with them yet.

"It doesn't matter," Simon said flippantly. "After I die, the title becomes extinct. And I for one couldn't be h-happier."

With that, he stalked out of the room, exiting through his dressing room, since Daphne was blocking the door.

Daphne sank down onto a chair, still wrapped in the soft linen sheet she'd yanked from the bed. What was she going to do?

She felt tremors spread through her body, a strange shaking over which she had no control. And then she realized she was crying. Without a sound, without even a caught breath, she was crying.

Dear God, *what* was she going to do?

Chapter 17

To say that men can be bullheaded would be insulting to the bull.

LADY WHISTLEDOWN'S SOCIETY PAPERS, 2 June 1813

In the end, Daphne did the only thing she knew how to do. The Bridgertons had always been a loud and boisterous family, not a one of them prone to keeping secrets or holding grudges.

So she tried to talk to Simon. To reason with him.

The following morning (she had no idea where he had spent the night; wherever it was, it hadn't been their bed) she found him in his study. It was a dark, overbearingly masculine room, probably decorated by Simon's father. Daphne was frankly surprised that Simon would feel comfortable in such surroundings; he hated reminders of the old duke.

But Simon, clearly, was not uncomfortable. He was sitting behind his desk, his feet insolently propped up on the leather blotter that protected the rich cherry wood of the desktop. In his hand he was holding a smoothly polished stone, turning it over and over in his hands. There was a bottle of whiskey on the desk next to him; she had a feeling it had been there all night.

He hadn't, however, drunk much of it. Daphne was thankful for small favors.

The door was ajar, so she didn't knock. But she wasn't quite so brave as to stride boldly in. "Simon?" she asked, standing back near the door.

He looked up at her and quirked a brow.

"Are you busy?"

He set down the stone. "Obviously not."

She motioned to it. "Is that from your travels?"

"The Caribbean. A memento of my time on the beach."

Daphne noticed that he was speaking with perfect elocution. There was no hint of the stammer that had become apparent the night before. He was calm now. Almost annoyingly so. "Is the beach very different there than it is here?" she asked.

He raised an arrogant brow. "It's warmer."

"Oh. Well, I'd assumed as much."

He looked at her with piercing, unwavering eyes. "Daphne, I know you didn't seek me out to discuss the tropics."

He was right, of course, but this wasn't going to be an easy conversation, and Daphne didn't think she was so much of a coward for wanting to put it off by a few moments.

She took a deep breath. "We need to discuss what happened last night."

"I'm sure you think we do."

She fought the urge to lean forward and smack the bland expression from his face. "I don't *think* we do. I *know* we do."

He was silent for a moment before saying, "I'm sorry if you feel that I have betrayed—"

"It's not that, exactly."

"—but you must remember that I *tried* to avoid marrying you."

"That's certainly a nice way of putting it," she muttered.

He spoke as if delivering a lecture. "You know that I had intended never to marry."

"That's not the point, Simon."

"It's exactly the point." He dropped his feet to the floor, and his chair, which had been balancing on its two back legs, hit the ground with a loud thunk. "Why do you think I avoided marriage with such determination? It was because I didn't want to take a wife and then hurt her by denying her children."

"You were never thinking of your potential wife," she shot back. "You were thinking of yourself."

"Perhaps," he allowed, "but when that potential wife became *you*, Daphne, everything changed."

"Obviously not," she said bitterly.

He shrugged. "You know I hold you in the highest esteem. I never wanted to hurt you."

"You're hurting me right now," she whispered.

A flicker of remorse crossed his eyes, but it was quickly replaced with steely determination. "If you recall, I refused to offer for you even when your brother demanded it. Even," he added pointedly, "when it meant my own death."

Daphne didn't contradict him. They both knew he would have died on that dueling field. No matter what she thought of him now, how much she despised the hatred that was eating him up, Simon had too much honor ever to have shot at Anthony.

And Anthony placed too much value on his sister's honor to have aimed anywhere but at Simon's heart.

"I did that," Simon said, "because I knew I could never be a good husband to you. I knew you wanted children. You'd told me so on a number of occasions, and I certainly don't blame you. *You* come from a large and loving family."

"You could have a family like that, too."

He continued as if he hadn't heard her. "Then, when you interrupted the duel, and begged me to marry you, I warned you. I told you I wouldn't have children—"

"You told me you *couldn't* have children," she interrupted, her eyes flashing with anger. "There's a very big difference."

"Not," Simon said coldly, "to me. I *can't* have children. My soul won't allow it."

"I see." Something shriveled inside Daphne at that moment, and she was very much afraid it was her heart. She didn't know how she was meant to argue with such a statement. Simon's hatred of his father was clearly far stronger than any love he might learn to feel for her.

"Very well," she said in a clipped voice. "This is obviously not a subject upon which you are open to discussion."

He gave her one curt nod.

She gave him one in return. "Good day, then."

And she left.

Simon kept to himself for most of the day. He didn't particularly want to see Daphne; that did nothing but make him feel guilty. Not, he assured himself, that he had anything to feel guilty about. He had told her before their marriage that he could not have children. He had given her every opportunity to back out, and she had chosen to marry him, anyway. He had not forced her into anything. It was not *his* fault if she had misinterpreted his words and thought that he was *physically* unable to sire brats.

Still, even though he was plagued by this nagging sense of guilt every time he thought of her (which pretty much meant all day), and even though his gut twisted every time he saw her stricken face in his mind (which pretty much meant he spent the day with an upset stomach), he felt as if a great weight had been lifted from his shoulders now that everything was out in the open.

Secrets could be deadly, and now there were no more between them. Surely that had to be a good thing.

By the time night fell, he had almost convinced himself that he had done nothing wrong. Almost, but not quite. He had entered this marriage convinced that he would break Daphne's heart, and that had never sat well with him. He liked Daphne. Hell, he probably liked her better than any human being he'd ever known, and that was why he'd been so reluctant to marry her. He hadn't wanted to shatter her dreams. He hadn't wanted to deprive her of the family she so desperately wanted. He'd been quite prepared to step aside and watch her marry someone else, someone who would give her a whole houseful of children.

Simon suddenly shuddered. The image of Daphne with another man was not nearly as tolerable as it had been just a month earlier.

Of course not, he thought, trying to use the rational side of his brain. She was his wife now. She was *his*.

Everything was different now.

He had known how desperately she had wanted children, and he had married her, knowing full well that he would not give her any.

But, he told himself, *you warned her*. She'd known exactly what she was getting into.

Simon, who had been sitting in his study, tossing that stupid rock back and forth between his hands since supper, suddenly straightened. He had not deceived her. Not truly. He had told her that they wouldn't have children, and she had agreed to marry him, anyway. He could see where she would feel a bit upset upon learning his reasons, but she could not say that she had entered this marriage with any foolish hopes or expectations.

He stood. It was time they had another talk, this one at his behest. Daphne hadn't attended dinner, leaving him to dine alone, the silence of the night broken only by the metallic clink of his fork against his plate. He hadn't seen his wife since that morning; it was high time he did.

She was his *wife*, he reminded himself. He ought to be able to see her whenever he damn well pleased.

He marched down the hall and swung open the door to the duke's bedroom, fully prepared to lecture her about *some*thing (the topic, he was sure, would come to him when necessary), but she wasn't there.

Simon blinked, unable to believe his eyes. Where the hell was she? It was nearly midnight. She should be in bed.

The dressing room. She had to be in the dressing room. The silly chit insisted upon donning her nightrobe every night, even though Simon wiggled her out of it mere minutes later.

"Daphne?" he barked, crossing to the dressing-room door. "Daphne?"

No answer. And no light shining in the crack between the door and the floor. Surely she wouldn't dress in the dark.

He pulled the door open. She most definitely wasn't present.

Simon yanked on the bellpull. Hard. Then he strode out into the hall to await whichever servant was unfortunate enough to have answered his summons.

It was one of the upstairs maids, a little blond thing whose name he could not recall. She took one look at his face and blanched.

"Where is my wife?" he barked.

"Your wife, your grace?"

"Yes," he said impatiently, "my wife."

She stared at him blankly.

"I assume you know about whom I am speaking. She's about

your height, long dark hair . . ." Simon would have said more, but the maid's terrified expression made him rather ashamed of his sarcasm. He let out a long, tense breath. "Do you know where she is?" he asked, his tone softer, although not what anyone would describe as gentle.

"Isn't she in bed, your grace?"

Simon jerked his head toward his empty room. "Obviously not."

"But that's not where she sleeps, your grace."

His eyebrows snapped together. "I beg your pardon."

"Doesn't she—" The maid's eyes widened in horror, then shot frantically around the hall. Simon had no doubt that she was looking for an escape route. Either that or someone who might possibly save her from his thunderous temper.

"Spit it out," he barked.

The maid's voice was very small. "Doesn't she inhabit the duchess's bedchamber?"

"The duchess's . . ." He pushed down an unfamiliar bolt of rage. "Since when?"

"Since today, I suppose, your grace. We had all assumed that you would occupy separate rooms at the end of your honeymoon."

"You did, did you?" he growled.

The maid started to tremble. "Your parents did, your grace, and—"

"*We are not my parents!*" he roared.

The maid jumped back a step.

"And," Simon added in a deadly voice, "I am not my father."

"Of- of course, your grace."

"Would you mind telling me which room my wife has chosen to designate as the duchess's bedchamber?"

The maid pointed one shaking finger at a door down the hall.

"Thank you." He took four steps away, then whirled around.

"You are dismissed." The servants would have plenty to gossip about on the morrow, what with Daphne moving out of their bedroom; he didn't need to give them any more by allowing this maid to witness what was sure to be a colossal argument.

Simon waited until she had scurried down the stairs, then he moved on angry feet down the hall to Daphne's new bedroom. He stopped outside her door, thought about what he'd say, realized he had no idea, and then went ahead and knocked.

No response.

He pounded.

No response.

He raised his fist to pound again, when it occurred to him that maybe she hadn't even locked the door. Wouldn't he feel like a fool if—

He twisted the knob.

She *had* locked it. Simon swore swiftly and fluently under his breath. Funny how he'd never once in his life stuttered on a curse.

"Daphne! Daphne!" His voice was somewhere between a call and a yell. "Daphne!"

Finally, he heard footsteps moving in her room. "Yes?" came her voice.

"Let me in."

A beat of silence, and then, "No."

Simon stared at the sturdy wooden door in shock. It had never occurred to him that she would disobey a direct order. She was his wife, damn it. Hadn't she promised to obey him?

"Daphne," he said angrily, "open this door this instant."

She must have been very close to the door, because he actually heard her sigh before saying, "Simon, the only reason to let you into this room would be if I were planning to let you into my bed, which I'm not, so I would appreciate it—indeed I believe the entire household would appreciate it—if you would take yourself off and go to sleep."

Simon's mouth actually fell open. He began to mentally weigh the door and compute how many foot-pounds per second would be required to bash the bloody thing in.

"Daphne," he said, his voice so calm it frightened even him, "if you do not open the door this instant I shall break it down."

"You wouldn't."

He said nothing, just crossed his arms and glared, confident that she would know *exactly* what sort of expression he wore on his face.

"Wouldn't you?"

Again, he decided that silence was the most effective answer.

"I *wish* you wouldn't," she added in a vaguely pleading voice.

He stared at the door in disbelief.

"You'll hurt yourself," she added.

"Then open the damned door," he ground out.

Silence, followed by a key slowly turning in the lock. Simon had just enough presence of mind not to throw the door violently open; Daphne was almost certainly directly on the other side. He shoved his way in and found her about five paces away from him, her arms crossed, her legs in a wide, militant stance.

"Don't you ever lock a door against me again," he spat out.

She shrugged. She actually shrugged! "I desired privacy."

Simon advanced several steps. "I want your things moved back into our bedroom by morning. And *you* will be moving back tonight."

"No."

"What the hell do you mean, no?"

"What the hell do you think I mean?" she countered.

Simon wasn't sure what shocked and angered him more—that she was defying him or that she was cursing aloud.

"No," she continued in a louder voice, "means no."

"You are my wife!" he roared. "You will sleep with me. In *my* bed."

"No."

"Daphne, I'm warning you . . ."

Her eyes narrowed to slits. "You have chosen to withhold something from me. Well, I have chosen to withhold something from you. Me."

He was speechless. Utterly speechless.

She, however, was not. She marched to the door and motioned rather rudely for him to go through it. "Get out of my room."

Simon started to shake with rage. "I own this room," he growled. "I own *you*."

"You own nothing but your father's title," she shot back. "You don't even own yourself."

A low roar filled his ears—the roar of red-hot fury. Simon staggered back a step, fearing that if he did not he might actually do something to hurt her. "What the *hell* do you m-mean?" he demanded.

She shrugged again, damn her. "You figure it out," she said.

All of Simon's good intentions fled the room, and he charged forward, grabbing her by her upper arms. He knew his grip was too tight, but he was helpless against the searing rage that flooded his veins. "Explain yourself," he said—between his teeth because he couldn't unclench his jaw. "Now."

Her eyes met his with such a level, knowing gaze that he was nearly undone. "You are not your own man," she said simply. "Your father is still ruling you from the grave."

Simon shook with untold fury, with unspoken words.

"Your actions, your choices—" she continued, her eyes growing very sad, "They have nothing to do with you, with what you want, or what you need. Everything you do, Simon, every move you make, every word you speak—it's all just to thwart him." Her voice broke as she finished with, "And he's not even *alive*."

Simon moved forward with a strange, predatory grace. "Not every move," he said in a low voice. "Not every word."

Daphne backed up, unnerved by the feral expression in his eyes. "Simon?" she asked hesitantly, suddenly devoid of the courage and bravado that had enabled her to stand up to him, a man twice her size and possibly thrice her strength.

The tip of his index finger trailed down her upper arm. She was wearing a silk robe, but the heat and power of him burned through the fabric. He came closer, and one of his hands stole around her until it cupped her buttock and squeezed. "When I touch you like this," he whispered, his voice perilously close to her ear, "it has nothing to do with him."

Daphne shuddered, hating herself for wanting him. Hating him for making her want him.

"When my lips touch your ear," he murmured, catching her lobe between his teeth, "it has nothing to do with him."

She tried to push him away, but when her hands found his shoulders, all they could do was clutch.

He started to push her, slowly, inexorably, toward the bed. "And when I take you to bed," he added, his words hot against the skin of her neck, "and we are skin to skin, it is just the two of—"

"No!" she cried out, shoving against him with all her might. He stumbled back, caught by surprise.

"When you take me to bed," she choked out, "it is never just the two of us. Your father is *always* there."

His fingers, which had crept up under the wide sleeve of her dressing gown, dug into her flesh. He said nothing, but he didn't have to. The icy anger in his pale blue eyes said everything.

"Can you look me in the eye," she whispered, "and tell me that when you pull from my body and give yourself instead to the bed you're thinking about *me*?"

His face was drawn and tight, and his eyes were focused on her mouth.

She shook her head and shook herself from his grasp, which had gone slack. "I didn't think so," she said in a small voice.

She moved away from him, but also away from the bed. She had no doubt that he could seduce her if he so chose. He could kiss her and caress her and bring her to dizzying heights of ecstasy, and she would hate him in the morning.

She would hate herself even more.

The room was deadly silent as they stood across from each other. Simon was standing with his arms at his sides, his face a heart-breaking mixture of shock and hurt and fury. But mostly, Daphne thought, her heart cracking a little as she met his eyes, he looked confused.

"I think," she said softly, "that you had better leave."

He looked up, his eyes haunted. "You're my wife."

She said nothing.

"Legally, I own you."

Daphne just stared at him as she said, "That's true."

He closed the space between them in a heartbeat, his hands finding her shoulders. "I can make you want me," he whispered.

"I know."

His voice dropped even lower, hoarse and urgent. "And even if I couldn't, you're mine. You belong to me. I could force you to let me stay."

Daphne felt about a hundred years old as she said, "You would never do that."

And he knew she was right, so all he did was wrench himself away from her and storm out of the room.

Chapter 18

Is This Author the only one who has noticed, or have the (gentle)men of the ton been imbibing more than usual these days?

LADY WHISTLEDOWN'S SOCIETY PAPERS, 4 June 1813

Simon went out and got drunk. It wasn't something he did often. It wasn't even something he particularly enjoyed, but he did it anyway.

There were plenty of pubs down near the water, only a few miles from Clyvedon. And there were plenty of sailors there, too, looking for fights. Two of them found Simon.

He thrashed them both.

There was an anger in him, a fury that had simmered deep in his soul for years. It had finally found its way to the surface, and it had taken very little provocation to set him to fighting.

He was drunk enough by then so that when he punched, he saw not the sailors with their sun-reddened skin but his father. Every fist was slammed into that constant sneer of rejection. And it felt good. He'd never considered himself a particularly violent man, but damn, it felt good.

By the time Simon was through with the two sailors, no one else dared approach him. The local folk recognized strength, but more importantly they recognized rage. And they all knew that of the two, the latter was the more deadly.

Simon remained in the pub until the first lights of dawn streaked the sky. He drank steadily from the bottle he'd paid for, and then, when it was time to go, rose on unsteady legs, tucked the bottle into his pocket, and made his way back home.

He drank as he rode, the bad whiskey burning straight to his gut. And as he got drunker and drunker, only one thought managed to burst through his haze.

He wanted Daphne back.

She was his wife, damn her. He'd gotten used to having her around. She couldn't just up and move out of their bedroom.

He'd get her back. He'd woo her and he'd win her, and—

Simon let out a loud, unattractive belch. Well, it was going to have to be enough to woo her and win her. He was far too intoxicated to think of anything else.

By the time he reached Castle Clyvedon, he had worked himself into a fine state of drunken self-righteousness. And by the time he stumbled up to Daphne's door, he was making enough noise to raise the dead.

"Daphneeeeeeeeeeee!" he yelled, trying to hide the slight note of desperation in his voice. He didn't need to sound pathetic.

He frowned thoughtfully. On the other hand, maybe if he sounded desperate, she'd be more likely to open the door. He sniffled loudly a few times, then yelled again, "Daphneeeeeeeee!"

When she didn't respond in under two seconds, he leaned against the heavy door (mostly because his sense of balance was swimming in whiskey). "Oh, Daphne," he sighed, his forehead coming to rest against the wood, "If you—"

The door opened and Simon went tumbling to the ground.

"Didja . . . didja hafta open it so . . . so *fast*?" he mumbled.

Daphne, who was still yanking on her dressing gown, looked at the human heap on the floor and just barely recognized it as her husband. "Good God, Simon," she said, "What did you—" She leaned down to help him, then lurched back when he opened his mouth and breathed on her. "You're drunk!" she accused.

He nodded solemnly. "'Fraid so."

"Where have you been?" she demanded.

He blinked and looked at her as if he'd never heard such a stupid question. "Out getting foxed," he replied, then burped.

"Simon, you should be in bed."

He nodded again, this time with considerably more vigor and enthusiasm. "Yesh, yesh I should." He tried to rise to his feet, but only made it as far as his knees before he tripped and fell back down onto the carpet. "Hmmm," he said, peering down at the lower half of his body. "Hmmm, that's strange." He lifted his face back to Daphne's and looked at her in utter confusion. "I could have sworn those were my legs."

Daphne rolled her eyes.

Simon tried out his legs again, with the same results. "My limbs don't sheem to be working properly," he commented.

"Your *brain* isn't working properly!" Daphne returned. "What am I to do with you?"

He looked her way and grinned. "Love me? You said you loved me, you know." He frowned. "I don't think you can take that back."

Daphne let out a long sigh. She should be furious with him—blast it all, she *was* furious with him!—but it was difficult to maintain appropriate levels of anger when he looked so pathetic.

Besides, with three brothers, she'd had some experience with drunken nitwits. He was going to have to sleep it off, that's all there was to it. He'd wake up with a blistering headache, which would probably serve him right, and then he would insist upon drinking some noxious concoction that he was absolutely positive would eliminate his hangover completely.

"Simon?" she asked patiently. "How drunk are you?"

He gave her a loopy grin. "Very."

"I thought as much," she muttered under her breath. She bent down and shoved her hands under his arms. "Up with you now, we've got to get you to bed."

But he didn't move, just sat there on his fanny and looked up at her with an extremely foolish expression. "Whydul need t'get up?" he slurred. "Can't you sit wi' me?" He threw his arms around her in a sloppy hug. "Come'n sit wi' me, Daphne."

"Simon!"

He patted the carpet next to him. "It's nice down here."

"Simon, no, I cannot sit with you," she ground out, struggling out of his heavy embrace. "You have to go to bed." She tried to move him again, with the same, dismal outcome. "Heavens above," she said under her breath, "why did you have to go out and get so drunk?"

He wasn't supposed to hear her words, but he must have done, because he cocked his head, and said, "I wanted you back."

Her lips parted in shock. They both knew what he had to do to win her back, but Daphne thought he was far too intoxicated for her to conduct any kind of conversation on the topic. So she just tugged at his arm and said, "We'll talk about it tomorrow, Simon."

He blinked several times in rapid succession. "Think it already is tomorrow." He craned his neck this way and that, peering toward the windows. The curtains were drawn, but the light of the new day was already filtering through. "Iz day all right," he mumbled. “See?” He waved his arm toward the window. “Tomorrow already.”

“Then we’ll talk about it in the evening,” she said, a touch desperately. She already felt as if her heart had been pushed through a windmill; she didn’t think she could bear any more just then. “Please, Simon, let’s just leave it be for now.”

“The thing is, Daphrey—” He shook his head in much the same manner a dog shakes off water. “DaphNe,” he said carefully. “DaphNe DaphNe.”

Daphne couldn’t quite stop a smile at that. “What, Simon?”

“The problem, y’see”—he scratched his head—“you just don’t understand.”

“What don’t I understand?” she said softly.

“Why I can’t do it,” he said. He raised his face until it was level with hers, and she nearly flinched at the haunted misery in his eyes.

“I never wanted to hurt you, Daff,” he said hoarsely. “You know that, don’t you?”

She nodded. “I know that, Simon.”

“Good, because the thing is—” He drew a long breath that seemed to shake his entire body. “I can’t do what you want.”

She said nothing.

“All my life,” Simon said sadly, “all my life he won. Didjou know that? He always won. This time I get to win.” In a long, awkward movement he swung his arm in a horizontal arc and jabbed his thumb against his chest. “Me. I want to win for once.”

“Oh, Simon,” she whispered. “You won long ago. The moment you exceeded his expectations you won. Every time you beat the odds, made a friend, or traveled to a new land you won. You did all the things he never wanted for you.” Her breath caught, and she gave his shoulders a squeeze. “You beat him. You won. Why can’t you see that?”

He shook his head. "I don't want to become what he wanted," he said. "Even though—" He hiccuped. "Even though he never expected it of m-me, what he w-wanted was a perfect son, someone who'd be the perfect d-duke, who'd then m-marry the perfect duchess, and have p-perfect children."

Daphne's lower lip caught between her teeth. He was stuttering again. He must be truly upset. She felt her heart breaking for him, for the little boy who'd wanted nothing other than his father's approval.

Simon cocked his head to the side and regarded her with a surprisingly steady gaze. "He would have approved of you."

"Oh," Daphne said, not sure how to interpret that.

"But"—he shrugged and gave her a secret, mischievous smile—"I married you anyway."

He looked so earnest, so boyishly serious, that it was a hard battle not to throw her arms around him and attempt to comfort him. But no matter how deep his pain, or how wounded his soul, he was going about this all wrong. The best revenge against his father would simply be to live a full and happy life, to achieve all those heights and glories his father had been so determined to deny him.

Daphne swallowed a heavy sob of frustration. She didn't see how he could possibly lead a happy life if all of his choices were based on thwarting the wishes of a dead man.

But she didn't want to get into all of that just then. She was tired and he was drunk and this just wasn't the right time. "Let's get you to bed," she finally said.

He stared at her for a long moment, his eyes filling with an ages-old need for comfort. "Don't leave me," he whispered.

"Simon," she choked out.

"Please don't. He left. Everyone left. Then I left." He squeezed her hand. "You stay."

She nodded shakily and rose to her feet. "You can sleep it off in my bed," she said. "I'm sure you'll feel better in the morning."

"But you'll stay with me?"

It was a mistake. She knew it was a mistake, but still she said, "I'll stay with you."

"Good." He wobbled himself upright. "Because I couldn't—I really—" He sighed and turned anguished eyes to her. "I need you."

She led him to her bed, nearly falling over with him when he tumbled onto the mattress. "Hold still," she ordered, kneeling to pull off his boots. She'd done this for her brothers before, so she knew to grab the heel, not the toe, but they were a snug fit, and she went sprawling on the ground when his foot finally slipped out.

"Good gracious," she muttered, getting up to repeat the aggravating procedure. "And they say women are slaves to fashion."

Simon made a noise that sounded suspiciously like a snore.

"Are you asleep?" Daphne asked incredulously. She yanked at the other boot, which came off with a bit more ease, then lifted his legs—which felt like deadweights—up onto the bed.

He looked young and peaceful with his dark lashes resting against his cheeks. Daphne reached out and brushed his hair off his forehead. "Sleep well, my sweet," she whispered.

But when she started to move, one of his arms shot out and wrapped around her. "You said you would stay," he said accusingly.

"I thought you were asleep!"

"Doesn't give you the right to break your promise." He tugged her at her arm, and Daphne finally gave up resisting and settled down next to him. He was warm, and he was hers, and even if she had grave fears for their future, at that moment she couldn't resist his gentle embrace.

Daphne awoke an hour or so later, surprised that she'd fallen asleep at all. Simon still lay next to her, snoring softly. They were both dressed, he in his whiskey-scented clothes, and she in her night-robe.

Gently, she touched his cheek. "What am I to do with you?" she whispered. "I love you, you know. I love you, but I hate what you're doing to yourself." She drew a shaky breath. "And to me. I hate what you're doing to me."

He shifted sleepily, and for one horrified moment, she was afraid that he'd woken up. "Simon?" she whispered, then let out a relieved exhale when he didn't answer. She knew she shouldn't have spoken words aloud that she wasn't quite ready for him to hear, but he'd looked so innocent against the snowy white pillows. It was far too easy to spill her innermost thoughts when he looked like that.

"Oh, Simon," she sighed, closing her eyes against the tears that were pooling in her eyes. She should get up. She should absolutely positively get up now and leave him to his rest. She understood why he was so dead set against bringing a child into this world, but she hadn't forgiven him, and she certainly didn't agree with him. If he woke up with her still in his arms, he might think she was willing to settle for his version of a family.

Slowly, reluctantly, she tried to pull away. But his arms tightened around her, and his sleepy voice mumbled, "No."

"Simon, I—"

He pulled her closer, and Daphne realized that he was thoroughly aroused.

"Simon?" she whispered, her eyes flying open. "Are you even awake?"

His response was another sleepy mumble, and he made no attempts at seduction, just snuggled her closer.

Daphne blinked in surprise. She hadn't realized that a man could want a woman in his sleep.

She pulled her head back so she could see his face, then reached out and touched the line of his jaw. He let out a little groan. The sound was hoarse and deep, and it made her reckless. With slow, tantalizing fingers, she undid the buttons of his shirt, pausing just once to trace the outline of his navel.

He shifted restlessly, and Daphne felt the strangest, most intoxicating surge of power. He was in her control, she realized. He was asleep, and probably still more than a little bit drunk, and she could do whatever she wanted with him.

She could *have* whatever she wanted.

A quick glance at his face told her that he was still sleeping, and she quickly undid his trousers. Underneath, he was hard and needy, and she wrapped her hand around him, feeling his blood leap beneath her fingers.

"Daphne," he gasped. His eyes fluttered open, and he let out a ragged groan. "Oh, God. That feels so damned good."

"Shhhh," she crooned, slipping out of her silken robe. "Let me do everything."

He lay on his back, his hands fisted at his sides as she stroked him. He'd taught her much during their two short weeks of marriage, and soon he was squirming with desire, his breath coming in short pants.

And God help her, but she wanted him, too. She felt so powerful looming over him. She was in control, and that was the most stunning aphrodisiac she could imagine. She felt a fluttering in her stomach, then a strange sort of quickening, and she knew that she needed him.

She wanted him inside her, filling her, giving her everything a man was meant to give to a woman.

"Oh, Daphne," he moaned, his head tossing from side to side. "I need you. I need you *now*."

She moved atop him, pressing her hands against his shoulders as she straddled him. Using her hand, she guided him to her entrance, already wet with need.

Simon arched beneath her, and she slowly slid down his shaft, until he was almost fully within her.

"More," he gasped. "Now."

Daphne's head fell back as she moved down that last inch. Her hands clutched at his shoulders as she gasped for breath. Then he was completely within her, and she thought she would die from the pleasure. Never had she felt so full, nor so completely a woman.

She keened as she moved above him, her body arching and writhing with delight. Her hands splayed flat against her stomach as she twisted and turned, then slid upward toward her breasts.

Simon let out a guttural moan as he watched her, his eyes glazing over as his breath came hot and heavy over his parted lips. "Oh, my God," he said in a hoarse, raspy voice. "What are you doing to me? What have you—" Then she touched one of her nipples, and his entire body bucked upwards. "Where did you learn that?"

She looked down and gave him a bewildered smile. "I don't know."

"More," he groaned. "I want to watch you."

Daphne wasn't entirely certain what to do, so she just let instinct take over. She ground her hips against his in a circular motion as she arched her back, causing her breasts to jut out proudly. She cupped both in her hands, squeezing them softly, rolling the nipples between her fingers, never once taking her eyes off Simon's face.

His hips started to buck in a frantic, jerky motion, and he grasped desperately at the sheets with his large hands. And Daphne realized that he was almost there. He was always so careful to please her, to make certain that she reached her climax before he allowed himself the same privilege, but this time, he was going to explode first.

She was close, but not as close as he was.

"Oh, Christ!" he suddenly burst out, his voice harsh and primitive with need. "I'm going to—I can't—" His eyes pinned upon her with a strange, pleading sort of look, and he made a feeble attempt to pull away.

Daphne bore down on him with all her might.

He exploded within her, the force of his climax lifting his hips off the bed, pushing her up along with him. She planted her hands underneath him, using all of her strength to hold him against her. She would not lose him this time. She would not lose this chance.

Simon's eyes flew open as he came, as he realized too late what he had done. But his body was too far gone; there was no stopping the power of his climax. If he'd been on top, he might have found the strength to pull away, but lying there under her, watching her tease her own body into a mass of desire, he was helpless against the raging force of his own need.

As his teeth clenched and his body bucked, he felt her small hands slip underneath him, pressing him more tightly against the cradle of her womb. He saw the expression of pure ecstasy on her face, and then he suddenly realized—she had done this on purpose. She had planned this.

Daphne had aroused him in his sleep, taken advantage of him while he was still slightly intoxicated, and held him to her while he poured his seed into her.

His eyes widened and fixed on hers. "How could you?" he whispered.

She said nothing, but he saw her face change, and he knew she'd heard him.

Simon pushed her from his body just as he felt her begin to tighten around him, savagely denying her the ecstasy he'd just had for himself. "How could you?" he repeated. "You knew. You *knew* th-that that I-I-I—"

But she had just curled up in a little ball, her knees tucked against her chest, obviously determined not to lose a single drop of him.

Simon swore viciously as he yanked himself to his feet. He opened his mouth to pour invective over her, to castigate her for betraying him, for taking advantage of him, but his throat tightened, and his tongue swelled, and he couldn't even begin a word, much less finish one.

"Y-y-you—" he finally managed.

Daphne stared at him in horror. "Simon?" she whispered.

He didn't want this. He didn't want her looking at him like he was some sort of freak. Oh God, oh God, he felt seven years old again. He couldn't speak. He couldn't make his mouth work. He was lost.

Daphne's face filled with concern. Unwanted, pitying concern. "Are you all right?" she whispered. "Can you breathe?"

"D-d-d-d-d—" It was a far cry from *don't pity me*, but it was all he could do. He could feel his father's mocking presence, squeezing at his throat, choking his tongue.

"Simon?" Daphne said, hurrying to his side. Her voice grew panicked. "Simon, say something!"

She reached out to touch his arm, but he threw her off. "Don't touch me!" he exploded.

She shrank back. "I guess there are still some things you can say," she said in a small, sad voice.

Simon hated himself, hated the voice that had forsaken him, and hated his wife because she had the power to reduce his control to rubble. This complete loss of speech, this choking, strangling feeling—he had worked his entire life to escape it, and now *she* had brought it all back with a vengeance.

He couldn't let her do this. He couldn't let her make him like he'd once been.

He tried to say her name, couldn't get anything out.

He had to leave. He couldn't look at her. He couldn't be with her. He didn't even want to be with himself, but that, unfortunately, was beyond his meager control.

"D-don't c-come n-near me," he gasped, jabbing his finger at her as he yanked on his trousers. "Y-y-y-you did this!"

"Did what?" Daphne cried, pulling a sheet around her. "Simon, stop this. What did I do that was so wrong? You wanted me. You know you wanted me."

"Th-th-this!" he burst out, pointing at his throat. Then he pointed toward her abdomen. "Th-th-that."

Then, unable to bear the sight of her any longer, he stormed from the room.

If only he could escape himself with the same ease.

Ten hours later Daphne found the following note:

> *Pressing business at another of my estates requires my attention. I trust you will notify me if your attempts at conception were successful.*
>
> *My steward will give you my direction, should you need it.*
>
> *Simon*

The single sheet of paper slipped from Daphne's fingers and floated slowly to the floor. A harsh sob escaped her throat, and she pressed her fingers to her mouth, as if that might possibly stem the tide of emotion that was churning within her.

He'd left her. He'd actually left her. She'd known he was angry, known he might not even forgive her, but she hadn't thought he would actually leave.

She'd thought—oh, even when he'd stormed out the door she'd thought that they might be able to resolve their differences, but now she wasn't so sure.

Maybe she'd been too idealistic. She'd egotistically thought that she could heal him, make his heart whole. Now she realized that she'd imbued herself with far more power than she actually possessed. She'd thought her love was so good, so shining, so pure that Simon would immediately abandon the years of resentment and pain that had fueled his very existence.

How self-important she'd been. How stupid she felt now.

Some things were beyond her reach. In her sheltered life, she'd never realized that until now. She hadn't expected the world to be handed to her upon a golden platter, but she'd always assumed that if she worked hard enough for something, treated everyone the way she would like to be treated, then she would be rewarded.

But not this time. Simon was beyond her reach.

The house seemed preternaturally quiet as Daphne made her way down to the yellow room. She wondered if all the servants had learned of her husband's departure and were now studiously avoiding her. They had to have heard bits and pieces of the argument the night before.

Daphne sighed. Grief was even more difficult when one had a small army of onlookers.

Or invisible onlookers, as the case may be, she thought as she gave the bellpull a tug. She couldn't see them, but she knew they were there, whispering behind her back and pitying her.

Funny how she'd never given much thought to servants' gossip before. But now—she plopped down on the sofa with a pained little moan—now she felt so wretchedly alone. What else was she supposed to think about?

"Your grace?"

Daphne looked up to see a young maid standing hesitantly in the doorway. She bobbed a little curtsy and gave Daphne an expectant look.

"Tea, please," Daphne said quietly. "No biscuits, just tea."

The young girl nodded and ran off.

As she waited for the maid to return, Daphne touched her abdomen, gazing down at herself with gentle reverence. Closing her eyes, she sent up a prayer. *Please God please*, she begged, *let there be a child.*

She might not get another chance.

She wasn't ashamed of her actions. She supposed she should be, but she wasn't.

She hadn't planned it. She hadn't looked at him while he was sleeping and thought—*he's probably still drunk. I can make love to him and capture his seed and he'll never know.*

It hadn't happened that way.

Daphne wasn't quite sure how it had happened, but one moment she was above him, and the next she'd realized that he wasn't going to withdraw in time, and she'd made certain he *couldn't . . .*

Or maybe— She closed her eyes. Tight. Maybe it had happened the other way. Maybe she *had* taken advantage of more than the moment, maybe she had taken advantage of *him.*

She just didn't know. It had all melted together. Simon's stutter, her desperate wish for a baby, his hatred of his father—it had all swirled and mixed in her mind, and she couldn't tell where one ended and the other began.

And she felt so alone.

She heard a sound at the door and turned, expecting the timid young maid back with tea, but in her stead was Mrs. Colson. Her face was drawn and her eyes were concerned.

Daphne smiled wanly at the housekeeper. "I was expecting the maid," she murmured.

"I had things to attend to in the next room, so I thought I'd bring the tea myself," Mrs. Colson replied.

Daphne knew she was lying, but she nodded anyway.

"The maid said no biscuits," Mrs. Colson added, "but I knew you'd skipped breakfast, so I put some on the tray, anyway."

"That's very thoughtful of you." Daphne didn't recognize the timbre of her own voice. It sounded rather flat to her, almost as if it belonged to someone else.

"It was no trouble, I assure you." The housekeeper looked as if she wanted to say more, but eventually she just straightened and asked, "Will that be all?"

Daphne nodded.

Mrs. Colson made her way to the door, and for one brief moment Daphne almost called out to her. She almost said her name, and asked her to sit with her, and share her tea. And she would have spilled her secrets and her shame, and then she would have spilled her tears.

And not because she was particularly close to the housekeeper, just because she had no one else.

But she didn't call out, and Mrs. Colson left the room.

Daphne picked up a biscuit and bit into it. Maybe, she thought, it was time to go home.

Chapter 19

The new Duchess of Hastings was spotted in Mayfair today. Philipa Featherington saw the former Miss Daphne Bridgerton taking a bit of air as she walked briskly around the block. Miss Featherington called out to her, but the duchess pretended not to hear.

And we know the duchess must have been pretending, for after all, one would have to be deaf to let one of Miss Featherington's shouts go unnoticed.

Lady Whistledown's Society Papers, 9 June 1813

Heartache, Daphne eventually learned, never really went away; it just dulled. The sharp, stabbing pain that one felt with each breath eventually gave way to a blunter, lower ache—the kind that one could almost—but never quite—ignore.

She left Castle Clyvedon the day after Simon's departure, heading to London with every intention of returning to Bridgerton House. But going back to her family's house somehow seemed like an admission of failure, and so at the last minute, she instructed the driver to take her to Hastings House instead. She would be near her family if she felt the need for their support and companionship, but she was a married woman now; she should reside in her own home.

And so she introduced herself to her new staff, who accepted her without question (but not without a considerable amount of curiosity), and set about her new life as an abandoned wife.

Her mother was the first to come calling. Daphne hadn't bothered to notify anyone else of her return to London, so this was not terribly surprising.

"Where is he?" Violet demanded without preamble.

"My husband, I presume?"

"No, your great-uncle Edmund," Violet practically snapped. "Of course I mean your husband."

Daphne didn't quite meet her mother's eyes as she said, "I believe that he is tending to affairs at one of his country estates."

"You *believe*?"

"Well, I know," Daphne amended.

"And do you *know* why you are not with him?"

Daphne considered lying. She considered brazening it out and telling her mother some nonsense about an emergency involving tenants and maybe some livestock or disease or *anything*. But in the end, her lip quivered, and her eyes started to prick with tears, and her voice was terribly small, as she said, "Because he did not choose to take me with him."

Violet took her hands. "Oh, Daff," she sighed, "what happened?"

Daphne sank onto a sofa, pulling her mother along with her. "More than I could ever explain."

"Do you want to try?"

Daphne shook her head. She'd never, not even once in her life, kept a secret from her mother. There had never been anything she didn't feel she could discuss with her.

But there had never been this.

She patted her mother's hand. "I'll be all right."

Violet looked unconvinced. "Are you certain?"

"No." Daphne stared at the floor for a moment. "But I have to believe it, anyway."

Violet left, and Daphne placed her hand on her abdomen and prayed.

Colin was the next to visit. About a week later, Daphne returned from a quick walk in the park to find him standing in her drawing room, arms crossed, expression furious.

"Ah," Daphne said, pulling off her gloves, "I see you've learned of my return."

"What the hell is going on?" he demanded.

Colin, Daphne reflected wryly, had clearly not inherited their mother's talent for subtlety in speech.

"Speak!" he barked.

She closed her eyes for a moment. Just a moment to try to relieve the headache that had been plaguing her for days. She didn't want to tell her woes to Colin. She didn't even want to tell him as much as she told her mother, although she supposed he already knew. News always traveled fast at Bridgerton House.

She wasn't really sure where she got the energy, but there was a certain fortifying benefit to putting up a good front, so she squared her shoulders, raised a brow, and said, "And by that you mean . . . ?"

"I mean," Colin growled, "where is your husband?"

"He is otherwise occupied," Daphne replied. It sounded so much better than, "He left me."

"Daphne . . ." Colin's voice held no end of warning.

"Are you here alone?" she asked, ignoring his tone.

"Anthony and Benedict are in the country for the month, if that's what you mean," Colin said.

Daphne very nearly sighed with relief. The last thing she needed just then was to face her eldest brother. She'd already prevented him from killing Simon once; she wasn't sure if she'd be able to manage the feat a second time. Before she could say anything, however, Colin added, "Daphne, I am ordering you right now to tell me where the bastard is hiding."

Daphne felt her spine stiffening. She might have the right to call her errant husband nasty names, but her brother certainly didn't. "I assume," she said icily, "that by 'that bastard' you refer to my husband."

"You're damned right I—"

"I'm going to have to ask you to leave."

Colin looked at her as if she'd suddenly sprouted horns. "I beg your pardon?"

"I don't care to discuss my marriage with you, so if you cannot refrain from offering your unsolicited opinions, you're going to have to leave."

"You can't ask me to leave," he said in disbelief.

She crossed her arms. "This is my house."

Colin stared at her, then looked around the room—the drawing room of the Duchess of Hastings—then looked back at Daphne, as if just realizing that his little sister, whom he'd always viewed as a rather jolly extension of himself, had become her own woman.

He reached out and took her hand. "Daff," he said quietly, "I'll let you handle this as you see fit."

"Thank you."

"*For now*," he warned. "Don't think I'll let this situation continue indefinitely."

But it wouldn't, Daphne thought a half hour later as Colin left the house. It couldn't continue indefinitely. Within a fortnight, she would know.

Every morning Daphne woke to find she was holding her breath. Even before her courses were due to arrive, she bit her lip, said a little prayer, and gingerly peeled back the covers of her bed and looked for blood.

And every morning she saw nothing but snowy white linen.

A week after her courses were due, she allowed herself the first glimmerings of hope. Her courses had never been perfectly punctual; they could, she reasoned, still arrive at any time. But still, she had never been quite *this* late . . .

After another week, though, she found herself smiling each morning, holding on to her secret as she would a treasure. She wasn't ready to share this with anyone yet. Not her mother, not her brothers, and certainly not Simon.

She didn't feel terribly guilty about withholding the news from him. After all, he had withheld his seed from her. But more importantly, she feared that his reaction would be explosively negative, and she just wasn't ready to let his displeasure ruin her perfect moment of joy. She did, however, jot off a note to his steward, asking that he forward Simon's new address to her.

But then finally, after the third week, her conscience got the better of her, and she sat down at her desk to write him a letter.

Unfortunately for Daphne, the sealing wax hadn't even dried on her missive when her brother Anthony, obviously returned from his sojourn in the country, came crashing into the room. Since Daphne was upstairs, in her private chamber, where she was *not* supposed to receive visitors, she didn't even want to think about how many servants he had injured on his way up.

He looked furious, and she knew she probably shouldn't provoke him, but he always made her slightly sarcastic, so she asked, "And how did you get up here? Don't I have a butler?"

"You *had* a butler," he growled.

"Oh, dear."

"Where is he?"

"Not here, obviously." There didn't seem any point in pretending she didn't know exactly who he was talking about.

"I'm going to kill him."

Daphne stood, eyes flashing. "No, you're not!"

Anthony, who had been standing with his hands on his hips, leaned forward and speared her with a stare. "I made a vow to Hastings before he married you, did you know that?"

She shook her head.

"I reminded him that I had been prepared to kill him for damaging your reputation. Heaven help him if he damages your soul."

"He hasn't damaged my soul, Anthony." Her hand strayed to her abdomen. "Quite the opposite, actually."

But if Anthony found her words odd, she would never know, because his eyes strayed to her writing table, then narrowed. "What is that?" he asked.

Daphne followed his line of vision to the small pile of paper that constituted her discarded attempts at a letter to Simon. "It's nothing," she said, reaching forward to grab the evidence.

"You're writing him a letter, aren't you?" Anthony's already stormy expression grew positively thunderous. "Oh, for the love of God, don't try to lie about it. I saw his name at the top of the paper."

Daphne crumpled the wasted papers and dropped them into a basket under the desk. "It's none of your business."

Anthony eyed the basket as if he were about to lunge under the desk and retrieve the half-written notes. Finally, he just looked back at Daphne, and said, "I'm not going to let him get away with this."

"Anthony, this isn't your affair."

He didn't dignify that with a reply. "I'll find him, you know. I'll find him, and I'll kill—"

"Oh, for goodness' sake," Daphne finally exploded. "This is *my* marriage, Anthony, not yours. And if you interfere in my affairs, so help me God, I swear I will never speak to you again."

Her eyes were steady, and her tone was forceful, and Anthony looked slightly shaken by her words. "Very well," he muttered, "I won't kill him."

"Thank you," Daphne said, rather sarcastically.

"But I will find him," Anthony vowed. "And I will make my disapproval clear."

Daphne took one look at his face and knew that he meant it. "Very well," she said, reaching for the completed letter that she'd tucked away in a drawer. "I'll let you deliver this."

"Good." He reached for the envelope.

Daphne moved it out of his reach. "But only if you make me two promises."

"Which are . . . ? "

"First, you must promise that you won't read this."

He looked mortally affronted that she'd even suggested he would.

"Don't try that 'I'm so honorable' expression with me," Daphne said with a snort. "I know you, Anthony Bridgerton, and I know that you would read this in a second if you thought you could get away with it."

Anthony glared at her.

"But I also know," she continued, "that you would never break an explicit promise made to me. So I'll need your promise, Anthony."

"This is hardly necessary, Daff."

"Promise!" she ordered.

"Oh, all right," he grumbled, "I promise."

"Good." She handed him the letter. He looked at it longingly.

"Secondly," Daphne said loudly, forcing his attention back to her, "you must promise not to hurt him."

"Oh, now, wait one second, Daphne," Anthony burst out. "You ask for too much."

She held out her hand. "I'll be taking that letter back."

He shoved it behind his back. "You already gave it to me."

She smirked. "I didn't give you his address."

"I can get his address," he returned.

"No, you can't, and you know it," Daphne shot back. "He has no end of estates. It'd take you weeks to figure out which one he's visiting."

"A-ha!" Anthony said triumphantly. "So he's at one of his estates. You, my dear, let slip a vital clue."

"Is this a *game*?" Daphne asked in amazement.

"Just tell me where he is."

"Not unless you promise—no violence, Anthony." She crossed her arms. "I mean it."

"All right," he mumbled.

"Say it."

"You're a hard woman, Daphne Bridgerton."

"It's Daphne Basset, and I've had good teachers."

"I promise," he said—barely. His words weren't precisely crisp.

"I need a bit more than that," Daphne said. She uncrossed her arms and twisted her right hand in a rolling manner, as if to draw forth the words from his lips. "I promise not to . . ."

"I promise not to hurt your bloody idiot of a husband," Anthony spat out. "There. Is that good enough?"

"Certainly," Daphne said congenially. She reached into a drawer and pulled out the letter she'd received earlier that week from Simon's steward, giving his address. "Here you are."

Anthony took it with a decidedly ungraceful—and ungrateful—swipe of his hand. He glanced down, scanned the lines, then said, "I'll be back in four days."

"You're leaving today?" Daphne asked, surprised.

"I don't know how long I can keep my violent impulses in check," he drawled.

"Then by all means, go today," Daphne said.

He did.

"Give me one good reason why I shouldn't pull your lungs out through your mouth."

Simon looked up from his desk to see a travel-dusty Anthony Bridgerton, fuming in the doorway to his study. "It's nice to see you, too, Anthony," he murmured.

Anthony entered the room with all the grace of a thunderstorm, planted his hands on Simon's desk and leaned forward menacingly. "Would you mind telling me why my sister is in London, crying herself to sleep every night, while you're in—" He looked around the office and scowled. "Where the hell are we?"

"Wiltshire," Simon supplied.

"While you're in Wiltshire, puttering around an inconsequential estate?"

"Daphne's in London?"

"You'd think," Anthony growled, "that as her husband you'd know that."

"You'd think a lot of things," Simon muttered, "but most of the time, you'd be wrong." It had been two months since he'd left Clyvedon. Two months since he'd looked at Daphne and not been able to utter a word. Two months of utter emptiness.

In all honesty, Simon was surprised it had taken Daphne this long to get in touch with him, even if she had elected to do so through her somewhat belligerent older brother. Simon wasn't exactly certain why, but he'd thought she would have contacted him sooner, if only to blister his ears. Daphne wasn't the sort to stew in silence when she was upset; he'd half expected her to track him down and explain in six different ways why he was an utter fool.

And truth be told, after about a month, he'd half wished she would.

"I would tear your bloody head off," Anthony growled, breaking into Simon's thoughts with considerable force, "if I hadn't promised Daphne I wouldn't do you bodily harm."

"I'm sure that wasn't a promise easily made," Simon said.

Anthony crossed his arms and settled a heavy stare on Simon's face. "Nor easily kept."

Simon cleared his throat as he tried to figure out some way to ask about Daphne without seeming too obvious. He missed her. He felt like an idiot, he felt like a fool, but he missed her. He missed her laugh and her scent and the way, sometimes in the middle of the night, she always managed to tangle her legs with his.

Simon was used to being alone, but he wasn't used to being this lonely.

"Did Daphne send you to fetch me back?" he finally asked.

"No." Anthony reached into his pocket, pulled out a small, ivory envelope, and slapped it down on the desk. "I caught her summoning a messenger to send you this."

Simon stared at the envelope with growing horror. It could only mean one thing. He tried to say something neutral, such as "I see," but his throat closed up.

"I told her I'd be happy to conduct the letter to you," Anthony said, with considerable sarcasm.

Simon ignored him. He reached for the envelope, hoping that Anthony would not see how his fingers were shaking.

But Anthony did see. "What the devil is wrong with you?" he asked in an abrupt voice. "You look like hell."

Simon snatched the envelope and pulled it to him. "Always a pleasure to see you, too," he managed to quip.

Anthony gazed steadily at him, the battle between anger and concern showing clearly on his face. Clearing his throat a few times, Anthony finally asked, in a surprisingly gentle tone, "Are you ill?"

"Of course not."

Anthony went pale. "Is Daphne ill?"

Simon's head snapped up. "Not that she's told me. Why? Does she look ill? Has she—"

"No, she looks fine." Anthony's eyes filled with curiosity. "Simon," he finally asked, shaking his head, "what are you doing here? It's obvious you love her. And much as I can't comprehend it, she seems to love you as well."

Simon pressed his fingers to his temples, trying to stave off the pounding headache he never seemed to be without these days. "There are things you don't know," he said wearily, shutting his eyes against the pain. "Things you could never understand."

Anthony was silent for a full minute. Finally, just when Simon opened his eyes, Anthony pushed away from the desk and walked back to the door. "I won't drag you back to London," he said in a low voice. "I should but I won't. Daphne needs to know you came for her, not because her older brother had a pistol at your back."

Simon almost pointed out that that was why he'd married her, but he bit his tongue. That wasn't the truth. Not all of it, at least. In another lifetime, he'd have been on bended knee, begging for her hand.

"You should know, however," Anthony continued, "that people

are starting to talk. Daphne returned to London alone, barely a fortnight after your rather hasty marriage. She's keeping a good face about it, but it's got to hurt. No one has actually come out and insulted her, but there's only so much well-meaning pity a body can take. And that damned Whistledown woman has been writing about her."

Simon winced. He'd not been back in England long, but it was long enough to know that the fictitious Lady Whistledown could inflict a great deal of damage and pain.

Anthony swore in disgust. "Get yourself to a doctor, Hastings. And then get yourself back to your wife." With that, he strode out the door.

Simon stared at the envelope in his hands for many minutes before opening it. Seeing Anthony had been a shock. Knowing he'd just been with Daphne made Simon's heart ache.

Bloody hell. He hadn't expected to miss her.

This was not to say, however, that he wasn't still furious with her. She'd taken something from him that he quite frankly hadn't wanted to give. He didn't want children. He'd told her that. She'd married him knowing that. And she'd tricked him.

Or had she? He rubbed his hands wearily against his eyes and forehead as he tried to remember the exact details of that fateful morning. Daphne had definitely been the leader in their lovemaking, but he distinctly recalled his own voice, urging her on. He should not have encouraged what he knew he could not stop.

She probably wasn't pregnant, anyway, he reasoned. Hadn't it taken his own mother over a decade to produce a single living child?

But when he was alone, lying in bed at night, he knew the truth. He hadn't fled just because Daphne had disobeyed him, or because there was a chance he'd sired a child.

He'd fled because he couldn't bear the way he'd been with her. She'd reduced him to the stuttering, stammering fool of his childhood. She'd rendered him mute, brought back that awful, choking feeling, the horror of not being able to say what he felt.

He just didn't know if he could live with her if it meant going back to being the boy who could barely speak. He tried to remind himself of their courtship—their mock-courtship, he thought with a smile—and to remember how easy it had been to be with her, to talk with her. But every memory was tainted by where it had all led—to Daphne's bedroom that hideous morning, with him tripping over his tongue and choking on his own throat.

And he hated himself like that.

So he'd fled to another of his country estates—as a duke, he had a number of them. This particular house was in Wiltshire, which, he had reasoned, wasn't too terribly far from Clyvedon. He could get back in a day and a half if he rode hard enough. It wasn't so much like he'd run away, if he could go back so easily.

And now it looked like he was going to have to go back.

Taking a deep breath, Simon picked up his letter opener and slit the envelope. He pulled out a single sheet of paper and looked down.

Simon,

My efforts, as you termed them, were met with success. I have removed myself to London, so that I might be near my family, and await your directive there.

Yours,
Daphne

Simon didn't know how long he sat there behind his desk, barely breathing, the cream-colored slip of paper hanging from his fingers. Then finally, a breeze washed over him, or perhaps the light changed, or the house creaked—but something broke him out of his reverie and he jumped to his feet, strode into the hall, and bellowed for his butler.

"Have my carriage hitched," he barked when the butler appeared. "I'm going to London."

Chapter 20

The marriage of the season seems to have gone sour. The Duchess of Hastings (formerly Miss Bridgerton) returned to London nearly two months ago, and This Author has seen neither hide nor hair of her new husband, the duke.

Rumor has it that he is not at Clyvedon, where the once happy couple took their honeymoon. Indeed, This Author cannot find anyone who professes to know his whereabouts. (If her grace knows, she is not telling, and furthermore, one rarely has the opportunity to ask, as she has shunned the company of all except her rather large and extensive family.)

It is, of course, This Author's place and indeed duty to speculate on the source of such rifts, but This Author must confess that even she is baffled. They seemed so very much in love . . .

LADY WHISTLEDOWN'S SOCIETY PAPERS,
2 August 1813

The trip took two days, which was two days longer than Simon would have liked to be alone with his thoughts. He'd brought a few books to read, hoping to keep himself distracted during the tedious journey, but whenever he managed to open one it sat unread in his lap.

It was difficult to keep his mind off Daphne.

It was even more difficult to keep his mind off the prospect of fatherhood.

Once he reached London, he gave his driver instructions to take him directly to Bridgerton House. He was travel-weary, and probably could use a change of clothing, but he'd done nothing for the past two days but play out his upcoming confrontation with Daphne—it seemed foolish to put it off any longer than he had to.

Once admitted to Bridgerton House, however, he discovered that Daphne wasn't there.

"What do you mean," Simon asked in a deadly voice, not particularly caring that the butler had done little to earn his ire, "the duchess isn't here?"

The butler took his deadly voice and raised him one curled upper lip. "I mean, your grace"—this was not said with particular graciousness—"that she is not in residence."

"I have a letter from my wife—" Simon thrust his hand into his pocket, but—damn it—didn't come up with the paper. "Well, I have a letter from her somewhere," he grumbled. "And it specifically states that she has removed herself to London."

"And she has, your grace."

"Then where the hell is she?" Simon ground out.

The butler merely raised a brow. "At Hastings House, your grace."

Simon clamped his mouth shut. There was little more humiliating than being bested by a butler.

"After all," the butler continued, clearly enjoying himself now, "she is married to *you*, is she not?"

Simon glared at him. "You must be quite secure in your position."

"Quite."

Simon gave him a brief nod (since he couldn't quite bring himself to thank the man) and stalked off, feeling very much like a fool. Of course Daphne would have gone to Hastings House. She hadn't *left* him, after all; she just wanted to be near her family.

If he could have kicked himself on the way back to the carriage, he would have done so.

Once inside, however, he did kick himself. He lived just across Grosvenor Square from the Bridgertons. He could have walked across the blasted green in half the time.

Time, however, proved not to be particularly of the essence, because when he swung open the door to Hastings House and stomped into the hall, he discovered that his wife was not at home.

"She's riding," Jeffries said.

Simon stared at his butler in patent disbelief. "She's riding?" he echoed.

"Yes, your grace," Jeffries replied. "Riding. On a horse."

Simon wondered what the penalty was for strangling a butler. "Where," he bit off, "did she go?"

"Hyde Park, I believe."

Simon's blood began to pound, and his breath grew uneven. Riding? Was she bloody insane? She was pregnant, for God's sake. Even *he* knew that pregnant women weren't supposed to ride.

"Have a horse saddled for me," Simon ordered. "Immediately."

"Any particular horse?" Jeffries inquired.

"A fast one," Simon snapped. "And do it now. Or better yet, I'll do it." With that, he turned on his heel and marched out of the house.

But about halfway to the stables, his panic seeped from his blood to his very bones, and Simon's determined stride turned into a run.

It wasn't the same as riding astride, Daphne thought, but at least she was going *fast*.

In the country, when she'd been growing up, she'd always borrowed Colin's breeches and joined her brothers on their hell-for-leather rides. Her mother usually suffered an attack of the vapors every time she saw her eldest daughter return covered with mud, and quite frequently sporting a new and startling bruise, but Daphne hadn't cared. She hadn't cared where they were riding to or what they were riding from. It had all been about speed.

In the city, of course, she couldn't don breeches and thus was relegated to the sidesaddle, but if she took her horse out early enough, when fashionable society was still abed, and if she made certain to limit herself to the more remote areas of Hyde Park, she could bend over her saddle and urge her horse to a gallop. The wind whipped her hair out of its bun and stung her eyes to tears, but at least it made her forget.

Atop her favorite mare, tearing across the fields, she felt free. There was no better medicine for a broken heart.

She'd long since ditched her groom, pretending she hadn't heard him when he'd yelled, "Wait! Your grace! Wait!"

She'd apologize to him later. The grooms at Bridgerton House were used to her antics and well aware of her skill atop a horse. This new man—one of her husband's servants—would probably worry.

Daphne felt a twinge of guilt—but only a twinge. She needed to be alone. She needed to move fast.

She slowed down as she reached a slightly wooded area and took a deep breath of the crisp autumn air. She closed her eyes for a moment, letting the sounds and smells of the park fill her senses. She thought of a blind man she'd once met, who'd told her that the rest of his senses had grown sharper since he'd lost his sight. As she sat there and inhaled the scents of the forest, she thought he might be right.

She listened hard, first identifying the high-pitched chirp of the birds, then the soft, scurrying feet of the squirrels as they hoarded nuts for the winter. Then—

She frowned and opened her eyes. Damn. That was definitely the sound of another rider approaching.

Daphne didn't want company. She wanted to be alone with her thoughts and her pain, and she certainly didn't want to have to explain to some well-meaning society member why she was alone in the park. She listened again, identified the location of the oncoming rider, and took off in the other direction.

She kept her horse to a steady trot, thinking that if she just got out of the other rider's way, he'd pass her by. But whichever way she went, he seemed to follow.

She picked up speed, more speed than she should have in this lightly wooded area. There were too many low branches and protruding tree roots. But now Daphne was starting to get scared. Her pulse pounded in her ears as a thousand horrifying questions rocked through her head.

What if this rider wasn't, as she'd originally supposed, a member of the *ton*? What if he was a criminal? Or a drunk? It was early; there was no one about. If Daphne screamed, who would hear her? Was she close enough to her groom? Had he stayed put where she'd left him or had he tried to follow? And if he had, had he even gone in the right direction?

Her groom! She nearly cried out in relief. It had to be her groom. She swung her mare around to see if she could catch a glimpse of the rider. The Hastings livery was quite distinctly red; surely she'd be able to see if—

Smack!

Every bit of air was violently forced from her body as a branch caught her squarely in the chest. A strangled grunt escaped her lips, and she felt her mare moving forward without her. And then she was falling . . . falling . . .

She landed with a bone-jarring thud, the autumn brown leaves on the ground providing scant cushioning. Her body immediately curled into a fetal position, as if by making herself as small as possible, she could make the hurt as small as possible.

And, oh God, she hurt. Damn it, she hurt everywhere. She squeezed her eyes shut and concentrated on breathing. Her mind flooded with curses she'd never dared speak aloud. But it hurt. Bloody hell, it hurt to breathe.

But she had to. Breathe. *Breathe, Daphne,* she ordered. *Breathe. Breathe. You can do it.*

"Daphne!"

Daphne made no response. The only sounds she seemed able to make were whimpers. Even groans were beyond her capability.

"Daphne! Christ above, Daphne!"

She heard someone jump off a horse, then felt movement in the leaves around her.

"Daphne?"

"Simon?" she whispered in disbelief. It made no sense that he was here, but it was his voice. And even though she still hadn't pried her eyes open, it *felt* like him. The air changed when he was near.

His hands touched her lightly, checking for broken bones. "Tell me where it hurts," he said.

"Everywhere," she gasped.

He swore under his breath, but his touch remained achingly gentle and soothing. "Open your eyes," he ordered softly. "Look at me. Focus on my face."

She shook her head. "I can't."

"You *can*."

She heard him strip off his gloves, and then his warm fingers were on her temples, smoothing away the tension. He moved to her eyebrows, then the bridge of her nose. "Shhhh," he crooned. "Let it go. Just let the pain go. Open your eyes, Daphne."

Slowly, and with great difficulty, she did so. Simon's face filled her vision, and for the moment she forgot everything that had happened between them, everything but the fact that she loved him, and he was here, and he was making the hurt go away.

"Look at me," he said again, his voice low and insistent. "Look at me and don't take your eyes off of mine."

She managed the tiniest of nods. She focused her eyes on his, letting the intensity of his gaze hold her still.

"Now, I want you to relax," he said. His voice was soft but commanding, and it was exactly what she needed. As he spoke, his hands moved across her body, checking for breaks or sprains.

His eyes never once left hers.

Simon kept speaking to her in low, soothing tones as he examined her body for injuries. She didn't appear to have suffered anything worse than a few bad bruises and having the wind knocked out of her, but one could never be too careful, and with the baby . . .

The blood drained from his face. In his panic for Daphne, he'd forgotten all about the child she was carrying. His child.

Their child.

"Daphne," he said slowly. Carefully. "Do you think you're all right?"

She nodded.

"Are you still in pain?"

"Some," she admitted, swallowing awkwardly as she blinked. "But it's getting better."

"Are you certain?"

She nodded again.

"Good," he said calmly. He was silent for several seconds and then he fairly yelled, "*What in God's name did you think you were doing?*"

Daphne's jaw dropped, and her eyelids started opening and closing with great rapidity. She made a strangled sort of sound that might have metamorphosed into an actual word, but Simon cut her off with more bellows.

"What the hell were you doing out here with no groom? And why were you galloping here, where the terrain clearly does not allow it?" His eyebrows slammed together. "And for the love of God, woman, what were you doing on a horse?"

"Riding?" Daphne answered weakly.

"Don't you even care about our child? Didn't you give even a moment's thought to its safety?"

"Simon," Daphne said, her voice very small.

"A pregnant woman shouldn't even get within ten feet of a horse! You should know better."

When she looked at him her eyes looked old. "Why do you care?" she asked flatly. "You didn't want this baby."

"No, I didn't, but now that it's here I don't want you to *kill* it."

"Well, don't worry." She bit her lip. "It's not here."

Simon's breath caught. "What do you mean?"

Her eyes flitted to the side of his face. "I'm not pregnant."

"You're—" He couldn't finish the sentence. The strangest feeling sank into his body. He didn't think it was disappointment, but he wasn't quite sure. "You lied to me?" he whispered.

She shook her head fiercely as she sat up to face him. "No!" she cried. "No, I never lied. I swear. I thought I'd conceived. I truly thought I had. But—" She choked on a sob, and squeezed her eyes shut against an onslaught of tears. She hugged her legs to her body and pressed her face against her knees.

Simon had never seen her like this, so utterly stricken with grief. He stared at her, feeling agonizingly helpless. All he wanted was to make her feel better, and it didn't much help to know that *he* was the cause of her pain. "But what, Daff?" he asked.

When she finally looked up at him, her eyes were huge, and full of grief. "I don't know. Maybe I wanted a child so badly that I somehow willed my courses away. I was so happy last month." She let out a shaky breath, one that teetered precariously on the edge of a sob. "I waited and waited, even got my woman's padding ready, and nothing happened."

"Nothing?" Simon had never heard of such a thing.

"Nothing." Her lips trembled into a faintly self-mocking smile. "I've never been so happy in my life to have nothing happen."

"Did you feel queasy?"

She shook her head. "I felt no different. Except that I didn't bleed. But then two days ago . . ."

Simon laid his hand on hers. "I'm sorry, Daphne."

"No you're not," she said bitterly, yanking her hand away. "Don't pretend something you don't feel. And for God's sake, don't lie to me again. You never wanted this baby." She let out a hollow, brittle laugh. "*This* baby? Good God, I talk as if it ever actually existed. As if it were ever more than a product of my imagination." She looked down, and when she spoke again, her voice was achingly sad. "And my dreams."

Simon's lips moved several times before he managed to say, "I don't like to see you so upset."

She looked at him with a combination of disbelief and regret. "I don't see how you could expect anything else."

"I—I—I—" He swallowed, trying to relax his throat, and finally he just said the only thing in his heart. "I want you back."

She didn't say anything. Simon silently begged her to say something, but she didn't. And he cursed at the gods for her silence, because it meant that he would have to say more.

"When we argued," he said slowly, "I lost control. I—I couldn't speak." He closed his eyes in agony as he felt his jaw tighten. Finally, after a long and shaky exhale, he said, "I hate myself like that."

Daphne's head tilted slightly as furrows formed in her brow. "Is that why you left?"

He nodded once.

"It wasn't about—what I did?"

His eyes met hers evenly. "I didn't like what you did."

"But that wasn't why you left?" she persisted.

There was a beat of silence, and then he said, "It wasn't why I left."

Daphne hugged her knees to her chest, pondering his words. All this time she'd thought he'd abandoned her because he hated her, hated what she'd done, but in truth, the only thing he hated was himself.

She said softly, "You know I don't think less of you when you stammer."

"I think less of myself."

She nodded slowly. Of course he would. He was proud and stubborn, and all the *ton* looked up to him. Men curried his favor, women flirted like mad. And all the while he'd been terrified every time he'd opened his mouth.

Well, maybe not every time, Daphne thought as she gazed into his face. When they were together, he usually spoke so freely, answered her so quickly that she knew he couldn't possibly be concentrating on every word.

She put her hand on his. "You're not the boy your father thought you were."

"I know that," he said, but his eyes didn't meet hers.

"Simon, look at me," she gently ordered. When he did, she repeated her words."You're not the boy your father thought you were."

"I know that," he said again, looking puzzled and maybe just a bit annoyed.

"Are you sure?" she asked softly.

"Damn it, Daphne, I know—" His words tumbled into silence as his body began to shake. For one startling moment, Daphne thought he was going to cry. But the tears that pooled in his eyes never fell, and when he looked up at her, his body shuddering, all he said was, "I hate him, Daphne. I h-h-h—"

She moved her hands to his cheeks and turned his face to hers, forcing him to meet her steady gaze. "That's all right," she said. "It sounds as if he was a horrid man. But you have to let it go."

"I can't."

"You *can.* It's all right to have anger, but you can't let that be the ruling factor in your life. Even now, you're letting him dictate your choices."

Simon looked away.

Daphne's hands dropped from his face, but she made sure they rested on his knees. She needed this connection. In a strange way she feared that if she let go of him right now she'd lose him forever. "Did you ever stop to wonder if *you* wanted a family? If you wanted a child of your own? You'd be such a wonderful father, Simon, and yet you won't even let yourself consider the notion. You think you're getting your revenge, but you're really just letting him control you from the grave."

"If I give him a child, he wins," Simon whispered.

"No, if you give *yourself* a child, *you* win." She swallowed convulsively. "We all win."

Simon said nothing, but she could see his body shaking.

"If you don't want a child because *you* don't want one, that's one thing. But if you deny yourself the joy of fatherhood because of a dead man, then you're a coward."

Daphne winced as the insult crossed her lips, but it had to be said. "At some point you've got to leave him behind and live your own life. You've got to let go of the anger and—"

Simon shook his head, and his eyes looked lost and hopeless. "Don't ask me to do that. It's all I had. Don't you see, it's *all I had*?"

"I don't understand."

His voice rose in volume. "Why do you think I learned to speak properly? What do you think drove me? It was anger. It was always anger, always to show him."

"Simon—"

A bubble of mocking laughter erupted from his throat. "Isn't that just too amusing? I hate him. I hate him so much, and yet he's the one reason I've managed to succeed."

Daphne shook her head. "That's not true," she said fervently, "you would have succeeded no matter what. You're stubborn and brilliant, and *I know you*. You learned to speak because of *you*, not because of him." When he said nothing, she added in a soft voice, "If he'd shown you love, it would have made it all the easier."

Simon started to shake his head, but she cut him off by taking his hand and squeezing it. "I was shown love," she whispered. "I knew nothing but love and devotion when I was growing up. Trust me, it makes everything easier."

Simon sat very still for several minutes, the only sound the low whoosh of his breath as he fought to control his emotions. Finally, just when Daphne was beginning to fear she'd lost him, he looked up at her with shattered eyes.

"I want to be happy," he whispered.

"You will be," she vowed, wrapping her arms around him. "You will be."

Chapter 21

The Duke of Hastings is back!
LADY WHISTLEDOWN'S SOCIETY PAPERS,
6 August 1813

Simon didn't speak as they slowly rode home. Daphne's mare had been found munching contentedly on a patch of grass about twenty yards away, and even though Daphne had insisted that she was fit to ride, Simon had insisted that he didn't care. After tying the mare's reins to his own gelding, he had boosted Daphne into his saddle, hopped up behind her, and headed back to Grosvenor Square.

Besides, he needed to hold her.

He was coming to realize that he needed to hold on to something in life, and maybe she was right—maybe anger wasn't the solution. Maybe—just maybe he could learn to hold on to love instead.

When they reached Hastings House, a groom ran out to take care of the horses, and so Simon and Daphne trudged up the front steps and entered the hall.

And found themselves being stared down by the three older Bridgerton brothers.

"What the hell are you doing in my house?" Simon demanded. All he wanted to do was scoot up the stairs and make love to his wife, and instead he was greeted by this belligerent trio. They were standing with identical postures—legs spread, hands on hips, chins jutted out. If Simon hadn't been so damned irritated with the lot of them, he probably would have had the presence of mind to have been slightly alarmed.

Simon had no doubt that he could hold his own against one of them—*maybe* two—but against all three he was a dead man.

"We heard you were back," Anthony said.

"So I am," Simon replied. "Now leave."

"Not so fast," Benedict said, crossing his arms.

Simon turned to Daphne. "Which one of them may I shoot first?"

She threw a scowl at her brothers. "I have no preference."

"We have a few demands before we'll let you keep Daphne," Colin said.

"What?" Daphne howled.

"*She is my wife!*" Simon roared, effectively obliterating Daphne's angry query.

"She was our sister first," Anthony growled, "and you've made her miserable."

"This isn't any of your business," Daphne insisted.

"*You're* our business," Benedict said.

"She's *my* business," Simon snapped, "so now get the hell out of my house."

"When the three of you have marriages of your own, then you can presume to offer me advice," Daphne said angrily, "but in the meantime, keep your meddling impulses to yourselves."

"I'm sorry, Daff," Anthony said, "but we're not budging on this."

"On what?" she snapped. "You have no place to budge one way or the other. This isn't your affair!"

Colin stepped forward. "We're not leaving until we're convinced he loves you."

The blood drained from Daphne's face. Simon had never once told her that he loved her. He'd shown it, in a thousand different little ways, but he'd never said the words. When they came, she didn't want them at the hands of her overbearing brothers; she wanted them free and felt, from Simon's heart.

"Don't do this, Colin," she whispered, hating the pathetic, pleading note of her voice. "You have to let me fight my own battles."

"Daff—"

"Please," she pleaded.

Simon marched between them. "If you will excuse us," he said to Colin, and by extension, to Anthony and Benedict. He ushered Daphne to the other end of the hall, where they might talk privately. He would have liked to have moved to another room altogether, but he had no confidence that her idiot brothers wouldn't follow.

"I'm so sorry about my brothers," Daphne whispered, her words coming out in a heated rush. "They're boorish idiots, and they had no business invading your house. If I could disown them I would. After this display I wouldn't be surprised if you *never* want children—"

Simon silenced her with a finger to her lips. "First of all, it's our house, not my house. And as for your brothers—they annoy the hell out of me, but they're acting out of love." He leaned down, just an inch, but it brought him close enough so that she could feel his breath on her skin. "And who can blame them?" he murmured.

Daphne's heart stopped.

Simon moved ever closer, until his nose rested on hers. "I love you, Daff," he whispered.

Her heart started again, with a vengeance. "You do?"

He nodded, his nose rubbing against hers. "I couldn't help it."

Her lips wobbled into a hesitant smile. "That's not terribly romantic."

"It's the truth," he said, with a helpless shrug. "You know better than anyone that I didn't want any of this. I didn't want a wife, I didn't want a family, and I *definitely* didn't want to fall in love." He brushed his mouth softly against hers, sending shivers down both of their bodies. "But what I found"—his lips touched hers again—"much to my dismay"—and again—"was that it's quite impossible *not* to love you."

Daphne melted into his arms. "Oh, Simon," she sighed.

His mouth captured hers, trying to show her with his kiss what he was still learning to express in words. He loved her. He worshipped her. He'd walk across fire for her. He—

—still had the audience of her three brothers.

Slowly breaking the kiss, he turned his face to the side. Anthony, Benedict, and Colin were still standing in the foyer. Anthony was studying the ceiling, Benedict was pretending to inspect his fingernails, and Colin was staring quite shamelessly.

Simon tightened his hold on Daphne, even as he shot a glare down the hall. "What the hell are the three of you still doing in my house?"

Not surprisingly, none of them had a ready answer.

"Get *out*," Simon growled.

"Please." Daphne's tone didn't exactly suggest politeness.

"Right," Anthony replied, smacking Colin on the back of the head. "I believe our work here is done, boys."

Simon started steering Daphne toward the stairs. "I'm sure you can show yourselves out," he said over his shoulder.

Anthony nodded and nudged his brothers toward the door.

"Good," Simon said tersely. "We'll be going upstairs."

"Simon!" Daphne squealed.

"It's not as if they don't know what we're going to do," he whispered in her ear.

"But still—They're my *brothers*!"

"God help us," he muttered.

But before Simon and Daphne could even reach the landing, the front door burst open, followed by a stream of decidedly feminine invective.

"Mother?" Daphne said, the word croaking in her throat.

But Violet only had eyes for her sons. "I knew I'd find you here," she accused. "Of all the stupid, bullheaded—"

Daphne didn't hear the rest of her mother's speech. Simon was laughing too hard in her ear.

"He made her miserable!" Benedict protested. "As her brothers, it's our duty to—"

"Respect her intelligence enough to let her solve her own problems," Violet snapped. "And she doesn't look particularly unhappy right now."

"That's because—"

"And if you say that's because you lot barged into her home like a herd of mentally deficient sheep, I'm disowning all three of you."

All three men shut their mouths.

"Now then," Violet continued briskly, "I believe it's time we left, don't you?" When her sons didn't move quickly enough to suit her, she reached out and—

"Please, Mother!" Colin yelped. "Not the—"

She grabbed him by his ear.

"Ear," he finished glumly.

Daphne grabbed Simon's arm. He was laughing so hard now, she was afraid he'd tumble down the steps.

Violet herded her sons out the door with a loud, "March!" and then turned back to Simon and Daphne on the stairs.

"Glad to see you in London, Hastings," she called, gifting him with a wide, brilliant smile. "Another week and I would have dragged you here myself."

Then she stepped outside and shut the door behind her.

Simon turned to Daphne, his body still shaking with laughter. "Was that your mother?" he asked, smiling.

"She has hidden depths."

"Clearly."

Daphne's face grew serious. "I'm sorry if my brothers forced—"

"Nonsense," he said cutting her off. "Your brothers could never force me to say something I don't feel." He cocked his head and pondered that for a moment. "Well, not without a pistol."

Daphne smacked him in the shoulder.

Simon ignored her and pulled her body against his. "I meant what I said," he murmured, wrapping his arms around her waist. "I love you. I've known it for some time now, but—"

"It's all right," Daphne said, laying her cheek against his chest. "You don't need to explain."

"Yes, I do," he insisted. "I—" But the words wouldn't come. There was too much emotion inside, too many feelings rocking within him. "Let me show you," he said hoarsely. "Let me show you how much I love you."

Daphne answered by tilting her face up to receive his kiss. And as their lips touched, she sighed, "I love you, too."

Simon's mouth took hers with hungry devotion, his hands clutching at her back as if he were afraid she might disappear at any moment. "Come upstairs," he whispered. "Come with me now."

She nodded, but before she could take a step, he swept her into the cradle of his arms and carried her up the stairs.

By the time Simon reached the second floor, his body was rock hard and straining for release. "Which room have you been using?" he gasped.

"Yours," she replied, sounding surprised that he'd even asked.

He grunted his approval and moved swiftly into his—no, *their*—room, kicking the door shut behind him. "I love you," he said as they tumbled onto the bed. Now that he'd said the words once, they were bursting within him, demanding a voice. He needed to tell her, make sure she knew, make sure she understood what she meant to him.

And if it took a thousand sayings, he didn't care.

"I love you," he said again, his fingers frantically working on the fastenings of her dress.

"I know," she said tremulously. She cupped his face in her hands and caught his eyes with hers. "I love you, too."

Then she pulled his mouth down to hers, kissing him with a sweet innocence that set him afire.

"If I ever, ever hurt you again," he said fervently, his mouth moving to the corner of hers, "I want you to kill me."

"Never," she answered, smiling.

His lips moved to the sensitive spot where her jaw met her earlobe. "Then maim me," he murmured. "Twist my arm, sprain my ankle."

"Don't be silly," she said, touching his chin and turning his face back to hers. "You won't hurt me."

Love for this woman filled him. It flooded his chest, made his fingers tingle, and stole his very breath. "Sometimes," he whispered, "I love you so much it scares me. If I could give you the world, you know I would do it, don't you?"

"All I want is you," she whispered. "I don't need the world, just your love. And maybe," she added with a wry smile, "for you to take off your boots."

Simon felt his face erupt into a grin. Somehow his wife always seemed to know exactly what he needed. Just when his emotions were choking him, bringing him dangerously close to tears, she lightened the mood, made him smile. "Your wish is my command," he said, and rolled to her side to yank the offending footwear off.

One boot tumbled to the floor, the other skittered across the room.

"Anything else, your grace?" he asked.

She cocked her head coyly. "Your shirt could go, too, I suppose."

He complied, and the linen garment landed on the nightstand.

"Will that be all?"

"These," she said, hooking her finger around the waistband of his breeches, "are definitely in the way."

"I agree," he murmured, shrugging them off. He crawled over her, on his hands and knees, his body a hot prison around her. "Now what?"

Her breath caught. "Well, you're quite naked."

"That is true," he concurred, his eyes burning down on hers.

"And I'm not."

"That is also true." He smiled like a cat. "And a pity it is."

Daphne nodded, completely without words.

"Sit up," he said softly.

She did, and seconds later her dress was whipped over her head.

"Now that," he said hoarsely, staring hungrily at her breasts, "is an improvement."

They were now kneeling across from each other on the massive four-poster bed. Daphne stared at her husband, her pulse quickening at the sight of his broad chest, rising and falling with each heavy breath. With a trembling hand, she reached out and touched him, her fingers lightly skimming over his warm skin.

Simon stopped breathing until her forefinger touched his nipple, and then his hand shot up to cover hers. "I want you," he said.

Her eyes flicked downward, and her lips curved ever so slightly. "I know."

"No," he groaned, pulling her closer. "I want to be in your heart. I want—" His entire body shuddered when their skin touched. "I want to be in your soul."

"Oh, Simon," she sighed, sinking her fingers in his thick, dark hair. "You're already there."

And then there were no more words, only lips and hands and flesh against flesh.

Simon worshipped her in every way he knew how. He ran his hands along her legs and kissed the back of her knees. He squeezed her hips and tickled her navel. And when he was poised to enter her, his entire body straining against the most all-consuming desire he'd ever felt, he gazed down upon her with a reverence that brought tears to her eyes.

"I love you," he whispered. "In all my life, it's been only you."

Daphne nodded and although she made no sound, her mouth formed the words, "I love you, too."

He pushed forward, slowly, inexorably. And when he was settled fully within her body, he knew he was home.

He looked down at her face. Her head was thrown back, her lips parted as she struggled for breath. He grazed her flushed cheeks with his lips. "You're the most beautiful thing I've ever seen," he whispered. "I've never—I don't know how—"

She arched her back in response. "Just love me," she gasped. "Please, love me."

Simon began to move, his hips rising and falling in time's most ancient rhythm. Daphne's fingers pressed into his back, her nails digging into his skin every time he thrust further into her body.

She moaned and mewled, and his body burned at the sounds of her passion. He was spiraling out of control, his movements growing jerky, more frenetic. "I can't hold on much longer," he gasped. He wanted to wait for her, needed to know that he'd brought her bliss before he allowed himself his own release.

But then, just when he thought his body would shatter from the effort of his restraint, Daphne shook beneath him, her most intimate muscles squeezing around him as she cried out his name.

Simon's breath stopped in his throat as he watched her face. He'd always been so busy making sure he didn't spill his seed inside of her that he'd never seen her face as she climaxed. Her head was thrown back, the elegant lines of her throat straining as her mouth opened in a silent scream.

He was awestruck.

"I love you," he said. "Oh, God, how I love you." Then he plunged deeper.

Daphne's eyes fluttered open as he resumed his rhythm. "Simon?" she asked, her voice tinged with a touch of urgency. "Are you sure?"

They both knew what she meant.

Simon nodded.

"I don't want you to do this just for me," she said. "It has to be for you, too."

The strangest lump formed in his throat—it was nothing like his stutters, nothing like his stammers. It was, he realized, nothing but love. Tears stabbed at his eyes, and he nodded, utterly unable to speak.

He plunged forward, exploding within her. It felt good. Oh God, it felt good. Nothing in life had ever felt that good before.

His arms finally gave out, and he collapsed atop her, the only sound in the room the rasp of his ragged breathing.

And then Daphne smoothed his hair from his forehead and kissed his brow. "I love you," she whispered. "I will always love you."

Simon buried his face into her neck, breathing in the scent of her. She surrounded him, enveloped him, and he was complete.

Many hours later, Daphne's eyelids fluttered open. She stretched her arms above her as she noticed that the curtains had all been pulled shut. Simon must have done that, she thought with a yawn. Light filtered around the edges, bathing the room with a soft glow.

She twisted her neck, working the kinks out, then slid out of bed and padded to the dressing room to fetch her robe. How unlike her to sleep in the middle of the day. But, she supposed, this hadn't been an ordinary day.

She pulled on her robe, tying the silken sash around her waist. Where had Simon gone off to? She didn't think he'd left the bed too long before she had; she had a sleepy memory of lying in his arms that somehow seemed too fresh.

The master suite consisted of five rooms altogether: two bedrooms, each with its own dressing room off to the side, connected by a large sitting room. The door to the sitting room was ajar, and bright sunlight streamed through the aperture, suggesting that the curtains inside had been pulled open. Moving on deliberately quiet feet, Daphne walked to the open doorway and peered inside.

Simon was standing by the window, staring out over the city. He'd donned a lush burgundy dressing gown, but his feet were still bare. His pale blue eyes held a reflective look, unfocused and just the slightest bit bleak.

Daphne's brow wrinkled with concern. She crossed the room

toward him, quietly saying, "Good afternoon," when she was but a foot away.

Simon turned at the sound of her voice, and his haggard face softened at the sight of her. "Good afternoon to you, too," he murmured, pulling her into his arms. Somehow she ended up with her back pressed up against his broad chest, gazing out over Grosvenor Square as Simon rested his chin on the top of her head.

It took Daphne several moments before she worked up the courage to ask, "Any regrets?"

She couldn't see him, but she felt his chin rub against her scalp as he shook his head.

"No regrets," he said softly. "Just . . . thoughts."

Something about his voice didn't sound quite right, and so Daphne twisted in his arms until she could see his face. "Simon, what's wrong?" she whispered.

"Nothing." But his eyes didn't meet hers.

Daphne led him to a love seat, and sat, tugging on his arm until he settled in beside her. "If you're not ready to be a father yet," she whispered, "that's all right."

"It's not that."

But she didn't believe him. He'd answered too quickly, and there'd been a choked sound to his voice that made her uneasy. "I don't mind waiting," she said. "Truth be told," she added shyly, "I wouldn't mind having a little time just for the two of us."

Simon didn't say anything, but his eyes grew pained, and then he closed them as he brought his hand to his brow and rubbed.

A ripple of panic washed over Daphne, and she started talking faster. "It wasn't so much that I wanted a baby right away," she said. "I just . . . would like one eventually, that's all, and I think you might, too, if you let yourself consider it. I was upset because

I hated that you were denying us a family just to spite your father. It's not—"

Simon laid a heavy hand on her thigh. "Daphne, stop," he said. "Please."

His voice held just enough agonized emotion to silence her immediately. She caught her lower lip between her teeth and chewed nervously. It was his turn to speak. There was obviously something big and difficult squeezing at his heart, and if it took all day for him to find the words to explain it, she could wait.

She could wait forever for this man.

"I can't say I'm excited about having a child," Simon said slowly.

Daphne noticed his breathing was slightly labored, and she placed her hand on his forearm to offer comfort.

He turned to her with eyes that pleaded for understanding. "I've spent so long intending never to have one, you see." He swallowed. "I d-don't know even how to begin to think about it."

Daphne offered him a reassuring smile that in retrospect, she realized was meant for both of them. "You'll learn," she whispered. "And I'll learn with you."

"I-it's not that," he said, shaking his head. He let out an impatient breath. "I don't . . . want . . . to live my life j-just to spite my father."

He turned to her, and Daphne was nearly undone by the sheer emotion burning on his face. His jaw was trembling, and a muscle worked frantically in his cheek. There was incredible tension in his neck, as if every ounce of his energy was devoted to the task of delivering this speech.

Daphne wanted to hold him, to comfort the little boy inside. She wanted to smooth his brow, and squeeze his hand. She wanted to do a thousand things, but instead she just held silent, encouraging him with her eyes to continue.

"You were right," he said, the words tumbling from his mouth. "All along, you've been right. About my father. Th-that I was letting him win."

"Oh, Simon," she murmured.

"B-but what—" His face—his strong, handsome face, which was always so firm, always so in control—crumpled. "What if . . . if we have a child, a-a-and it comes out like me?"

For a moment Daphne couldn't speak. Her eyes tingled with unshed tears, and her hand moved unbidden to her mouth, covering lips that had parted in shock.

Simon turned away from her, but not before she saw the utter torment in his eyes. Not before she heard his breath catch, or the shaky exhale he finally expelled in an attempt to hold himself together.

"If we have a child who stutters," Daphne said carefully, "then I shall love him. And help him. And—" She swallowed convulsively, praying that she was doing the right thing. "And I shall turn to you for advice, because obviously you have learned how to overcome it."

He turned to face her with surprising swiftness. "I don't want my child to suffer as I have suffered."

A strange little smile moved across Daphne's face without her even realizing it, as if her body had realized before her mind that she knew exactly what to say. "But he wouldn't suffer," she said, "because you'll be his father."

Simon's face did not change expression, but his eyes shone with an odd, new, almost hopeful light.

"Would you reject a child who stuttered?" Daphne asked quietly.

Simon's negative reply was strong, swift, and accompanied by just a touch of blasphemy.

She smiled softly. "Then I have no fears for our children."

Simon held still for one moment more, and then in a rush of movement pulled her into his arms, burying his face in the crook of her neck. "I love you," he choked out. "I love you so much."

And Daphne was finally certain that everything was going to be all right.

Several hours later, Daphne and Simon were still sitting on the love seat in the sitting room. It had been an afternoon for holding hands, for resting one's head on the other's shoulder. Words hadn't been necessary; for both it had been enough simply to be next to the other. The sun was shining, the birds were chirping, and they were together.

It was all they needed.

But something was niggling at the back of Daphne's brain, and it wasn't until her eyes fell on a writing set on the desk that she remembered.

The letters from Simon's father.

She closed her eyes and exhaled, summoning the courage she knew she'd need to hand them over to Simon. The Duke of Middlethorpe had told her, when he'd asked her to take the packet of letters, that she'd know when the time was right to give them to him.

She disentangled herself from Simon's heavy arms and padded over to the duchess's chamber.

"Where are you going?" Simon asked sleepily. He'd been dozing in the warm afternoon sun.

"I—I have to get something."

He must have heard the hesitation in her voice, because he opened his eyes and craned his body around to look at her. "What are you getting?" he asked curiously.

Daphne avoided answering his question by scurrying into the next room. "I'll just be a moment," she called out.

She'd kept the letters, tied together by a red-and-gold ribbon—the ancestral colors of Hastings—in the bottom drawer of her desk. She'd actually forgotten about them for her first few weeks back in London, and they'd lain untouched in her old bedroom at Bridgerton House. But she'd stumbled across them on a visit to see her mother. Violet had suggested she go upstairs to gather a few of her things, and while Daphne was collecting old perfume bottles and the pillowcase she'd stitched at age ten, she found them again.

Many a time she'd been tempted to open one up, if only to better understand her husband. And truth be told, if the envelopes hadn't been closed with sealing wax, she probably would have tossed her scruples over her shoulder and read them.

She picked up the bundle and walked slowly back to the sitting room. Simon was still on the couch, but he was up and alert, and watching her curiously.

"These are for you," she said, holding up the bundle as she walked to his side.

"What are they?" he asked.

But from the tone of his voice, she was fairly certain he already knew.

"Letters from your father," she said. "Middlethorpe gave them to me. Do you remember?"

He nodded. "I also remember giving him orders to burn them."

Daphne smiled weakly. "He apparently disagreed."

Simon stared at the bundle. Anywhere but at her face. "And so, apparently, did you," he said in a very quiet voice.

She nodded and sat next to him. "Do you want to read them?"

Simon thought about his answer for several seconds and finally settled on complete honesty. "I don't know."

"It might help you to finally put him behind you."

"Or it might make it worse."

"It might," she agreed.

He stared at the letters, bundled up by a ribbon, resting innocently in her hands. He expected to feel animosity. He expected to feel rage. But instead, all he felt was . . .

Nothing.

It was the strangest sensation. There before him was a collection of letters, all written in his father's hand. And yet he felt no urge to toss them in the fire, or tear them to bits.

And at the same time no urge to read them.

"I think I'll wait," Simon said with a smile.

Daphne blinked several times, as if her eyes could not believe her ears. "You don't want to read them?" she asked.

He shook his head.

"And you don't want to burn them?"

He shrugged. "Not particularly."

She looked down at the letters, then back at his face. "What do you want to do with them?"

"Nothing."

"Nothing?"

He grinned. "That's what I said."

"Oh." She looked quite adorably befuddled. "Do you want me to put them back in my desk?"

"If you like."

"And they'll just sit there?"

He caught hold of the sash on her dressing robe and started pulling her toward him. "Mmm-hmm."

"But—" she spluttered. "But—but—"

"One more 'but,' " he teased, "and you're going to start to sound like me."

Daphne's mouth fell open. Simon wasn't surprised by her reaction. It was the first time in his life he'd ever been able to make a joke out of his difficulties.

"The letters can wait," he said, just as they fell off her lap onto the floor. "I've just finally managed—thanks to you—to boot my father from my life." He shook his head, smiling as he did so. "Reading those now would just invite him back in."

"But don't you want to see what he had to say?" she persisted. "Maybe he apologized. Maybe he even groveled at your feet!" She bent down for the bundle, but Simon pulled her tightly against him so she couldn't reach.

"Simon!" she yelped.

He arched one brow. "Yes?"

"What are you doing?"

"Trying to seduce you. Am I succeeding?"

Her face colored. "Probably," she mumbled.

"Only probably? Damn. I must be losing my touch."

His hand slid under her bottom, which prompted a little squeal. "I think your touch is just fine," she said hastily.

"Only fine?" He pretended to wince. " 'Fine' is so pale a word, don't you think? Almost wan."

"Well," she allowed, "I might have misspoken."

Simon felt a smile forming in his heart. By the time it spread to his lips, he was on his feet, and tugging his wife in the general direction of his four-poster bed.

"Daphne," he said, trying to sound businesslike, "I have a proposition."

"A proposition?" she queried, raising her brows.

"A request," he amended. "I have a request."

She cocked her head and smiled. "What kind of request?"

He nudged her through the doorway and into the bedroom. "It's actually a request in two parts."

"How intriguing."

"The first part involves you, me, and"—he picked her up and tossed her onto the bed amidst a fit of giggles—"this sturdy antique of a bed."

"Sturdy?"

He growled as he crawled up beside her. "It had better be sturdy."

She laughed and squealed as she scooted out of his grasp. "I think it's sturdy. What's the second part of your request?"

"That, I'm afraid involves a certain commitment of time on your part."

Her eyes narrowed, but she was still smiling. "What sort of commitment of time?"

In one stunningly swift move, he pinned her to the mattress. "About nine months."

Her lips softened with surprise. "Are you sure?"

"That it takes nine months?" He grinned. "That's what I've always been told."

But the levity had left her eyes. "You know that's not what I mean," she said softly.

"I know," he replied, meeting her serious gaze with one of his own. "But yes, I'm sure. And I'm scared to death. And thrilled to the marrow. And a hundred other emotions I never let myself feel before you came along."

Tears pricked her eyes. "That's the sweetest thing you've ever said to me."

"It's the truth," he vowed. "Before I met you I was only half-alive."

"And now?" she whispered.

"And now?" he echoed. " 'Now' suddenly means happiness, and joy, and a wife I adore. But do you know what?"

She shook her head, too overcome to speak.

He leaned down and kissed her. " 'Now' doesn't even compare to tomorrow. And tomorrow couldn't possibly compete with the next day. As perfect as I feel this very moment, tomorrow is going to be even better. Ah, Daff," he murmured, moving his lips to hers, "every day I'm going to love you more. I promise you that. Every day . . ."

Epilogue

It's a boy for the Duke and Duchess of Hastings!

After three girls, society's most besotted couple has finally produced an heir. This Author can only imagine the level of relief in the Hastings household; after all, it is a truth universally acknowledged that a married man in possession of a good fortune must be in want of an heir.

The name of the new babe has yet to be made public, although This Author feels herself uniquely qualified to speculate. After all, with sisters named Amelia, Belinda, and Caroline, could the new Earl Clyvedon be called anything but David?

LADY WHISTLEDOWN'S SOCIETY PAPERS,
15 December 1817

Simon threw up his arms in amazement, the single-sheet newspaper flying across the room. "How does she know this?" he demanded. "We've told no one of our decision to name him David."

Daphne tried not to smile as she watched her husband sputter and storm about the room. "It's just a lucky guess, I'm sure," she said, turning her attention back to the newborn in her arms. It was far too early to know if his eyes would remain blue or turn brown like his older sisters', but already he looked so like his father; Daphne couldn't imagine that his eyes would spoil the effect by darkening.

"She must have a spy in our household," he said, planting his hands on his hips. "She must."

"I'm sure she doesn't have a spy in our household," Daphne said without looking up at him. She was too interested in the way David's tiny hand was gripping her finger.

"But—"

Daphne finally lifted her head. "Simon, you're being ridiculous. It's just a gossip column."

"Whistledown—ha!" he grumbled. "I've never heard of any Whistledowns. I'd like to know who this blasted woman is."

"You and the rest of London," Daphne said under her breath.

"Someone should put her out of business once and for all."

"If you wish to put her out of business," Daphne could not resist pointing out, "you shouldn't support her by buying her newspaper."

"I—"

"And don't even try to say that you buy *Whistledown* for me."

"You read it," Simon muttered.

"And so do you." Daphne dropped a kiss on the top of David's head. "Usually well before I can get my hands on it. Besides, I'm rather fond of Lady Whistledown these days."

Simon looked suspicious. "Why?"

"Did you read what she wrote about us? She called us London's most besotted couple." Daphne smiled wickedly. "I rather like that."

Simon groaned. "That's only because Philipa Featherington—"

"She's Philipa Berbrooke now," Daphne reminded him.

"Well, whatever her name, she has the bloodiest big mouth in London, and ever since she heard me calling you 'Dear Heart' at the theater last month, I have not been able to show my face at my clubs."

"Is it so very unfashionable to love one's wife, then?" Daphne teased.

Simon pulled a face, looking rather like a disgruntled young boy.

"Never mind," Daphne said. "I don't want to hear your answer."

Simon's smile was an endearing cross between sheepish and sly.

"Here," she said, holding David up. "Do you want to hold him?"

"Of course." Simon crossed the room and took the baby into his arms. He cuddled him for several moments, then glanced over at Daphne and grinned. "I think he looks like me."

"I know he does."

Simon kissed him on the nose, and whispered, "Don't you worry, my little man. I shall love you always. I'll teach you your letters and your numbers, and how to sit on a horse. And I shall protect you from all the awful people in this world, especially that Whistledown woman . . ."

And in a small, elegantly furnished chamber, not so very far from Hastings House, a young woman sat at her desk with a quill and a pot of ink and pulled out a piece of paper.

With a smile on her face, she set her quill to paper and wrote:

Lady Whistledown's Society Papers
19 December 1817

Ah Gentle Reader, This Author is pleased to report . . .

Dear Reader,

Have you ever wondered what happened to your favorite characters after you closed the final page? Wanted just a little bit more of a favorite novel? I have, and if the questions from my readers are any indication, I'm not the only one. So after countless requests from Bridgerton fans, I decided to try something a little different, and I wrote a "2nd Epilogue" for each of the novels. These are the stories that come after the stories.

At first, the Bridgerton 2nd Epilogues were available exclusively online; later they were published (along with a novella about Violet Bridgerton) in a collection called The Bridgertons: Happily Ever After. *I'm delighted that each is now included with the novel it follows. I hope you enjoy Daphne and Simon as they continue their journey.*

Warmly,
Julia Quinn

The Duke and I: The Second Epilogue

Mathematics had never been Daphne Basset's best subject, but she could certainly count to thirty, and as thirty was the maximum number of days that usually elapsed between her monthly courses, the fact that she was currently looking at her desk calendar and counting to forty-three was cause for some concern.

"It can't be possible," she said to the calendar, half expecting it to reply. She sat down slowly, trying to recall the events of the past six weeks. Maybe she'd counted wrong. She'd bled while she was visiting her mother, and that had been on March twenty-fifth and twenty-sixth, which meant that . . . She counted again, physically this time, poking each square on the calendar with her index finger.

Forty-three days.

She was pregnant.

"Good God."

Once again, the calendar had little to say on the matter.

No. No, it couldn't be. She was forty-one years old. Which wasn't to say that no woman in the history of the world had given birth at forty-two, but it had been seventeen years since she'd last conceived. Seventeen years of rather delightful relations with her husband during which time they had done nothing—absolutely nothing—to block conception.

Daphne had assumed she was simply done being fertile. She'd had her four children in rapid succession, one a year for the first four years of her marriage. Then . . . nothing.

She had been surprised when she realized that her youngest had reached his first birthday, and she was not pregnant again. And then he was two, then three, and her belly remained flat, and Daphne looked at her brood—Amelia, Belinda, Caroline, and David—and decided she had been blessed beyond measure. Four children, healthy and strong, with a strapping little boy who would one day take his father's place as the Duke of Hastings.

Besides, Daphne did not particularly enjoy being pregnant. Her ankles swelled and her cheeks got puffy, and her digestive tract did things that she absolutely did not wish to experience again. She thought of her sister-in-law Lucy, who positively glowed throughout pregnancy—which was a good thing, as Lucy was currently fourteen months pregnant with her fifth child.

Or nine months, as the case might be. But Daphne had seen her just a few days earlier, and she *looked* as if she were fourteen months along.

Huge. Staggeringly huge. But still glowing, and with astonishingly dainty ankles.

"I can't be pregnant," Daphne said, placing a hand on her flat belly. Maybe she was going through the change. Forty-one did seem a bit young, but then again, it wasn't one of those things anyone ever talked about. Maybe lots of women stopped their monthly courses at forty-one.

She should be happy. Grateful. Really, bleeding was such a bother.

She heard footsteps coming toward her in the hallway, and she quickly slid a book on top of the calendar, although what she thought she might be hiding she had no idea. It was just a calendar. There was no big red X, followed by the notation, "Bled this day."

Her husband strode into the room. "Oh good, there you are. Amelia has been looking for you."

"For me?"

"If there is a merciful God, she is not looking for *me*," Simon returned.

"Oh, dear," Daphne murmured. Normally she'd have a more quick-witted response, but her mind was still in the possibly-pregnant-possibly-growing-very-old fog.

"Something about a dress."

"The pink one or the green one?"

Simon stared at her. "Really?"

"No, of course you wouldn't know," she said distractedly.

He pressed his fingers to his temples and sank into a nearby chair. "When will she be married?"

"Not until she's engaged."

"And when will that be?"

Daphne smiled. "She had five proposals last year. You were the one who insisted that she hold out for a love match."

"I did not hear you disagreeing."

"I did not disagree."

He sighed. "How is it we have managed to have three girls out in society at the same time?"

"Procreative industriousness at the outset of our marriage," Daphne answered pertly, then remembered the calendar on her desk. The one with the red X that no one could see but her.

"Industriousness, hmmm?" He glanced over at the open door. "An interesting choice of words."

She took one look at his expression and felt herself turn pink. "Simon, it's the middle of the day!"

His lips slid into a slow grin. "I don't recall that stopping us when we were at the height of our industriousness."

"If the girls come upstairs . . ."

He bound to his feet. "I'll lock the door."

"Oh, good heavens, they'll *know*."

He gave the lock a decisive click and turned back to her with an arched brow. "And whose fault is that?"

Daphne drew back. Just a tiny bit. "There is no way I am sending any of my daughters into marriage as hopelessly ignorant as I was."

"Charmingly ignorant," he murmured, crossing the room to take her hand.

She allowed him to tug her to her feet. "You didn't think it was so charming when I assumed you were impotent."

He winced. "Many things in life are more charming in retrospect."

"Simon . . ."

He nuzzled her ear. "Daphne . . ."

His mouth moved along the line of her throat, and she felt herself melting. Twenty-one years of marriage and still . . .

"At least draw the curtains," she murmured. Not that anyone could possibly see in with the sun shining so brightly, but she would feel more comfortable. They were in the middle of Mayfair, after all, with her entire circle of acquaintances quite possibly strolling outside the window.

He positively dashed over to the window but pulled shut only the sheer scrim. "I like to see you," he said with a boyish smile.

And then, with remarkable speed and agility, he adjusted the situation so that he was seeing *all* of her, and she was on the bed, moaning softly as he kissed the inside of her knee.

"Oh, Simon," she sighed. She knew exactly what he was going to do next. He'd move up, kissing and licking his way along her thigh.

And he did it *so* well.

"What are you thinking about?" he murmured.

"Right now?" she asked, trying to blink her way out of her daze. He had his tongue at the crease between her leg and her abdomen and he thought she could *think*?

"Do you know what I'm thinking?" he asked.

"If it's not about me, I'm going to be terribly disappointed."

He chuckled, moved his head so that he could drop a light kiss on her belly button, then scooted up to brush his lips softly against hers. "I was thinking how marvelous it is to know another person so completely."

She reached out and hugged him. She couldn't help it. She buried her face in the warm crook of his neck, inhaled the familiar scent of him, and said, "I love you."

"I adore you."

Oh, so he was going to make a competition of it, was he? She pulled away, just far enough to say, "I fancy you."

He quirked a brow. "You *fancy* me?"

"It was the best I could summon on such short notice." She gave a tiny shrug. "And besides, I do."

"Very well." His eyes darkened. "I *worship* you."

Daphne's lips parted. Her heart thumped, then flipped, and any facility she might have possessed for synonym retrieval flew right out of her. "I think you've won," she said, her voice so husky she barely recognized it.

He kissed her again, long, hot, and achingly sweet. "Oh, I know I have."

Her head fell back as he made his way down to her belly. "You still have to worship me," she said.

He moved lower. "In that, your grace, I am ever your servant."

And that was the last thing either of them said for quite some time.

Several days later Daphne found herself staring at her calendar once more. It had been forty-six days now since she'd last bled, and she still had not said anything to Simon. She knew that she should, but it felt somewhat premature. There could be another explanation for the lack of her courses—one had only to recall her last visit with her mother. Violet Bridgerton had been constantly fanning herself, insisting that the air was stifling even though Daphne had found it to be perfectly pleasant.

The one time Daphne had asked someone to light a fire, Violet had countermanded her with such ferocity that Daphne had half expected her to guard the grate with a poker.

"Do not so much as strike a match," Violet had growled.

To which Daphne had wisely replied, "I do believe I shall fetch a shawl." She looked at her mother's housemaid, shivering next to the fireplace. "Er, and perhaps you should, too."

But she did not feel hot *now*. She felt . . .

She did not know what she felt. Perfectly normal, really. Which was suspicious, as she had never felt the least bit normal while pregnant before.

"Mama!"

Daphne flipped over her calendar and looked up from her writing desk just in time to see her second daughter, Belinda, pause at the entrance of the room.

"Come in," Daphne said, welcoming the distraction. "Please."

Belinda sat down in a nearby comfortable chair, her bright blue eyes meeting her mother's with her usual directness. "You must do something about Caroline."

"*I* must?" Daphne queried, her voice lingering ever-so-slightly longer on the "I."

Belinda ignored the sarcasm. "If she does not stop talking about Frederick Snowe-Mann-Formsby, I shall go mad."

"Can't you simply ignore her?"

"His *name* is Frederick Snowe . . . Mann . . . *Formsby*!"

Daphne blinked.

"Snowman, Mama! Snowman!"

"It *is* unfortunate," Daphne allowed. "But, Lady Belinda Basset, do not forget that you could be likened to a rather droopy hound."

Belinda's gaze grew very jaded, and it became instantly clear that someone had indeed likened her to a basset hound.

"Oh," Daphne said, somewhat surprised that Belinda had never told her about it. "I'm so sorry."

"It was long ago," Belinda said with a sniff. "And I assure you, it was not said more than once."

Daphne pressed her lips together, trying not to smile. It was definitely not good form to encourage fisticuffs, but as she had fought her way to adulthood with seven siblings, four of them brothers, she could not help but utter a quiet "Well-done."

Belinda gave her a regal nod, then said, "Will you have a talk with Caroline?"

"What is it you wish for me to say?"

"I don't know. Whatever it is you usually say. It always seems to work."

There was a compliment in there somewhere, Daphne was fairly certain, but before she could dissect the sentence, her stomach did a nasty flip, followed by the oddest sort of squeeze, and then—

"Excuse me!" she yelped, and she made it to the washroom just in time to reach the chamber pot.

Oh dear God. This wasn't the change. She was pregnant.

"Mama?"

Daphne flicked her hand back at Belinda, trying to dismiss her.

"Mama? Are you all right?"

Daphne retched again.

"I'm getting Father," Belinda announced.

"No!" Daphne fairly howled.

"Was it the fish? Because I thought the fish tasted a bit dodgy."

Daphne nodded, hoping that would be the end of it.

"Oh, wait a moment, you didn't have the fish. I remember it quite distinctly."

Oh, bugger Belinda and her bloody attention to detail.

It was not the most maternal of sentiments, Daphne thought as she once again heaved her innards, but she was not feeling particularly charitable at the moment.

"You had the squab. I had the fish, and so did David, but you and Caroline ate only squab, and I think Father and Amelia had both, and we all had the soup, although—"

"Stop!" Daphne begged. She didn't want to talk about food. Even the mere mention . . .

"I think I had better get Father," Belinda said again.

"No, I'm fine," Daphne gasped, still jerking her hand behind her in a shushing motion. She didn't want Simon to see her like this. He would know instantly what was about.

Or perhaps more to the point, what was about to happen. In seven and a half months, give or take a few weeks.

"Very well," Belinda conceded, "but at least let me fetch your maid. You should be in bed."

Daphne threw up again.

"After you're through," Belinda corrected. "You should be in bed once you're through with . . . ah . . . *that*."

"My maid," Daphne finally agreed. Maria would deduce the

truth instantly, but she would not say a word to anyone, servants or family. And perhaps more pressing, Maria would know exactly what to bring as a remedy. It would taste vile and smell worse, but it would settle her stomach.

Belinda dashed off, and Daphne—once she was convinced there could be nothing left in her stomach—staggered to her bed. She held herself extremely still; even the slightest rocking motion made her feel as if she were at sea. "I'm too old for this," she moaned, because she was. Surely, she was. If she remained true to form—and really, why should this confinement be any different from the previous four—she would be gripped by nausea for at least two more months. The lack of food would keep her slender, but that would last only until mid-summer, when she would double in size, practically overnight. Her fingers would swell to the point that she could not wear her rings, she would not fit into any of her shoes, and even a single flight of stairs would leave her gasping for breath.

She would be an elephant. A two-legged, chestnut-haired elephant.

"Your grace!"

Daphne could not lift her head, so she lifted her hand instead, a pathetic silent greeting to Maria, who was by now standing by the bed, staring down at her with an expression of horror . . .

. . . that was quickly sliding into one of suspicion.

"Your grace," Maria said again, this time with unmistakable inflection. She smiled.

"I know," Daphne said. "I know."

"Does the duke know?"

"Not yet."

"Well, you won't be able to hide it for long."

"He leaves this afternoon for a few nights at Clyvedon," Daphne said. "I will tell him when he returns."

"You should tell him now," Maria said. Twenty years of employment did give a maid some license to speak freely.

Daphne carefully edged herself up into a reclining position, stopping once to calm a wave of nausea. "It might not take," she said. "At my age, they very often don't."

"Oh, I think it's taken," Maria said. "Have you looked in the mirror yet?"

Daphne shook her head.

"You're green."

"It might not—"

"You're not going to throw the baby up."

"Maria!"

Maria crossed her arms and speared Daphne with a stare. "You know the truth, your grace. You just don't want to admit it."

Daphne opened her mouth to speak, but she had nothing to say. She knew Maria was right.

"If the baby hadn't taken," Maria said, a bit more gently, "you wouldn't be feeling so sickly. My mum had eight babies after me, and four losses early on. She never was sick, not even once, with the ones that didn't take."

Daphne sighed and then nodded, conceding the point. "I'm still going to wait, though," she said. "Just a bit longer." She wasn't sure why she wanted to keep this to herself for a few more days, but she did. And as she was the one whose body was currently trying to turn itself inside out, she rather thought it was her decision to make.

"Oh, I almost forgot," Maria said. "We received word from your brother. He's coming to town next week."

"Colin?" Daphne asked.

Maria nodded. "With his family."

"They must stay with us," Daphne said. Colin and Penelope did not own a home in town, and to economize they tended to stay with either Daphne or their oldest brother, Anthony, who had inherited the title and all that went with it. "Please ask Belinda to pen a letter on my behalf, insisting that they come to Hastings House."

Maria gave a nod and departed.

Daphne moaned and went to sleep.

By the time Colin and Penelope arrived, with their four darling children in tow, Daphne was throwing up several times a day. Simon still didn't know about her condition; he'd been delayed in the country—something about a flooded field—and now he wasn't due back until the end of the week.

But Daphne wasn't going to let a queasy belly get in the way of greeting her favorite brother. "Colin!" she exclaimed, her smile growing positively giddy at the familiar sight of his sparkling green eyes. "It has been much too long."

"I fully agree," he said, giving her a quick hug while Penelope attempted to shoo their children into the house.

"No, you may not chase that pigeon!" she said sternly. "So sorry, Daphne, but—" She dashed back out onto the front steps, neatly nabbing seven-year-old Thomas by the collar.

"Be grateful your urchins are grown," Colin said with a chuckle as he took a step back. "We can't keep—Good God, Daff, what's wrong with you?"

Trust a brother to dispense with tact.

"You look awful," he said, as if he hadn't made that clear with his first statement.

"Just a bit under the weather," she mumbled. "I think it was the fish."

"Uncle Colin!"

Colin's attention was thankfully distracted by Belinda and Caroline, who were racing down the stairs with a decided lack of ladylike grace.

"You!" he said with a grin, pulling one into a hug. "And you!" He looked up. "Where's the other you?"

"Amelia's off shopping," Belinda said, before turning her attention to her little cousins. Agatha had just turned nine, Thomas was seven, and Jane was six. Little Georgie would be three the following month.

"You're getting so big!" Belinda said to Jane, beaming down at her.

"I grew two inches in the last month!" she announced.

"In the last year," Penelope corrected gently. She couldn't quite reach Daphne for a hug, so she leaned over and squeezed her hand. "I know your girls were quite grown-up last time I saw them, but I swear, I am still surprised by it every time."

"So am I," Daphne admitted. She still woke some mornings half expecting her girls to be in pinafores. The fact that they were ladies, fully grown . . .

It was baffling.

"Well, you know what they say about motherhood," Penelope said.

" 'They'?" Daphne murmured.

Penelope paused just long enough to shoot her a wry grin. "The years fly by, and the days are endless."

"That's impossible," Thomas announced.

Agatha let out an aggrieved sigh. "He's so literal."

Daphne reached out to ruffle Agatha's light brown hair. "Are you really only nine?" She adored Agatha, always had. There was something about that little girl, so serious and determined, that had always touched her heart.

Agatha, being Agatha, immediately recognized the question as rhetorical and popped up to her tiptoes to give her aunt a kiss.

Daphne returned the gesture with a peck on the cheek, then turned to the young family's nurse, standing near the doorway holding little Georgie. "And how are you, you darling thing?" she cooed, reaching out to take the boy into her arms. He was plump and blond with pink cheeks and a heavenly baby smell despite the fact that he wasn't really a baby any longer. "You look scrumptious," she said, pretending to take a nibble of his neck. She tested the weight of him, rocking slightly back and forth in that instinctive motherly way.

"You don't need to be rocked anymore, do you?" she murmured, kissing him again. His skin was so soft, and it took her back to her days as a young mother. She'd had nurses and nannies, of course, but she couldn't even count the number of times she'd crept into the children's rooms to sneak a kiss on the cheek and watch them sleep.

Ah well. She was sentimental. This was nothing new.

"How old are you now, Georgie?" she asked, thinking that maybe she *could* do this again. Not that she had much choice, but still, she felt reassured, standing here with this little boy in her arms.

Agatha tugged on her sleeve and whispered, "He doesn't talk."

Daphne blinked. "I beg your pardon?"

Agatha glanced over at her parents, as if she wasn't sure she should be saying anything. They were busy chatting with Belinda and Caroline and took no notice. "He doesn't talk," she said again. "Not a word."

Daphne pulled back slightly so that she could look at Georgie's face again. He smiled at her, his eyes crinkling at the corners exactly the same way Colin's did.

Daphne looked back at Agatha. "Does he understand what people say?"

Agatha nodded. "Every word. I'm sure of it." Her voice dropped to a whisper. "I think my mother and father are concerned."

A child nearing his third birthday without a word? Daphne was *sure* they were concerned. Suddenly the reason for Colin and Penelope's unexpected trip to town became clear. They were looking for guidance. Simon had been just the same way as a child. He hadn't spoken a word until he was four. And then he'd suffered a debilitating stutter for years. Even now, when he was particularly upset about something, it would creep back over him, and she'd hear it in his voice. A strange pause, a repeated sound, a halting catch. He was still self-conscious about it, although not nearly so much as he had been when they'd first met.

But she could see it in his eyes. A flash of pain. Or maybe anger. At himself, at his own weakness. Daphne supposed that there were some things people never got past, not completely.

Reluctantly, Daphne handed Georgie back to his nurse and urged Agatha toward the stairs. "Come along, darling," she said. "The nursery is waiting. We took out all of the girls' old toys."

She watched with pride as Belinda took Agatha by the hand. "You may play with my favorite doll," Belinda said with great gravity.

Agatha looked up at her cousin with an expression that could only be described as reverence and then followed her up the stairs.

Daphne waited until all the children were gone and then turned back to her brother and his wife. "Tea?" she asked. "Or do you wish to change out of your traveling clothes?"

"Tea," Penelope said with the sigh of an exhausted mother. "Please."

Colin nodded his agreement, and together they went into the drawing room. Once they were seated Daphne decided there was no point in being anything but direct. This was her brother, after all, and he knew he could talk to her about anything.

"You're worried about Georgie," she said. It was a statement, not a question.

"He hasn't said a word," Penelope said quietly. Her voice was even, but her throat caught in an uncomfortable swallow.

"He understands us," Colin said. "I'm sure of it. Just the other day I asked him to pick up his toys, and he did so. Immediately."

"Simon was the same way," Daphne said. She looked from Colin to Penelope and back. "I assume that is why you came? To speak with Simon?"

"We hoped he might offer some insight," Penelope said.

Daphne nodded slowly. "I'm sure he will. He was detained in the country, I'm afraid, but he is expected back before the week's end."

"There is no rush," Colin said.

Out of the corner of her eye, Daphne saw Penelope's shoulders slump. It was a tiny motion but one any mother would recognize. Penelope knew there was no rush. They had waited nearly three years for Georgie to talk; a few more days wouldn't make a difference. And yet she wanted so desperately to do *some*thing. To take an action, to make her child whole.

To have come this far only to find that Simon was gone . . . It had to be discouraging.

"I think it is a very good sign that he understands you," Daphne said. "I would be much more concerned if he did not."

"Everything else about him is completely normal," Penelope said passionately. "He runs, he jumps, he eats. He even reads, I think."

Colin turned to her in surprise. "He does?"

"I believe so," Penelope said. "I saw him with William's primer last week."

"He was probably just looking at the illustrations," Colin said gently.

"That's what I thought, but then I watched his eyes! They were moving back and forth, following the words."

They both turned to Daphne, as if she might have all the answers.

"I suppose he might be reading," Daphne said, feeling rather inadequate. She wanted to have all the answers. She wanted to say something to them other than *I suppose* or *Perhaps*. "He's rather young, but there's no reason he couldn't be reading."

"He's very bright," Penelope said.

Colin gave a look that was mostly indulgent. "Darling . . ."

"He is! And William read when he was four. Agatha, too."

"Actually," Colin admitted thoughtfully, "Agatha did start to read at three. Nothing terribly involved, but I know she was reading short words. I remember it quite well."

"Georgie is reading," Penelope said firmly. "I am sure of it."

"Well, then, that means we have even less to be concerned about," Daphne said with determined good cheer. "Any child who is reading before his third birthday will have no trouble speaking when he is ready to do so."

She had no idea if this was actually the case. But she rather thought it ought to be. And it *seemed* reasonable. And if Georgie turned out to have a stutter, just like Simon, his family would still love him and adore him and give him all the support he needed to grow into the wonderful person she knew he would be.

He'd have everything Simon hadn't had as a child.

"It will be all right," Daphne said, leaning forward to take Penelope's hand in hers. "You'll see."

Penelope's lips pressed together, and Daphne saw her throat tighten. She turned away, wanting to give her sister-in-law a moment to compose herself. Colin was munching on his third biscuit and reaching for a cup of tea, so Daphne decided to direct her next question to him.

"Is everything well with the rest of the children?" she asked.

He swallowed his tea. "Quite well. And yours?"

"David has got into a bit of mischief at school, but he seems to be settling down."

Colin picked up another biscuit. "And the girls aren't giving you fits?"

Daphne blinked with surprise. "No, of course not. Why do you ask?"

"You look terrible," he said.

"Colin!" Penelope interjected.

He shrugged. "She does. I asked about it when we first arrived."

"But still," his wife admonished, "you shouldn't—"

"If I can't say something to her, who can?" he said plainly. "Or more to the point, who *will*?"

Penelope dropped her voice to an urgent whisper. "It's not the sort of thing one talks about."

He stared at her for a moment. Then he looked at Daphne. Then he turned back to his wife. "I have no idea what you're talking about," he said.

Penelope's lips parted, and her cheeks went a bit pink. She looked over at Daphne, as if to say, *Well?*

Daphne just sighed. Was her condition *that* obvious?

Penelope gave Colin an impatient look. "She's—" She turned back to Daphne. "You are, aren't you?"

Daphne gave a tiny nod of confirmation.

Penelope looked at her husband with a certain degree of smugness. "She's pregnant."

Colin froze for about one half a second before continuing on in his usual unflappable manner. "No, she's not."

"She is," Penelope replied.

Daphne decided not to speak. She was feeling queasy, anyway.

"Her youngest is seventeen," Colin pointed out. He glanced over at Daphne. "He is, isn't he?"

"Sixteen," Daphne murmured.

"Sixteen," he repeated, directing this at Penelope. "Still."

"Still?"

"Still."

Daphne yawned. She couldn't help it. She was just *exhausted* these days.

"Colin," Penelope said, in that patient yet vaguely condescending tone that Daphne *loved* to hear directed at her brother, "David's age hardly has anything to do with—"

"I realize that," he cut in, giving her a vaguely annoyed look. "But don't you think, if she were going to . . ." He waved a hand in Daphne's general direction, leaving her to wonder if he could not bring himself to utter the word *pregnant* in relation to his own sister.

He cleared his throat. "Well, there wouldn't have been a sixteen-year gap."

Daphne closed her eyes for a moment, then let her head settle against the back of the sofa. She really *should* feel embarrassed. This was her brother. And even if he was using rather vague terms, he was talking about the most intimate aspects of her marriage.

She let out a tired little noise, something between a sigh and a hum. She was too sleepy to be embarrassed. And maybe too old, too. Women ought to be able to dispense with maidenly fits of modesty when they passed forty.

Besides, Colin and Penelope were bickering, and that was a good thing. It took their minds off Georgie.

Daphne found it rather entertaining, really. It was lovely to watch any of her brothers stuck in a stalemate with his wife.

Forty-one definitely wasn't too old to feel just a little bit of pleasure at the discomfort of one's brothers. Although—she yawned again—it would be more entertaining if she were a bit more alert to enjoy it. Still . . .

"Did she fall asleep?"

Colin stared at his sister in disbelief.

"I think she did," Penelope replied.

He stretched toward her, craning his neck for a better view. "There are so many things I could do to her right now," he mused. "Frogs, locusts, rivers turning to blood."

"Colin!"

"It's so tempting."

"It's also proof," Penelope said with a hint of a smirk.

"Proof?"

"She's pregnant! Just like I said." When he did not agree with her quickly enough, she added, "Have you ever known her to fall asleep in the middle of a conversation?"

"Not since—" He cut himself off.

Penelope's smirk grew significantly less subtle. "Exactly."

"I hate when you're right," he grumbled.

"I know. Pity for you I so often am."

He glanced back over at Daphne, who was starting to snore. "I suppose we should stay with her," he said, somewhat reluctantly.

"I'll ring for her maid," Penelope said.

"Do you think Simon knows?"

Penelope glanced over her shoulder once she reached the bell-pull. "I have no idea."

Colin just shook his head. "Poor bloke is in for the surprise of his life."

When Simon finally returned to London, fully one week delayed, he was exhausted. He had always been a more involved landowner than most of his peers—even as he found himself approaching the age of fifty. And so when several of his fields flooded, including one that provided the sole income for a tenant family, he rolled up his sleeves and got to work alongside his men.

Figuratively, of course. All sleeves had most definitely been down. It had been bloody cold in Sussex. Worse when one was wet. Which of course they all had been, what with the flood and all.

So he was tired, and he was still cold—he wasn't sure his fingers would ever regain their previous temperature—and he missed his family. He would have asked them to join him in the country, but the girls were preparing for the season, and Daphne had looked a bit peaked when he left.

He hoped she wasn't coming down with a cold. When she got sick, the entire household felt it.

She thought she was a stoic. He had once tried to point out that a true stoic wouldn't go about the house repeatedly saying, "No, no, I'm fine," as she sagged into a chair.

Actually, he had tried to point this out twice. The first time he said something she had not responded. At the time, he'd thought she hadn't heard him. In retrospect, however, it was far more likely that she had *chosen* not to hear him, because the second time he said something about the true nature of a stoic, her response had been such that . . .

Well, let it be said that when it came to his wife and the common cold, his lips would never again form words other than "You poor, poor dear" and "May I fetch you some tea?"

There were some things a man learned after two decades of marriage.

When he stepped into the front hall, the butler was waiting, his face in its usual mode—that is to say, completely devoid of expression.

"Thank you, Jeffries," Simon murmured, handing him his hat.

"Your brother-in-law is here," Jeffries told him.

Simon paused. "Which one?" He had seven.

"Mr. Colin Bridgerton, Your Grace. With his family."

Simon cocked his head. "Really?" He didn't hear chaos and commotion.

"They are out, your grace."

"And the duchess?"

"She is resting."

Simon could not suppress a groan. "She's not ill, is she?"

Jeffries, in a most un-Jeffries-like manner, blushed. "I could not say, your grace."

Simon regarded Jeffries with a curious eye. "Is she ill, or isn't she?"

Jeffries swallowed, cleared his throat, and then said, "I believe she is tired, your grace."

"Tired," Simon repeated, mostly to himself since it was clear that Jeffries would expire of inexplicable embarrassment if he pursued the conversation further. Shaking his head, he headed upstairs, adding, "Of course, she's tired. Colin's got four children under the age of ten, and she probably thinks she's got to mother the lot while they're here."

Maybe he'd have a lie-down next to her. He was exhausted, too, and he always slept better when she was near.

The door to their room was shut when he got to it, and he almost knocked—it was a habit to do so at a closed door, even if it did lead to his own bedchamber—but at the last moment he instead gripped the doorknob and gave a soft push. She could be sleeping. If she truly was tired, he ought to let her rest.

Stepping lightly, he entered the room. The curtains were partway drawn, and he could see Daphne lying in bed, still as a bone. He tiptoed closer. She *did* look pale, although it was hard to tell in the dim light.

He yawned and sat on the opposite side of the bed, leaning forward to pull off his boots. He loosened his cravat and then slid it off entirely, scooting himself toward her. He wasn't going to wake her, just snuggle up for a bit of warmth.

He'd missed her.

Settling in with a contented sigh, he put his arm around her, resting its weight just below her rib cage, and—

"Grughargh!"

Daphne shot up like a bullet and practically hurled herself from the bed.

"Daphne?" Simon sat up, too, just in time to see her race for the chamber pot.

The chamber pot????

"Oh dear," he said, wincing as she retched. "Fish?"

"Don't say that word," she gasped.

Must have been fish. They really needed to find a new fishmonger here in town.

He crawled out of bed to find a towel. "Can I get you anything?"

She didn't answer. He hadn't really expected her to. Still, he held out the towel, trying not to flinch when she threw up for what had to be the fourth time.

"You poor, poor dear," he murmured. "I'm so sorry this happened to you. You haven't been like this since—"

Since . . .

Oh, dear God.

"Daphne?" His voice shook. Hell, his whole body shook.

She nodded.

"But . . . how . . . ? "

"The usual way, I imagine," she said, gratefully taking the towel.

"But it's been— It's been—" He tried to think. He couldn't think. His brain had completely ceased working.

"I think I'm done," she said. She sounded exhausted. "Could you get me a bit of water?"

"Are you certain?" If he recalled correctly, the water would pop right back up and into the chamber pot.

"It's over there," she said, motioning weakly to a pitcher on a table. "I'm not going to swallow it."

He poured her a glass and waited while she swished out her mouth.

"Well," he said, clearing his throat several times, "I . . . ah . . ." He coughed again. He could not get a word out to save his life. And he couldn't blame his stutter this time.

"Everyone knows," Daphne said, placing her hand on his arm for support as she moved back to bed.

"Everyone?" he echoed.

"I hadn't planned to say anything until you returned, but they guessed."

He nodded slowly, still trying to absorb it all. A baby. At his age. At *her* age.

It was . . .

It was . . .

It was *amazing.*

Strange how it came over him so suddenly. But now, after the initial shock wore off, all he could feel was pure joy.

"This is wonderful news!" he exclaimed. He reached out to hug her, then thought better of it when he saw her pasty complexion. "You never cease to delight me," he said, instead giving her an awkward pat on the shoulder.

She winced and closed her eyes. "Don't rock the bed," she moaned. "You're making me seasick."

"You don't get seasick," he reminded her.

"I do when I'm expecting."

"You're an odd duck, Daphne Basset," he murmured, and then stepped back to A) stop rocking the bed and B) remove himself from her immediate vicinity should she take exception to the duck comparison.

(There was a certain history to this. While heavily pregnant with Amelia, she had asked him if she was radiant or if she just looked like a waddling duck. He told her she'd looked like a radiant duck. This had not been the correct answer.)

He cleared his throat and said, "You poor, poor dear."

Then he fled.

Several hours later Simon was seated at his massive oak desk, his elbows resting atop the smooth wood, his right index finger ringing the top of the brandy snifter that he had already refilled twice.

It had been a momentous day.

An hour or so after he'd left Daphne to her nap, Colin and Penelope had returned with their progeny, and they'd all had tea and biscuits in the breakfast room. Simon had started for the drawing room, but Penelope had requested an alternative, someplace without "expensive fabrics and upholstery."

Little Georgie had grinned up at him at that, his face still smeared with a substance Simon hoped was chocolate.

As Simon regarded the blanket of crumbs spilling from the table to the floor, along with the wet napkin they'd used to sop up Agatha's overturned tea, he remembered that he and Daphne had always taken their tea here when the children were small.

Funny how one forgot such details.

Once the tea party had dispersed, however, Colin had asked for a private word. They had repaired to Simon's study, and it was there that Colin confided in him about Georgie.

He wasn't talking.

His eyes were sharp. Colin thought he was reading.

But he wasn't talking.

Colin had asked for his advice, and Simon realized he had none. He'd thought about this, of course. It had haunted him every time Daphne had been pregnant, straight through until each of his children had begun to form sentences.

He supposed it would haunt him now. There would be another baby, another soul to love desperately . . . and worry over.

All he'd known to tell Colin was to love the boy. To talk to him, and praise him, and take him riding and fishing and all those things a father ought to do with a son.

All those things his father had never done with him.

He didn't think about him often these days, his father. He had Daphne to thank for that. Before they'd met, Simon had been obsessed with revenge. He'd wanted so badly to hurt his father, to make him suffer the way he had suffered as a boy, with all the pain and anguish of knowing he had been rejected and found wanting.

It hadn't mattered that his father was dead. Simon had thirsted for vengeance all the same, and it had taken love, first with Daphne and then with his children, to banish that ghost. He'd finally realized that he was free when Daphne had given him a bundle of letters from his father that had been entrusted into her care. He hadn't wanted to burn them; he hadn't wanted to rip them to shreds.

He hadn't particularly wanted to read them, either.

He'd looked down at the stack of envelopes, tied neatly with a red and gold ribbon, and realized that he felt nothing. Not anger, not sorrow, not even regret. It had been the greatest victory he could have imagined.

He wasn't sure how long the letters had sat in Daphne's desk.

He knew she'd put them in her bottom drawer, and every now and then he'd taken a peek to see if they were still there.

But eventually even that had tapered off. He hadn't forgotten about the letters—every now and then something would happen that would spring them to mind—but he'd forgotten about them with such constancy. And they had probably been absent from his mind for months when he opened his bottom desk drawer and saw that Daphne had moved them there.

That had been twenty years ago.

And although he still lacked the urge to burn or shred, he'd also never felt the need to open them.

Until now.

Well, no.

Maybe?

He looked at them again, still tied in that bow. *Did* he want to open them? Could there be anything in his father's letters that might be of help to Colin and Penelope as they guided Georgie through what might be a difficult childhood?

No. It was impossible. His father had been a hard man, unfeeling and unforgiving. He'd been so obsessed with his heritage and title that he'd turned his back on his only child. There could be nothing—nothing—that he might have written that could help Georgie.

Simon picked up the letters. The papers were dry. They smelled old.

The fire in the grate felt new. Hot, and bright, and redemptive. He stared at the flames until his vision blurred, just sat there for endless minutes, clutching his father's final words to him. They had not spoken for over five years when his father died. If there was anything the old duke had wanted to say to him, it would be here.

"Simon?"

He looked up slowly, barely able to pull himself from his daze. Daphne was standing in the doorway, her hand resting lightly on the edge of the door. She was dressed in her favorite pale blue dressing gown. She'd had it for years; every time he asked if she wanted to replace it, she refused. Some things were best soft and comfortable.

"Are you coming to bed?" she asked.

He nodded, coming to his feet. "Soon. I was just—" He cleared his throat, because the truth was—he wasn't sure what he'd been doing. He wasn't even sure what he'd been thinking. "How are you feeling?" he asked her.

"Better. It's always better in the evening." She took a few steps forward. "I had a bit of toast, and even some jam, and I—" She stopped, the only movement in her face the quick blink of her eyes. She was staring at the letters. He hadn't realized he was still holding them when he stood.

"Are you going to read them?" she asked quietly.

"I thought . . . perhaps . . ." He swallowed. "I don't know."

"But why now?"

"Colin told me about Georgie. I thought there might be something in here." He moved his hand slightly, holding the stack of letters just a little bit higher. "Something that might help him."

Daphne's lips parted, but several seconds passed before she was able to speak. "I think you might be one of the kindest, most generous men I have ever known."

He looked at her in confusion.

"I know you don't want to read those," she said.

"I really don't care—"

"No, you do," she interrupted gently. "Not enough to destroy them, but they still mean something to you."

"I hardly ever think about them," he said. It was the truth.

"I know." She reached out and took his hand, her thumb moving lightly over his knuckles. "But just because you let go of your father, it doesn't mean he never mattered."

He didn't speak. He didn't know what to say.

"I'm not surprised that if you do finally decide to read them, it will be to help someone else."

He swallowed, then grasped her hand like a lifeline.

"Do you want me to open them?"

He nodded, wordlessly handing her the stack.

Daphne moved to a nearby chair and sat, tugging at the ribbon until the bow fell loose. "Are these in order?" she asked.

"I don't know," he admitted. He sat back down behind his desk. It was far enough away that he couldn't see the pages.

She gave an acknowledging nod, then carefully broke the seal on the first envelope. Her eyes moved along the lines—or at least he thought they did. The light was too dim to see her expression clearly, but he had seen her reading letters enough times to know exactly what she must look like.

"He had terrible penmanship," Daphne murmured.

"Did he?" Now that he thought about it, Simon wasn't sure he'd ever seen his father's handwriting. He must have done, at some point. But it wasn't anything he recalled.

He waited a bit longer, trying not to hold his breath as she turned the page.

"He didn't write on the back," she said with some surprise.

"He wouldn't," Simon said. "He would never do anything that smacked of economization."

She looked up, her brows arched.

"The Duke of Hastings does not need to economize," Simon said dryly.

"Really?" She turned to the next page, murmuring, "I shall have to remember that the next time I go to the dressmaker."

He smiled. He loved that she could make him smile at such a moment.

After another few moments, she refolded the papers and looked up. She paused briefly, perhaps in case he wanted to say anything, and then when he did not, said, "It's rather dull, actually."

"Dull?" He wasn't sure what he had been expecting, but not this.

Daphne gave a little shrug. "It's about the harvest, and an improvement to the east wing of the house, and several tenants he suspects of cheating him." She pressed her lips together disapprovingly. "They weren't, of course. It is Mr. Miller and Mr. Bethum. They would never cheat anyone."

Simon blinked. He'd thought his father's letters might include an apology. Or if not that, then more accusations of inadequacy. It had never occurred to him that his father might have simply sent him an accounting of the estate.

"Your father was a very suspicious man," Daphne muttered.

"Oh, yes."

"Shall I read the next?"

"Please do."

She did, and it was much the same, except this time it was about a bridge that needed repairing and a window that had not been made to his specifications.

And on it went. Rents, accounts, repairs, complaints . . . There was the occasional overture, but nothing more personal than *I am considering hosting a shooting party next month, do let me know if you are interested in attending*. It was astounding. His father had not only denied his existence when he'd thought him a stuttering idiot, he'd managed to deny his own denial once Simon was speaking clearly and up to snuff. He acted as if it had never happened, as if he had never wished his own son were dead.

"Good God," Simon said, because *some*thing had to be said.

Daphne looked up. "Hmmm?"

"Nothing," he muttered.

"It's the last one," she said, holding the letter up.

He sighed.

"Do you want me to read it?"

"Of course," he said sarcastically. "It might be about rents. Or accounts."

"Or a bad harvest," Daphne quipped, obviously trying not to smile.

"Or that," he replied.

"Rents," she said once she'd finished reading. "And accounts."

"The harvest?"

She smiled slightly. "It was good that season."

Simon closed his eyes for a moment, as a strange tension eased from his body.

"It's odd," Daphne said. "I wonder why he never mailed these to you."

"What do you mean?"

"Well, he didn't. Don't you recall? He held on to all of them, then gave them to Lord Middlethorpe before he died."

"I suppose it was because I was out of the country. He wouldn't have known where to send them."

"Oh yes, of course." She frowned. "Still, I find it interesting that he would take the time to write you letters with no hope of sending them to you. If I were going to write letters to someone I couldn't send them to, it would be because I had something to say, something meaningful that I would want them to know, even after I was gone."

"One of the many ways in which you are unlike my father," Simon said.

She smiled ruefully. "Well, yes. I suppose." She stood, setting the letters down on a small table. "Shall we go to bed?"

He nodded and walked to her side. But before he took her arm, he reached down, scooped up the letters, and tossed them into the fire. Daphne let out a little gasp as she turned in time to see them blacken and shrivel.

"There's nothing worth saving," he said. He leaned down and kissed her, once on the nose and then once on the mouth. "Let's go to bed."

"What are you going to tell Colin and Penelope?" she asked as they walked arm in arm toward the stairs.

"About Georgie? The same thing I told them this afternoon." He kissed her again, this time on her brow. "Just love him. That's all they can do. If he talks, he talks. If he doesn't, he doesn't. But either way, it will all be fine, as long as they just love him."

"You, Simon Arthur Fitzranulph Basset, are a very good father."

He tried not to puff with pride. "You forgot the Henry."

"What?"

"Simon Arthur *Henry* Fitzranulph Basset."

She pfffted that. "You have too many names."

"But not too many children." He stopped walking and tugged her toward him until they were face to face. He rested one hand lightly on her abdomen. "Do you think we can do it all once more?"

She nodded. "As long as I have you."

"No," he said softly. "As long as I have *you*."

About the Author

#1 *New York Times* bestselling author JULIA QUINN began writing one month after graduating from college and, aside from a brief stint in medical school, she has been tapping away at her keyboard ever since. Her novels have been translated into forty-three languages and are beloved the world over. A graduate of Harvard and Radcliffe Colleges, she lives with her family in the Pacific Northwest.

hastings house
Bridgerton house
aubrey hall
my cottage
number five
Bridgerton house
bloomsbury
berkeley square
greenwich
hampstead heath
Daphne
falls in love with
Simon
1784
1792
Anthony
falls in love with
Kate
1784
1793
Benedict
falls in love with
Sophie
1786
1794
Colin
falls in love with
Penelope
1791
1796
the Bridgerton family
"You are a Bridgerton. You will always be a Bridgerton."

my cottage
romney hall
mayfair
kilmartin house
kilmartin
danbury house
FLYING PEA
st clair house
hastings house
aubrey hall
mayfair
number five
fensworth house
hyde park
Gregory
falls in love with
Lucy
ah-choo!
ah-choo!
ah-choo!
Francesca
falls in love with
Michael
Eloise
falls in love with
Phillip
Hyacinth
falls in love with
Gareth
E+V
the Duke and I
etc